Praise for *Etruscans*

"[A] sturdy historical fantasy novel. . . . Horatius grows persuasively as a character as well as in age . . . and the final sequence in the underworld is well up to Llywelyn's usual vivid standard."
—*Publishers Weekly*

"The fast-paced plot, the large cast of characters, and the colorful settings certainly will appeal to readers of romantic fantasy. Many bodices are ripped, bloody intrigues are revealed, and the conclusion leaves room for a sequel."
—*VOYA*

Praise for Morgan Llywelyn

"She weaves the tapestry of her story with intelligence and skill."
—*San Diego Union-Tribune* on *1916*

"A masterpiece is how best I can describe this latest novel from the pen of Morgan Llywelyn . . . . It is a difficult undertaking to get the facts right yet have a rip-roaring yarn. A marvelous achievement."
—*Republican News* (Dublin) on *1916*

Praise for Michael Scott

"Michael Scott is the King of Fantasy in these Isles."
—*The Irish Times*

"Scott is a master of the naturally unfolding mystery, and the tension never lets up."
—Orson Scott Card on *October Moon*

BY MORGAN LLYWELYN FROM TOM DOHERTY ASSOCIATES

FICTION

Bard

Brian Boru

The Elementals

Finn Mac Cool

Lion of Ireland

Pride of Lions

Strongbow

1916

1921

NONFICTION

The Essential Library for Irish Americans

ETRUSCANS

BELOVED OF THE GODS

MORGAN LLYWELYN

AND

MICHAEL SCOTT

A TOM DOHERTY ASSOCIATES BOOK
NEW YORK

ETRUSCANS

Edited by David G. Hartwell.

A Tor Book
Published by Tom Doherty Associates, LLC
175 Fifth Avenue
New York, NY 10010

www.tor.com

Tor® is a registered trademark of Tom Doherty Associates, LLC.

ISBN: 0-812-58012-5

First edition: March 2000
First mass market edition: December 2001

Printed in the United States of America

0 9 8 7 6 5 4 3 2 1

Earthworld
Otherworld
Netherworld

These are the realms of our existence
These are the worlds that bind us
Flesh is tied to Earthworld
Spirit to Otherworld
Death to Netherworld
Between the three, only the Ais *travel*
without restriction.

Etruscan proverb, Second Century, B.C.

PROLOGUS

Extracted from LIBRI FATALES,
The Hidden Will of the Gods,
as found in the ETRUSCA DISCIPLINIA

A NEW TRANSLATION BY LLYWELYN & SCOTT

We have always been.

We, the Ais, *existed even before the beginning. But it was humankind who named us gods, assigning us form and attributing omnipotence to us as well. Then they bowed before us and we were pleased by the taste of worship.*

When humans learned to fear the gods we reached the zenith of our power.

Although we are what man aspires to become, in many ways we resemble humankind. We are fickle. The Ais *can love and hate, destroy life and create it anew. We amuse ourselves by elevating our favorites and tormenting those we do not like, and occasionally, just to vary the entertainment, we reverse their positions.*

Ostensibly humans are the slaves and we the masters; yet in truth the relationship is far more complex. Some of the Ais *say we would be better off without humans because their incessant demands are a nuisance and a distraction. Others, however, point out the ways in which we depend upon humankind and insist we dare not destroy them. The argument between the two points of view has raged for eons.*

Humans will always require gods.

We give their lives a meaning: often we are the meaning. Our existence is taken as their command to exist. We provide them with someone to blame other than themselves. We satisfy their inborn need of ritual. We give them reasons to celebrate.

But we, the Ais, *also need humankind. Without them we have no definition. Human imagination imbues us with form and face, shape and substance.*

Interaction with the Earthworld has become an imperative for us, involved as we are in such a symbiotic relationship. Over the millennia we have grown dangerously dependent. We stimulate awe, and resultant faith through demonstrations of power such as storms and plagues and celestial marvels. We must, because if humankind stops believing in us the Ais *may cease to be gods.*

Man born of dust is incorrigibly cunning. Like the rat, he sniffs out the smallest advantage. He constantly strives to overcome his limitations and enlarge his sphere of influence by manipulating the gods through his priests. Usually we ignore the pious mouthings of the priesthood, which have little to do with our own intentions and desires. On the occasions when the two do coincide, however, and we appear to be answering some human prayer, man invariably claims he has influenced the gods. This makes him more arrogant than ever.

Nor is man above trying to create gods who are more amenable to his wishes than we are. For this purpose even his dead ancestors are employed. Unfortunately, the same belief with which man shapes us can transform one of his own into a deity . . . of sorts.

Such man-made gods have abilities exceeding those of mere mortals and in addition embody all the vices of humankind. They inevitably hate the Ais, *whom they see as rivals and superiors.*

We call them siu, *the evil ones.*

Demons.

ONE

Silent, deadly, and immense, they came whispering out of the bright sky with talons extended. By their unnatural size and behavior he recognized the great white owls for what they were: minions of the dark goddess.

Their golden eyes burned with ferocity. Their silver claws sank into his scalp and the shoulders of his naked body, ripping his flesh. He bit down hard on the inside of his cheek until he tasted blood to keep himself from crying out. If she was watching from the Otherworld, he refused to grant her that satisfaction.

At some distance beyond the trees, he detected a faint but unmistakable glow that could only mean one thing: he must be approaching an area of Sacred Space.

He stumbled as the ground beneath his feet turned to a gelatinous morass, sucking him down, then solidified almost instantly to trap his feet and ankles. With the palm of his hand he struck the earth, spending a valuable portion of his remaining energy to break the surface tension and release himself.

As he pulled his legs free, he felt the draught of wings brush his face. He promptly threw himself back down and cradled his head with his arms. The trio of hunters swept in low above him, the susurration of their wings all the more menacing for its softness.

At the last instant he surged to his feet. With flailing fists he struck one of the birds in the chest, bringing it down in an explosion of feathers. Before it could hit the ground he snatched up the creature and held it to his face. The distinctive, musty odor flooded his mouth and throat as he sank his teeth into the owl's neck. Trying not to gag on the cloud of plumage, he clamped down hard and inhaled deeply.

The owl screeched and writhed.

He took another, even deeper breath, forcibly drawing into his lungs a thin vapor torn from the very core of his victim. He was ravenous for the creature's *hia,* the living spirit it contained.

As he inhaled its essence, the energy that animated the owl began to replenish his waning strength. But one breath was not enough, he must have more. The pursuit had been so long; he was so weary. . . .

Sensing his intent, the owl redoubled its struggles. Its legs extended abnormally until they could reach around his torso and tear the flesh from his back in order to lay bare the spine, to seize and crush the vertebrae with its mighty talons. But he did not give it the chance. Opening his jaws, he twisted the bird's head to one side and snapped its neck with his bare hands.

Swiftly he sucked the last of the *hia* from the dying body, even as the creature shriveled and decomposed in his hands. Then with a cry of disgust he flung the liquefying object from him.

Drawing on his new strength he ran on, pushing his way through closely spaced ranks of sentinel trees. He had escaped the Otherworld, tearing through the fabric that separated it from the Earthworld only to find the earth itself conspiring against him. Could the dark goddess extend her reach so far?

As if in answer, branches twisted into skeletal limbs that clutched at him, holding him back. A coiling root emerged from the soil, catching his foot and sending him crashing to the ground. As he fell he was already wrapping his arms around his body and beginning to roll. If he gave up now the forest would claim him as its victim before his pursuers could.

At least he would have the small satisfaction of cheating her minions.

Lurching to his feet, he risked a glance backward. Thus he stood clearly revealed to his pursuers; a slender, swarthy man of somewhat less than average height, with a hooked nose and sensual lips. His eyes were almond shaped, his flesh fine-grained. But that flesh looked old, worn, almost as if it had long ago turned to parchment. And his eyes, rimmed around with scars, were very tired.

The remaining owls ghosted toward him on silent wings, banking sharply to clear the trees. Their pale plumage glimmered as they passed through patches of shade. To a casual observer they might have seemed beautiful.

But no normal owl would hunt during the day.

Fighting back fear—but not regret; no, never regret—he staggered on.

Sacred Space lay ahead. Once there he would be safe from their attack because no matter what form they took, these creatures were animated by *hia*. A *hia* might be the ghost of someone who had died, or the life force waiting to occupy a person as yet unborn. It could belong to an animal or a tree or a flower, for no life was possible without spirit. Nor were *hia* exclusive to the Earthworld; quite the contrary. In the Otherworld there were many spirits who would never manifest themselves in tangible bodies. But all *hia* had one limitation. Without invitation or very special powers they could not enter space consecrated to the gods.

No such restriction applied to the *Ais,* of course. If the goddess who was now his enemy chose, she could come after him herself, even into Sacred Space. He had no doubt that she was angry enough.

Why had she sent the owls instead?

He must recover and decide what to do next. He had to find sanctuary, if only for a little while.

As he burst from the forest, his thoughts were so firmly fixed on this goal that he reached the riverbank before he knew it. The muddy verge was treacherous. At his first step it slid away beneath his feet and plunged him headfirst into the Tiber. The icy shock drove the breath from his lungs and stole the warmth of *hia* energy from his body, leaving him weak again.

A powerful current battered him, dragging him away from the bank. Small round mouths lined with vicious teeth gaped just beneath the surface as ribbonlike eels fixed on his flesh. Pain seared up his legs. Frantically he fought to keep his balance while he pulled off the sucking eels. If he went under he would never resurface.

A whisper on the air warned him just in time. Turning from one battle to another, he struck the owl in midair and sent it spiraling down to the water. As it fell, the creature made a desperate effort to recapture its long-lost human shape. Swirling, melting, it presented a blurred image of a woman with the talons and snowy plumage of an owl and panicky golden eyes set in a human face. Embodied in this hybrid form the *hia* had neither the advantages of the owl nor the human.

With a terrific splash it fell into the river, the unforgiving waters swallowing its scream.

The eels were distracted from their original prey by the floundering of this new victim. Flowing away from him, they attacked the owl-thing before it could recover. They circled the dazed form, entwined themselves around its limbs, and dragged the hapless creature beneath the surface, where larger, darker creatures lurked.

Splashing wearily out of the river, he dragged himself up the bank on the far side. His breath was coming in sobs. The flesh of his legs was red from the cold and redder still from the blood pouring from scores of ragged wounds. The owls had torn his body and the eels had shredded his lower limbs. As he staggered on, drops of blood spattered the soil.

Deep in the earth something shifted, as his blood excited ancient memories. The banks of the sentient rivers throbbed with somnolent life, which normally required great amounts of blood and passion to rouse it to full consciousness. But this blood was different; vibrant with spiritual energy and fragrant with the scent of the Otherworld.

A shudder ran through the ground like the first tremor of a quake.

When he had dragged himself to the top of the rise he saw Sacred Space just ahead. He narrowed his eyes to call upon the weary remnants of his Otherworld sight for a better look. The sanctuary's glow was blurred, its holy radiance not fully developed. Consecration of the *templum* was not complete then. But that did not matter. He would be safe enough there for as long as he needed.

He had only moments left. He could feel the ground beneath his feet moving and shifting, rippling in long, slow waves. The air began to tremble as before a storm. Who knew what ancient madness lurked in the earth in this place?

Caution dictated that he advance warily; there were undoubtedly traps in the lush landscape ahead of him. But there was no time for caution. Summoning the last of his energy, he broke into a shambling run toward the *templum* while behind him the earth began to rise in a great, curling wave. A few steps, just a few more . . .

He had almost reached safety when the last of the

owls struck him. It swooped out of the sky to sink triumphant talons deep into his flesh.

His cry of pain was swallowed as he pitched forward and fell headlong to the ground.

TWO

Beyond the bend of the river, Vesi strolled in the sunshine. She loved being out under the bright blue sky. Let others shelter themselves in houses, in cities. Above all things she enjoyed unfettered freedom.

Suddenly she detected a change in the atmosphere. An unexpected chill, though the day was warm; a brief bitterness on the wind, overriding the perfume of ripening grapes. Vesi shivered in spite of herself, then laughed off the sensation. She would not let anything spoil her mood on this radiant late summer day.

Tossing back hair the color of a moonless midnight, the girl closed her eyes. Wide-set eyes, dark and bright as onyx. Her sheer *peplos* was dyed with saffron, complementing her olive complexion. A crimson scarf was draped across her shoulders. Strings of tiny silver bells were laced around her throat and wrists, making music with her slightest movement.

The bells tinkled as she breathed deeply, savoring the sweetness of the air. Without visual distraction her other senses came to the fore. She measured the weight of the wind on her shoulders, as light as a lover's caress, and turned her face to welcome its breath. Warm again. The momentary cold had been just an aberration. Thankfully, the girl abandoned herself to the delights of the season.

With a delicate sniff she identified the smells of summer one by one. Dew-drenched grass, sun-warmed earth, flowers in the meadow, droppings of sheep and scat of fox, the odor of a young bullock grazing not far away, and an old wolf bitch tardily coming into season. Underlying these was the verdant scent of trees at the edge of the forest and the fecund mud of the nearby river.

A hundred fragrances assailed Vesi's nostrils, each telling their story of life.

There was just one smell she did not recognize.

A faint but acrid tang still lay like a stain on the air. She curled her lip in distaste. How monstrous that something ugly should mar the otherwise perfect day! She would ignore it and surely it would go away.

Tilting her head, the young woman redirected her concentration to the natural music surrounding her. She could recognize sixty species of bird by their song, differentiating between those that were native to Etruria and those that merely visited the lush meadows on their way to the northern Darklands or south to the realm of Aegypt, the fabled Black Land.

One by one, Vesi sorted through various sounds until she found one she could not identify . . . a distant, labored gasping, occasionally punctuated with a groan.

An injured wild boar perhaps. But no, this was no animal. Vesi knew all the animal voices. Perhaps she was hearing a member of one of the primitive tribes her people had dispossessed in claiming this land long ago.

Her forebears styled themselves the Rasne, the Silver People, although others referred to them simply as the Etruscans. In a time recalled only by storytellers they had moved into the territory between the rivers Magra and Rubicon. Eventually their control was total in an area bordered by the Arno on the north and the Apennines and Tiber to the east and south, extending as far as Latium. Force of arms and superior intellect made the land theirs. None had been able to stand against them, neither the indigenous inhabitants nor the subhuman beasts who infested the mountain wildernesses.

Not all the vanquished had left the land. Those who remained, in the high mountains and primeval forests, were in the process of creating legends. Tales of the Silver People.

Opening her eyes, Vesi blinked against the bright sunlight, then shaded her face with both hands and gazed toward the south.

The bitter smell and gasping breath both seemed to emanate from the site of the incomplete *spura,* the Rasne city being built beyond the bend of the river. But the place was uninhabited at the moment. Although the ground had been cleared and the *purtani,* the priests, had blessed the boundaries, the final sacrifices had yet to be made. Vesi knew that none of the Rasne would break the taboo and enter unhallowed Sacred Space without being accompanied by a *purtan.*

Yet someone was there.

As she stood, puzzled, the wind changed, carrying to her the unmistakable odor of fresh blood.

Drawing her long-bladed knife from its tooled leather sheath, Vesi glided silently forward. Since earliest childhood she had loved to play at hunting, like a boy—to the despair of her mother, who wanted her daughter to be feminine and delicate. Rasne women were works of art.

But Vesi had no desire to be a work of art. Such a static image bored her. Life was to be *lived.* She thrilled to the prospect of adventures. Now her callused bare feet slid through the long grass, testing every step before trusting her weight. One could never be too cautious. A patch of quicksand might be anywhere. *Spurae* were sometimes sited to take advantage of such natural defenses.

She drew another questing breath. The blood-smell was stronger now, identifiably human but disgustingly tainted with something foul.

Another groan sounded. There was no mistaking the voice of a man in pain. Abandoning caution, the girl started forward just as a rising wind whipped her hair into her eyes. It might have been an omen; the Rasne believed the gods spoke to them in such signs and portents. The girl paused long enough to take a gleaming silver fillet from the leather purse she wore at her waist. She settled the band firmly on her brow to hold her hair in place.

Then she began to run.

Since none of her people would have ventured on their own into the unfinished *spura,* she assumed the groaning man must belong to one of the native tribes. Or, more dangerously, be a hawk-faced Roman from Latium, an advance scout for an army hoping to extend Rome's territory. Such raiders had become a constant threat. Once the Etruscans had feared no one, dominating not only Etruria but much of Latium. With increasing prosperity their aggressive impulses had diminished however. The Rasne had become tired of war, tired of the casual butchery, the stink of the dead and the dying. They had taken their martial arts and turned them inward, using them to create rather than destroy, to build rather than pull down.

And now the jackals were gathering.

Vesi hefted the knife in her hand, her thumb caressing the hilt with its encrusted carnelians. But she did not hesitate. At the back of her mind was some romantic, childish notion of taking an injured Roman warrior prisoner at knife point and leading him home in triumph. No Rasne woman had ever done such a thing before.

She sprinted up a hill, then dropped flat at the crest so she would not be silhouetted against the sky. From this vantage point she could look down upon the *spura* spread out below like some child's toy.

The area had been cleared, foundations dug, drains installed, streets laid out. Each house, shop, and public building was already allocated a site that would contribute to the symmetry of the whole. Squares and rectangles were pegged with fluttering strips of pale cloth. Stone footings would be placed to support walls of sunbaked brick covered with tinted plaster. Courtyards and roofs would be tiled; murals would be painted on every available surface. Terra-cotta piping was stacked to one side, waiting to serve the fountains that would sparkle throughout the city.

The choicest site of all was reserved for the great *templum* at the center of the *spura.* Plinths would be placed at intervals along the approaching avenue; statues of the *Ais* would stand there, gazing down with blind eyes upon their people. But before this could happen, the entire area must be consecrated with blood and flesh and smoke. Then a city wall would be raised to protect Sacred Space and construction could begin in earnest.

The result would be the finest *spura* ever built, even more elegant than Veii, which was celebrated as the most beautiful city in Etruria. And as everyone knew, Etruria was the most beautiful land in the world. Its inhabitants were the special favorites of the *Ais.*

"Great are the gods and precious their love," Vesi murmured automatically.

She shaded her eyes with one hand so she could make out details of the scene below.

There!

In the center of the site designated for the *templum* lay a huddled body. Desecration! When Vesi leaped to her feet with a yelp of outrage she accidentally dropped her dagger. It struck the soft earth point first and stood there quivering.

She was quivering herself, with indignation. Injured or not, the man had gone beyond all bounds of decency! The most Sacred Space of all had been defiled. The priests would not use it now; the lengthy process of selecting another site for the city would have to be undertaken. It might be many seasons before an equally propitious location was determined.

To add to Vesi's dismay, she glanced down to discover that her knife was stabbing the earth. With a soft moan the girl stooped and withdrew the blade. She removed the clinging soil with reverent fingertips, then tenderly pressed the tiny particles back into the ground as she murmured a prayer to the goddess Ops. "May the earth spirits forgive my carelessness; I meant them no harm."

Straightening, she drew a deep breath.

The blood-smell was stronger than ever. The figure lying in the center of the *templum* space was not moving.

Keeping a firm hold on her knife, Vesi trotted down the hill toward the *spura.* When she reached the edge of the first marked foundation she stopped, reluctant to cross the invisible line that bordered the most dangerous of Sacred Space: unhallowed ground, designated but not protected from the more inimical inhabitants of the Otherworld.

Pacing along the line, she stared at the man lying on what should have become the floor of the *templum.* From a distance she had thought he wore a tattered cloak; now she saw it was the flesh of his naked back, torn in bizarre strips. Vesi wondered what animal could have inflicted such wounds. Neither bear nor boar nor aurochs, whose marks she recognized. Could it be one of the legendary monsters said to inhabit the mountains of Latium? Would such a creature have come this far into Etruria in search of prey? Surely not.

Yet obviously some predator had been at work. The injured man must have been caught and mauled and then dragged here, suffering terribly.

Vesi caught her lower lip between her teeth as she pondered a new mystery.

Where was the trail of blood?

Crimson had seeped from the man's body to puddle beneath him, yet there was no gory pathway across flattened grass to the place where he now lay. An animal dragging him would have left one. Instead there were only spattered droplets, indicating he had walked there by himself. Furthermore he looked wet, as if he had recently emerged from the nearby Tiber. Swimming? So wounded?

Suddenly the fallen man gave an appalling shriek and convulsed like a fish on a hook. Fresh blood began oozing from his wounds.

His anguish was so acute Vesi could almost feel it herself. She could go for help, but by the time she returned he would surely be dead. Fortunately she was not afraid of blood. Had she not watched from hiding as the *purtani* set the silver plate into her father's crushed skull after the hunting accident that eventually claimed his life? She could help this man if he was not too far gone, if he had not lost too much blood.

Vesi looked over her shoulder. The rolling hills were tapestried with flowers, many of them possessing healing properties. She could cleanse the wounds and apply a poultice to staunch the bleeding. The *purtani* would criticize her for usurping their healing functions and probably punish her for entering unhallowed Sacred Space. But if she were to allow a man to die needlessly when she might have saved him . . . was that not the greater crime?

Vesi pressed her forefinger and middle finger to her lips, kissed them, and bowed her head in reverence. "Culsan, the god of destiny; Tuflas, goddess of healing, guide me. What I do now, I do through you."

Then she stepped over the line.

Walking through the unmade city was terrifying. In unhallowed Sacred Space the fabric between the worlds was very thin. Vesi was certain she could hear *hia* and *siu* whispering in the Otherworld.

She could even catch the faintest scent of the Netherworld where Satres ruled and Veno protected the dead. As long as she was alive its mysteries were denied her. But the perfumes that wafted from that dark kingdom were spiced with myrrh and cinnamon and subtler, more alluring fragrances that promised and beguiled. She felt their temptation, potent as a stirring in the loins.

Death, the Aegyptians claimed, was a jewel of incomparable brilliance.

On every side shadows twisted and dissolved, hinting at wonders, each one attempting to draw her into the darkness from which she knew she would never return.

Fragments of songs, ghosts of winds, the distant trilling of unknown birds called to her, and behind them the faintest whispers that might have been prayers, incantations, secrets. . . .

With an effort Vesi forced herself to concentrate on the injured man. To allow her spirit to be distracted would leave her vulnerable to vengeful spirits lurking in wait for the unwary. The young woman was trembling with tension as finally she stepped into the rectangle of the *templum.*

It was as if she had walked into a maelstrom.

Dark hair tore free of her silver fillet; saffron *peplos* molded itself to her body. The air within the area was so thick she had to force herself through invisible density. The beings lurking beyond human sight in the Otherworld were frenzied as she had never known them to be . . . but then she had never walked through unhallowed Sacred Space before. They clustered and gibbered at the very edges of her vision, vanishing when she turned to look at them, reappearing as writhing shadows when she looked away.

The absence of a bloody trail was more puzzling now, but only because there was so much blood around the man's body. Vesi forced herself to kneel beside him, drawing her linen skirt up onto her thighs to keep from staining it any more than necessary. She gently examined the wounds on his back—deep punctures and long, raking claw marks that flayed the flesh. Then, sliding her hands under the man's body, she turned him over.

She was startled to find the broken body of a huge white owl underneath him, downy feathers plastered to his bloody chest. Then when she looked upon his face, she realized this was no ordinary man.

Vesi was about to scream when he opened his eyes.

THREE

Though he was half a mile from the river, Artile caught a whiff of the tainted breeze. Instinctively he dropped to the ground and rolled a short distance down the terraced slope. Yet even as he rolled, the stench followed him.

Twice before he had encountered a similar putrid chill. The first time had been when a Babylonian magus loosed a minor *utukki,* an *ummu* demon, on a caravan Artile was leading across the Great Sand Waste. The *utukki*'s presence had been heralded by a foul, icy breeze. Artile had smelled the odor again many seasons later on the day he came upon the remains of a human sacrifice high in the Black Mountains. Although the day had been warm, the telltale chill had lingered around the butchered corpses.

The *purtani* said the foul wind slipped through whenever the fabric between the worlds was torn.

Lying flat on the ground, Artile raised his head cautiously and sniffed. The air around him smelt only of loamy earth and healthy grapevines. The noxious odor had vanished.

And yet . . .

Artile fumbled for his pruning knife and got to his feet with the inadequate weapon clutched in his hand. He crouched like a man ready to run; there was no shame in running. In his youth he had been a mariner, a guide, and a mercenary warrior, surviving all three dangerous occupations because he had learned to trust his instincts . . . and run when the occasion warranted.

His instincts were telling him now that something was wrong, terribly wrong.

Shading his eyes with one hand, he turned full circle. His vineyard spread out before him, vines laden with grapes just beginning to ripen. In the distance he could see some of the workers moving slowly along the rows and filling their baskets. None of them appeared uneasy.

Beyond his land a fold of hills sloped to meet the forest and the river. Nothing disturbed the scene. No spiral of smoke warned of fire among the trees. The Tiber was as placid as a snake basking in the sun.

Artile looked up. The birds that circled in the sky above, always hopeful of snatching some fruit, seemed equally untroubled.

Perhaps he was imagining things; were his aging senses at last beginning to betray him?

Tightening his lips, Artile gave a firm shake of his head. He could not accept the possibility; he had not imagined that odor. His nose was still sensitive enough to detect the first hint of rot upon the vine or the telltale sliminess of diseased soil. His other senses might fail, but that of smell would be reliable until the end.

Limping slightly, he walked the width of the vineyard terrace and climbed the hill beyond. His left thigh muscle had been torn by a Nubian spear eight seasons past. The *purtani* had healed the injury, but the residual awkwardness finally convinced him he was getting too old to be a mercenary. So using the small fortune he had secreted away over the years, he purchased a vineyard with a modest but comfortable villa. There he had settled down to spend the rest of his life getting acquainted with peace.

The gods, Artile told everyone, had been good to him. But the *Ais* were fickle; they could rescind their kindness at any time, as he knew.

At the top of the hill he paused to catch his breath. Automatically he glanced northward, in the direction where the new *spura* soon would rise almost on the boundary of his vineyards. Another gift of the gods, the opportunity to sell his wines so close to home. He would . . .

The man grunted in surprise. There was a moving splash of color—gold and green and red—against the cleared earth. He rubbed his eyes, then looked again.

Someone was crossing unhallowed Sacred Space.

Keeping his eyes fixed on the distant *spura,* Artile hurried forward as swiftly as his game leg would allow. Those colors indicated a woman; the female costumes of the Rasne were famous for their exuberant hues.

Surely none of the Silver People would knowingly enter unhallowed Sacred Space!

Yet he was seeing a woman there, of that Artile was certain. His mobility was impaired, but the keen sight that had stood him in good stead for so many years was undiminished. Once it had been his proud boast that he could tell if the eyes of an eagle flying overhead were yellow or gray.

The woman seemed to be moving toward a dark form in the very center of the *spura.* The old man frowned, trying to make sense of the vaguely human shadow. Artile saw the woman pause, bend over . . . then the path dipped and the scene was hidden from him by the next hill. Cursing under his breath, he hastened forward.

Before he reached the summit of the hill he heard her scream. The sound was high-pitched, terrified . . . and abruptly cut off.

Without hesitation, Artile tried to run.

When he could see the *spura* again, only the figure in bright clothing lay on the cleared earth. The dark form she had been examining had vanished.

Artile's heart was pounding fearfully in his chest by the time he reached the margins of the *spura*. He hesitated, unwilling to enter until he realized that Sacred Space had already been compromised. No city would be built here now, he thought with a pang of disappointment. No market on his doorstep. Then he berated himself for his petty and selfish thoughts. Limping, he hurried across the foundations toward the area designated for the *templum*.

The still figure within was lying on her stomach with her head twisted to one side. What he could see of her face was puffed and bruised; dark hair was matted to her skull by blood. Torn from her body and strewn on the ground beside her were the tatters of her bright clothing.

Artile's fist closed with the index and little fingers extended. He brought his hand to his mouth and breathed an ancient prayer into the fingers, warding off evil.

Kneeling beside the woman, he gently turned her over. The breath caught in his throat. He knew her. She was Vesi, a maiden, a daring girl who played games and ran races like a boy, a girl filled with spirit and courage. Of all the children of the Rasne, Vesi was among the brightest. Watching her had made him long for a daughter of his own, though Fate and old war wounds had decreed he had none. Now to see her like this . . . !

Artile had traveled far and fought in many battles, and more than once had observed what men inflamed by blood lust could do to a woman. Yet never had he seen a woman so peculiarly mutilated.

Deep parallel gouges ran the length of the girl's body, slicing open her breasts and cutting deeply into the soft flesh of her belly. On closer inspection, they looked as if they had begun low on her abdomen and ripped *upward*. He measured them with his broad hands. There were four cuts spaced wider than the span of human fingers. More blood stained her thighs.

Making sympathetic noises deep in his throat, Artile removed his cloak. She was a strong girl and well-nourished; with his bad leg he would not be able to carry her all the way back to his villa. He must go for help. But he could not leave her naked amid the gaudy ruins of her dress.

As he was tucking his cloak around her, the crushed remains of a bird fluttered from her hands. From the feathers Artile identified the corpse as that of an owl.

The old man picked up a feather and turned it in his gnarled fingers. A white owl, in a land without white owls.

FOUR

Long before consciousness returned, Vesi could hear voices. Dream voices circled and spun around her, some murmuring almost inaudibly in a misty distance, others loud and immediate. A few she recognized. Her mother's was suffused with anger. The *purtan* was soft-spoken in counterpoint, conciliatory.

There was another whose words were like the crack of a whip, Pepan, Lord of the Rasne.

Vesi grew dimly aware of the hiss of candle flame somewhere nearby, of water tinkling from a fountain a little farther away, of the particular ambient sound of space embraced by stuccoed walls. From beyond those walls came a low buzz, as of a distant crowd.

Through ears that never slept, such details informed that level of Vesi's mind that also never slept. The sounds created a pattern she recognized. She knew this place by heart, was familiar with each crack in the plaster and every tile on the floor.

As with most Etruscan houses, the structure was a hollow square with stone foundations and walls of unfired brick, built around a roofless courtyard that provided both light and air to the interior. The rooms that comprised three sides of the house gave onto this space. At the rear a solid wall formed the fourth side of the square. A fountain in the courtyard kept the house filled with the delicate tinkle of water music, and the air was perfumed by flowering plants growing in terra-cotta tubs. Beyond the entrance door at the front of the dwelling lay the *spura* of Vesi's birth. She was in the main room of the house she had lived in for all of her fourteen years. She was . . . home.

Safe.

Following that first conscious thought, her other senses began to awaken one by one. She caught a whiff of the herbs and spices used in Etruscan cooking, then the lush fragrance of the flowers blooming in the courtyard. Gradually, feeling began to return to her nerve endings. At first she was but dimly aware that she lay on a couch piled high with cushions, but then . . .

. . . with the restoration of total tactile sensation came *pain,* an explosion of agony that enfolded her body like a sheet of flame!

Vesi screamed.

"I tell you no man could have done this," Repana was saying angrily to Caile, the *purtan.* A big-boned, middle-aged woman in a sky blue gown of elaborately pleated linen, Repana prided herself on being considered still handsome. Surely someday Pepan would notice.

But her own appearance had become irrelevant. She fixed her eyes on the *purtan*'s face rather than look any longer at the damage that had been done to her daughter's body.

The paunchy priest was an easterner, not a full-blooded Etruscan, and excessively fond of the pleasures of the vine and the table. His thick lips were still glistening with grease from his most recent meal as he replied, "The man who found your daughter is a former mercenary, and we all know what they're like. I feel quite certain he was the one who. . ."

Pepan dropped his hand onto the *purtan*'s shoulder as lightly as if the touch might soil his fingers. A slender man with long-lidded eyes and a thrusting, aquiline nose, the Lord of the Rasne moved with the deceptive languor common to his race. He could be identified as a prince of Etruria by the way he wore his beard. All facial hair was plucked from his cheeks and upper lip, but from his chin hung a precisely coiled pair of dark brown curls. His clothing consisted of a narrow, short-sleeved white robe with a red border over which he wore a triangle of darker red, finely woven wool, drawn to one side and fastened high on the shoulder with a silver brooch set with lapis and carnelians.

"The man who found Vesi is Artile the winemaker," Pepan told the priest in crisp tones, "and is well known to me. A man of impeccable honor. I trust him implicitly, and on his behalf I resent your slander."

Caile widened his eyes. "I meant no harm, my lord! Certainly not! It was just a suggestion . . . one looks first at the most obvious. . ."

Pepan locked his hands on either side of Caile's head before the other man had time to flinch. He forced him to bend over the young woman lying on the bed. "Then look at the obvious!" Pepan commanded.

Roughly he thrust the *purtan* down, holding his face just above the girl's torn breasts. When the priest squeezed his eyes shut, pressure from Pepan's thumbs made him open them again. "Look, you coward," snarled the Lord of the Rasne. "Does this damage resemble the work of any human weapon . . . or human hand?"

The *purtan* focused his eyes to find himself a mere finger's length from mutilated flesh. He wrinkled his nose at the scent of blood and a smell as foul as excrement. His stomach heaved.

"Repana is right, no man did this," Pepan asserted, satisfied to have made his point. "We must seek elsewhere for Vesi's attacker." He released the *purtan* and stepped back, deliberately wiping his fingers on the red wool as if the touch of the priest's flesh had insulted him. "I need some fresh air." Folding his arms across his chest, he stalked into the courtyard and stared up at the twilight sky.

The evening was sweet with summer, the first stars a handful of jewels flung against a peacock blue dome. Normally such beauty enthralled Etruscans. They composed countless poems to celebrate the first star, the warm night wind, the constantly changing hues of the heavens.

But this evening Pepan's outraged senses took no pleasure from beauty.

A widower, he had long admired the widowed Repana. At the most unexpected moments he found himself thinking of her warm smile, her long-fingered hands. His sons and daughters were grown, and his house and his heart were lonely. He could not simply take Repana as wife however. Under the law, first the spirits of his own dead mate and Repana's would have to be located in the Netherworld and propitiated, and these arrangements took time. The Lord of the Rasne had many responsibilities and put his responsibility to himself at the bottom of the list, something he would get around to . . . in the future.

So he had done nothing as yet about his feelings for Repana. But he had developed a paternal affection for her daughter; if—when—he wed Repana, Vesi would become his child. He could taste, as bitter as bile on his tongue, fury at the wanton damage that had been inflicted upon the lovely young woman.

"If no man is responsible, then the girl must have been mauled by a beast," Caile was saying in an effort to regain his dignity. "That stench, that wild smell, could come from a bear or. . . "

Repana uttered such an exclamation of disgust that the *purtan* backed away from her, fearing she might strike him. "Look around, what do you see?" she demanded to know, making a graceful gesture that included the entire house. "The fur rugs underfoot, the tusks of boar and horns of aurochs that hang on the walls . . . every one of those trophies was taken by my husband. He prided himself on his skill with the spear; it was an art form, he said.

"Usually he killed his prey and made a sacrifice of propitiation to its spirit. But sometimes the beasts left their mark on him. I have tended and stitched many such wounds, including the one that ultimately proved fatal when a bear ripped off the top of his skull. I also saw the damage done by the pack of wild boar that killed my sons when they tried to follow in his footsteps as a matter of family pride. You might say I am an expert on hunting injuries," she added, with a bitter twist of her mouth.

Pointing toward the four terrible raking wounds on her daughter's body, she concluded, "I tell you, priest, there is no wild animal in Etruria that leaves marks like these."

"If it was neither man nor animal, it must have been some monster that strayed into our territory," Caile suggested. "Perhaps a creature from the Darklands, one of those things with the head of a boar and the body of a lion and great leathery wings. We know such monsters live there."

"*We* know?" Pepan called scornfully from the courtyard, not even deigning to look over his shoulder at the *purtan*. "Who is this 'we,' priest? You never venture outside the *tular spural*, the city boundaries. I have scouted the forests and mountains and found them inhabited by debased tribes one could scarcely call human, yet they fear us more than we fear them. In all my travels I have seen no such monster as you describe. Nor have I seen anything like what has been done to this girl."

"But if you eliminate man and beast and monster," the *purtan* argued, throwing up his hands, "what does that leave? What else is there?"

"Hia," breathed Repana. Suddenly her courage failed her. *"Hia!"*

To the terror of all, occasionally some corrupted *hia* would break through from the Otherworld or, more terribly, from the Netherworld. Ravening and uncontrollable, the thing might fasten upon a living person. Once it had selected a victim, it would use its malign influence to drive the unfortunate to commit the most appalling acts, even self-mutilation. But Vesi could not possibly have done this to herself . . . and Artile had seen another . . . if the old man had not disturbed her attacker, Vesi might have endured a fate beyond imagining. The thought sickened Repana.

But as she shuddered with horror, a cracked whisper said, "No, this is not the deed of a mere *hia.*"

Repana whirled around as Caile dropped to his knees and pressed his forehead to the floor. In the courtyard, Pepan did the same. A slight, bent figure stood in the doorway of the house, ignoring the men who prostrated themselves in reverence.

"Not *hia?"* Repana asked hoarsely.

"No. Something worse, I suspect. Much worse." The shape at the door moved and an old woman hobbled into the room. She was almost hairless with age, her skin taut across the bones of her face, giving the impression of a skull.

"Uni Ati," Repana murmured. She attempted to kneel, but the old woman placed a restraining hand on her arm.

"Stand with me, daughter. Lend me your support while I examine the child."

In silence the two women gazed down upon the suffering girl. After her one scream Vesi had made no further sound. Tears seeped from beneath her closed eyelids however.

"Leave us," the old woman ordered the men. "We have no need of you now. I can do whatever needs to be done for this girl."

Without protest, the *purtan* and the Lord of the Rasne scrambled to their feet and left the house to join the crowd gathered outside. Not only the Rasne, but even the humblest of their slaves had been drawn by news of Vesi's injury—and the more astonishing and unprecedented visit of the Uni Ati to a private residence.

The Uni Ati, whose title meant First Mother, was the oldest of all the Silver People. She had been the senior elder of the Council for as long as anyone could remember. The most serious disputes of the Rasne were referred to her; her judgment was final and irrevocable. In addition, she was a skillful healer, and many who had been given up as hopeless by the *purtani* were taken to her and subsequently cured.

It was claimed that she never changed the rags she wore nor left the hillside cave that was her only home. Yet she had come to Repana's house this evening.

"No *hia* caused this," the old woman repeated. Extending her left hand palm downward, she rotated it in a sunwise circle above Vesi's torn body. Her knuckles and joints were so knotted with age as to resemble the mangled claws of birds. But when she moved her fingers through the air, the bones glowed through her skin with an eerie green light.

Vesi convulsed.

Repana tried to gather her daughter in her arms but the old woman blocked her with her own body. "No!" she cried, continuing to make gestures above the girl's torso. "These are not fatal injuries," she remarked after a time, "only very painful ones. But. . . " She drew a deep breath and moved her hand in a different pattern, allowing it to rest for a moment above Vesi's torn belly. Once she darted a glance at Repana and swiftly looked away. Moments later, she grunted as if confirming some suspicion.

With a sigh, the Uni Ati folded her hands and withdrew them into the sleeves of her tattered robe. "Your daughter was attacked and violated by a *siu,*" she told Repana. "That is demon's stink on her flesh." One hand reemerged from the sleeve of her robe holding a ceremonial knife with a curved bronze blade. "She would be better off dead."

"No!" Repana gasped. "No, First Mother, she is everything to me! I gave birth to four children: three boys and this girl. Over the years I have attended the dying not only of my husband but also my beloved sons. I am not ready to put my last child into her tomb. Can you understand? I want to enjoy her living. Please! Why do you want to do this?"

Still holding the knife aloft, the old woman replied, "I tell you your daughter has been impregnated by a *siu.* Even now the demon's seed swells within her; she will give birth to an abomination. Is that what you want for her? Do you wish her to be feared and loathed by the rest of the Rasne? Do you think they will even allow the two of you to remain in this *spura*?"

Pressing the knife into Repana's numb hand, the Uni Ati closed the woman's fingers around the handle. "It is up to you to sacrifice your daughter," she said. "You must offer her to Veno and request that your ancestors be allowed to come for her. Assure her of a proper dying, and implore the *Ais* to destroy the *siu* spawn."

Repana was very pale. "What if I refuse?"

"Then someone else will do the deed, for it must be done. But remember—only Vesi's nearest kin can summon the *hia* of her ancestors to conduct her spirit to sanctuary in the Netherworld. Without such guides, she is not likely to find her way there alone. She could be lost to wander frightened and confused through the Otherworld instead, a helpless ghost. There she would easily fall prey to evil spirits."

From the hollows of her sunken eyes, the Uni Ati gave Repana a searing look. "You have no choice," she said. Then she hobbled from the house.

As Repana stood beside her daughter, clutching the knife in fingers turned to ice, she could hear the old woman's cracked tones beyond the door. "Caile, we will require your services after all. Dress yourself in your ceremonial robes and summon the townspeople. There is to be a Dying."

"A Dying? But why?" Pepan demanded to know. "Appalling as they are, Vesi's injuries need not be fatal. You can heal them, First Mother. Your skills are. . . "

"Be silent and do not interrupt me! Repana has chosen to give the girl to Veno because she is carrying the spawn of a *siu,*" the old woman snapped. "Were Vesi to live, her child would bring disaster to the race of the Rasne."

FIVE

From its source on the northwestern slope of the Apennines the water flowed relentlessly downward. At first an inconsequential rivulet that sang to itself in the sun, the stream gathered force as it descended. In time a mighty river swept seaward to a raw young city sprawling across seven hills.

Long before the birth of Rome, the Etruscans had named the river Tiber, meaning notched. Of all the watercourses that flowed through their land, this was the most important: Father Tiber.

Like fertile Sister Nile and dark Brother Styx, the Tiber was both a barrier and a conduit. Unpolluted and pristine, the living waters of the great rivers straddled the divide between the worlds of flesh and spirit. Strange beings inhabited the three realms—Earthworld, Otherworld, Netherworld—traversed by these rivers.

Only rarely did the occupants of one realm venture into another.

The great river gave life and took life. On its journey

to the sea it drained meadowland and fed marsh; incubated dragonflies, dissolved the flesh of carrion, and scrubbed the bones clean. Some worshipped it, some feared it, and only the fool ignored it.

The river was unforgiving.

Denizens of the Otherworld clustered most thickly around the Tiber's banks, and Earthworld hunters found the richest bounty there.

Wulv pressed the tip of his bronze dagger into the pile of dung in the center of the path. The outer crust cracked open to reveal a moist and steaming interior. The man smiled to himself, but the expression was distorted by the scars that covered the left side of his face, pulling his lips away from his teeth in a permanent leer. Unkempt hair straggled to his shoulders; eyebrows as tangled as briar thickets overhung his deep-set brown eyes. Even among his own tribespeople, the Teumetes, Wulv was considered ugly.

But he knew how to track animals.

The boar had passed this way recently and was keeping to the trail, a well-worn animal trail winding through the forest west of the Tiber. If the beast followed the usual pattern, it was heading for a familiar lair.

Of course, there was always the possibility that it would break with the pattern. Throughout his life Wulv had hunted bear, wolf, and wildcat, but of all creatures, boar were the most unpredictable. Bears were not much better, however. The bear that had torn open his face should have been hibernating when a much younger Wulv stumbled across its den. The bear had taken his face—but he had taken its hide. Made into a mantle, the trophy still hung across his broad shoulders.

Wulv had been tracking this particular boar for three days, patiently, biding his time. Any other hunter would have abandoned the pursuit and returned to the comfort of friends and family, but Wulv had neither to distract him. All he had was single-minded determination.

The boar he was following had rampaged through the fields bordering the Teumetes village on the fringe of the Great Forest. What the animal had not eaten, it had trampled in wanton destruction. A hunting party composed of the young men of the village had gone out and eventually killed a boar—a young, wiry-bristled female they'd trapped in a patch of marshland. They had hurled as many spears into the animal as the fingers on two hands, slung the dead boar from a pole, and carried the carcass back in triumph to their village.

One look at the beast convinced Wulv it was the wrong animal. The slain boar had a broken hoof that would have left a distinctive track and was not nearly as heavy as the animal that had ravaged the crops. But when Wulv called attention to these facts, he was shouted down by the triumphant hunters. Their beardless leader even threatened him. Only the patience Wulv had learned while waiting for his bear injuries to heal had prevented him from removing the youth's liver with his knife.

Instead he had gone home to wait. He did not live in the village, but some distance away on an islet in the middle of a marshy lake at the very edge of the Great Forest. Wulv preferred to spend his days where no man would laugh at his ugliness and no woman would shrink from his touch.

Four days later the village elders paid him an unprecedented visit. They implored him to forgive the rash behavior of the young men and begged him to go in search of the original boar. The beast had returned, doing even more damage than before. In addition, it had killed a tiny boy child whose mother was working in the fields. The sight of her half-eaten toddler had, the elders related, driven the woman to madness.

Wulv listened without comment, his arms folded and his eyes staring into some misty distance. He let his visitors work up a sweat as they strove to persuade him and accepted, with apparent reluctance, the bribes they pressed upon him. Then at last he gathered his weapons and a few supplies and set off—as he had meant to do all along.

The boar was a challenge.

As if the beast knew it was now being hunted by an expert, it abandoned the area, moving deeper and deeper into the forest. Wulv had no difficulty picking up its trail. Perhaps, he speculated, the boar was deliberately leading him somewhere for reasons of its own. The creature was intelligent and cunning, and obviously learned from experience.

He must be doubly wary.

Determined to maintain a precise distance, a margin of safety, between himself and his quarry, Wulv ate as he traveled, satisfying his hunger with strips of dried meat he had brought with him and berries snatched from bushes he passed.

In the middle of the third day of his hunt, the man halted and took a half step off the trail. In his bearskin mantle and untanned leather tunic he blended into the forest background. Turning his face up, he peered through the branches of the giant trees above him until he was able to locate the Great Sky Father. Past High Day it was. Great Sky Father had begun his journey down to the horizon.

Wulv came to a decision: If he had not tracked the boar to its lair by nightfall, he would turn back. Three days was long enough to be wandering through the forest without feeling sun on his head. He was growing bored.

As the afternoon wore on, the temperature fell and what little light penetrated to the forest floor soon vanished. Wulv caught the scent of rain on the air. The hard rain typical of the region could obliterate all traces of the boar, dissolving fresh spoor and washing away its characteristic odor. A less experienced hunter might have tried to close up the space between himself and his quarry so as not to lose the trail, but Wulv had learned caution the hard way.

Unconsciously, he rubbed at the scars on his face.

Borne on a howling wind, the rain swept in from the north. Icy drops as vicious as stones slashed through the canopy of the leaves, driving earthward at an angle. Wulv paused long enough to unsling the leather pack on his back and remove a piece of oiled deerhide, which he carefully wrapped around the head of his spear.

Some of the mountain tribes still used blades of flint or obsidian, but the Teumetes were proud of their metal weapons and intensely protective of them, knowing their worth to be greater than jewels.

With the rain now at his back, the hunter moved even more cautiously. The wind was blowing his scent up the trail; surely the boar had already picked it up. Wulv had heard of a boar turning aside from a track and waiting until its hunter passed by, then lunging out to kill the man with its savage tusks.

One foot set precisely in front of the other, Wulv continued to advance. His wary eyes peered out from beneath his tangled brows; his spear was balanced in his hand, ready for action.

Lightning flashed, illuminating the forest in stark black and white. The God Who Roars boomed an angry response. Wulv halted abruptly and made the Sign of Horns, index and little finger pointing straight out to ward off evil. It was not good to be in the way when the God Who Burns and the God Who Roars stalked the land, warring between themselves. Capricious and deadly, they trampled man underfoot as carelessly as a man trod on ants.

Lightning cracked again. In that instant, Wulv saw the boar. The beast was standing immobile in the track ahead of him, with its body at an angle, its great head bowed, razor tusks gleaming. He saw the boar start to turn . . . and at that moment the lightning exploded again and the world vanished in white brilliance as the boar began its charge.

The hunter's eyes were seared by the light. Momentarily blinded, he hurled his spear.

SIX

Some distance to the south, a lone figure was sitting on his haunches in a small cave. He appeared to be human: a slender man somewhat less than middle height, with almond-shaped eyes and swarthy skin as worn and crumpled as old parchment.

Drawing upon inhuman abilities lingering from his Otherworld existence, the *siu* had reformed the walls of the cave to glassy smoothness. This vitreous substance rendered him invisible from any prying eyes that could see beyond the physical.

Secure within this stronghold, he sat.

In the sky above the cave clouds gathered; thunder rumbled.

On reflection, his earlier actions now dismayed him. But they were not his fault; nothing was ever his fault. The minions of the *Ais* had hunted him relentlessly until he became so desperate and exhausted he could not think. By the time he escaped from the Otherworld into the Earthworld he was acting on sheer instinct. Encountering the human girl had been . . . his mouth twisted in an ironic grimace . . . like a gift from the gods.

An incomplete gift, unfortunately. Eating the still-living heart of a virgin should have been sufficient to restore him to full strength. But a moment's intense excitement, a loss of control . . . when he had a warm human female in his hands once more after so long a time, he had been unable to resist the temptation to rape her. The mistake would have been rectified by devouring her heart afterward and thus killing her. But as he was about to tear out the organ, the limping man had come hurrying toward them. Knowing he still lacked the strength for a confrontation, the *siu* had been forced to abandon the girl and flee.

Leaving a part of himself in her living body.

Mistake, mistake!

In spite of the distance between them, he was physically aware of the child that had been conceived. The call of its unborn spirit drew him like a beacon.

In another age the demon might have allowed his seed to mature to birthing. He would either have been indifferent to the child or taken malicious pleasure in teaching it evil.

But the era when humans and inhabitants of the Otherworld could freely mingle with one another was over. As a result of manipulation by the *Ais,* the different planes inhabited by sentient beings had boundaries now. A demon could exert influence in the Earthworld, but he, or she, could no longer take a tangible form there. Thus had the gods ruled.

This particular *siu* had willfully ignored their ruling and made himself part of the Earthworld with a tangible body. The Earthworld he had once walked as a human man himself. The Earthworld for which he still lusted.

Here he could act with impunity, knowing that little could harm him . . . except the flesh of his own flesh. As a carnate element of the *siu,* his spawn made the demon vulnerable.

The unborn infant and the woman who carried it must be found and destroyed. As long as the child existed it posed a very real threat, one he could not tolerate.

Closing his eyes, the scarred flesh wrinkling and twisting, the being in the cave concentrated on the faint but distinctive song of the unborn life, tracing it to its source. Occasionally he paused to scratch himself, tiny slivers of skin peeling off beneath his nails. Too many centuries had passed since he was truly a man; now he was vaguely uncomfortable in skin. To the casual glance his looked like human flesh, but with a decidedly greenish cast he could not eradicate. And it was very dry, which annoyed him. Any small failing on his part made him angry.

There! The telltale song of life, a wondrous threnody that never failed to infuriate him.

Lightning flashed across the sky.

He began a low, monotone humming as he expanded his inner sight to encompass territory far beyond the cave. He knew where they were now; it only remained to find a form in which to attack and destroy them.

Lightning flashed again. The final flash blinded not only Wulv but the boar as it charged. In that instant it was slain. By sheerest accident the hunter's spear entered its left eye and pierced its brain.

Before it could even feel the pain of the fatal blow, the great beast crashed to the ground. Heart stilled, lungs frozen. A gush of bright blood poured from its nostrils. For a few moments there was no sound but the gurgle of organs dying within the carcass.

Slowly Wulv regained his sight, searing monochrome fading to familiar colors. He approached the body one wary step at a time, intending to reclaim his spear and collect his trophies. Sometimes an animal could play dead until the hunter was right on top of it. But not this one. A once-in-a-lifetime throw and the beast had run right onto the spear, driving it deeper. The boar was slain. Wulv was silently exulting as he reached for his spear.

With a shudder, the dead boar staggered to its feet.

Wulv flung himself backward, scrabbling for his knife.

The first tottering steps the boar took were as uncertain as those of a newborn. It lurched, almost fell, gathered itself, and lurched on. The beast's mouth opened but no breath emerged. Its right eye continued to glaze; no lashes batted across the fixed stare. The thing paid no attention to Wulv however.

There was one brief moment when the shadows around the creature suggested a crouching man. Then the image vanished as if absorbed into the beast's body. Sullen red coals began to glow deep within its undamaged eye. Giving a toss of its mighty head, it slammed its skull against a tree trunk and dislodged the encumbering spear.

Then the slain boar trotted into the forest and disappeared.

For a time Wulv could only stare after the beast. Cold sweat was running down his spine and his legs were trembling. He should turn and walk away, forget what he had seen. But he was no coward . . . and he was curious. Curiosity had always been a weakness of his.

At last he clenched his jaw, reclaimed his spear, wiped its bloodied head on the leaves, and set off on the boar's trail.

Repana caught her daughter's hand and squeezed it as hard as she could, but the girl was unresponsive. Vesi seemed half asleep, unaware of the branches that scratched her skin or the brambles that tore her bare legs. She had already been so injured that she did not feel the lesser wounds. All her concentration was required to put one foot after the other as her mother demanded.

Looking up, Repana tried to judge time through the dense canopy of oak and elm leaves high above the forest floor. The pursuit might already be underway.

The woman narrowed her eyes in thought, considering her situation. The Uni Ati had intended to preside over Vesi's Dying, cocelebrating the event with the *purtan.* Normally any of the Rasne would have welcomed such an honor. Nothing in the lives of the Silver People was as important as the end of life itself, a highly formalized ritual circumscribed by rites and observances. Families went to the greatest lengths to ensure that a departing member was committed to the care of the ancestors and welcomed by Veno in the Netherworld. The Netherworld was fraught with hazards. Only the powerful Protectress of the Dead could keep a spirit safe there.

But Repana was not willing to surrender her last surviving child to Veno. Not yet.

While pretending to accede to the Uni Ati's demand, she had secretly given Vesi a draught of oil of poppy, then put clothes on the girl as the narcotic was taking effect. Working swiftly and silently, Repana had gathered a small bundle of food and herbs and the few essentials they would need to make good their escape. When all was in readiness, she had gone to the door of the house and requested a sacrificial knife. She spoke with pride, as befitted a mother preparing to give her child a great gift.

The Uni Ati had replied, "You have my knife already," in a querulous voice that scratched the air like a sliver of glass.

Repana had bowed her head respectfully. "I return your knife to you, First Mother, and ask that I may have another to use. One which I may keep for myself afterward, as a holy relic of my daughter."

Such a request could not be refused. Head wobbling atop her thin neck, Uni Ati nodded agreement. "When we bring a child into the world," she said, "we grant it the gift of life borne of blood. Now you, Repana, have a final gift of blood to give your daughter. Those whose deaths we make beautiful will reward us when our own time comes; they will be waiting with loving arms outstretched to guide us safely to Veno in the Netherworld.

"Give your daughter her Dying as you choose. We support you and commend you. When she has departed, we will sing songs and hold funeral games in her honor. Great will be our joy at imagining the existence awaiting her with Veno in a nightless land of fruit and music."

The assembled people murmured among themselves. Most of the Rasne and not a few of their slaves had children; all wondered if they would have the courage now being required of Repana.

Without a word, Pepan stepped forward and handed Vesi's mother a large ebony-handled knife with a curved blade. As her eyes met his he gave a slight but deliberate nod, then silently mouthed the words "glade of stones."

With an effort, Repana kept her face impassive. Any reaction on her part could arouse suspicion and she did not wish to have Pepan implicated. She was grateful however. The Lord of the Rasne seemed to be the only one who cared what she was feeling and who was willing to take her side.

Carrying his knife, she went back inside the house and closed the door, the only door. She and her child were alone together within the windowless walls. It was to be expected that she would want privacy until the mortal wound was delivered. Then she would summon the others and they would form a triumphal procession to carry Vesi to the *templum.*

There was no limit on the time allowed for a ritual of Dying. It could take a matter of moments, it could occupy an entire day. There were a hundred ways to make a Dying, from the swift and painless, which was favored for the very old or the very young, to the most ancient rite in which the victim was allowed to bleed to death over a long period of time. This was the way favored by traditionalists, who insisted that only blood could be certain of attracting the favor of Veno.

Repana never intended to find out.

Even if Pepan had not called her attention to the sacred glade deep in the forest, which was famed as a sanctuary, she had already chosen that as her destination. Hers and Vesi's. But first they must escape the *spura.*

The rear of Repana's house was actually the high wall that encircled the Rasne city. The house consisted of three small wings surrounding the courtyard, but its size was a blessing for a widow with only one child. There was another advantage, however, which Repana now appreciated for the first time.

She stood quietly for a moment, looking down at Vesi. From outside came the voices of the crowd raised in supplication to the gods as Caile led them in a wailing singsong that grated on Repana's nerves. Bending, she wrapped her semiconscious daughter in a cloak, then somehow got the girl to her feet. "It hurts," Vesi whimpered, but only once. Whimpering was not part of her nature.

Through a combination of cajoling and brute force Repana succeeded in hoisting Vesi through a narrow vertical opening let into the city wall. Intended as a loophole to allow javelin throwers to defend the Rasne *spura,* the shaft was not meant to accommodate a human body. When Repana followed she found it a very tight squeeze. For a moment she panicked. What if she got stuck and they broke into the house and found her?

Then with one final, desperate wriggle, she was through, emerging in an angle of the wall screened from casual view by a clump of shrubbery. There she found Vesi slumped on the ground, her figure no more than a dark huddle in the darker night. Her mother caught her by the shoulders and dug in her fingernails, hoping to rouse the girl with pain. When Vesi murmured an inarticulate protest, Repana whispered urgently, "Stand up, child. I can't carry you; you will have to walk . . . or die. Walk, I tell you. Now! Walk!"

Without a backward look, Repana had led her daughter away from the only home they had ever known, across the fields and into the black maw of the forest. From behind them came the sound of chanting slowly rising toward an inevitable crescendo: the Song of a Dying.

As she made her way into the forest, Repana could not remember the last time anyone had defied a Uni Ati. Such a deed would merit the most dire punishment. Nor could she recall any Etruscan ever exiling themselves from one of their *spurae.* Immersed in beauty and comfort, they were the god-chosen, the god-blessed, the god-loved. In living memory none of her race had turned their back on such a heritage.

But sometimes slaves attempted to escape. Or thieves. Then the great hunting dogs came into their own. No one escaped the massive hounds with their sensitive noses and long, silken ears. And sharp fangs.

Repana could feel a prickling of the skin on her back as if the hounds were already right behind her. She tried to get Vesi to hurry, but the girl could barely walk. In addition, the footing was treacherous, the forest so dark that each step had to be felt out with a tentative foot. When they had gone far enough that they could no longer hear the chanting, Repana allowed her daughter to stop. While the girl leaned panting against the bole of a huge tree, her mother scooped out a shallow bed for them between the roots. There they hid until dawn, concealed beneath dead branches.

When the first daylight filtered into their sanctuary they were up again. Vesi's injuries forced them to travel very slowly; they seemed to be inching through the forest rather than running away. More than once Repana ground her teeth with impatience. When a storm overtook them, thunder and lightning signaling the fury of the gods, she did not dare stop to propitiate the elements. She and Vesi must keep going. Their defection would not be forgiven by the Rasne, whose threat seemed the more immediate.

When the storm abated the two women hardly noticed. But in the silence following the thunder, Repana heard sounds in the distance that convinced her the hounds were on their trail. Holding Pepan's knife in one sweating hand, she gripped her daughter's arm with the other and dragged Vesi on. If only they could reach the glade, they might be safe from the hounds.

And if they did not . . . well, there was no shame in being taken down by the famous hunting dogs of the Rasne. Death would be swift and sure; the animals were well trained. And it would mean Repana did not have to kill her own daughter.

At least, she told herself, they would die together. Without a formal Dying their spirits would wander aimlessly. But they would have each other . . . and hope. It was common knowledge that those who died together in such circumstances were often rebirthed together, returning to the Earthworld if they found no home in the Netherworld.

The pursuing beasts were getting closer; she could hear them crashing through the undergrowth.

Repana frowned. The hounds of the Rasne were not usually so clumsy.

As something came rushing toward them, Repana whirled around, pushing Vesi behind her. The girl stumbled and fell with a loud cry.

Repana had been expecting dogs, but instead found herself facing an enormous, battle-scarred wild boar. Cruel yellow tusks protruded from its gaping mouth. She screamed . . . and in that final, terrible moment, noticed that something was wrong with its eyes. One was blasted open and suppurating. The other was opaque and glazed, like that of something dead.

Holding Pepan's knife in both hands, Repana called aloud upon Veno and prepared to die.

SEVEN

Six hooded figures stood wordlessly staring into the pool that dominated the long oval hall. A solid beam of intense white light shafted down from a circular opening in the ceiling, turning the water milky.

Sacred water, touching both Earthworld and Otherworld.

In the distance a wild dog howled. Shadows flickered across the beam of light as bats winged their way through the warm night air.

A single bubble rose to the surface of the water, gathered, then burst, sending concentric ripples flowing outward. The silent figures turned their backs on the pool and bent their heads.

Another bubble burst on the surface and then another. Soon the pool was heaving and boiling as if with a life of its own.

Abruptly, opalescent water cascaded off polished obsidian.

A smooth head emerged from the center of the pool. A flat forehead. Blind, slanted eyes. A long, narrow jaw, a slash of a mouth. White water flowed down the black surface of what appeared to be a statue as the image was more fully revealed. The slender column of a neck, sloping shoulders, and then, like a cluster of monstrous fruit, a ribcage covered by swollen black breasts tipped by enormous ruby nipples . . . with one exception. A single breast was flat and withered, the nipple desiccated.

The statue spoke.

Her voice was sibilant but slurred, as if every word was an effort. "I have work for you."

The six figures kept their heads bent to avoid sight of the presence in the pool. "We hear, O Great Pythia," one, older than the others, murmured.

The dark goddess spoke again. "A particularly vicious and cunning *siu* has committed a crime against me. This demon is known to you by his original name of Bur-Sin. Until recently he was an acolyte of mine, the one I held in special favor. Then he robbed me. He took advantage of my trust to get close enough to me to fasten his mouth on my breast."

The listeners shuddered in a mixture of religious ecstasy and terror.

"Each of my breasts has its own attributes, as you know," the voice went on. "The one he drained has given him powers to which he was not entitled."

The six waited, but she did not elaborate.

"I sent Otherworld minions in pursuit," said the carven image, "but the *siu* escaped them in the Earthworld. During the chase they did succeed in injuring his bodily form however. To restore his strength he intended to tear out and eat the living heart of a human virgin. He was disturbed by the approach of another human before he had done more than open her flesh. He abandoned her and fled, but even now his child quickens within her body."

A crescent of darkness edged the milky pool as the moon made its way through the sky, altering the angle of the shaft of light. The obsidian image, which had never risen above waist height, began to slip back into the water. Her dark form glimmered dimly through the translucent liquid.

The words were coming quicker as the level of the water began to rise. "I charge you to seek out this *siu* in the Earthworld. Take him captive to hold for my punishment. Locate his spawn first—you will find the impregnated woman among the Rasne—then use the child as a lure to trap the father. He dare not allow it to live and thrive. Once you have the demon, destroy his child and summon me to complete his punishment. Go now . . . and fail at your peril!" she added harshly.

"We will not fail, O Great Pythia," one of the six whispered.

White water closed over a blind black head. The ripples died away, leaving the surface of the pool as smooth as polished glass.

The shaft of moonlight narrowed, disappeared.

Six hooded figures left the chamber without a backward glance, moving through pitch-black corridors without the benefit of torches. Their kind had no need of light.

EIGHT

Lowering its head, the boar charged.

Repana crouched reflexively as she struggled to recall anything useful her husband might have said about the habits of wild boar. Had he once remarked that a wild boar usually veered to the left, hooking upward with its tusks to disembowel its victim? Frantically she ransacked her memory for an echo of his words, some guidance from the Netherworld where he surely watched and waited.

She would have one chance. She must turn her body sideways to make the smallest possible target and in the same move step to the right, plunging the dagger she carried into the base of the boar's skull as it charged past.

If she failed . . .

The boar thundered across the glade; she could feel the ground shake beneath its hooves. But its behavior was most unnatural. The animal's one-eyed stare was fixed and blind, no foam flecked its lips, no breath hissed from its nostrils. When it was five paces from her, she could smell the unmistakable odor of putrefaction. The boar was dead and rotting . . . yet still moving.

"May the *Ais* protect us!" Repana gasped. The dagger shifted in sweat-slick hands. "Ancestors guide us. . . "

There was a blur of movement from her left.

Pepan's bronze-headed hunting spear buried itself to the haft in the beasts heavily muscled shoulder.

The boar should have squealed and turned toward its attacker or dropped to the ground and rolled to dislodge the weapon. It did neither. Instead it kept advancing with terrible intent, head lowered, dead eyes fixed on Vesi.

The Lord of the Rasne hurled himself forward, recklessly throwing his body onto the boar's back, using his weight in a desperate attempt to force it to the ground. He meant to dig his heels into the earth and try to get enough leverage to snap the animal's neck.

The boar jolted to a halt so abruptly that Pepan was thrown off in an unintentional somersault. Scrambling to his feet, he reached for his dagger, only to realize belatedly that he had given it to Repana the previous day. It was in her hand now. He could not reach it before the boar got him.

His hunting spear was lying in the long grass a little to one side. Closer than Repana and his knife . . . but still too far.

The boar shuddered and lifted its head, flinging it angrily from side to side. Pepan blinked at the wash of foul air the beast exuded. Patches of the boar's flesh sloughed off with its violent movements. The Lord of the Rasne discovered that the film of grease and hair on his hands was composed of decomposing flesh. As he watched in horror, a flap of skin on the boar's jaw dissolved into stringy pulp, clinging to the bone by a viscous thread. Teeth gleamed yellow in the gap.

"Walk away," Pepan said over his shoulder. He kept his eyes fixed on the beast, not daring to turn and look at the women.

"We can't," gasped Repana. "Vesi can go no farther."

"Then drag her! Wrap her hair around your hands and drag her to the lake. Wade out into the water; the boar will not follow you there. Even if it does," he added grimly, "I think the rest of its flesh would fall away at the touch of clean water."

Still Repana hesitated. "Did the Uni Ati send this thing after us, Pepan?"

"Even the Uni Ati cannot work such magic. This creature is possessed. Now go!" He heard Vesi moan and risked a quick glance over his shoulder. Repana was trying to maneuver her daughter onto her feet, but the girl resisted.

In that moment the boar gathered itself and charged again.

A terrific blow to the belly forced the air from Pepan's body, doubling him over, sending him sliding on the damp earth. He staggered to his feet with his hands pressed to his stomach. Repana was screaming behind him and there was a deeper, inner roaring as blood surged in his ears. When he tried to straighten up the pain was excruciating.

The boar was directly in front of him. Its grotesque head swayed from side to side as more gobbets of flesh fell away. The skull beneath was stark in the fading light. There was blood on the grass and blood on the creature's muzzle. For an instant Pepan thought he had injured the monster . . . until he realized the blood was his own.

The boar's tusks had torn a ragged hole through his tunic and the skin beneath. Probing with his fingertips, he felt rib bones grate together. When he lifted his hand to his face, his palms were dark with gore.

He knew all too well the signs of fatal injury. So he would die. He was not afraid. Even if his ancestors were not summoned for him, even if he were not guided to safety in the Netherworld, he had faith in his own ability to cope. His *hia* would survive.

The boar took a shaky step forward. Pepan distinctly heard a bone snap in its body and it lurched sideways. Its left hind leg was now dragging.

The Lord of the Rasne felt a surge of hope. If only he could keep the beast at bay for a few more moments, accelerated putrefaction would render the creature harmless. All he had to do was to keep it away from the women until it collapsed.

The boar staggered forward, enveloping Pepan in its nauseating miasma. Its jaws gaped, baring the cruel tusks.

At that moment a hand fell on his shoulder. He looked around to find Repana standing beside him, holding his hunting spear. "Go now," he urged her. He was shocked to find his voice so weak; shocked too at the black wall of pain that was slowly enveloping him. "Run before it charges again."

"I will not leave you." The big woman planted the spear solidly on the ground before Pepan with its triangular head facing the boar.

"You must. My wound is fatal."

"We will stand together," Repana vowed grimly.

The crippled boar lunged . . . straight onto the spearhead, which entered the animal's throat and erupted between the shoulder blades. The crossbar set onto the shaft should have prevented the boar from charging up the shaft to attack the hunter, but the beast's disintegrating flesh simply flowed around the obstacle.

In less than a heartbeat it was upon them.

Releasing Repana's hand, Pepan threw himself into the boar's gaping maw.

NINE

Because he had not stopped for food or rest, Wulv was growing very tired, but he no longer had any thought of giving up. The chase was too interesting. The thing he was tracking followed no normal pattern, meandering instead in a disoriented way as if it did not have total control of its faculties. Which, he thought, was not surprising. But whatever the boar was, living or dead, natural or unnatural, Wulv had marked it as his quarry. His tenacity was a source of pride. He would destroy the monster no matter what and celebrate victory afterward.

The beast had become progressively easier to track as it disintegrated. By the time he finally caught up with it, he was afraid there would be little left to . . . kill? But he would claim a trophy anyway; the tusks, perhaps. Properly cleaned, at least they would not stink.

He was actually imagining the arm-ring he would

make of them when he heard a male cry of pain just ahead.

Wulv ran forward with his spear balanced in his hand, ready for the throw. As he burst through the screening undergrowth he tried to see everything at once so as not to be taken by surprise, but it was hard not to be surprised by the sight that greeted him.

A tall old man had flung himself straight at the moving boar in a desperate attempt to stop it. He was obviously trying to protect a woman in a sodden blue gown. Off to one side a younger woman half-slumped against a tree, with one hand pressed over her mouth and her eyes wide with terror.

"Duck!" screamed Wulv. For the second time he hurled his spear at the boar; for the second time the weapon found its target. The beast's rotten flesh no longer had enough tensile strength to offer any resistance to the spear. With a shriek like a deflating bladder, it collapsed as the force that had animated the body fled.

For a brief moment the shadows around the creature suggested a crouching man.

Then only a pile of rotten flesh remained.

Wulv drew a shaky breath. After his last experience he was reluctant to approach the boar again. Instead he turned toward its intended victims. By the richness of their clothing and the craftsmanship of their jewelry he knew them as Etruscans. "Are you all right?" he asked abruptly.

"I am," replied the woman in blue. "But my daughter . . . come here, Vesi, come here to me. It's over now." She opened her arms and the younger woman stumbled into them.

"There, there," Repana murmured, stroking the girl's sweat-matted hair. Giving her daughter a hug, she turned toward Pepan and what she saw wrung a soft cry from her. She flung herself on the ground beside the man and tenderly cradled his head in her lap. "My lord, my lord Pepan!"

The man struggled to open his eyes. His chest felt like broken pottery. "At last . . . ," he whispered.

"What?" She bent closer. "At last, what?"

"I am in your arms," he said almost inaudibly.

"You sacrificed your life to save ours!"

Pepan summoned another tiny surge of strength, enough to ask, "Was I . . . successful?"

Repana's eyes filled with tears. "You were," she told him. She did not mention the hunter with the spear.

But Pepan's pain-dimmed eyes moved past her and, with an effort, focused on Wulv. "You," he said.

"I, lord?" Wulv sounded nervous. He was not accustomed to having Etruscan nobility speak to him. The tribes of Etruria regarded the Teumetes as little better than beasts of the field and forest.

"You were the one who saved them. I am . . . grateful."

Wulv hardly knew where to look. The woman in blue was also staring at him, but he dared not meet her eyes. She must be a queen. Surely his damaged face and crude clothing disgusted her.

"You helped save us," she said in a low voice. "I too am grateful."

For the first time he could remember, Wulv felt a blush heat his face.

Pepan attempted to sit up. "Help me," he urged Repana. He slid a massive ring from one of his fingers and held it toward Wulv. "Take this," said the Lord of the Rasne, "as a token of my gratitude. And as payment for a further service you may do me."

Wulv echoed numbly, "A further service?"

"These women—Repana and her daughter, Vesi—are dear to me, and they are in danger. I must entrust them to your keeping. I bid you take them deeper into the forest, all the way to the glade of stones. You know the place? Hide them there; protect them from those who pursue them."

"I, lord?"

A little of Pepan's old command returned to his voice. "You are of the Teumetes, are you not? Therefore you know your way around the forest, and you are good with spear and knife."

Abashed, Wulv nodded.

"I cannot command you to do this. I ask you as one man to another. You have proved you are a man of honor; a lesser man would have run away. Will you do as I ask?"

The hunter nodded again. The ring was heavy in his hand.

"I will not ask you for your word," said the dying Rasne. "I will not bind you thus."

"My word is given. I will protect them."

Repana was weeping now. "But what of you, my lord?" she asked Pepan.

He tried to sound strong as he answered, "I go in a different direction to throw them off your trail. When it is safe, I will return to the *spura* and say you have escaped. I will insist that no further effort be made to pursue and punish you."

"But the Uni Ati. . . "

"Even if she does not believe me, she will not dare call me a liar in public. Go now, the pair of you. Go with . . . what is your name?"

"Wulv." Even as he spoke he recognized how harsh, how barbaric his name sounded.

But Pepan did not seem to hold it against him. "Go with our friend Wulv and be safe," he told Repana.

"I would not leave you before. What makes you think I will leave you now?" Her eyes flashed; she was ready to fight.

For the first and last time he told her, "Because I love you, and this is what I ask of you."

Repana caught Pepan's bloody hand and brought it to her lips. "Let me stay," she breathed, her breath moist against his flesh.

"If you stay, then all of this will have been in vain. And Vesi will still be slain."

Slowly Repana got to her feet. She backed away from the wounded Etruscan lord and gathered her daughter into her arms. "Will we meet again?" she asked Pepan.

"We will," he promised. "I swear it. I will always be with you. Now go. Go!"

As Wulv shepherded his new charges deeper among the trees, Repana looked back. She saw Pepan on his feet, standing erect and proud, leaning on his spear.

In the cave with glassy walls the *siu* lay stretched on the earth, recovering. The expenditure of energy required for possession was not normally so exhausting. But finding himself in a suddenly dead body had been a shock. His hold on the flesh had been tenuous, and his struggles to maintain it had only succeeded in speeding up the processes of decay. The hunter's second spear cast had been more than he could counteract, forcing him to flee in order to recoup.

In all his long experience, nothing quite like that had happened before. It did not weaken his resolve to find and kill his spawn however. If anything, his anger at being thwarted was an added stimulus.

Meanwhile six hooded figures made their way through the forest pursuing their own hunt. They did not speak, having no need to confer for they acted with one will. The command had been given; they had no choice but to obey.

TEN

Had Pepan not been Lord of the Rasne, he would have died where the boar first struck him. His wounds were mortal; he knew he was bleeding internally. But he must live up to his nobility and therefore was obliged to attempt the impossible. Besides, he was one of the Silver People who believed that one's Dying was the most important aspect of one's Living and must be accomplished in a particular way. He had to reach his own *spura*.

His extremities were cold and numb and he was only able to walk by a supreme effort of will, clasping his locked fingers together across his abdomen and breathing between the stabs of pain. Something gurgled deep in his lungs with each breath he drew.

The injured Vesi had recently covered the same distance. So he could do it. He must.

He went on. When he could no longer stand, he crawled.

* * *

Through the roaring in his ears he began to hear the sibilant snickering of malevolent spirits watching from the Otherworld, hopeful of seizing and feasting upon his *hia* if it left his body without protection.

Pepan was on his hands and knees when the hounds found him. The posture bewildered them. By his scent they knew he was not their quarry but the Two-Legs whom the other Two-Legs considered dominant. The hounds dare not be other than submissive in his presence. Yet how did it happen that he was walking like one of them?

Whining with uncertainty they capered around him, wagging their tails to demonstrate their friendship and licking at his bloodied face and hands. This was the scene that greeted their handlers when they arrived. They could only stare, as baffled as their dogs.

The Lord of the Rasne managed to groan, "Pursue the women no more. Just carry me to . . . Sacred Space," before his final collapse.

Caile prepared for the Dying of the Lord of the Rasne with exceptional care. *Purtani* came into their own at a Dying, the focal point of their profession. But when the Dying was for a noble lord, a priest must excel himself. In a crimson robe of heaviest silk rewoven with silver thread, and wearing a headpiece of silver set with lapis lazuli, Caile was more vividly attired than any woman. This Dying demanded an explosion of joy.

Even before he left his chamber and made his way toward the *templum,* he began to sing. He called first on Pepan's nearest living kin, his sons and daughters, to summon them formally. They fell into step behind him. They too were clothed in their best as befitted the occasion. Silver glinted on throats and sparkled on fingers and dangled from earlobes, gemstones glowed in arm-rings, hair was pomaded and curled and coiled into a dozen elaborate shapes.

They were people on their way to a celebration.

As they passed through the streets of the city, every door was thrown open. The Rasne—male and female, old and young—came flocking out of their houses to join the parade, taking up the glad song.

The Etruscan *templum* was large enough to accommodate the population of the city. A structure of flawless symmetry, it was built of the finest materials and followed a design handed down for untold generations. A deep, colonnaded portico ran the width of the building, allowing the maximum number of people to stand beneath the roof of the *templum*. Within the sacred precincts themselves, a long flight of steps approached a high podium upon which the final rites of Dying were celebrated. The atmosphere was at once solemn and joyous, as befitted a place where people celebrated kinship with the immortals.

If a city outgrew its Sacred Space, a new *spura* had to be built and a new and larger *templum* constructed according to the same plan, for it was unthinkable that even one person be denied access to the rituals. The throng that gathered for Pepan's Dying could barely crowd under the roof, straining forward so as not to miss a thrilling moment.

Only the Uni Ati was not present. Her absence was interpreted as censure. As he lay dying Pepan had sent for her and demanded she forgive Repana, but the ancient crone had merely listened in silence then returned to her lonely cave.

There she now did her own praying to the *Ais*.

Meanwhile Caile led the Rasne in Songs of Summoning to the dead kin of the dying man. Their *hia* must make the journey from the Netherworld and be near when Pepan's spirit left his body, to accompany it safely back to Veno. Sacrifices were offered to lure them; incense was burned to guide them.

Tingling with anticipation, the Silver People prepared to celebrate the advancement of their lord to a higher, richer state of existence. Children vied with adults for the best places in the *templum* in order to be the first to feel the rush of invisible forces gliding past. The exact moment Pepan's *hia* sprang free of his ruined body would signal a great outpouring of joy.

Oblivious, the Lord of the Rasne lay stretched on an elaborately carved cedarwood altar in the *templum*, beneath a purple canopy embroidered with sacred symbols of sky and river and sea. A wisp of life remained to him. Like a curl of smoke it extended from his body into a hazy distance, already halfway to the Netherworld. He had only to let go and be drawn along that nebulous pathway.

But he was not ready to let go. His kin had not arrived; he could not sense their *hia*. So he waited, caught between life and death.

In the cave with the glassy walls, the being who lay there became aware of a vortex of forces gathering in the distance. Someone was initiating a Dying. He forced himself to focus, gathering the last of his depleted energy, allowing his consciousness to expand, to take in the surrounding forests and mountains, the rivers and valleys. Tiny spots of vibrating light shimmered and danced, pulsing with life and living.

Where . . . ah, yes . . . there! The city beyond the river was beginning to vibrate with a ritual summoning of the Rasne's dead ancestors.

The prospect was tempting. If he timed it right, he could arrive before the ancestors, invade the Dying ceremonies, and snatch the departing spirit from the very grasp of its kinfolk. Such a trophy was the envy of every other demon.

The *siu* had a more immediate need however, to destroy the life he had inadvertently planted in the human female. The child's fleshly link with him was too dangerous. And he had not the energy to do battle with the enraged ancestors of the dead.

There would be other Dyings, other chances for pleasurable predation. The Etruscans were preoccupied with death and all its trappings. He could remain here and feed off their dead, growing ever stronger and more powerful. Before he could take advantage of them, however, he must seek out the young woman he had violated. Her and her unborn child.

As his thoughts lingered on the woman, he became aware that she was the object of other thoughts. He was not alone in seeking her.

A surprising number of others seemed to be looking for her as well!

Wulv did not know just who was pursuing Repana and her daughter. Neither they nor Pepan had told him. Perhaps it was not even necessary that he know. Protection was protection, and he would defend them against all dangers. He had given his word and that was enough.

For the first time in his life the scarred Teumetian felt important. The Lord of the Rasne had entrusted him with an important mission . . . but more importantly, he had looked beyond the ruined face, the unkempt hair, and the crude clothing to see the man beneath. And had trusted him.

But as he led the way through the lightless depths of the Great Forest, Wulv could not quench his curiosity. Later, when they had stopped to rest the wearied young woman, whose name he gathered was Vesi, he asked the older woman, "What are you running from? Thieves? Romax invaders? A jealous husband? It would help if I knew what pursued us."

Repana hesitated before replying. "My daughter and I defied the traditions of our people."

Wulv waited, but she told him no more. He understood the power of traditions however. They were more important than laws, since they were enforced with emotions rather than regulations. One could disregard a law; one could not flout a tradition. Repana and Vesi were being pursued by their own people, then, who would probably hound them to their dying day.

Wulv nodded bitterly; one's own tribe could be the cruelest of all.

When Vesi finally collapsed with exhaustion, he made camp for the three of them and stood guard. Repana fed herself from the supplies she carried and urged a few bites on her daughter, feeding her by hand, but Wulv rejected the food she offered him. Rasne food was sweetened and spiced, as if its natural flavor was not good enough. To eat such things would make a strong man weak. Instead he speared a rabbit for himself and roasted it over a small fire, devouring it when it was still half raw. He refused even to season the meat with some of Repana's salt, though he appreciated the generous gesture. The possession of a commodity as valuable as salt confirmed what he already knew: his charges were nobility.

After Vesi fell asleep, Wulv tried to talk with her mother. They had little common ground. Repana was plainly uncomfortable with anyone so crude, though she tried to conceal her distaste. But when she unthinkingly drew aside the hem of her stained and torn gown rather than let it be contaminated by his foot, Wulv felt the gesture like a knife to the heart. Once such an occurrence would have aroused him to a terrible anger, but now . . . now it merely saddened him. Perhaps he was getting old.

At length Repana asked, "How long will it take us to reach the glade of stones?"

Sucking on one of his broken teeth, Wulv calculated distances. "Traveling as slow as your daughter does, we can't be there much before tomorrow sunset."

"She is injured; she can go no faster," Repana said.

"And besides. . . " She broke off abruptly, realizing that in her weariness she was about to say too much.

But Wulv would not let it be. His hunter's instincts were alerted. "Besides what? Is there anything else I need to know that might be important if I am to protect you?"

She turned and looked squarely at him in the somber glow of the dying campfire. He truly was an ugly creature, with that scarred face and twisted smile, and the dancing firelight lent his features a macabre cast. She came of a race devoted to beauty, mistrusting and abhorring ugliness as an abomination before the *Ais*. But these were hunting scars—bears' claws, she thought—and thus honorably earned. Her own late husband had been scarred . . . and Pepan had trusted . . .

Repana could not bear to think of Pepan. "My daughter is with child," she said in a voice so low Wulv could hardly hear her. "A most undesirable child. Our people want to kill her with the infant in her womb."

Wulv thought he understood. Some inferior, a slave perhaps, had defiled Vesi, and now both she and the unborn infant were outcasts.

His heart went out to them. He was to some degree an outcast himself. "While I live your daughter and her baby will come to no harm," he vowed. "I am strong and I know the ways of the forest. I can protect you from the wild animals and from outlaws; I can find food for you and show you where there is pure water to drink. You can trust Wulv; he will never let you down."

His voice rang with such unsuspected fervor that Repana was taken aback. Tentatively, she laid one hand on the arm of their new ally. "I thank you, Wulv."

Touching him was not as unpleasant as she expected. His face was hideous but his skin was warm; he felt like any other man.

ELEVEN

Although they were Rasne and the hunter had always been a little contemptuous of the effete Silver People, Wulv had to admit he was impressed by Vesi's courage. When time came to be on the move again, she got to her feet without complaining in spite of her pain. He watched as her mother tended her wounds, so he saw how terrible they were.

But when he asked Repana what beast had caused them, she merely pressed her lips together and shook her head. "No animal did this," she said shortly.

"No beast either," replied Wulv.

"An . . . enemy," Repana reluctantly admitted.

"You do have dangerous enemies," Wulv conceded. "But you'll be safe from them at the glade of stones."

Or so he hoped. He was beginning to get an itchy feeling at the base of his skull, an old hunter's wordless warning. As they forced their way through the dense thickets of the Great Forest, he kept his spear at the ready. His movements were stealthy, cautious; his gaze ceaselessly examined the dense undergrowth. Nothing attacked them, yet he felt the weight of watching eyes.

They reached the glade of stones, as he had predicted, late in the day. Gesturing to the women to stay in the shelter of the trees, Wulv went forward to reconnoiter the time-honored sanctuary before he would allow them to join him.

He walked into an eerie stillness.

This place always chilled him, so in the past he had avoided it whenever possible. A blood-red sun was setting, casting a lurid hue over the scene. The glade contained a circle of standing stones each as high as Wulv's head, so roughly hewn that it was impossible to tell whether their shape was natural or carved. In the crimson twilight, with the shadows writhing down the ancient stones, they resembled a circle of gnarled and twisted old men. Local lore named these stones the Twelve Whisperers. At certain times of night and certain times of year, or so folk claimed, a question whispered into the ear of the tallest stone would result in a whispered response.

Wulv only half-believed that it was the wind.

But he knew that nothing living occupied the glade.

Relieved, Wulv beckoned to the women.

They set up camp between the stone circle and the trees. Wulv used fallen branches to build a wattle shelter and made a surprisingly comfortable bed for Vesi and her mother out of boughs and leaves.

"You are very skilled. And you are being very kind to us," Repana said, as she observed the little touches he added: the crushed flowers and herbs among the boughs to scent them, the mud chinked into the walls of the shelter to keep out the wind.

The Teumetian mumbled something in embarrassment and looked away. But he was pleased she'd noticed.

"We will stay here," he told the woman, "until. . . "

"Until what?"

"We receive word from your friend that it is . . . safe."

A twinge of pain tightened the skin around Repana's eyes. She doubted that they would ever receive word of any sort from Pepan. She knew also, from the look in the hunter's eyes, that he too believed that Pepan was dead.

I will never see him alive again, she mourned silently. Oh, my love! My lost and never-to-be love. Why did I not speak to you as I should? Why did you not speak to me?

Guided by the sound of chanting, six hooded figures made their way toward the Rasne city. They moved slowly, with a peculiar gliding motion, but they never stopped. When they saw the walls ahead of them, glowing with the pale golden hue of delicately tinted brick, they lowered their hoods and exchanged congratulatory glances. Gathering closer to one another, they offered silent prayers to Pythia. Then they raised their hoods once more and approached the city.

The single guard remaining on duty at the gates of the *spura* was feeling sorry for himself. He resented being excluded from the Dying. There had been no Dying for several moons. He had felt cheated when the Repana woman ran off with her daughter rather than providing such a ceremony.

When he saw the six approach, he reacted more aggressively than he normally would have. "Halt!" he cried, striding toward them and dramatically flourishing his spear. Pilgrims, farmers, brigands—they could be anyone; they had no business in the *spura* when a Dying was in progress. As he drew nearer to them, however, the quality of the cloth in the heavy robes they wore put him in mind of the last Roman trade delegation to visit the city. Best to address them carefully. "Halt and state your business," he called in measured tones.

The six continued to advance. He could not see their

faces, overshadowed as they were by the large hoods, but a hollow voice replied, "We are looking for someone."

The guard leveled his spear at the speaker. "Who?"

Again the answer came: "We are looking for someone."

"I have to have a name," insisted the guard, taking one prudent step backward but continuing to point his spear. The voice set his teeth on edge and caused a peculiar unease in the pit of his stomach, as if he had eaten spoiled meat. "I cannot let just any stranger off the road come in here."

"We are not just any strangers; we mean to enter," replied the hollow voice.

As they continued toward him, the guard grew nervous. There were six of them to one of him, and though they did not appear to be armed, their attitude implied menace.

He reached for the horn hanging at the side of the gate to warn of intruders.

A nauseating odor swept over him. Suddenly his head seemed full of swirling mist. He drew a breath to cry out but that only sucked the foul air deeper into his lungs. As he choked, the lead figure had almost casually brushed aside his leveled spear. The other five followed.

Within the *templum* Caile and his fellow *purtani* were chanting incantations over braziers clustered at one end of a high podium to form a five-pointed star. At the other end was an altar on which a motionless Pepan lay. When the Dying was successfully completed, the emptied husk would be placed in an elaborately painted and decorated tomb, there to spend all eternity surrounded by beauty.

In a precise order the priests alternately trickled powders and water into the flames of the braziers. Scented smoke billowed; colored flames plumed. The sons and daughters of Pepan promptly used consecrated scarves to wave the smoke toward the doorways, while they repeated their own chants of summoning.

Supine on the altar, Pepan lay beneath his purple canopy and felt no sense of time passing. He was suspended between worlds. The weight of his flesh seemed an increasingly slight impediment. Soon he would break his last bonds with his physical body and go. And he would be pleased to go. He had no fear of Death. His only regret was that he had been unable to help Repana when she most needed him. It gave him some consolation to know the hunter would look after them however. Obviously this path was ordained by the gods. Though he had often doubted them during his lifetime, here and now Pepan found it easy to believe in the *Ais*.

Suddenly rising voices interrupted the ceremony. They buzzed like insects around Pepan. He just wanted to drift . . . away . . . away . . .

"Who are those strangers?" someone was asking.

Another replied, "I felt dizzy the moment they passed under the portico."

"Where did they come from?"

"They have a dreadful smell about them, did you notice?"

"How silently they move. Have they no feet?"

"How dare they enter Sacred Space uninvited!"

"Are they . . . gods?"

Reluctantly Pepan became aware of six dark shadows looming like vultures around the altar. He could feel cold thoughts probing his dying brain, unnatural ideas and bizarre images flickering behind his fading eyes. Panic rose in him. These must be *siu,* come to claim him. . . .

Though the *hia* of his dead kin had not arrived to protect him from the encroaching Otherworld and guide him safely to Veno in the Netherworld, he could wait no longer.

With a great burst of energy Pepan leaped free of his body and fled along the nebulous, misty pathway that opened up before him. In the distance he could see dim shapes; he prayed they were the *hia* of his ancestors approaching.

Behind him, clustered around the empty shell of his flesh like carrion crows, the shadows gathered.

The six surrounding the altar turned as one, filed down the steps, and left the *templum*. An unspoken thought was shared between them: We have failed; the one we seek is not in this place. Pythia will be displeased.

Silently they returned through the city, making their way toward the gates. People from the *templum* started to run after them; some fell back as their minds were gripped by an inexplicable awe, leaving them weeping and shaken on the streets.

"The moment the strangers gathered around him, Lord Pepan died," one person whispered to another. "They must indeed be gods."

Several bowed down and touched their foreheads to the ground, pressing their flesh into the soil recently walked upon by the gods.

Embarrassed by his earlier fear and terrified anew by the reappearance of the six, the guard at the gate made no effort to stop the six from going out the gateway. But when the Rasne came staggering up, he gathered the remnants of his courage, strode boldly into the road, and hurled his spear after the last figure.

With a solid thud the weapon sank into the cloaked back, impaling him; arms flung wide, crucified on the air, he fell silently. Without breaking stride, his companions caught his body beneath the arms and dragged him away with them.

A heavily armed company from the *spura* soon set out after them but came to a dead end. The peculiarly imprecise footprints of the six simply vanished off the dusty track. The Rasne searched for a while, then had to admit defeat. They returned to their city with a sense of persistent unease.

* * *

With the resilience of the young, Vesi began to recover as soon as she had some rest and food. Wulv worked to make their shelter a secure hut without defiling the sacred nature of the place. With additional leaves and branches he camouflaged the hut so skillfully that it looked like nothing more than a windblow of forest debris. Inside it was dry and snug, with enough headroom and even a smokehole so they could build a tiny fire, the opening canted at an angle to allow the smoke to drift away horizontally, rather than straight up into the heavens.

That evening, following their supper of rabbit, berries, and a nourishing broth of roots, they sat around the tiny thread of a fire and talked. Their voices were whispers in the gloom, only their eyes visible in the shadows.

"I have known about this place all my life," said Wulv, "but I never entered the circle of stones before."

"Are your people, the Teumetes, afraid of the stones?"

"Not afraid, exactly; we revere them. This is a place of sanctuary. We shed no blood within the circle, and any animal that flees a hunter is safe as long as it shelters here. To my people, this is sacred space."

"Do you know why the glade is sacred, Wulv?" Vesi wanted to know. Her voice was thready and weak, but at least she was beginning to show interest.

"My people have their legends, as I'm sure the Rasne have."

Repana smiled. She needed to keep Vesi awake and interested in her surroundings; anything to prevent her dwelling on the horror that had occurred. The older woman leaned toward Wulv. "Time spent waiting is long indeed. Shorten it for us. Tell us the stories of your tribe."

Wulv was flattered. To the best of his knowledge, no

member of the Silver People had ever shown the slightest interest in the history or customs of the Teumetes.

He gently stirred the fire with a stick, careful not to raise any sparks that might ignite the thatch. Then he cleared his throat several times and, rather self-consciously, began. "When I was a child I used to listen to the elders of my tribe talk. That was before my scars made me so ugly my people scorned me."

Repana made a small sound of sympathy in her throat. It was, Wulv thought, the first such sound he had heard from a woman in many years.

"The ancestors of the Teumetes lived in forests even darker and denser than this one. We were the Children of the Bear. That was our name because we were not men and women, you see. We walked upright but our bodies contained the spirits of bears."

"Hia," Vesi murmured. Her mother gave her a sharp look.

Wulv nodded. "Our bear-spirits were fierce and brave, *hia* a man would be proud to welcome into his body. But then a new people came up from the south, following the seacoast in boats made of timber and reeds. They also walked upright but their spirits were those of the river serpent. Members of a subtle, cunning race, they invaded our homeland in search of certain herbs and stones, metals and crystals to use in their rituals.

"The Serpent People could not outfight the Children of the Bear but they were far more clever. In the fighting that followed, my ancestors were defeated. They fled their home forests and at last reached this region, only to find it was already inhabited by an ancient and venerable tribe who practiced a form of magic involving the spirits of the stones. They tolerated us as long as we respected their customs and did not desecrate their sacred sites.

"We were weary of running, so we stayed. A few of the Serpent People pursued us almost this far, but they would not go near the sacred sites of the stone-magicians. Eventually they went back across the mountains to the land they had stolen from us. In the seasons that followed we waged constant war with the serpent folk, harrying them along the rivers that bordered the two lands. As time went by, they changed: they were no longer as cunning, no longer as fast or as deadly . . . but we had changed too; we were no longer powerful and virile. So there came a time when the descendants of the serpent folk simply disappeared from our lands. But by then there was no going back for us; we had become men and women. Our bear-spirits simply . . . faded away." The hunter touched his scarred flesh. "Though bears are with us still," he added somewhat ruefully.

Repana understood more of Wulv's simple tale than he knew. The Silver People had legends of their own origin that were not totally dissimilar, stories of an era when existence had been in a state of flux, with flesh and spirit interchangeable. The ancestors of the Etruscans had, of course, been nothing so crude as bears or serpents. In ancient times the *Ais* had invaded their bodies and minds, impregnating them with the divine. Thus the Etruscans became the embodiment of all that was fine and noble, avatars of love and war and wisdom transcending mortal limitations. They could interpenetrate the various planes of existence at will, wearing their flesh into the Otherworld or reclaiming their *hia* from the Netherworld.

Slowly, choosing her words with care, Repana tried to explain this to Wulv, so he would understand the natural superiority of herself and Vesi. But he had the sort of blunt and basic mind that kept asking irritating questions.

"Why can't you still do that?" he wanted to know. "If the Etruscans are almost gods, why can't you move instantly from place to place without needing either protection or a guide?"

"The *Ais* are easily bored," Repana replied, speaking as patiently as to a child, "so all things change after a time. For their own reasons the gods chose to alter the relationship between flesh and spirit. Some of our ancestral *hia* were permanently lodged in mortal form, becoming the tribes of Etruria. The best of them, of course, became the Rasne, my own people. Other *hia* retained an independent existence. They never put on flesh; they never accepted mortal limitations.

"The men and women of Etruria revered their ancestors, as they should. These were beings who had been almost gods. But this competing homage made the *Ais* jealous. By way of retaliation they caused some ancestral *hia* to embody all the vices of humankind but none of the virtues. Thus were the *siu* created, to keep us torn between good and evil."

Repana glanced sidelong at her daughter. "And the *siu,* like the *Ais,* are with us always. Each cruelty, every crime, has, at its heart, a *siu.*"

At this the girl entered the conversation. "The people your ancestors found when they first came here—were they Etruscan?" she asked Wulv.

The Teumetian shook his head. "I don't think so. The Etruscans began somewhere to the east, or so the stories of my people claim. They settled here later. They are a very different race from the stone-magicians."

"Then what happened to the stone-magicians?"

"I don't know. Some of our elders believe they simply melted into their stones," Wulv concluded in a hushed voice. He glanced out into the night, fingers touching the bone amulets stitched into his clothing.

Silence filled the hut, a silence permeated with invisible beings who must be taken into account and ancient events that continued to affect the present. Only the little fire dared to hiss.

TWELVE

The five cloaked beings were not accustomed to running, but now they ran, seeking a place where they could learn the extent of their comrade's injuries in safety. There was always the chance that the Rasne might send armed warriors after them. The awe they had sought to exude through sheer mental power obviously did not work equally on all the Silver People, as the guard's action had shown.

If they fell, they would have failed Pythia. Then even death might not protect them from her anger.

They set out toward the nearest river, the Tiber, to seek aid. Water was sacred to Pythia. Certain rivers had special powers, not the least of which was the ability to cure followers of the dark goddess. Or so her acolytes believed. The time had come to put that belief to the test.

The one they dragged made no sound. He might already be dead, but was at least beyond feeling pain.

They stopped long enough to shoulder him like a sack of meal, then hurried on. The last in line kept turning back to watch for the pursuit that never came.

As he recovered from the shock he had endured, the being in the cave grew increasingly hungry. He was now afraid to return to the Otherworld; she was surely waiting there to exact her punishment. But if he remained in the Earthworld, the flesh he had acquired at such cost must be nourished.

He began to lust for food.

He allowed his consciousness to roam into the forest beyond the cave, seeking a developed life-form. He could subsist off the flesh and spirits of birds and beasts, but they provided insufficient energy. He needed richer fare.

Gradually he became aware of the existence of the six. Though still some distance away they were headed in his direction and one was seriously wounded. Its life force was bleeding away.

Gathering himself, the *siu* left the cave. Sustenance must not be wasted.

By the time the five reached the river, all semblance of life had left their comrade. Without hesitation they plunged down the bank anyway, intending to immerse the body in the water and beseech holy Tiber to restore him. But the task that awaited them was not an easy one. Yesterday's storm had swollen the Tiber to flood strength and now it rushed headlong between its banks, hissing like an angry serpent. The five struggled to keep their footing on the muddy bank while lowering their companion into the river.

Abruptly, his robe ballooned as water flowed beneath the fabric. Within moments he was torn from their grasp. The rampaging river whirled the body away, tossing it like a log in the current, sending it spinning down the river course to disappear around the nearest bend.

Only a short distance below the bend, the being from the cave trotted along the riverbank, anxious eyes searching.

He stopped abruptly and scanned the river.

The Tiber was carrying an appalling mass of tree branches and uprooted bushes toward him. The *siu* ignored the debris, his attention arrested by someone caught in the flood. As he watched, the river tossed the body of its helpless victim to and fro. The flailing limbs provided a spurious life that excited the *siu* almost beyond bearing. He began to run along the bank in hot pursuit. Food! *Energy!*

The river course narrowed, the water boiling white through a defile. The body tumbled in the rapids and then paused, snagged on an outcropping of stone. To the *siu* watching anxiously from the riverbank, it appeared as if the figure in the water had caught hold of the rocks to save itself.

The *siu* eagerly waded into the river to claim his prize.

The pure water of the Tiber shrank from his glaucous flesh. But he managed to catch one end of the sodden robe and drag the body onto shore, hauling it through mud and briars with apparent ease. Grinning, the *siu* crouched to examine his catch.

The corpse's hood had become dislodged. A thin patina of serpentine scales covered his flattened, almost triangular skull.

The *siu* spat in disgust. He knew these creatures of old and considered them abominations. He should cast this one back into the river. But he hungered, hungered desperately for the life he thought the body still contained.

Losing control of his greed, he tore off gobbets of flesh and thrust them into his mouth while he dug for the heart. It was not the meat he craved, but the living essence. He chewed perfunctorily, then gulped, swallowing hard . . . and gagged violently as a shudder ran through him.

There was no essence of life.

The only essence was death.

He had ingested dead flesh!

Abandoning his prey, he staggered away from the river. Twice in a short period of time the *siu* had joined himself not with life but with death. First with the boar, now with this creature. Slow black waves rolled through his body, battering at his consciousness, leaching away his personality, his memories.

He was . . .

He was . . .

He . . .

As the madness claimed him, the violence of his derangement sent a shrill discord jangling through the Otherworld. Those who heard and understood the sound laughed at his pain.

Thoughts flowed around Pepan; he swam through them as through water. He had a sense of millions of swarming intellects, some sparkling like fireflies, others as dull and muddy as frog spawn. This was a plane separate from, yet impinging upon, the reality he knew. The consciousness of Earthworld trees and plants cast constantly changing reflections here, and the movement of every Earthworld animal caused a parallel vibration in the invisible realm.

Looking down at himself, Pepan discovered that an image of his body continued to cling to his spirit like the afterimage of the sun on one's eyeballs. He also became aware that his *hia* was sending out an auditory signal as distinctive as birdsong, a deep, musical ululation that echoed through the Otherworld. This was the song of his soul.

Pepan's call was soon answered. A dense cloud materialized in the distance, pulsing with a rhythmic beat as familiar as his own heartbeat had been. Without even thinking about it, he recognized the sound and knew its source, listened as his own sound melded and became part of the greater symphony. His ancestors were coming for him . . .

Abruptly Pepan's attention was distracted by a faint and very different signal coming from the opposite direction.

A mere thread of music, lyrical and heartbreakingly sweet, it evoked a powerful response in Pepan.

Three strains in delicate harmony, soaring together. They were not his family, yet he recognized them with a loving heart.

Repana.

Vesi.

And the child!

The child already quickened within her then. So soon . . .

Separated from them by death, Pepan felt more concerned about them than ever. In the Otherworld everything touched upon everything else, so perhaps he could continue to have influence on their lives. Perhaps he could finish what he had set out to do: protect Repana and Vesi . . . and the baby.

With this thought uppermost he hurried to intercept his escort, eager to explain what he required of them.

THIRTEEN

"The child is growing far too fast," Wulv told Repana. "I have had little experience in such matters, but I know a woman should not swell like that. Not so soon, so quickly."

Repana cast a critical eye toward her daughter. The Teumetian was right; he had confirmed what she had only suspected. After only a few days Vesi's belly was already large enough to contain a seven months' child. Had it been the siring of a human father such development would have been frighteningly abnormal.

The father was not human.

But she did not want to admit this to Wulv. How could she admit to this primitive woodsman that her daughter was carrying a demon's child? Such an admission to one's inferior would be extremely embarrassing. And who knew how he might react? Those like him were superstitious brutes. He might slay them out of hand; she dare not take the chance. "My daughter has probably been pregnant for longer than anyone thought," she said. "It is easy to misjudge such events."

Wulv was saying, "Only yesterday her belly was almost flat."

"Sometimes that happens," Repana replied with a calm she did not feel. "Infants grow in spurts, you know."

He looked dubious. "I've watched the breeding of animals. The unborn inside them grow slow and steady."

"My daughter is not some beast!" Repana snapped. "I ask you to remember that she is Rasne." The woman turned away before Wulv could ask any more awkward questions.

Vesi was aware of the child's extraordinary swelling within her. She knew she should feel terror at the very thought, but onrushing motherhood produced a calming effect. Whatever the baby's sire, the unborn was also part of her and she could not fear part of her own self. Sometimes she just sat beside the fire with her fingers laced across her rounded stomach and crooned to the child inside, promising to love it no matter what its nature might be.

Watching her, Repana wanted to cry, remembering the times she had sat before a fire, cradling her own stomach, murmuring to the infant Vesi within. She had wanted so much for her only daughter, had promised her so much. Now those dreams and promises would come to naught because of another child . . . the demon's child.

At night she lay on the bed of boughs and held her daughter in her arms. "There are ways," she whispered, "of getting rid of the child if you want to. Herbal preparations I can concoct for you or a diffusion of hazel bark with. . . "

Vesi stiffened. "No. It is my child."

"But. . . "

"No!"

"It might be a monster. You know that."

"If I had been deformed in your womb—and you knew it—would you have gotten rid of me?"

By way of answer Repana simply clutched Vesi harder, unwilling to answer. The Rasne worshipped beauty. No mother ever wanted to be forced to use her sacrificial knife.

Traveling, Pepan discovered, was not the same in the Otherworld. Time and distance were measured differently. But that did not mean his *hia* enjoyed unhampered freedom of movement. As he tried to reach his ancestors, a peculiar viscosity wrapped itself around him, forming a barrier that he thrust against until it gave like a weakened membrane. He slipped through to find himself in what appeared to be a long tunnel. Translucent walls surrounded him, yet when he reached out to try to touch one he felt nothing.

Just ahead he could see the cloud that contained his kinsmen, but reaching them required a complex set of trial-and-error maneuvers. It was like learning to walk all over again, and he was elated at each small success.

Nearing the cloud, he tried to get some idea of its size. But its opaque mass constantly expanded and contracted. At the end of one of these contractions a form emerged.

My son, said a voice without words.

The form flickered and . . . Pepan found himself gazing upon the face of his father, Zivas, former Lord of the Silver People. A gifted linguist, Zivas had studied and mastered the languages of a dozen other tribes, even those in Latium, for no reason other than the joy of learning. He displayed the characteristic long-lidded eyes and aquiline nose that marked their family, but his visage was slightly faded, like mosaic tiles that had been too long in the sun.

Is it really you? Pepan wanted to know, reaching out. Then he peered eagerly over his father's shoulder. *Is Mother with you?*

Zivas gestured toward the cloud behind him. *Only one from each generation of the bloodline responds to a Dying. Your mother is safe with Veno in the Kingdom of the Dead. Come now; she is eager to welcome you.*

Pepan strove to understand the details of this new existence. *If one from each generation is with you, does that mean your sire, and your grandsire, and . . .*

By way of answer his father moved backward and the cloud swallowed him, expanded, contracted, and a new figure emerged. These features also bore the familial stamp, only more faded still.

I am your grandfather's grandfather. Within our bloodlines is carried the history of the Rasne. My immortal spirit is that of the warrior I once was when under my command Etrurians stood shoulder to shoulder with allies from the Attic nations and beat the Carthaginians to their knees. I returned home in triumph only to discover an invasion force from Latium had attacked our city in my absence. After I had driven them away, we held a festival of celebration and sacrificed to the Ais. *Then we rebuilt our* spura *on undefiled ground according to the plans long ago set forth by my revered ancestor. . . .*

The cloud convulsed, another figure replaced his and went on, the words blending into a lyrical paean.

I am the Planner. From the talents the gods gave me sprang the great cities of Etruria, during the glory days when we spread out across this land. Whenever our warriors claimed new territory, I oversaw preparation of the most auspicious site the priests could identify, then laid out streets and drainage systems, designed buildings, and selected construction materials. In the blink of an eye I could envision an elaborate plan and know just how to bring it to fruition. So it was that the mark of the Silver People was carved into the very stones of this country, as long ago foreseen by . . .

Almost instantly he was replaced by yet another form, one so faint Pepan could scarcely see it at all. In the tones of a woman this new image told him, *I am the Prophet. In my day the* Ais *spoke directly to us. We were not so proud then as we later became,* the voice added regretfully. *We were willing to listen.*

In the reign of Atys, *Son of Ghosts, the place in which we lived suffered a great famine. But by following the direction of the gods we were led out of starvation to this much more fertile region, where we grew and prospered. Life became more pleasant; we no longer had to struggle just to survive.*

Then the Ais *encouraged us to develop a sense of beauty so we could appreciate them more fully. Under their tutelage we developed our arts until eventually we became known as the Silver People.*

Another voice interjected, *Generations of craftsmen such as myself have captured stunning images of the* Ais *in sculpture—some no larger than a thumb. We have designed jewelry beyond compare for our beautiful women; we have decorated our tombs with images of the dear dead so lifelike they almost breathe. Far beyond our borders the Rasne are famed for luxury and elegance. But all that we achieve is simply a gift from the gods, who love us.*

The gods who love us, echoed the Prophet.

Marveling, Pepan realized he was in the presence of the most able of his race. Just when he needed them.

Using his new-found ability to speak without words, he struggled to communicate his problem. *There are two exiled women, Repana and her daughter, Vesi, who are very dear to me and are in great trouble. I want to help them, but I am new to this state of being, I do not know what abilities I may possess here. I ask you, my ancestors, to teach me. Help me to help my friends.*

Why should we involve ourselves? The women you name are not your wife and daughter, his warrior ancestor pointed out. *They are not our bloodline. They have their own ancestors.*

But they are Rasne, Pepan argued, *so we must share common ancestors.*

A multitude of voices debated among themselves. Then, sounding faintly amused, the female voice of the Prophet spoke from within the cloud. *Some of us had many children. All rivers are born from the same rain.*

Pepan said eagerly, *You will do as I ask then?*

Because you ask it, his father's voice replied, *and I could never refuse my sons anything.*

The voice of the Planner countered, *If we do this, will you come with us afterward?*

Instinct told him he could not lie to the dead. *I cannot say. I only know I cannot go to the Netherworld leaving things as they are.*

The Prophet intoned, *You would not be the first who remained behind to conclude unfinished business.*

But will he come afterwards? someone demanded to know.

Possibly. He is guided by love. The ability to love even after death is common to all hia *and is the one emotion no* siu *can feel. Pepan invokes the love we bear him and asks us to extend it to those he loves. I say we shall.*

The cloud roiled and from its depths came the sounds of not three or four but hundreds of voices, some little more than animalistic grunts. Pepan could tell some mighty argument was taking place. He waited, unable to measure the passage of time in a world where time was not, until at last the Prophet spoke to him again. *All things happen as they should,* she said. *Lead us.*

It was easier to move now that he had had some practice. He still had no sense of direction however, and when the Prophet bade him to lead them he was momentarily uncertain. Then he heard once more that lovely, distant music and followed it eagerly.

As he approached the glade, he discovered that the circle of stones continually emitted a humming sound. At close range the hum distorted the music that guided him and set up a disturbing vibration in the Otherworld. That vibration could repel many entities. Pepan forced himself to go on.

At his back pulsed the opaque cloud.

Wulv lay on the ground just outside the shelter he had built for the women. Clothed in leather and bearskin, he looked like a wild animal himself. Pepan hovered over him long enough to ascertain that he was sleeping peacefully, then entered the hut.

Walls were no longer a barrier. The *hia* of the dead Rasne passed effortlessly through interlaced branches and chinked mud. Inside he found Repana and Vesi lying in each other's arms. Each was contributing a note to the Otherworld music that had guided him this far. Repana's identifying sound was rich and melodious; Vesi had a higher, clearer note, achingly pure in spite of all that had happened to her.

But it was their physical voices that caught Pepan's attention. He arrived just in time to overhear the conversation between mother and daughter about the possibility of aborting the infant. To his surprise, he felt their pain as sharply as if it were his own. Since he had no flesh to serve as a buffer, their emotion came into him naked and raw.

Vesi obviously cherished the unborn infant, but Repana secretly regarded it with resentment amounting to loathing. The child would begin life with every possible disadvantage. Like its mother it would be an exile with no property, no status—and the added curse of a demon father. Only the *Ais* knew what face it would wear in the world or what deformities of body or spirit it might carry. Pepan could understand Repana's reservations, but life was sacred, even this life. He must do what he could to ease the way.

Silently he called out to the unseen cloud that had taken up a position in the center of the circle of stones. *This is the woman I should have wed. This girl should have become my daughter. I did not give them enough of myself in life, but I would rectify that now. Help me. Help us.*

It has never been done . . .

Never been done . . .

Never. . . .

When the argument raged into silence, the Prophet said simply, *Put your hand on her belly.*

Pepan protested, *I have no hands now.*

His grandfather replied, *The memory of your earthly body is still strong and we will add all our force to yours. It will be enough.*

Pepan did as he was instructed and approached Vesi. His fingers were as transparent as glass when he held them up to his face; through them he could dimly see Vesi's body, as if she were made of slightly thicker mist. When he laid his palm—delicately, tentatively—on her mounded flesh he had no sensation of solidity. There seemed nothing to keep him from reaching farther, from reaching inside her and actually putting his hand on the womb. As he stared at her belly, its flesh became translucent and he could see the shape of the baby within.

Yes, said the voice of the Prophet, *that is what you must do. Reach inside, feel the child.*

Pepan obeyed. Neither of the two women on the bed seemed aware of the invasion, but the infant floating in its small, warm universe responded to his touch by opening its eyes.

Beyond the shelter, the stone circle began to hum.

The unborn child heard. Its eyes opened wider, looking upon scarlet and crimson tides as its tiny hands clutched at the mist of Pepan's fingers.

Do not move now, Pepan, commanded the Prophet.

The cloud within the circle began to glow with a lambent green flame, while sparkling white fire shivered across the stones.

In his dreams, Wulv stirred and mumbled but did not awake.

The cloud contracted violently then expanded to cover the hut. Tiny emerald fires flickered over the carefully arranged branches. The air smelled of storm. A rushing wind howled through the primeval forest, whipping the trees until they groaned in protest, sending the forest creatures scurrying for shelter.

Pepan felt a great weight descend upon him, as if he had been floating in the river for a long time and just come out on land again. The weight pressed down unbearably, threatening to crush him though he had no body. Desperately he fought to remain upright and stay still—until the weight flowed through him and his *hia* caught fire.

This he could feel. He writhed like the storm-tossed trees in an agony beyond description. His spirit was burning hotter than the forge, hotter than the sun, consuming him.

The essence of a people was raging through him.

And from him, into the woman and her unborn child.

Chieftain and warrior, craftsman and Planner and Prophet and all the generations before them poured along the conduit Pepan provided, emptying their knowledge into Vesi's womb.

The baby convulsed. Vesi sprang up with a shriek, clutching at her belly. "It's being born!" she cried. "It's being born now!"

FOURTEEN

As with a Dying, there were certain rituals that must attend a Birthing. The newborn *hia* required protection as it entered the Earthworld from a very different plane. It would take awhile before he or she learned the rules governing this new type of existence. But the more immediate problem was the danger imposed by malign inhabitants of the Otherworld.

Siu, as well as corrupted *hia* who had never made their way safely to the Netherworld, were very aware of a newborn's vulnerability. While a mother was still in labor they crowded close, hoping to subsume the baby's spirit and thus acquire a being of flesh and blood who would obey their dictates.

If Vesi had given birth at home, midwives and *purtani* would have been with her constantly, caring for flesh and spirit. Protective symbols would be painted on her belly and on the special birthing stool handed down from mother to daughter. Priests would chant and burn incense whose sweet smoke dulled the pain. Silver bells would ring to ward off evil spirits, while elsewhere in the *spura* young goats were sacrificed to lure them to other prey.

Instead she was alone in a crude hut in the forest with only her mother and a primitive Teumetian—and the combined wisdom of a hundred generations of Rasne.

As Pepan watched, Repana worked over her daughter. Wulv had been awakened by the girl's shrieks but was forbidden to enter the hut. "You would just get in my way!" Repana shouted at him.

Hurt, the woodsman sat on the ground outside and sulked. From time to time he flexed his callused hands with their dirt-rimmed fingernails and stared at them, unable to comprehend their uselessness in the current situation.

Pepan understood the impotence Wulv felt. All he could do now was defend the little family against the Otherworld predators already swarming toward the site.

The atmosphere had grown thick with demonic shapes. *Siu* hissed and growled, writhing obscenely as they advanced. Instead of bodies, in the Otherworld they displayed grotesque manifestations of their favorite vices. Some appeared as gaping mouths with slimy tongues and endlessly working jaws. Others were little more than oversized genital organs, throbbing with lusts that could never be eased.

Hia were different. Many had never been embodied but existed as pure, crackling energy. *Hia* who had been corrupted by *siu* gave off a distinct smell of decay. They tended to stay close to their corrupters, basking in the sulfurous glow of concentrated evil.

As this hideous assemblage gathered, Pepan braced himself. He still did not know enough about the Otherworld to know how to fight them but was trusting to instinct. And the ancestors. But they seemed to be drawing back, pulling away.

From within the hovering cloud came the voice of the

Prophet. *The child is not without resources of its own,* she said. *Watch . . . and learn.*

When labor began, the infant had ceased to emit its characteristic tonal signal. For a time it was silent, all its energies focused on the convulsive struggle to escape the womb. The birthing was swift, but no sooner had the child emerged from Vesi's body than it sent out a new signal, a layered, complex chord of ineffable sweetness that rose and fell with its lusty cries.

The sound rang like a chime through the Otherworld.

The rapacious horde halted abruptly. A few—the older, more experienced—even turned back. The others milled around in confusion, snarling and snapping at one another but advancing no farther.

Pepan asked, *What happened? I do not understand.*

A small part of each of us is now in that child, replied the voice of the Prophet, *making him more powerful than any single member of our race has ever been. Demons and those they influence are destructive rather than creative. A lack of creativity means a lack of imagination. Without imagination they cannot encompass a new idea—and this child represents a new idea. He frightens them.*

Abruptly, the sound the child was making changed, becoming a deep growl that provided a startling counterpoint to the original sweetness of tone. The effect was disturbing; one by one the gathered *hia* and *siu* turned and melted back into the Otherworld.

What's wrong? Pepan asked the ancestors.

Demon-song, his father replied. *You did not tell us the infant was* siu-*spawn.* Although there was no inflection in his voice, Pepan could sense his anger. *We have gifted the offspring of a demon. My son, do you know what you have done?*

Will you take back your gifts because of it? Pepan countered.

The cloud roiled again. At last the Prophet spoke. *All things happen as they should. What we have given, we do not reclaim. But although we return to the Netherworld, you are commanded to stay close to this child. The gifts that burn within him must have every possible good influence to counterbalance the evil. He will have further need of you . . . and so will our people.*

Pepan turned away to hide his delight. *If it is my destiny . . . then so be it.*

The voice of the Prophet darkened. *The threads of destiny grow very knotted, Pepan.*

Beware.

FIFTEEN

As soon as she was able, Vesi reached for her baby. Wordlessly Repana put the infant into her arms. The two women stared down at the head nuzzling Vesi's breast. Aside from a downy cap of lustrous dark hair, the infant looked like any other newborn, red faced and wrinkled. Vesi gave a great sigh of relief. "I was afraid. . . "

"I know. So was I. But he is no monster," Repana added to reassure her daughter in spite of the lurking doubts she herself still harbored. "You have given birth to a healthy boy who looks as normal as any other." She didn't add that she had checked the babe for additional fingers or toes and its spine for a tail.

As if to prove her words, the infant opened his mouth and gave a lusty bellow. Both women laughed. "Little man," Vesi murmured fondly. "My little man."

"Men need names. What will you call him?"

"I do not know, Mother. There are no *purtani* to take

the auguries, so how am I to know what sort of name he needs?"

"You must give him a name of your own choosing then."

Vesi blinked. "That is too great a responsibility. Names have so much power over those who bear them. What if I choose wrong and do him damage?"

Unseen, Pepan bent over them. The girl feared the responsibility but he did not; he knew what name the child should have. With all his strength he tried to shout it loud enough so she could hear. *Hora Trim!*

But his strength was not enough. Though the shout resonated throughout the Otherworld, Vesi barely heard a whisper. She turned her head quickly, eyes wide. "Was that the wind?" she asked her mother.

"I heard nothing. There was a storm earlier but it is over now."

Hora Trim!

Vesi shivered. "There is a draught here."

HORA TRIM!

Abruptly Vesi smiled, lips moving as she formed words. "Hora . . . trim." She looked up at her mother. "I will call my son Horatrim."

Repana raised a quizzical eyebrow. "Meaning spirit of heroes?"

"Is that not a perfect name for a little boy?"

As she gazed down at the child, Repana was not so sure. His Rasne forebears were undoubtedly heroic, but the infant's sire was very different. Yet perhaps Horatrim was a good choice. "Such a noble name just might help counteract the influence of the *siu,*" she told Vesi.

At the mention of the *siu* the young woman stiffened; her eyes became distant and glazed. "No demon had anything to do with my son. Nothing, I tell you!" Her voice rose shrilly, startling the baby, who began to cry. Vesi's eyes were wide and wild. She was as brittle as glass, threatening to shatter at the slightest blow. Her mother feared she might lose her mind.

"Of course, my child," Repana hastily agreed. "I am simply weary and made a foolish slip of the tongue. I meant to say the name would protect your son against any demons he might encounter when he is older. It is a good name, a fine name. Rest now. You have done well." She stroked Vesi's forehead and murmured soothingly until both mother and infant grew calmer.

But long after Vesi fell asleep, Repana was still trembling.

The physical attack must have been terrible indeed, she thought, *but to relive it unbearable. I have to be careful with Vesi. We must find a safe place to raise the child where no one will mention its origins and bring the memories flooding back.* Repana realized they could not return to their *spura*. Even if Pepan had succeeded in getting the others to forgive them, there was always the danger someone would say something.

When Repana announced to Wulv that the baby was alive and well, he was eager to see the infant at once. But Repana discouraged him; she was uncomfortable with the idea of allowing the woodsman too near a new baby. "They're both sleeping," she said. "There is something you can do, however. We will need moss for diapering, can you find some?"

Wulv looked almost insulted. "Some? How much do you want?"

"As much as you can carry," Repana said with a hint of a smile.

Delighted to be of use, he set off at once and soon brought back not only moss but a freshly snared rabbit for Vesi's dinner. "Meat makes milk," he assured Repana as he showed her his prize at the entrance to the hut.

"I suppose you have a great experience of nursing infants?" she remarked sarcastically.

He took no offense. "Hunters have to be observant. I

have seen what the women in my tribe do. I have watched the beasts of the field feed their young."

Repana bit back an angry retort. "My daughter is Rasne, which of course means she has delicate sensibilities," she said firmly. "Vesi prefers fish. White fish."

"This deep in the forest she had better eat what she can get. We're not on the banks of the Tiber now. When you go home you can—"

"We will not be going back to our *spura.* Even . . . even if the Lord of the Rasne sends for us himself."

Wulv stared at Repana. "But I thought. . . "

"Our lives there are over."

"Then where will you go? You can't stay here forever. The forest is full of dangerous beasts who won't respect the sanctuary of the stones. And I can't protect you night and day; I have to sleep sometime."

"Are you saying you would abandon us?"

"I am not. I gave my word to the Rasne lord. I may not have much, but I have my honor."

Repana nodded. "We will rely upon it then. Pepan recognized your quality and I trust his judgment. But tell me, Wulv—you have a home elsewhere, do you not? Someplace safer, where we could go?"

"I can't take you there."

"Why not?"

"It's . . . well, it isn't much of a place, nothing like I'm sure you're used to. There's a hut like this one only bigger and made to stand winter weather. It's part of a compound with a shed for storing hides and a smokehouse for fish, all on an island I built up in the middle of some swampy ground that floods a lot. In fact, my home is usually surrounded by a lake. People leave me alone there, which is the way I like it."

Repana clapped her hands together. "It sounds perfect!"

Wulv was disconcerted. But before he could think of a way to discourage them, he heard a voice. Not a human voice, it sounded more like the soughing of the wind through the leaves, yet it spoke in clearly distinct human syllables.

Take them.

Wulv grabbed his knife and glanced wildly around. He saw only Repana, the hut, the circle of stones, and the forest beyond. Yet with a hunter's infallible instinct, he was aware of another presence. He touched the bear's claw amulet on his belt. This was indeed a cursed place.

Take them, the voice repeated. *Whatever Repana wants, you must do. Your future lies with them.*

Wulv had to fight back an almost overwhelming desire to throw himself on the ground and do worship. Surely one of the gods was speaking directly to him. In the memory of his tribe, such a thing had never happened to one of the Teumetes before. He was simultaneously terrified and elated.

"What is wrong with you?" asked Repana. "The color has left your face."

You must take them with you, insisted the implacable voice.

"I will. Oh, I will!"

Repana was perplexed. "You will what?"

"Take you to my home as soon as your daughter can travel. That's what you wanted, isn't it?"

She gave him a hard look. But just then Vesi called to her, and forgetting everything else, Repana ducked inside the hut.

Once more Wulv swept his eyes around the glade. There was nothing noteworthy, only the sentinel stones standing their eternal vigil. A bird's cry drew Wulv's attention upward. Although the sky was a delicate eggshell blue, a gathering of clouds portended rain. One in particular puzzled him. Its shape changed so swiftly. One moment it looked like soft billows of foam, the next it resembled rugged mountain peaks. As Wulv watched, the mountains became an army marching away into the distance.

* * *

From the Otherworld things looked different.

Wulv, the hut, even the circle of stones were to Pepan no more than misty and somewhat indistinct shapes. The cloud, however, was very solid.

Pepan, intoned the voice of the Prophet, *we must go now.*

What will happen to me if I stay here?

You are vulnerable in the Otherworld, Pepan. A siu *could contaminate your* hia, *making you one like them. It would be a great pity to see such a noble spirit corrupted. Your ancestors would grieve; our happiness in the Netherworld would be marred.*

But I cannot die?

No, his father's familiar tones replied, *you cannot die. Only flesh can die, and you are done with that.*

Then I will watch over the women and the infant all their lives. I am strong, stronger than any demon.

The hovering cloud darkened. *You are also overconfident,* proclaimed yet another voice in accents he could hardly understand. *I was like you once, a thousand years ago. But you will learn, Pepan. We all learn.*

With a mighty roar the cloud turned an inky purple and began to twist into a giant knot. The roar increased. The cloud convulsed, folding in upon itself. Abruptly came a sound like the boom of a monstrous drum and the knot unwound into a long, thin rope the color of spring violets, stretching all the way from the circle of stones to the horizon.

The sky shimmered with rainbows.

The air smelled of the distant sea.

A hush fell upon the Otherworld.

As Pepan watched, the violet rope grew thinner and thinner until only one filament remained. Then that too was gone and he was alone.

Alone in a way he had never been before.

Within the hut, the baby began to cry.

SIXTEEN

Throughout his life, Wulv had lived intimately with nature. Later he told Repana, "I've seen every weather there is and every sort of cloud too. But never one like that one. It was unnatural."

"How can a cloud be unnatural? The Rasne believe that clouds are nothing more than heated water, rising as steam."

Wulv looked shocked. "The Teumetes know that clouds are the exhalations of our gods." His voice trailed away as he gazed, awestruck, into the heavens once more. "The gods spoke to me from the clouds. I swear it. And that one cloud in particular sailed away in the direction of my home. I am to take you both there as soon as possible. Do you think your daughter will be strong enough to leave here tomorrow?"

Repana of the Silver People was not about to argue with one who had a message from the gods, his or anyone else's. "We will see how she feels in the morning, Wulv."

As it happened they had to wait a few more days until Vesi was able for the journey. Childbirth combined with her injuries had weakened her more than she would admit, but her mother's keen eye would not be fooled as to her condition. "When my daughter is strong," she argued with Wulv, "she will be able to travel faster. As it is, we would have to stop too often to let her rest, we would hardly make any progress. So go and bring us some fresh meat. I will make her a nourishing broth. You will eat some too; you look as if you need it."

On the morning before they set out for Wulv's home, the Teumetian carefully demolished the little hut in the glade, smoothing away every trace of its existence.

"This is a sacred place," Wulv pointed out. "We must leave it as we found it."

Repana nodded. The Rasne understood all too well the importance of keeping any sacred space undefiled . . . unlike the brutal and warlike Romans, who were said to burn other people's temples and throw down their gods.

Carrying her baby close to her breast, crooning constantly to it, Vesi followed Wulv with her mother at her back as they made their way along the narrow forest trails. Even at High Day it was very dark beneath the primordial oaks. Repana kept glancing over her shoulder, convinced she could hear something behind her. But there was nothing she could see, only a few thin shafts of light slanting down through the canopy of the leaves overhead. Yet each time she looked back she felt certain there was more undergrowth than she remembered and the forest had a more pungent, fecund odor.

As he followed the little party, the *hia* energy that Pepan radiated left its mark on the forest. Branches dipped greedily to absorb some of it; leaves burgeoned and grew glossy with their share. In Pepan's wake, roots clawed through the soil, clutching after the last tendrils of the nourishing force. The *hia* of the dead fed the living, who in turn would die, decay, and feed new lifeforms in a never-ending cycle. The integrity of the whole depended upon the death and rebirth of its parts.

The only constant was change.

Pepan's strength was continually dissipated and then restored by the surging emerald energy of the living forest.

Just when it was most needed, Wulv called a halt. "I'll find some drinking water for Vesi," he said. "You sit here with your back against this big tree and close your eyes and rest. I'll be only a shout away." Not for the first time, Repana was impressed by Wulv's consideration.

When weariness began to take its toll on Vesi, he volunteered to carry little Horatrim. She demurred. "What can he know about babies?" she hissed to her mother, her whisper loud enough for Wulv to hear. "You carry him," she said, thrusting the child into Repana's arms.

But Repana was weary as well. When she stumbled and almost dropped the infant, Wulv caught her and steadied her, then gently eased the babe from her arms. "I won't hurt him," he insisted. "I like babies."

Repana raised an eyebrow. "Have you ever held one before?"

The Teumetian thrust forward his lower jaw in a way she was coming to recognize. "I like babies," he repeated stubbornly.

"But have you ever. . ."

"I've held bear cubs and fox kits, day-old wolves and orphaned fawns. I know what to do," he said, wrapping the baby in his bearskin mantle.

Too tired to argue, the women gave in. For the rest of the journey their guide carried Horatrim as carefully as any mother could wish. From time to time he even murmured to the baby and was rewarded by a gurgle that pleased him inordinately. "I think he likes me," Wulv confided shyly.

Shortly before sunset the forest gave way to a marshy expanse fed by a tributary of the Tiber. Wulv stopped and pointed. At the marsh's lowest point a lake glinted; a tiny islet was barely discernible in its midst. "My home," he announced with shy pride. "I built it myself. Piled up earth and rocks until I had a raised place that was always dry. Made that causeway leading to it too, so I can get home even in time of flood."

Repana was too tired to be interested in the details of the place. It looked appallingly primitive, but at least it was a sanctuary. "How much farther?" she wanted to know.

"We'll be there before dark. Take care to follow in my footsteps. If you step off the path you could find yourself neck deep in water."

Now Repana was doubly glad that Wulv was carrying the baby.

The path twisted and turned, dipped and doubled back on itself in an ever more intricate pattern meant to confuse invaders. Beyond the forest marsh grass took over, slender, supple leaves that gradually grew higher and higher, until they were walking through a verdant tunnel. The ground underfoot was boggy in places, making every step an effort. The Teumetian moved with confidence, barely glancing at the route he followed. He was concentrating on the baby in his arms. Finally, he stopped and allowed the women to catch up. "Welcome," he said simply, stepping aside at the neck of the narrow causeway that ran out to the artificial island in the center of the lake. Several thatched huts stood on the island. "All this is mine," the Teumetian added, indicating the little compound with a wave of his hand.

Gratefully, Repana and Vesi stumbled along the causeway and collapsed together on the bed inside the largest hut. As Repana's eyelids drifted closed, the last thing she saw was Wulv carefully handing Horatrim to his mother.

In the morning, while Vesi was nursing Horatrim, Repana allowed Wulv to show her around his little domain. Although it was very crude, Repana was forced to admit to herself that Wulv had achieved a surprising level of domesticity.

"The spit over the firepit rotates—look, I'll show you; it works with this foot treadle I made—so meat roasts evenly," he explained proudly. "And in this shed here, where I smoke fish, I've arranged flaps in the roof so I can control the amount of smoke."

"Is there only one way onto this island of yours?"

"Only one. And I can barricade the causeway if wolves or bears get too close."

"What about two-legged predators?" wondered Repana. "What is to stop them from swimming across?"

"Nothing—except for the pointed stakes I sunk into the mud around the margins of the lake. And the water here is full of eels. I feed them on blood and scraps of meat. If any attacker were to jump into the lake and injure themselves, the eels would be drawn by the blood and do a bit of attacking of their own."

"Eels cannot kill a man," protested Repana.

"No, but it would take an extraordinarily brave man to attempt to swim through a swarm of biting eels," Wulv told her with a grin.

Repana subsequently commented to Vesi, "He is a resourceful man and more intelligent than he looks. In fact, if I did not know Wulv was a Teumetian I would not take him for a savage."

"Perhaps the Teumetes are not savages," Vesi suggested.

Repana's eyebrows flew toward her hairline. "Of course they are! You heard what Wulv said about being descended from bears." But privately she was beginning to have doubts as to just what constituted a savage.

In the days and moons and seasons that followed, Repana's good opinion of Wulv continued to grow. She and Vesi found him unfailingly courteous according to his own standard and gifted with a sense of humor that made their exile more bearable. When winter closed in, he brightened the long nights by telling rambling jokes that had no point but were somehow very funny and singing bawdy, equally funny songs in a husky voice.

Repana tried to pretend she did not understand their meaning, but sometimes she blushed.

Wulv found her blushes beguiling. At night he lay sleepless thinking about them, and when spring came he brought her armloads of wildflowers. "There are more flowers around the lake than I ever saw before," he commented.

"What am I to do with these?" asked Repana, bending her head to sniff their fragrance.

"I don't know. I just thought you would enjoy . . . something beautiful, after looking at my scarred old face all winter."

"I stopped looking at your face a long time ago," Repana said quietly. "My people worship beauty in all of its forms, but you have taught me that there is a deeper beauty, a beauty of spirit. I think our people lack that, and we are the poorer for it."

Wulv bowed, his cheeks flushed. He did not entirely understand what Repana was saying, but he understood the emotion behind the words.

"You like him very much," Vesi remarked.

The older woman shrugged and concentrated on gathering the flowers together. "He is good to us."

* * *

Pepan also was aware of a burgeoning affection between Wulv and Repana. In the Otherworld the emotional attraction was expressed as a lyrical strand of melody whenever their eyes met. The former Lord of the Rasne was astonished that Repana could so react to a primitive woodsman. He was not exactly jealous; the longer he was in the Otherworld, the more such emotions seemed irrelevant. Rather he felt a fading, wistful envy. Life was going on without him. How strange.

Yet he remained involved, watching with something akin to paternal pride as the infant Horatrim crawled, then stood, then took his first precocious steps. There was no doubt the boy was developing with astonishing rapidity. One could almost see him grow.

Meanwhile Vesi's youthful face took on more matronly plumpness, and a sheen of silver frosted Repana's hair.

Because in the Otherworld Pepan had no sense of time, each change took him by surprise. The swiftness of the changes surprised him even more. During his life in the Earthworld, had things altered so quickly? Had time passed with such extraordinary rapidity? Perhaps it had . . . and perhaps he had been too busy to notice the changes.

Eventually he realized he was having his own effect on the Earthworld. The energy of his *hia,* remaining in one place as it now did, was causing an explosion of growth most clearly demonstrated by the vegetation surrounding Wulv's lake. Ancient marsh willows that had been on the verge of dying reclothed themselves with new leaves. Spindly seedlings developed into luxuriant shrubbery in less than a season. Vivid, fleshy orchids of gold and azure blossomed along stems the length of a spear shaft, while from early spring until late autumn the air was perfumed by masses of white roses.

And day after day, Wulv brought Repana flowers. When she took them from him, their hands touched and lingered. In the morning there would be more blossoms for the Teumetian to bring to Repana.

Horatrim continued to grow with astonishing rapidity. The first words he spoke were, "Give me!" as he reached for his grandmother's flowers, displaying early the Rasne passion for beauty.

The three adults laughed with delight.

In the Otherworld Pepan laughed too, a rich warm sound.

Laughter was not irrelevant, for while it lasted the sound of joy acted as a shield that kept dark forces at bay. The musical chord of Horatrim's spirit had the same effect, Pepan observed. In the immediate vicinity of the child no *siu* lurked; no corrupted *hia* sniggered. But he knew they were not far away, circling, stalking. Rapacious.

There were other watchers as well. He was aware of them as vast shapes on the horizon emitting a sound like the ringing of silver bells, a barely perceptible tintinnabulation that underlay all other sounds: this was the song of the *Ais,* the music of the gods. Their looming presence made Pepan uneasy. He was willing to challenge a *siu* but he had no illusions about his strength compared to one of the *Ais.* They could crush him without a thought if they chose, if his actions displeased them. So far they had not interfered, but he had no way of knowing what they might do in the future.

He wondered why they were also taking an interest in the demon-sired child.

SEVENTEEN

The half-human child of a siu *has always been considered an abomination, a creature who belongs in neither world.*

Yet would we be justified in destroying such a child?

He is innocent of his father's crime. Because of her own sense of outrage, Pythia wants the boy Horatrim killed. But if we do so, we will be no better than the siu, *matching one destruction with another.*

There is also the matter of the child's exceptional heritage.

A powerful spirit, newly entered into the Otherworld, gave the unborn infant an assortment of gifts donated by older, even more powerful spirits from the Netherworld. Thus the child is special to Veno, Protectress of the Dead. Veno argues for the boy's survival as forcibly as Pythia argues against it.

We, the Ais, *shape all three worlds according to our own designs, which humankind can never understand. Humans have their own effect on the Earthworld, of course . . . and on us, who conform in some degree to the images they give us. So one influences the other.*

The outcome is not certain.

Wild forces and inexplicable energies are gathering about the boy called Horatrim. We feel their power but are uncertain how to proceed. Although we pretend to omnipotence, we have to admit among ourselves that even we do not know everything.

Therefore we agree that it would be a mistake to move against these forces until we understand them better. Such an action might not only destroy Horatrim, but also destroy the delicate balance he represents between the three worlds. The risk is too great.

We shall content ourselves with watching, and waiting . . . for a while.

EIGHTEEN

"Romax!"

Even before Wulv reached his native village, he heard the first shouts. Those living in outlying areas were swiftly passing the word.

"Romax," they warned, using the Teumetian name for the most powerful tribe in Latium. "Romax warriors are headed this way!"

It was high summer and Wulv was making a rare journey to his birth village to trade pelts from the forest for wool and linens with which Repana could make new clothes. Three years had passed since she and Vesi had fled the Rasne *spura,* and the gowns they were wearing had long since worn out. They were, as they frequently told Wulv, tired of improvising with scraps.

Little Horatrim was happy enough to wear furs and leather like his hero Wulv, but women required something more.

As time passed Wulv was learning quite a bit about

women—and small boys. They had become his family, the only family he would ever know. Whatever any of them wanted, he felt obliged to provide. But for their own protection he had never told anyone about them and allowed no one from outside to approach the island.

For once, when he entered the village no one called out, "Here comes Scarface. Hide the women so he doesn't frighten them into fits." It was an old joke and not a funny one. But this time the Teumetians had something more urgent on their minds.

"Five or six raiding parties have been seen in our territory," Wulv was told by the headman, a grizzled veteran of many battles. "As usual they're looting and burning, then trying to claim the land for their own. But they won't succeed here!" The headman brandished his favorite battle-ax by way of emphasis. Several strips of dried and blackened skin were knotted together just below the ax head, trophies taken from the backs of old enemies.

The Romax were the most hated enemy of all, the mere sight of one arousing the Teumetes to blood-fury.

"Stay here and stand with us," the elders implored Wulv. "There will be plenty of good fighting."

"I can't. I have to go back."

"Go back to what? That swamp you live in? You stupid maggot. If you stay here and fight with us, you can have your pick of the Romax weapons we capture. Forged metal!"

But Wulv was stubborn. "I don't need metal. I have this great lump of precious metal right here to use for trade." He held out the ring Pepan had given him. "I want to exchange this for wool and linen to make clothes."

The headman sneered, although he took the ring readily enough, holding it to the light before pressing it between the nubs of his worn teeth. "Wool and linen?

Why? What happened to that filthy bearskin mantle you usually wear? Getting soft in your old age, eh?"

"The weather is too hot now. Besides, I need something better than that for my women."

"Your what?" The elders gaped at him, but the headman burst into laughter. "Wulv, with women! I don't believe it. Who would have anything to do with you? Your scars aren't even wounds of victory; you got them in some battle you lost."

"A fight with a bear," Wulv corrected, "which I didn't lose. I made his pelt into that mantle you mentioned, and he's kept me warm every winter since. But Rasne women are used to finer fabrics so I need—"

"You don't have any Rasne women. You're lying."

Wulv growled and locked his fingers around the other man's throat, but at that moment a cry from the sentry at the gate rang through the village. "Smoke! There's a fire in the distance. The Romax must be heading this way."

Dropping his hand, pushing the headman away from him, Wulv whirled around to look. A column of black smoke was rising toward the sunny sky—from the direction of his lake and island. Without a word, he turned and fled.

Horatrim had been disappointed that morning when Wulv refused to take him to the village. "I've never met any other people," he had complained. "I've only heard you talk about them. I want to know what they look like. I want to see how they live."

But his grandmother was adamant that he be kept hidden away. With the passing of the seasons Repana had grown accustomed to their isolation and increasingly fearful of any exposure. Meanwhile Vesi's bright, adventurous spirit had been subdued by her misfortunes, leaving her content to bow to her mother's authority. She rarely spoke and was content with sitting quietly by herself, humming tunelessly. At night, her dreams were often troubled.

"You're better off here," Repana told Horatrim, "where you are safe."

"Wulv can keep me safe," Horatrim had insisted. "Wulv can do anything. Tell them," he appealed to the Teumetian.

"Your grandmother's right," Wulv affirmed.

But in the end Wulv went off without him, leaving the little boy to amuse himself. His mother and Repana were busy grinding emmer wheat in a stone quern that they had set out in the sunshine, so for want of anything better to do, he ambled over to watch them. The ground wheat would make dumplings for the main meal of the day, but that, Horatrim thought regretfully, was a long time away.

His small round belly rumbled. "Dumplings taste better with meat," he remarked to his mother.

There was no response and although Vesi's hands were busy, her eyes were distant and lost, seeing another time and another place where her dream lover took her to his couch of silken sheets.

Horatrim appealed to higher authority. "Grandmama? I can get us meat."

"You're too little," Repana said automatically.

He thrust out his lower lip. "Am not."

The pouting little face was so comical Repana bit the inside of her cheek to keep from laughing. He had the appearance of a boy of seven or eight, though only three years had passed since his birth. The three adults were with him all the time so hardly noticed how exceptional his growth was. But once in a while his grandmother took a long, serious look at him and marveled. Life was, indeed, full of mysteries, including the mystery of the way her own feelings toward the child had changed.

It was impossible to continue to resent such an engaging little fellow. Sometimes Repana just wanted to grab him in her arms and hug him. She did not always resist the impulse, but today she was trying to be serious. "You're just a child, Horatrim. Providing meat is man's work."

"I am a man!" he flung at her, standing with his legs wide apart and his pudgy fists braced on his hips. "Almost."

Repana shook her head. When the boy was in a stubborn mood, there was no dissuading him. "All right then, bring us a bit of meat if you can. But don't wander far away and be careful in the forest. If you see any strangers, hide, or I will never let you go off on your own again."

Horatrim ran to collect the slingshot and miniature fishing spear Wulv had made for him before she could change her mind.

He was still a child. When he he stood on tiptoe the top of his head came only to his mother's breast. Yet under the tutelage of the Teumetian he had learned to kill hares and spear fish in the streams that fed into the marsh. He was not big enough to hunt for the venison and wild boar that Wulv brought down, but he could pretend they were his quarry.

The day was blindingly hot. Almost every afternoon in summer a spectacular storm would erupt somewhere in the area, sending great white spiders stalking across the land on their long legs. The touch of one of those legs was known to be fatal. Each morning Vesi and Repana offered a sacrifice of burned feathers to Tinia, the deity of lightning, to spare their home, and whenever he left the island they warned young Horatrim to avoid the trees if a storm broke.

But he was a boy who tended to forget the warnings of women.

Now, carrying his spear lightly balanced in his hand, the boy trotted along the bank of his favorite fishing stream. The stream was not swift running but quite deep and snaked its way in and out of the edge of the forest.

Where it ran close to the trees, fat fish lurked in caverns beneath thirsty roots reaching down into the water.

Today Horatrim had decided to trace the water all the way to its source. He had never seen the birthplace of a stream before and the prospect excited him. He had a remarkable ability to find adventure where no one else thought to look.

A sturdy little boy with dark hair and eyes and the olive complexion of the Rasne, Horatrim himself did not appear remarkable—except to the watcher from the Otherworld.

Pepan could see the *hia* encased in the boy's body and there was nothing childish about that spirit. Enriched by the talents and abilities of a pantheon of gifted ancestors, Horatrim's *hia* was already more powerful than Pepan's. A hundred forms of genius fed its flame.

You do not yet know what you are, Pepan thought. *When you do, that body will be too small to hold you.*

He watched in fascination as the child painstakingly traced the stream. At one point Horatrim picked up a large piece of bark and, using a sharp stone, began drawing a map of the watercourse with all the detail and accuracy of an adult planning a drainage system for a city. As he worked he hummed to himself in a childish treble. But the tune he was creating was one of the ancient love songs of the Silver People, a song the boy had never heard before.

Pepan was aware of the Roman scouting party long before Horatrim was. A brazen clanging rang through the Otherworld, destroying harmonies.

Beware! he called silently to the boy.

Horatrim tensed.

Throughout his short life he had been aware of certain intuitions he could not explain, of half-glimpsed images, barely heard sounds, snatches of conversation, the intentions of animals. Now, suddenly intuition was warning him to hide, so without hesitation he abandoned the open ground beside the stream and ran toward the nearby forest. Panting, he dived into the first thicket.

No sooner had the child burrowed into the undergrowth than the leaves swelled and expanded, hiding him.

He heard the invaders coming long before he saw them.

Tramping feet, marching to a rhythm. They too were following the open ground beside the streambed but approaching from the opposite direction.

Cautiously, the little boy parted the leaves and peered out.

A company of men was passing no more than a spear's throw from Horatrim's hiding place. Could they be the Romax Wulv spoke of with such loathing? They wore molded tunics of boiled leather and metal helms with flaps that protected the backs of their necks. They walked two abreast, each carrying a round shield on his back and wearing a short sword in a scabbard at his hip. In front of them their captain marched alone, with sword drawn.

"Are we near Etruria yet?" a man in the third row called up to the first. His clipped, abrupt speech was unfamiliar, yet to his surprise Horatrim could understand the language. "I want to see one of those rich Etruscan cities."

"Forget about the cities; I want to get my hands on one of those perfumed Etruscan women," remarked another man. "They have skin like thick cream, or so I've heard. Can you imagine nuzzling into. . . "

"You think their fathers and husbands will just hand them over to us?"

"I don't mind fighting for a woman; I've done it often enough before."

The captain said over his shoulder, "You won't have to fight for women. I know the Etruscans; their men have become as idle and pleasure loving as any female. There was a time when they joined with the Hellenes to extend their influence from the Darklands to the Sunlands. But success went to their heads. They stopped trying so hard and devoted themselves to wine cups and banquet tables and dancing. Now it takes intervention by the gods to force any of them to fight. The Etruscans are said to be the most religious people on earth," he remarked as an afterthought, "for whatever that's worth."

There was coarse laughter from the rear. "They'll be praying to their gods right enough when we get through with them!"

"We won't see them for a while," retorted the captain. "We're in a pocket of Teumetian territory now and those square-headed bastards love to fight, so keep your weapons at the ready."

Hidden by the sheltering leaves, the little boy watched the company pass by. He found them very strange. They made no effort to muffle their footfalls. Twigs snapped loudly beneath their tramping feet. Their leather creaked, their metal clanged. Since earliest childhood Horatrim had been taught by Wulv to move as silently as any forest creature, and he found the actions of these strangers disturbing, a desecration of the peaceful countryside. One even took a swing with his shortsword at a little willow sapling, cutting the young tree in half for no reason. He brayed with laughter.

Horatrim was horrified. He felt the willow's pain and heard its anguished cry.

The wind shifted, carrying a wave of pungent body odors to the boy. The Romax stink, he observed. His nose twitched with disgust at the smells of garlic and sweat and long-unwashed clothing.

Mama and Grandmama insisted Horatrim bathe every day, and fresh clothing always awaited him. "You are Rasne," Grandmama frequently reminded him. She had even encouraged Wulv to begin bathing.

He was not too sure what "being Rasne" meant. But he felt confident it was something very different from the nature of the invaders crashing through the countryside. He would be glad when they were gone. He had wanted to see others like himself, but these men were not like him at all. And he had no desire to be like them.

When the last sounds of their passing died away, he crept from his hiding place and resumed tracing the watercourse. The sky was darkening with a summer storm and he knew he should head for home, but he was stubborn. What he began, he would finish.

Yet his mind kept skittering back to the strangers. What sort of place did they come from? He would ask Wulv about them when he returned. Wulv would know. Wulv knew everything.

NINETEEN

Wulv ran as hard as he could, while with every step his foreboding increased. Dark clouds gathering overhead added to his sense of impending doom. He regretted having built his sanctuary so far from the village. At a walking pace it had always seemed a satisfying distance, assuring him privacy and freedom from the pitying stares of others. But he was running at top speed now.

Even at that he was too late however. He burst from the forest at the edge of the marsh to discover that his home was ablaze. The island was swarming with Romax warriors. Several were silhouetted against the flames of his burning house as they busied themselves with the two women.

Vesi lay unconscious beneath her ravager, but Repana was fighting back.

"Monsters!" Wulv screamed at the top of his lungs. "Monsters!" He hurled himself forward with no sense of personal danger, only a vast, reddening rage.

Within that rage a great shadow took form. As Wulv, roaring with fury, pounded across the causeway, the nearest Romax turned around in time to see a human running toward him embedded in what appeared to be the transparent image of a giant bear.

"Ho . . . !" cried the startled warrior. But he made no further sound. Wulv struck him such a mighty blow across the throat that his vocal cords were paralyzed. A second blow snapped his spine, sending him spinning into the lake, which immediately boiled with wriggling eels.

The nearby warriors were so taken aback that they hesitated, and in that slim space of time Wulv killed two more. Then they closed on him, swords thrusting, spears jabbing. Screams and grunts tore through the air as a company of highly trained warriors attacked, and were attacked by, something that might have been a huge and savage bear—or one desperate man.

"Repana!" Wulv called with all his might from the heart of the fray. He thought a faint voice answered.

The Teumetian was hopelessly outnumbered, yet somehow he stayed on his feet. A blade sliced through the big muscle in his upper left arm but the pain never reached his brain. Anger blocked all sense of agony; he felt only a desperate desire to get to his women.

Repana had heard him call out to her and it gave her renewed strength. From the moment the warriors had emerged from the forest she had anticipated her fate, but she was determined not to give up her life without a struggle. Life, to her surprise, had become very sweet again, even though Pepan was lost to her forever.

Besides, she had her daughter to protect.

"Kick and bite," she had instructed Vesi when the warriors first approached the causeway. "Vomit on them if they try to rape you; that puts men off. Get your hands on a weapon, any weapon, and take as many into the Netherworld with you as you can."

"And you, Mother," gritted the younger woman as she

rummaged through the household's meager supply of implements in search of weapons. She equipped herself with a fish scaler and gave her mother a hand ax. Shoulder to shoulder they stood waiting in the sunshine for the enemy.

They had not long to wait.

With howls of delight the war party had pounded across the causeway and attacked the compound. The women fought back with a ferocity that gave the lie to the Roman belief that Etruscans were weak and soft, but soon they were overcome by superior numbers.

"Now you'll lick my feet, you scrawny bitch!" a warrior had demanded as he ripped the fish scaler from Vesi's fingers and flung her backward onto the ground. He hurled himself on top of her, neither noticing nor caring that she had struck her head on the stone quern as she fell. Panting, he tore at her helpless and unmoving body.

Meanwhile others had pillaged the compound. When they found nothing of value they set fire to the buildings and amused themselves by taking turns with the women. Vesi remained lifeless and unrewarding, so was spared the worst of it. Repana proved a more worthy trophy, fighting like a tigress. Each new man had to subdue her in turn, and she left the mark of her teeth and nails on every one. But she was growing tired, terribly tired. It was only a matter of time before pain and shock released her to unconsciousness, perhaps to death.

When at last Wulv's cry reached her ears, she struggled to free herself from her latest rapist and get to the Teumetian somehow. She meant to shout his name . . . but instead she heard herself scream, "Pepan!"

TWENTY

He never left Horatrim, yet part of him was always with Repana. His *hia* became aware of her pain. Then he heard her call his name, a cry of distress winging to him through the Otherworld. He had no flesh with which to go to her aid, but he had another resource.

Horatrim! Pepan shouted voicelessly. *Horatrim, listen to me!*

The child stopped in his tracks.

You must go home. Now!

The little boy cocked his head to one side, listening. But all his ears heard was the singing of the stream, the sighing of the wind.

Go home!

Now!

Dropping his fishing spear, Horatrim whirled around and began to run.

As he sped back the way he had come, the sound of the wind turned into the malicious hiss and snicker of a thousand evil voices.

The boy's heart began to pound in his breast. His feet thudded a frantic rhythm on the stream bank. The sky continued to darken as a massive summer storm advanced, but it was not fear of the storm that propelled him.

Hurry, urged the silent intuition that drove him on. *Faster, faster!*

He had not realized how far he had come; the journey back seemed to take forever. But at last he saw the lush marshland spread before him, with the small lake, shallow in the heat of summer, at its center. Relieved, he raced toward the glint of water. And stopped in horror.

Wulv's compound was ablaze. Invaders swarmed over the little island like ants, and in their midst some sort of struggle was taking place. With sweat pouring into his eyes Horatrim could not tell just what was happening until he wiped his forearm across his face. Then he saw all too clearly.

Outlined against the purple storm clouds a creature like a huge bear stood on its hind legs, surrounded by warriors. Roaring in fury, it flung itself from one side to the other while they slashed and jabbed at it with their weapons. A woman was staggering toward the creature, holding out her arms imploringly. Her clothing was bloody and torn to ribbons, exposing her bare breast. Long strands of gray hair streamed wildly over her shoulders. As the child watched she fell to her knees with her arms still outstretched, and her wail of despair drifted across the lake.

"Grandmother!" screamed Horatrim.

He must get to her, but there were warriors on the causeway so he flung himself into the lake instead. Thrashing wildly through water up to his chest, he waded toward the island. The eels surged toward him, then writhed in agony when they touched his flesh. Horatrim was unaware of them. Too late he remembered his abandoned fishing spear. What could one unarmed little boy do against a company of warriors? Remembering the stakes Wulv had driven into the mud, he reached down and wrenched one free with surprising strength.

The boy pushed through the water. But the viscous mud at the bottom of the lake sucked greedily at his feet, holding him back. He gave a violent lunge to free himself.

From nowhere a shrill, mirthless laugh sounded in his ears. Something was watching; something was enjoying.

The sound distracted him. At that moment he lost his balance and tumbled face forward, inadvertently swallowing a mouthful of brackish liquid.

Choking, strangling, fighting panic, Horatrim struggled to get his feet under him. When his head at last broke the surface he desperately gulped air into his lungs. It burned like fire but it was better than drowning. The dark water terrified him; it seemed determined to claim him as a victim before he could reach Repana. And his mother . . .

"*Ais,* help me!" gasped the little boy.

His mother and grandmother believed in the gods implicitly and made sacrifices to them for every occasion. Aside from standing obediently silent throughout the rituals, he had never taken part in their devotions, which seemed very adult and mystifying. But if ever there was a time to seek supernatural aid, this was it.

"Help me," he repeated urgently. "I'm frightened!"

You must not be afraid, replied a voice. He could not tell where it came from; it was simply there. In him, around him . . . almost a part of him.

Fear can cripple you, the voice warned.

Before Horatrim could recover from his astonishment a different voice spoke up, enunciating as if with great effort, *Fear is something you can step out of as a beetle leaves its shell. Walk away from your fear. Leave it behind you and never look back.*

"I can't!"

You can. I did. And, having mastered the technique myself, I have given you that ability, it was my gift to you.

"But. . ."

Stop resisting! You make this too difficult. Just listen. Listen!

Never before had Horatrim conversed with *Ais,* but he was certain the gods were talking to him now. In their divine wisdom they were assuring him he could walk away from fear.

Your fear is like a shadow that is always with you. Look around. See the darkness that hovers close by? That is your fear.

The boy did as he was told. A faint, smoky cloud hung like a stain on the air beside him.

Now that you have seen it, recognize it for what it is, the voice instructed. *Then walk away. Leave your fear behind you.*

. . . and so he did.

Gritting his teeth, Horatrim floundered out of the shallow lake and onto the rocky but solid earth of the islet. Behind in the mud he left his capacity for fear, never to be reclaimed.

What he saw next would indeed have crippled him if terror still had any power over him. A sudden blast of lightning against the storm dark sky illuminated the scene with painful clarity.

The thing that Horatrim had mistaken for a bear was only Wulv—valiant Wulv—locked in a fight to the death with a score of men who were systematically hacking him to bits.

Thunder boomed.

Repana, obviously dying, was trying to crawl forward to meet her fate with the Teumetian. Beyond them Horatrim glimpsed the figure of Vesi lying on the earth like a broken branch while one of the warriors kicked her.

The lightning struck again, very close. Horatrim felt

the hair lift on his scalp and forearms, then a great shudder ran through him.

Wulv's fading cries were nothing compared to the roar that now burst from Horatrim's throat. It was not the shriek of a child but the full-blooded howl of an enraged man. His vocal cords swelled to accommodate the sound; his neck thickened, his shoulders broadened accordingly.

Faster than he had ever thought before, his racing brain analyzed the situation and made a decision. Wulv and Repana were almost beyond help, but Vesi's condition was uncertain. She might be saved. Horatrim raced toward her, the pointed stake clutched in one white-knuckled hand.

But they were not the hands of a little boy. The Romax who was kicking Vesi, more out of frustration than cruelty, stared in disbelief as a figure came toward him. With every step the child grew larger, older. The warrior's foot paused in midswing. The boy—the youth—the young man hurled himself forward in a great leap calculated to disable.

As Horatrim left the ground he heard yet another voice instructing, *Swing your arms for balance.*

He landed easily before the Romax.

Twist, then kick.

His left foot shot out, slamming hard into the Romax's unprotected kneecap. The sound of breaking bone was clearly audible, and the warrior pitched forward.

Now use your weapon, drive it up beneath the chin.

Horatrim rammed the stake into the Romax's throat, pushing it up through the roof of the mouth and into the brain. The man was dead before he hit the ground.

Horatrim bent over Vesi. She was still breathing, though both her eyes were swollen shut and a thin trickle of blood ran from the corner of her mouth.

Put your fingers to her throat and feel how the blood

pulses, said another of his voices. *Ah, she is strong. She will recover in time if no further harm comes to her. Go to the others now.*

Leaving his mother, Horatrim ran toward Repana and Wulv. With a coldness that surprised himself his brain was planning strategy to free them from their tormentors. One piercing cry caught the attention of the warriors surrounding Wulv and they turned toward the newcomer.

On their faces Horatrim saw blank surprise. He would never know what they saw, for as he approached they began scrambling backward. When he was within a couple of paces of them, he pretended to lunge to the right, then darted to the left instead and scooped Repana into his arms. The child Horatrim would never have thought of lifting his grandmother; the young man he had become did so easily.

"Who are you?" she managed to gasp through bloody lips.

"Vengeance," replied a voice—a voice she recognized even in her extremity, for it was Pepan's. Yet the face looking down at her belonged to the child Horatrim. But the features had matured inexplicably however, as if years had passed since the morning. Now he was both man and boy, familiar and a stranger.

Moaning, Repana closed her eyes.

Horatrim's actions caught the warriors off balance. One of them took a wild swing at him with his sword, but he easily ducked beneath the blow and in the same movement laid Repana at Wulv's feet. The mortally wounded Teumetian slumped down beside her and cradled her against his chest with a little sigh that might have been contentment.

The Roman warriors were tough and experienced; they swiftly regrouped. In a unit they rushed at him, then separated to flow around him like a river around a rock in order to trap him within their circle.

A child would have been overwhelmed by the strategy. The person Horatrim had become found himself drawing on the experiences of men who had been dead five hundred years. He fell to the ground, hugging his knees and rolling between pairs of running legs, then as soon as he was in the clear he was on his feet and turning to fight.

He had no weapons but his spirit and all it now contained: the accumulated wisdom of generations of people who had lived intimately with the gods.

Balancing a spear, a cursing warrior took aim at the man-boy who had appeared so unexpectedly. Horatrim met the man's eyes, then glanced up almost casually. "Tinia," he murmured as if calling to an old friend.

A bolt of blinding light seared out of the boiling clouds to detonate at the feet of the Roman and engulf him in a ball of fire. In the resulting dazzle Horatrim envisioned a flame-haired figure with no face, no indication of gender, and yet a terrible beauty. In one hand the figure held a whip. When the whip was cracked, lightning crackled and snapped.

Cowering, the Romans shrank back as the smell of their comrade's crisping flesh tainted the air.

"Tinia," Horatrim murmured again in acknowledgment and gratitude. Then from deep within himself came other names. "Sethlan, god of metals, give me fists of iron. Tuflas, goddess of healing, let me not feel my wounds. Culsan, god of destiny, grant me victory. Sancus, god of cities; Satres, ruler of the Netherworld; Ani, guardian of the gates; Veno, Protectress of the Dead; all you who are sacred to my people, be with me. I honor you now and fight in your name!"

His mother and grandmother had spoken those names within the hearing of the child Horatrim. Now he identified them with the multitude he felt inside himself. He had long been aware of the crowd of presences flooding his mind and his muscles, filling him with strength and cleverness and courage. He had never known their origins, but now he made the assumption that they were gods.

Surely the *Ais* were with him.

How could a mere band of mortal warriors hope to stand against one whom the gods loved?

He attacked in fury, and in terror the Romans attempted to flee from him. They saw what he did not.

Behind the infuriated youth, bearing down upon them, strode a whole army. Led by the image of an aging figure dressed in the garments of a nobleman of Etruria, a shadowy host of men and women marched implacably forward. Through their spectral flesh could be seen the dying fires of the compound behind them. Spears hurled at them passed through them as if through thin air.

The youth from the lake commanded an army of ghosts.

"Manes!" shrieked the Roman captain. His eyes rolled in his head. *"Manes!"*

Without effort, Horatrim understood what the word *manes* meant. But why did the man claim he was seeing ghosts? Was it supposed to be a trick? "Fool," Horatrim muttered contemptuously. Locking his fists together, he slammed them against the Roman captain's temple and grinned with satisfaction as the man slumped to the ground.

Being a warrior is fun, thought what was left of the little boy inside Horatrim. He looked for the next man to hit.

Storm clouds had swallowed the sun, and smoke from the burning compound further obscured the scene. In such a premature twilight it was hard to tell what was happening. Horatrim knew only that he fought and fought, knocking down one man after the other. With every blow he landed he seemed to grow stronger.

He never thought to look behind him.

* * *

In his wake, specters strode among the fallen Romans, extracting a terrible vengeance and taking more than lives. Souls were torn from the stunned bodies Horatrim left behind him; souls bound and ensnared by magic that was ancient when the world was young. The *hia* of the Roman warriors belonged to the shades of long-dead Etruscans now, forced forever to do their bidding. But their captors did not content themselves with taking slaves. Lovers of beauty, they must create beauty where none had existed before. The *hia* of the Rasne had spent many centuries in the Netherworld perfecting their talents. Moments of terminal terror were extracted from dying minds by the most skilled physicians, twisted and shaped into intricate, bloody beads by the greatest artisans, strung onto wire spun by the finest craftsmen from filaments of pain.

When the Etruscan spirits were finished, only the man-boy and the mortally injured bodies of Wulv and Repana and the unconscious Vesi remained. No Roman flesh, no spilled blood spattered the earth where moments before a company of trained warriors had been slaughtered.

Horatrim stood rocking slightly on his heels, rubbing his knuckles and looking around with a dazed expression. "Where did everyone go?" he asked in bewilderment.

There was no answer.

A faint groan caught his attention. He dropped to his knees beside Repana and Wulv, who looked up at him with glazing eyes. "Don't touch her," snarled the Teumetian.

"Wulv . . . it's me, Horatrim."

"Horatrim?" The Teumetian scowled. "You're not Horatrim."

"I am, but something happened to me," the boy replied. "And I came too late," he added miserably. Suddenly he was a child again, eyes brimming with tears. He reached for Repana.

Wulv twisted sideways, interposing his body between them. "Leave her! She's mine now."

"I only want to help; she's my grandmother."

Wulv responded by clutching Repana still more tightly to his chest and baring his teeth like a wild animal. It was obvious he no longer recognized the child he had helped raise.

Repana turned her head and tried to look into Horatrim's face, but the effort was too much for her. She uttered one soft moan, then slumped lifeless.

Wulv's scarred features blurred with a grief too great to survive. He struggled into a sitting position and shook the still body. "No! You have to live, you have to live for me! With me! I'll do better. I'll get you soft cloth. I'll catch such lovely fish for your meal. Please. Oh, please. My. . . "

The Teumetian drew a long, anguished breath. In his throat Horatrim could hear the death rattle. Wulv made a final effort. "My dear one," he murmured, the words of tenderness crossing his lips for the first and last time. Then he too was gone.

At the moment of Repana's dying, Horatrim had felt a pain as if something had torn loose inside him. The sensation was not repeated when Wulv died, but his sorrow was just as intense. Fighting back tears, he turned away—so he did not see two shadowy figures slowly materialize to bend over the woman who lay on the earth. One was tall and elegant, the other stocky and coarsely formed. Each held out a hand to her.

Repana's *hia* hesitated, then accepted them both. Like a scarf of sheerest silk it floated upward from her corpse and, together with her two companions, faded into the Otherworld.

Meanwhile Horatrim, wiping furiously at his eyes, was stumbling back to his mother. Vesi was still unconscious but at least she was alive. He was determined to keep her that way.

TWENTY-ONE

The Roman garrison occupied a hill fort overlooking the river. Built many years before by a now vanquished tribe, the fort had been modified and reinforced by the victorious Romans to take full advantage of its position. A high timber palisade surmounted walls of rammed earth and rubble. New timber gates had been installed and secured by massive bars. Pyramids of stones warned of ballistae mounted atop the walls.

From a level summit the hill fell sharply away, with clumps of parched cedar clinging to its steep flanks. Treacherous scree made any approach to the top difficult. Bronze-helmeted guards were stationed at the gates at all times, each equipped with a two-edged sword in a scabbard, a dagger, and a pair of throwing spears. Over linen undervests and woolen tunics they wore corselets of hammered bronze plates fastened together with rings to allow for mobility, while scarves around their necks served to keep the armor from cutting into their skin. The entire outfit was meltingly hot in the summer sun, bitterly cold in winter.

Because the garrison was situated north of Rome on a tribal frontier, the guards were under orders to be constantly vigilant. They were human; occasionally their attention wavered.

"This isn't a frontier, it's a backwater," Paulus complained to Sextus as they stood on either side of the main gate. "There's no fighting, no action. No opportunity for loot," he added petulantly. "There're rich pickings on all the other borders—I've heard of men making fortunes in Thrace, where even the slaves are bedecked in gold. But here. . . " He shook his head and spat into the dust. "The Samnites haven't come down from their mountains recently because they're too scared of us, the Vestini are subdued, and as for the Etruscans, they've gone as soft as melting wax. The king says we'll be overrunning them soon."

"You can be burned by melting wax," Sextus reminded him. He had stood this watch with Paulus every day for a month and was weary of the younger man's constant complaining. Paulus wanted most desperately to be in the midst of battle; he longed for the clash of weapons and the stink of blood and the promise of loot. Since joining the military his only assignment had been guard duty, and he was frustrated.

Sextus, on the other hand, had fought in many campaigns and had his belly full of battle and bloodshed. Paulus did not appreciate how lucky they were to be simply standing here, doing nothing. He now tried to transmit this to his companion. "I fought the Etruscans. . . " he began.

Paulus groaned audibly. He had heard the tales of Sextus's exploits a hundred times.

"I know the Etruscans well," Sextus continued undeterred. "If they should decide to declare war on Rome before our king marches on Veii, we had better be ready."

"I'll wager anything you care to name that it never happens." Yawning, Paulus scratched himself in the armpit. A trickle of sweat ran down under his body armor and he dug with one forefinger in an unsuccessful attempt to reach his upper ribs. "The Etruscans have no interest in Rome. I've heard descriptions of the cities in Etruria. They have brick cities with public buildings as fine as temples and private houses fit for princes. What would they want with an overgrown village of mud-and-timber shacks on seven rocky hills? You worry unnecessarily, Sextus. In the meantime I'm mightily bored and that sun is too damned hot. There's no one in sight. Why not step into the shade of the wall and have a quick game of dice? We can see just as well from there, and I'd welcome the chance to win that cloak I lost to you in the barracks last night."

A sharp voice cut through the stifling air. "If either of you desert your post for an instant, I'll personally skewer your guts."

Paulus and Sextus froze as their captain, Antoninus, strode through the gateway with a grim expression on his sunburned, hawk-nosed face. "You're supposed to be standing guard, attentive and watchful. All I can hear is your chatter. And you underestimate the Etruscans," he told Paulus. "They may seem peaceful now, but I wouldn't trust one of them if we had exchanged a blood oath and I was married to his sister. Guile is as natural to them as fighting is to us. They are an ancient, decadent race; they make the Egyptians look honest. Their current nonaggression could be just a clever ploy to make us relax our vigilance. While you two are dicing your pay away, a whole army could be sneaking past us under cover of those willows along the river down there, determined to sack and loot Rome."

"That's hardly likely; we're not the only guards," Paulus replied, smiling easily. His cousin was married to the captain's son, and he imagined it allowed him a certain familiarity.

Antoninus's backhanded blow drove him to the ground. "When you stand at this gate you stand as if you are the only guards between the barbarians and the gates of Rome. So keep a sharp lookout. And let me hear nothing further about playing dice!" Antoninus added as he walked away. "You ignorant whelps may not realize it, but the Etruscans you sneer at *invented* dice!"

Below the garrison, the Tiber undulated lazily through a land baked ochre by the relentless sun. Only the sway of willow branches against the wind betrayed any activity, but by the time Sextus and Paulus resumed their silent surveillance of the terrain, the trees were immobile. The bird song, which was the eternal heartbeat of the region, had been stilled.

The dark-haired young man leading the woman along the river's edge was careful to keep the trees between himself and the fort on the hill. Seeking cover in unfamiliar territory was as natural to him as breathing.

Vesi had been badly damaged in the raid. Her distraught son had held her in his arms and tended her wounds as best he could, using mud and leaves and scraps of half-remembered lore, lore that he should not know, had never been taught. Yet it came to him in his need and he accepted gratefully.

Horatrim had poured his love into his mother and was finally rewarded when she opened her eyes with a weary sigh. But when he looked into her eyes they were blank. No matter how much he pleaded with her to come back to him, there was no spark there, no sign of recognition. Yet she was alive; he comforted himself with that much. She was at least alive.

When Vesi had regained enough physical strength, Horatrim had taken her away from the island and its unbearable memories. He had set off through the forbidding, endless expanse of the Great Forest with no real destination in mind.

Then at night Horatrim began having vivid dreams of a wide river running through a fertile valley of rich black earth. In this unfamiliar land, exotically robed, dark-skinned healers worked in high-ceilinged temples. As he watched, they cured the sick and repaired the injured with incredible skill.

Where such dreams came from he did not know. But he awoke convinced the healers existed. Somewhere. In the Black Land, wherever that was. If he could only find them, perhaps they could help his damaged mother.

In the meantime, however, he decided to take Vesi to her own people. They might be able to heal her themselves, or they could at least look after her while he went in search of the Black Land and the wondrous healers of his dreams.

He did not discuss his plans with Vesi. Conversation was no longer possible with his mother. She could only be gently guided, told to sit here, lie there, eat this, drink that. He fed her by hand, pressed soft food into her mouth, then waited while she chewed slowly and swallowed, then fed her some more. When she soiled herself he cleaned and bathed her, unaware how recently she had been doing the same for him. Obedient as a child, Vesi followed his instructions. Sometimes she made small, erratic gestures or gaped dumbly with her mouth hanging ajar. But she did not speak; she had not spoken since that terrible day when Wulv and Repana died.

Slowly, limited by Vesi's ability to travel, they had made their way through the forest. Thanks to the hunting and foraging skills Wulv had taught him, Horatrim was able to keep them both fed. He asked for nothing but directions from the occasional Teumetians they encountered.

During endless, sleepless nights, he tormented himself with memories of his grandmother and Wulv and the life they had led together before the coming of the Romax. The little family on the island had bothered no one, done no damage. In retrospect he realized they had been happy.

Yet the Romax had destroyed all that for the sheer pleasure of destruction. His stubborn mind re-created the images of that last terrible day again and again, refusing to accept them, refusing to forget.

He was taller than his mother, taller than most of the hunters or trappers or even the occasional Romax scout they encountered. He had burst from his clothes and been forced to make new ones from hides and pelts he trapped along the way, stitching the pelt with tiny neat stitches although he had never sewn before. Almost overnight his body had turned into that of a powerful young man. Yet deep inside a small boy still lived, peering out at the world through wondering, baffled eyes, and with the universal question of the child: Why?

Why had the Romax come?

Why had his grandmother and Wulv been slain?

Most important of all, where had his mother gone?

They had been traveling for the best part of a ten-day journey when they had stumbled—almost accidentally—upon a Teumetian village deep in the heart of the forest. While Vesi sat on a log, Horatrim chopped wood, using an ax with fluid ease, in return for some cheese and bread and sour wine.

Later that day, as he was being paid, the Teumetian headman had looked at him appraisingly, admiring the breadth of the young man's shoulders, the rippling muscles in his bare arms, the brawny length of his legs.

"Stay with us and join our warrior band," the headman urged Horatrim. "We could use a big powerful fellow like you to stand with us. And in return you would enjoy the safety of our village. Wandering the forest is no longer safe; every year there seem to be more raiders from Latium. These are dangerous times."

"I cannot," Horatrim replied. "We are going to find my mother's people."

"And who are they?"

"The Rasne. They have some sort of . . . of city, I believe my grandmother once said. On the other side of the Great Forest. We will be safe there."

"I wouldn't expect to find safety among the Silver People," advised the bandy-legged village chieftain. "The Etruscans produced great warriors—once. But not anymore. Now they lack the will to resist any determined effort at conquest. And conquest is what the Romax intend. They won't always be satisfied with raiding. Why settle for some loot when you can have all of it? The Teumetes will prove too tough for them, but remember my words, we'll see the day when they swarm over the Etruscan cities and make them their own. The Romax may be maggots, but at least they're lively maggots. The Silver People have become slugs."

"That may be. But I have to take my mother to her own people. You see how she is; I cannot care for her by myself."

"You won't get any help from the Etruscans. Just look at her, dressed in rags and as mad as a mouse under the full moon. The Silver People want everything to be perfect; they'll never accept her as one of their own. They'll either turn her away or sacrifice her to one of their gods."

The headman rubbed his hands together, skin rasping. "But you're right," he went on, "a young man like you should not be looking after a grown woman. I'm sure you have better things to do. Tell you what; I'm a generous man. Although I've already got two wives, I'll take her off your hands." He grinned toothlessly. "Wouldn't mind having a woman who can't talk."

The man's eyes glinted lasciviously; a thread of saliva drooled from his lips. Horatrim, repelled, took a step backward, pulling Vesi with him. The chieftain had followed. In one hand he brandished a knife; with the other he reached for the woman. "Even a madwoman has her uses."

But just as his grimy hand clutched the front of her gown, Horatrim's fingers closed around the man's hand. He squeezed so tightly he could hear the bones grinding together. "I think not," he said softly.

For a single heartbeat the chieftain had contemplated driving the knife in his free hand into the youngster's chest, but the look in Horatrim's eyes stopped him. He knew without the slightest doubt that the boy could and would kill him first. He spun around and scuttled back to his village, leaving the young man and his mother standing alone.

That night as he had made camp for the pair of them in a forest glade, Horatrim thought over what the chieftain had said. What if Vesi's people would not accept her? Absentmindedly he scratched the stubble that had recently bloomed on his jaws. His body was becoming a man's, and men were supposed to know what to do. Wulv would have known.

In the dark, in the night, alone with the massive responsibility of his helpless mother, Horatrim felt like a very small boy indeed. Tears prickled at the back of his eyes, but he brushed them away with the back of his hand. He had used that same angry movement almost from the moment he learned to walk, whenever tears threatened. He had never seen Wulv cry.

"I'm worried, Mother," he reluctantly admitted as he fed small sticks to the fire. "I fear nothing for myself, but I am concerned about you. The world is a dangerous place. Until the Rasne take us in, we have no one but ourselves."

Vesi had sat cross-legged beside him, fingers idly pleating the threadbare fabric of her gown, staring eyes fixed on the flames. She did not think, did not feel, did not care. From the moment her head struck the stone quern in Wulv's compound she had been little more than an empty vessel, a woman's body with no functioning intelligence inside. The bright, brave girl was gone. But on some level deeper than thought the mother had responded to the son's anxiety. A prayer was formulated in her blood and bones. And into her emptiness, something came, using her . . .

Her disused throat worked convulsively.

Forget about the Rasne, said a voice.

Horatrim jumped. The voice was not Vesi's, was hardly even human. He dropped the sticks to crouch before his mother, taking her cold hands in his. "What did you say? Mother, did you speak?"

She sat unresponsive. He was beginning to think he'd imagined it when he saw the flesh of her throat working.

Forget about finding the Rasne. You have a different future. In Latium. Among the Romans.

Horatrim had seized his mother's hands. They were icy cold. Her eyes did not meet his; she seemed as stupefied as ever. Yet though her lips barely moved, she was undeniably speaking. The voice was thin, strained, without gender or emotion. Yet curiously it reminded him of the voices that had spoken to him the day Wulv's island was raided, the same voices he sometimes thought he heard whispering to him at the very edges of his consciousness.

Desperately trying to establish some conscious contact, Horatrim had squeezed her hands hard enough to cause pain. She never flinched. "Are you talking about the Romax, the ones who hurt you?"

In Latium they are known as Romans.

"You want vengeance, is that it?"

Listen.

Speaking directly is difficult, though we find it easier through this woman because she does not resist us. You must go to Rome. Your future is there.

"Mine? How can that be? And what about you, Mother, what am I to do with you? I do not understand what you want."

A silence had followed while Horatrim waited patiently, eyes fixed on his mother's throat and lips, waiting for them to move.

You must. For the first time there was emotion in the voice, an imperative command.

And take me with you.

There was no further sound but the crackle of the fire, the calls of the night birds, the distant yapping of a fox.

Horatrim did not hear them. He sat with his elbows propped on his knees and stared at his mother.

She did not speak again.

The next morning they resumed their travels. Eventually they emerged from the Great Forest to find themselves on a deeply rutted dirt road that bore signs of frequent cart travel. Horatrim had looked both ways, up and down, but saw no one, no indication of habitation in either direction. Yet this was a road; it must lead somewhere. But in which direction? Stooping, he examined the ground, sensitive fingers tracing the cracked lines in the earth.

Knowledge came unbidden: cart wheels generally turned outward, so they were deeper on that side, and laden carts would usually be heading toward a town. With a boyish grin, Horatrim caught his mother by the hand and set off down the road. After the first time Vesi stepped in a rut and almost turned her ankle, he was careful to keep her to the center of the track, which provided a relatively level surface.

Before long they had begun encountering other travelers, as many as three or four in a day. Instead of asking for the city of the Rasne, Horatrim had sought directions to a place called Rome. To his own astonishment, he found himself speaking to each traveler in that person's own language. The courtesy earned him a friendly response and occasionally a cart ride or a meal as well.

"Rome! You don't want to go to Rome. The Romans

are the most aggressive of all the Italic tribes," he was informed by a Picene merchant making his way west with a train of oxcarts driven by whip-scarred slaves. "They've subdued most of their neighbors already. They claim to be descended from twins who were suckled by a wolf, if you can believe it. One of the twins was known as Romulus so they call their stronghold Rome after him. Their current king is Tarquin the Superb."

"Superbius," corrected a Campanian merchant heading east the following day. "He styles himself Lucius Tarquinius Superbius, a name meant to impress the *plebeians,* the commoners. He boasts of having royal Etruscan blood but he's really just the latest in a long line of opportunists. Kings come and go. Romans are difficult to govern; the place is always a nettlepatch of intrigue. Look for a better destination, young man, unless you're interested in trade. Rome loves doing business." He had glanced sidelong at the silent Vesi. "Maybe you want to sell this woman in the slave market. If you do, Rome is where you'll get the best price."

Horatrim had listened to this advice without comment, but after they left the merchant he said to Vesi, "Are you certain you want to go to Rome?"

She did not answer. Her mouth hung ajar like the door to an abandoned house.

"We can turn back," her son suggested, wiping a trail of spittle from her chin.

In response the woman had shuddered as if a cold wind blew through her. She straightened until she stood perceptibly taller. Her chin came up, her shoulders went back. From somewhere deep inside had issued one of the voices he was coming to know.

We never turn back.

He did not question the voice. Command was implicit in every syllable.

"We never turn back," he had repeated. On his lips the words became a vow.

* * *

Thirty days after leaving Wulv's ruined fort, Horatrim and Vesi were skirting a garrisoned hill; a garrison on the frontier of Rome. The man-boy paused to listen to the voices of the guards carrying on the still air. Peering through the screening willows, he watched the captain appear and wondered yet again at the wisdom of traveling into the city.

Then he glanced down at his mother. Vesi was sitting contentedly on the earth beside him, picking at the countless tiny flowers that had sprung up around his sandaled feet.

He crouched beside the woman and lifted her chin to look into her empty eyes.

"Rome lies ahead. Are you still sure?" he asked.

Vesi ignored him and concentrated on weaving the flowers into an intricate garland.

Horatrim looked back over his shoulder. But that way lay the past, with its bitter memories of pain and death. Rome was waiting. Whatever it contained could not be worse than what they had already experienced.

"We never turn back," he whispered, lifting Vesi gently to her feet. As his head was bent, she slipped the garland of flowers around his neck. For an instant he thought he saw a ghost of a smile on her lips.

TWENTY-TWO

In the beginning Pepan's *hia* had been content merely to follow them. As long as there was no actual danger to the woman or her son he remained a passive observer. But when the Teumetian chieftain openly lusted after Vesi, Pepan had responded.

With an effort of will, he had concentrated all his thought on a summoning. A sound like a trumpet rang through the Otherworld. From the mist shapes had appeared, dim shapes that had no faces, but faces were not needed. Form was important, and these had the form of an army.

As Horatrim spoke with the Teumetian an invisible army of ghosts had materialized at Vesi's back. Gray, wraithlike shapes had raised their arms in silent menace and a cold wind had blown out of nowhere, lifting the hair on their heads so it writhed like snakes.

The startled chieftain forgot all about Vesi's round hips.

When Horatrim led his mother safely away, a peal of

laughter had reverberated through the Otherworld. *I am still involved with life!* Pepan had crowed with delight.

The nearer Horatrim drew to the borders of Latium, the more closely his invisible watcher followed. He wondered if Horatrim was thinking of revenge. If he were still a living man, Pepan would have desired revenge himself.

Repana—his Repana—had lost her life to the Romans, and though her spirit continued to exist, the path of her destiny was forever altered. Wulv was part of her future now. Having died together, they were linked in a way Pepan and Repana were not. He knew that once they got used to the changed condition of being dead, they would have gone off together to the next stage of being. Wistfully, Pepan wondered if he would ever have that luxury. But he had chosen his own path. Now he must follow it wherever it might lead.

We never turn back.

That had been his credo in life—the credo of the Rasne—and he had carried it with him into death. Now Horatrim had taken the oath as his own.

Life, Pepan mused, *is strange, and afterlife is stranger still. Death is the true meaning of life.*

In addition to Pepan, other beings were following Horatrim. After the death of one of their number, the surviving minions of Pythia had retired from the pursuit of the *siu*'s child—for a time—to recover themselves. One of their own had been slain. The loss was almost incomprehensible.

Returning to the long oval hall with the moon pool, they performed the summoning ritual and awaited their goddess. When the surface of the water stirred they prudently turned their backs.

From the depths of the milky pool an obsidian image rose. Droplets of opalescent water clung to the ruby nipples of her multiple breasts like obscene milk. Her mouth was an angry slash from which a voice hissed in anger.

"So you have not succeeded?"

"We were thwarted, O Great Pythia, by—"

The dark goddess interrupted, "Out of cowardice you abandoned your mission, that is all there is to say. You were to find the *siu* and kill its spawn and you have not done so."

"We did find the *siu,* O Noble Queen," began the leader of the five. "But he. . . "

The statue's voice had dropped to a liquid purr more frightening than its former sibilance. "Perhaps you should die instead," murmured Pythia. "I could take my pleasure from your torment."

"That will not be necessary, Divine Goddess! We will resume our quest at once!" Flinging themselves to their knees, they had groveled in the dirt, being careful to keep their backs turned at all times toward the fearsome figure in the pool. To gaze upon her was to court destruction.

"I am merciful—foolish with my mercy perhaps—it has always been my greatest failing. I will allow you to return to your quest because I know you will not fail me again." The goddess paused. "Now that you know how vulnerable you are, you will be more careful. Remember, everything that walks the Earthworld can be slain in the Earthworld. Including you."

As the goddess began to sink back into the pool, she added, "Usually creatures in the Earthworld die only once. But fail me again, and I will take pleasure in killing you a thousand times. I can promise you an eternity of the most exquisite agony."

With these chilling words ringing in their ears, the five set out again upon their quest. The trail had grown cold, however, and they dared not call upon the goddess for help.

There followed a frustrating time of trial and error, questions asked and bribes paid. The seasons raced by.

The five were painfully aware of the goddess watching. But the quarry they sought seemed to have disappeared from the earth.

Then at last, on the far edge of the Great Forest, they picked up the trail again. In that remote region they learned of Wulv's compound and succeeding in tracing the fugitive Vesi to the islet in the marsh. But they arrived too late. The ashes had been cold for a long time.

They fell upon the nearest Teumetian village instead and destroyed it in a blind rage, torturing the inhabitants for the slightest scrap of information. In an effort to save his own life, the last survivor told the five of a muscular youth and a mute, mindless woman who had fled the territory after the Romax raid. The woman was reputedly Rasne, he said, and they were last seen heading south.

In payment for this information the Teumetian was ritually slaughtered as a sacrifice to the dark goddess. The five then feasted upon his liver.

"We have them!" the leader of the five exulted. "That is surely the youngster we seek, for he has grown more quickly than any human offspring could. When we find him we can be certain his sire will not be far behind. Demons follow their own."

Eyes glinting with a fanatic light, the five then made their way south. Toward Latium and Rome.

Horatrim and Vesi were still within sight of the Roman garrison on the hilltop when she gave a hollow groan. At once he put his arm around her. "What is it, Mother?"

Danger, said one of the voices he believed to be gods. *You are being pursued.*

"Pursued by who?"

Five.

"I can fight five," he confidently declared.

These are not ordinary warriors. You could not hope to stop them all.

"Then what am I to do?" It did not occur to Horatrim that it was foolish to ask advice from a madwoman. By now he understood he was not talking to Vesi, but to something else.

Five cannot stand against two score, came the cryptic reply.

"What are you saying?"

Leave me here and double back. Go up the side of yonder hill, but do not follow one of the obvious approaches. Drag your feet, scuffle dirt. Then halfway up, stop leaving a trail and return to me.

Obediently, Horatrim worked his way up the southeast face of the hill toward a blank garrison wall, dislodging stones and crushing small clumps of cedar with deliberate clumsiness. Before he reached the top he veered off sharply and made his way down again as light footed as a deer, using the techniques Wulv had taught him. He ran silently to the willows where he had secreted Vesi. Finding her mute and unresponsive once more, he took her hand and led her away.

It was almost twilight before the five cloaked figures came within sight of the Roman garrison. They searched the surrounding area until the one with sharpest eyes discovered Horatrim's trail going up the hill to the fort. "This way, we have him now."

Paulus and Sextus were still on guard at the gates, though the day was almost over. The enervating heat lingered however. The ground seethed; the horizon shimmered. Sticky inside their clothes and with pounding headaches, both men were in bad humor. Twice more Antoninus had emerged from the fort to bawl orders at them, finding fault with everything they did, from the way they stood to the angle of their spears.

Once the sun extinguished itself in a sea of flame beyond the western hills, the guard would change. Already the two men were anticipating their daily ration of beer and meat. "I could drink goat piss, I'm that thirsty," Paulus remarked.

"The beer they give us is goat piss, do you think frontier guards rate barley brew? I tell you, it wouldn't take much to induce me to throw down my weapons and go back to . . . Ho! What's that?"

"I don't see anything, Sextus."

"Some fool's trying to sneak up on us. Off there to the side, down below that outcropping. Look where I'm pointing, will you?"

Taking a step forward, Paulus peered down to discover several cloaked figures crawling up the hillside on hands and knees and bellies. Delighted with something to do, something to relieve the boredom, he promptly whipped his sword from its scabbard, hammered it against his shield, shouting, "Attack! Attack!"

Gate guards were chosen for their carrying voices. A moment later his cry was taken up inside, followed by a clashing of weapons and a thunder of feet as the entire garrison came pouring through the gates. There were only forty of them, but they were tough, aggressive veterans bored with inactivity. The intention to kill was stamped on every sunburned face. They could successfully have fought a number half again as large as their own.

At the first sight of them, the five cloaked figures halfway up the hill realized they stood no chance. With a wail of "Pythia protect us!" their leader jumped up and turned to run. His companions followed. But their talents did not include fleetness of foot. The first Roman caught up with the last of them and delivered a savage swordblow through the cloak to the flesh beneath. A scream rang across the hillside.

The angle had been calculated to chop off his leg at the knee, yet the wounded figure continued to run although something flopped on the ground behind him. When the Roman paused in midstride to pick up the severed limb, he gave a gasp of revulsion and flung it from him.

What he had amputated was no leg, but a muscular, scaly tail as long as his arm.

By that time Horatrim was a considerable distance away, but the sound of the scream was borne to him on a rising wind. He stopped and turned to his mother. "Did you hear that?"

She did not answer. She stood beside him with head bowed and hands hanging.

"There's fighting back there," he told her as he listened intently. "Whoever was chasing us must have met the Romans instead. Like running into a nest of hornets, I would say from the sound of it." He smiled, thinly. "That was a clever plan, Mother."

He knew the plan was not Vesi's, but how else was he to address her? And where, he found himself wondering, did she go when someone else was speaking through her?

Suddenly the little boy inside him wanted to weep. Vesi might still walk and breathe, but his mother was irrevocably lost to him.

Stumbling and slithering, the mutilated creature fled down the hill with his four companions. Behind him he left a trail of thick, brownish ichor smeared across the sunbaked earth.

The Romans pursued halfheartedly. The horror of the severed tail demoralized even such hard-bitten warriors; no one really wanted to catch up with the cloaked figures. They shouted threats and beat their swords against their shields, but when the order came to turn back they responded with enthusiasm. They had been raised on stories of the creatures of myth that inhabited the dark northern forests.

"What in the name of Great Mars was that thing, do you suppose?" Paulus asked Sextus as they trudged back up the hill.

Wiping his sword blade again and again on every stunted cedar they passed, Sextus replied, "I don't know and I don't want to know. I never saw anything so awful in my life." Lifting his sword, he examined the blade ruefully. The metal was pitted as if it had been dipped in acid.

Antoninus, who was hardly less shaken than his men, said in an unsteady voice, "It was a demon. They were all demons, that's why I gave the order to turn back. You can't kill demons."

Paulus gazed down at an ugly smear on the ground before him, the viscous, stinking ooze from the wounded creature. "Perhaps they were demons and perhaps not. Look there, Sextus."

His friend kept his eyes fixed on the garrison ahead of them. "I don't want to."

"You certainly did the thing great damage; you should be proud."

"I'm scared, that's what I am. What if it comes after me seeking revenge?"

Paulus's own courage was seeping back. He managed a lopsided grin as he punched his friend on the arm. "At least you can't say you've been bored today."

Sextus glared at him. "I don't think that's funny."

Emboldened, Paulus teased, "Where did you throw that tail? We should keep it as a trophy."

"Leave it alone, will you!"

"A demon's tail? I think not. I want it if you don't. We can hang it on the wall of the barracks along with the captured trophies." Paulus made a great show of searching among the rocks and bushes while some of the other Romans sniggered at Sextus's discomfort. But just as Paulus found what he sought half-concealed in a clump of cedar, Antoninus barked, "Get on, you lot, I want us all back inside the walls before the dark catches us.

Those things might come back . . . with reinforcements," he added for emphasis.

Paulus reached for the severed tail. On closer inspection it did not appear to be a tail, but more nearly resembled the nether part of some huge serpent. He did not want to touch the repellent object but he could not back down now; he had carried the joke too far.

His fingers had barely grazed the scaly surface when the thing whipped around his wrist and crushed every bone.

TWENTY-THREE

It was important to take care of the family.

Whenever Young Ones wandered away from the mouth of the cave, He would growl and wiggle his eyebrows, and She would run after their errant offspring, chittering anxiously. She was responsible for herding Young Ones back to safety. He did not tend Young Ones. He provided meat and mounted She whenever She invited him.

He remembered an Old One like himself who had brought meat to the cave when He was little. And an old She with drooping dugs who chased himself and other Young Ones. There had been more like them living in other caves throughout the hills. But not now.

Where had they gone?

When He tried to think about them his head hurt. It was not easy to construct a thought. Hunting was easier and required no thought. He liked hunting. Whenever He returned with meat, He would devour his fill, then let

She take her turn. Afterward they would sit in the sun outside the cave and watch Young Ones rend and tear what remained of the bloody flesh. Sun was good. A full belly was good.

Mounting She was good; locking his fingers in the shaggy yellow hair that grew along her shoulders and sides, thrusting deep into her, feeling the bursting feeling. Afterward He liked to sleep. She liked to sleep then, too, but Young Ones would take advantage and run outside and She would have to go after them.

Young Ones were a lot of trouble. They made a lot of noise racing and romping in the cave.

The cave smelled good. It smelled of rotten meat and dried blood, reminding He that his belly was empty. But no matter how He searched, there were no shreds of meat to be found. Not even a cracked marrowbone. All gone. Young Ones had eaten the last of the food.

One of them came too close and He growled and cuffed it with the back of his hand, but not too hard. Young One ran and hid behind She, peering out with bright, beady eyes. He growled again. Young One blinked.

She growled back at He, warning him not to threaten her baby. In response He showed her his teeth but She only growled again. Usually She would back down, but not where Young Ones were concerned.

He sighed and began picking through the thick mat of russet hair on his torso in search of fleas. She came over to him then and made a whimpering noise. When She pressed insistently against him He began grooming her, catching her fleas between thumb and forefinger and popping them into his mouth. But they were too small. They did not fill the belly. He must go in search of more meat now or sleep hungry.

When He pushed her away and stood up on his two bowed legs, She gave a grunt of protest that He ignored. From a pile of debris at the mouth of the cave, He took a gnarled branch He often used as a club. If He hit meat on the head, meat would fall down and die. He swung the branch onto his shoulder and strode away without looking back.

She stood in the cave entrance and watched him go down the hill in the twilight with his peculiar, rolling gait. Soon He disappeared into a stand of cedar trees.

Licking her lips in anticipation, She sat down to wait. She knew what it meant when He took the club.

They would eat soon.

TWENTY-FOUR

The Roman matron called Delphia was stout and handsome, with oiled hair arranged in sculptured curls across her brow in a style copied from an Etruscan wall-hanging. Silver Etruscan beads hung in graduated strands around her neck. Like her husband Propertius, she exuded an air of prosperity. As she reclined at her ease in the cart, she was chattering merrily and examining her hennaed fingernails.

The couple was returning from a trip to view their latest acquisition, an estate near the border of Roman territory. Propertius sat facing his wife, going over accounts in his head and wondering whether their hired driver would try to extort more money from them before they got home. He was annoyed to realize they would not reach the gates of Rome until well after dark, and beginning to worry. He hated traveling at night. In spite of the warriors the city assigned to patrol the approaches to Rome, the roads were not safe. The most trusted drivers had been known to betray their passengers to outlaws for a share of the profits.

As a member of the Roman Senate and the owner of a far-flung trading business, Propertius Cocles sometimes engaged in a bit of spying. Following his recent report on current Etruscan military strength, he had been rewarded by King Tarquinius with an estate in the country. The understanding was that in return, Propertius would put his property at the service of Tarquinius whenever required. Roman kings occasionally found themselves in need of a secret hideaway.

In truth the estate was little more than a sprawling farm bisected by a tributary of the Tiber, but the soil was fertile and with enough slaves, a man could produce an excellent profit. And there were always enough slaves, more than ever now that Rome was beginning to expand.

As they jolted along in the high-wheeled wooden cart behind a bristle-maned Thracian horse, Delphia was enthusing, "Now that I've seen the land I have so many ideas, Propertius. We must build a villa for ourselves overlooking the river, so we can get away from the heat of Rome in the summer. It never seems to bother you, of course, but myself and the children suffer dreadfully. I want an enclosed garden where the younger children can play, and separate slave quarters, and perhaps a. . . "

Propertius was used to Delphia's chatter. The bulk of her conversation consisted of demands to which he responded with unfailing agreement—although he never really listened. He would build what he wanted and his wife would have to . . .

"What is that? Gods defend us!"

Propertius's musings were cut short by Delphia's shriek of horror. At the same time their driver began furiously plying the whip, but the Thracian horse was fat and sleepy. It broke into a trot instead of the gallop the situation demanded.

The monstrosity that came hurtling toward them

down the cedar-covered slope was enough to chill the spine. Though man-shaped, it was not a man but a massive shaggy horror. The curious rolling gait of the thing was deceptively swift; in spite of the driver's frantic efforts, in a few moments it had reached the road and was bounding toward the cart in prodigious leaps.

Only then did Propertius's numbed brain realize that one of the monster's disproportionately long forelimbs was carrying a club.

Springing to his feet, the Roman shouted, "Help! Someone help us!" as loud as he could. But there were no patrols within range of his voice. The hilly, wooded countryside through which they were passing was empty except for occasional scattered farmsteads. There was no one nearby to save them—and their hired driver was useless. He could only gape in horror as their attacker leaped for the horse.

Too late the animal realized its danger and plunged forward. Simultaneously the shaggy creature hit it between the eyes with a mighty blow. The sickening smash of the skull was clearly audible, even above Propertius's calls for help. The horse fell dead in the traces, bringing the cart to a shuddering halt.

Lifting the club to its mouth, the monster licked at the blood and brain matter clinging to the wood and grunted with pleasure. It might have been satisfied with its equine prey had not the driver panicked and leaped out of the cart at that moment, slashing at the creature with his knife. With a roar, the thing took a swipe at the man that knocked his head from his shoulders.

Delphia's screams drew the creature's attention to the white-faced passengers. Curious, it started toward the cart, nostrils flaring, trying to decide if these hairless ones were its own kind or simply meat. The brute was making appalling noises, a combination of growls and grunts that so unnerved Propertius that his knees gave way. He slumped back onto the seat, moaning in terror and clutching his chest.

Seeing her husband on the verge of fainting had quite the opposite effect on Delphia. Her terrified shrieks were transformed into an ear-splitting yowl of anger as she snatched up the whip the driver had dropped and lashed it across the face of the monster. The brute paused for the briefest moment, staring at her in obvious surprise. An overlong pink tongue traced the bloody cut on its hairy cheek.

Then, with a grunt, it scrambled over the side of the cart.

Seen up close, the creature was even more horrific than Delphia had realized. Its skull was grotesquely large, back-slanting, with a shelflike brow extending over sunken eyes. The broad, flat nose had cavernous nostrils, the slobbering mouth stretched in a disgusting grin. Except for its face, the monster was covered with filthy reddish hair, and the breath that washed over Delphia was so foul she thought she would vomit.

Worst of all, however, were the eyes. Staring at her with an expression of murderous hunger, they were obviously intelligent and very close to being human. At this realization, Delphia came close to fainting herself.

The monster's grin stretched even further to display cruel yellow fangs. Leaning back to give itself room in the cramped confines of the cart, it raised the club for the killing blow—just as the first stone hit it in the back of the head.

He gave a grunt of surprise. Turning, He saw another hairless one running toward him. With incredible agility the human was scooping up rocks from the road as he ran and hurling them one after another.

The next hard-flung stone struck He squarely on the nose. His roar of pain echoed across the countryside. When the sound reached the cave on the distant hillside and his waiting She, the female responded.

Her mate was in danger!

Frantically, She called to him again and again, raising her voice in an eerie, ululating cry that rebounded from hill to hill; a cry born of the swiftly descending night and an even more ancient darkness.

It was the loneliest sound in the world.

When the stranger leaped into the cart to grapple with the pain-dazed monster, Delphia seized the opportunity to scramble out. Then she reached over the side and tugged desperately at her husband. "Come, Propertius, hurry! While they're fighting we can get away."

The Roman almost fell as he stepped to the ground; only his wife's outstretched arms saved him.

Meanwhile the stranger had succeeded in wrenching the club away from the monster. The thing possessed extraordinary strength, but its reactions were slow. When he pried the club from its grip and threw it as far from the cart as possible, the brute turned to watch it rather than concentrating on fighting its opponent.

In that moment Horatrim wrapped his hands around the creature's neck.

TWENTY-FIVE

From the moment he heard the first screams for help, he had been aware of a singing in his blood. "Stay here and stay out of sight, Mother," he had told Vesi, seating her on a large stone behind a screen of cedars. Then he began to run in the direction of the screams.

Pepan's *hia* followed.

The singing had intensified as Horatrim ran. It became the sound of a thousand bees—or a thousand voices—humming confidently through his veins, giving specific directions to his limbs and muscles. By the time he came in sight of the cart on the roadway, his body had known exactly what to do.

The stones Horatrim threw distracted and then briefly disabled the monster, allowing him to enter the cart and close with it. His hands were hardly large enough to encompass the massive, muscular throat, but his fingers knew just where the nerves and veins were located beneath the skin. He pinched the windpipe shut, then compressed the thick artery that brought blood to the brain.

The creature slumped immediately, not unconscious but shocked by the pain and confused by the shadows that had gathered so quickly, the numbness that threatened its limbs.

Step by step Horatrim forced it backward, out of the cart. They staggered together to the ground. Once it felt solid earth under its feet, the creature erupted in a frenzy. It broke free of Horatrim and ran off into the darkness, leaving him holding a handful of russet hair and a patch of flesh torn from its hide. As it ran the monster emitted another chilling, inhuman cry. In the distance, something answered.

Horatrim threw down the hair and torn flesh in disgust and turned to the couple from the cart. They were both trembling but unhurt. Gently, he led them away from the road and helped them sit down. They wrapped their arms around each other and sat watching him like two terrified children as he went back to the cart to examine first the driver, then the horse. Nothing could be done for either.

Horatrim returned to the pair he had rescued. "You cannot stay out here in the open tonight," he said to the man, a short, stocky individual with a fringe of graying hair around a head rapidly going bald. The man merely stared at him. Horatrim tried again, finding a different language on his tongue. "Where were you going when you were attacked?" he asked.

Propertius shook himself as if awakening from a bad dream. A sense of relief washed over him. Their rescuer was not only a man like himself, but also spoke Latin, albeit with a strange accent, a man of some learning. "My wife and I were returning to Rome," he replied in a voice that still quavered slightly. "I am called Propertius Cocles, and I am in your debt for saving our lives."

"The . . . the gods were with me. They sent me to

you. You owe me nothing. But come, we should move away from here; the bodies will bring scavengers." He urged the couple down the road toward the hiding place where he had left Vesi.

"I am in your debt," Propertius insisted on repeating as they walked. "I am a man of no small importance, and my honor is precious to me. I always pay what I owe. You can ask anything of me and it is yours. Just tell me your name and family, that I may do you—and them—proper honor."

"I am called Horatrim. As for my family. . . " The young man hesitated, then went on, still guided by the strange music surging through him, "My mother is my only family. We are Rasne. Travelers on our way to Rome."

The woman brightened. "Etruscan? How wonderful! I do admire the Etruscans, they are so very elegant." Delphia, a person of warm affections and instant enthusiasms, was ready to welcome this new hero unreservedly.

Her husband was more cautious. Horatrim's background gave him pause. For generations there had been sporadic conflict between Etruria and the tribes of Latium, although never enough to put an end to trade. Frequent intermarriage had done little to lessen the tension. The Etruscans resented the rise of a more vigorous culture, the people of Latium were jealous of past Etrurian achievements.

In spite of this stormy relationship, in Roman society an ancient Etruscan bloodline was highly desirable. To be considered *patrician,* a member of the nobility, it was almost essential to have at least one Etruscan antecedent. The present king was a perfect example. Lucius Tarquinius Superbius frequently called attention to the pedigree of his Etruscan father and tended to overlook his mother's Latin family.

Years of experience trading with the tribes of Etruria had made Propertius wary however. The Etruscans believed that every aspect of their lives was influenced by gods and demons, by the shades of their ancestors and the malice of disembodied spirits. The result was a complicated culture where countless invisible entities had to be placated before the smallest action could be taken. It often got in the way of business.

Propertius mistrusted mysticism; he put little faith in things he could not see and count. In this he differed from most of his contemporaries. Burgeoning Rome was seeking an enhanced spiritual identity. Simple pastoral gods of field and forest were being superseded by more esoteric deities, each with its own priests and rituals shrouded in mystery, though as a businessman, Propertius could appreciate that there was money in religion.

In the privacy of his own home Propertius scoffed at the proliferating religions. He was particularly contemptuous of the Cult of Magna Dea to which many of the women, including his wife, were devoted. "It's nothing more than the attempt of idle women to usurp power for themselves," he said. "The only god Romans need is Mars. War is good for business."

Still, one must admit Etruria had attained a level of prosperity that was the envy of Latium. For generations wealth had poured into their cities from copper, lead, and iron mines, from farms and vineyards, from Eastern trade and Western piracy. The Etruscans insisted they owed their entire success to the benevolence of their gods.

Now this young man had appeared just in time to save the Roman and his wife from a monster. He had accomplished the feat with extraordinary skill and agility and was not even breathing hard afterward. "The gods were with me," was all he offered by way of explanation.

Propertius was prepared only to believe in what he could see and touch. Tonight, perhaps, he had seen a miracle: the gods working directly with and through a human. An Etruscan. A young, handsome Etruscan, obviously educated and therefore from a good family.

Propertius had a daughter of marriageable age.

Arranging his face in his best trust-me-I'm-an-honest-trader smile, he said, "Since you're going to Rome anyway, Horatrim, we would be grateful if you would accompany us. I fear we shall have to travel on foot the rest of the way, but it's not far now. You will stay the night with us of course; in fact, I insist you stay for as long as it pleases you. I want to hear more about these gods of yours." He eyed his rescuer's filthy clothing of uncured hides. "And surely we can find you something better to wear. I have a son almost your size."

"I would be happy to see you safely home, but I'm not alone. I have my mother with me. I left her at a safe distance when I heard the screaming."

"Bring her too!" Propertius insisted. "Any woman who gave birth to such a hero is welcome under my roof. We'll treat her with every courtesy, I assure you. Where is she? I want to congratulate her on her son."

Horatrim hesitated. Here was an offer of shelter and protection for Vesi, but it was coming from one of the Romans. Yet was he not being led into the very heart of the Roman world anyway? The knowledge that mysteriously had been imparted to his muscles was of no help in this situation. He needed to confer with Vesi—or rather, with the gods who spoke through Vesi. But he dare not leave the Roman couple alone, not with the monster's voice still reverberating across the hills.

"Come with me," Horatrim said to Propertius and his wife. "I'll take you to my mother."

Night had fallen by this time; a humid, overcast night, an obsidian night in which unseen entities whispered and rustled. He was accustomed to a presence at his back that he assumed was that of the gods, the *Ais.* But there were other invisibles too, less benign ones. He could feel them, watching, waiting.

Horatrim was anxious to get back to Vesi.

* * *

When Horatrim had run off in the direction of the screams, Vesi had waited patiently where he left her. Waiting did not bother her. Nothing bothered her. The boulder on which she sat radiated residual warmth from the sun.

When the hooded figures slunk out of the night, she paid them no attention.

They had been trying to find a safe place where their injured comrade could be left to recover, if possible. They stumbled upon Vesi quite by accident. It was one of the tenets of their religion that nothing ever happened by accident however. Finding the woman was surely part of the goddess' plan. So while Vesi looked on mute and uncomprehending, the hooded beings addressed their deity and asked for guidance.

An answer came, very soon.

They were delighted to discover that Pythia was no longer displeased with them; in fact, she congratulated them for having done well indeed.

Then she took control of the situation.

Horatrim found Vesi just as he had left her, sitting on a boulder in the darkness with her fingers laced around her knees. Hurrying to her side, he put his fingers under her chin and turned her face up toward him. She did not speak but he liked to believe that she recognized him. He needed to believe.

"This is Vesi of the Silver People," he told the two Romans.

The woman on the rock said nothing.

Propertius leaned forward to peer at her in the gloom. "Is she ill?"

"No, just . . . quiet. We were . . . attacked by brigands, and she was badly injured some time ago. As a result she stopped speaking."

"Ah, that's a pity. Have you had a physician look at her? We have several in Rome who might be able to help. I will arrange for the best of them for you."

"Truly we have been led to you by the gods," replied Horatrim.

He put his hand under Vesi's elbow and lifted, and she came obediently to her feet. "We are going now, Mother. These kind people have offered us aid and shelter."

"I am Propertius, dear lady," the beaming Roman introduced himself. "And this is my wife, Delphia. I hope you will consider us your friends."

"We are indebted to your son for our lives," the woman added. "What he did was so wonderful; you should have seen him!"

Vesi said nothing.

Delphia turned to Horatius. "Does she never speak?"

"Rarely."

"And you have been looking after her for how long?"

"Most of my adult life," Horatrim replied with truth.

"You are indeed a hero," declared Delphia. Her voice choked. "A son any mother should be proud of."

TWENTY-SIX

Horatrim kept his arm around his mother, Propertius had his around Delphia. The road was deeply rutted with cart and chariot tracks and difficult to walk upon, and occasionally the Roman or one of the women stumbled. But Horatrim never stumbled.

The warm night air smelled of cedar and cypress.

At last Propertius exclaimed thankfully, "See there, ahead? The gates of Rome!"

By comparison with the *spurae* of Etruria, Rome was very crude. To anyone who had seen stately, symmetrical Veii, Rome was a confused jumble of ramshackle huts and half-built halls, its lack of planning all too obvious. But Horatrim had seen no Etruscan cities. He walked along open-mouthed, swiveling his head from side to side in astonishment at the size of the place, the crowds, the noise. . . .

At night the narrow streets were alight with flaring torches and bustling with people. "This is the city that never sleeps," Propertius announced proudly.

Many of the buildings were constructed of timber and sods plastered with river mud, giving them the look of something thrown up in a hurry. Houses and shops and flat-roofed warehouses crowded together, clinging to the hillsides and to one another as if fearful they would slide down. Rome smelled of cooked food and rotting fruit and olive oil and animal dung and raw timber, of new construction and old midden heaps.

Hawkers thronged the streets in spite of the lateness of the hour, trying to persuade people to buy jellied eels and cheap trinkets. Garishly painted women stood outside the numerous *tavernae,* beckoning in a way Horatrim did not understand. A burst of profanity erupted from the open door of one *taverna;* a woman's laugh gurgled merrily from another direction. Elsewhere someone was playing a pipe with a shrill, brassy tone that grated on the eardrum.

Suddenly Vesi's feet slid out from under her and she almost fell. Horatrim caught her before she could hit the ground. Gathering her into his arms, he stroked her hair and murmured soothingly. Then, indicating the torrent of raw sewage flowing down the street and turning its mud into slime, he asked Propertius, "Why don't they pave these streets and install gutters?" He did not know where the concept came from; it simply appeared in his mind.

Propertius paused in midstep. "Pavement? Here? Impossible, the streets are too steep and too crooked."

As if he were listening to someone else, Horatrim heard himself say with explanatory gestures, "You could begin with a series of temporary timber supports laid at angles . . . like this . . . then dig out above them and set permanent stone slabs across like this.. . . "

The Roman was looking at him thoughtfully. "You are the most astonishing young man. I want my brother to meet you. Like myself, Severus is a member of the Senate, but he's also the king's chief builder. Tarquinius is constantly demanding new schemes to improve

Rome—for his own greater glory, of course—and it's Severus's responsibility to find them. I think he will be very interested in what you have to say. But that is all for the morrow. First, however, we all need a bath and a good night's rest."

Propertius led the way up first one narrow street and then another, eventually reaching a hilltop overlooking the city. The summit was crowned with houses. He halted before a door let into a plastered wall and beat a tattoo with his fist. After a time, the door creaked open. A slave holding an oil lamp stood in the doorway, blinking uncertainly. "Master? Master!"

"Of course it's me. Let us in, you fool. We're exhausted and we want to go to bed."

Guiding his mother by the elbow, Horatrim followed the Romans inside.

Pepan had never dreamed his *hia* would someday enter Rome. But where Horatrim and Vesi went, he followed. The nearer he got to the city, the more he disliked the sound that characterized Rome and Romans in the Otherworld, a brazen, strident staccato of muscle and might.

Viewed from the Otherworld, the house of Propertius was a mere translucent shell. Pepan easily penetrated the walls. Finding himself in the large, square room that formed the bulk of the dwelling, he surveyed his surroundings with distaste. No murals were painted on the walls, no tiled mosaics set in the floors. There were no flowers, no fountains, and only one statue, a crude clay representation of Mars in a small niche off to one side. Where was the household art? How could people survive without a clutter of beautiful things around them?

These people are pitifully unpolished, he thought with contempt. *The few pleasing things they possess, like the jewelry the woman wears, are merely copies of*

Etruscan styles. Do Romans create nothing worthwhile of their own? Or do they steal it all?

As he mused, Pepan became aware of a swirling viscosity slowly filling the room. Like himself, other intangible beings had penetrated the walls. They were never far away, the denizens of the Otherworld. Lacking palpable bodies, they could have no physical effect on humankind. But that did not prevent their having influence.

Since joining their number, Pepan had witnessed demonstrations of their power. Disembodied spirits could fill a living human with elation or dread, could make the imagination soar or turn dreams into unrelenting nightmares. More to be feared than sword or spear, *siu* and corrupted *hia* could induce an insanity from which there was no returning.

And they were always vigilant, awaiting their chance. The bright lights of the physical world drew them like moths to a flame. So Pepan must be vigilant too. Never for a moment could he cease watching over Horatrim and Vesi, protecting them from all the things they could not see. He regretted that he was unable to protect them from physical dangers as well, but the gifts of the ancestors that surged through Horatrim's body were doing a good enough job of that.

The invisible beings that invaded the Roman house in Horatrim's wake had followed him from the northern verdant forests. Latium was not their natural home; the sunbaked hills were foreign to creatures of mist and mystery. But they were here now, prancing and gibbering and beckoning, flinging their snares, competing furiously with one another over the extraordinarily endowed spirit of Vesi's son.

Someone else thought young Horatrim well endowed.

In spite of the lateness of the hour when Propertius and Delphia returned home, their older children thronged around them. When Propertius told them of the attack and rescue, all eyes turned toward Horatrim.

One pair of eyes belonged to a girl Propertius identified as his eldest daughter, Livia. Aside from a few coarse-featured girls hiding behind their glowering and suspicious mothers in a Teumetian village, Horatrim had never seen a young woman before. At sixteen years of age, with a well-developed figure and a generous mouth, Livia already had considerable experience of young men. But she had seen no one like Horatrim; no one whom her father glowingly described as a hero.

She sidled close to him and gazed up from under her dark lashes. "Did you really save my parents from a monster?" Her voice was soft and sweet, with a delicious little trill at the end. She spoke in such a soft whisper that Horatrim had to lean forward to hear her—a trick she had learned from her maid.

Horatrim was quite unprepared for the effect she had upon him. He had reached physical maturity in an astonishingly short time; his emotions had lagged behind. Now they were beginning to catch up. His throat closed; his mouth went dry. He was certain she could hear his heart pounding.

"I . . . uh . . . that is. . . " Where were those voices in his head when he needed them? Why had they no guidance to offer now? He cast a beseeching glance toward his mother, but Vesi was equally noncommittal. She stood where he had left her, just inside the door. Her blank gaze took in the entire room and saw nothing.

Delphia was at no loss for words however. She already had decided that a brave young Etruscan would be a fine catch for one of her daughters and bring a touch of ancient elegance to the family. Her friends would be so jealous; they were already envious of the Etruscan baubles Propertius brought back to her from his travels. "Horatrim not only saved us both," she told Livia, "but has agreed to accept our hospitality so we can repay him properly. He—and his dear mother, of course—will be staying here with us for a while. We want you to make them feel welcome."

The girl smiled at Horatrim and dipped her head so that she could look at him through overlong lashes. "There is nothing I would like more," she said for his ears alone.

The bedazzled Horatrim grinned back.

Pepan, watching, was filled with misgivings. He did not want Vesi and her son to be in this city or this house. Rome was too raw and too new, the Romans too hungry for conquest. His *hia* was made uncomfortable by the strident martial music that identified them in the Otherworld, drowning out all other sounds. Why, he wondered, had the ancestors been so determined to bring Horatrim here? What had Rome ever meant for anyone—but trouble? What Rome could not assimilate, it destroyed.

TWENTY-SEVEN

Livia liked to sleep late. Yet this morning she rose early, bathed carefully, and paid particular attention to her cosmetics, squinting at her reflection in the polished silver mirror. Having learned from one of the house slaves that Horatrim was in the garden, she managed "accidentally" to find him there. He was sitting on a bench in the sun at the side of the house tenderly feeding Vesi.

She observed him critically in the early morning light. His jaws were freshly shaven. A slave had attempted to perform the service for him, but Horatrim had refused. "I can do it myself; I know how to use knives." He did not want any stranger close to his bare throat with a naked blade in his hand; Wulv would never have approved. Now his cheeks were bare of stubble although a plethora of cuts and nicks showed he still had to master the technique.

For clothing he wore a toga borrowed from Livia's

brother Quintus, a plump and petulant youth. A slave had folded the garment around Horatrim's body in the precise pleats of current Roman fashion, which he thought a bit silly. What use were pleats, he wondered? He only tolerated the fashion because it was part of learning about Rome.

His heavily callused feet were strapped into leather sandals. He had never worn shoes before and disliked them intensely. From time to time he stopped feeding Vesi long enough to scratch his calves, which were irritated by the snug sandal thongs.

"Can't your mother feed herself?" Livia asked as she watched him.

Horatrim shook his head. "She has no interest in food. If I don't put it into her mouth, she doesn't eat." Using a round-bowled olivewood spoon he tipped some lentil porridge into Vesi's mouth, then offered her a sun-ripened fig. She would not bite into the fruit; he had to tear off a tiny bit and place it on her tongue, but then she chewed and swallowed. Vesi was wearing one of Delphia's old gowns. Neither of them knew that it was cut in the Etruscan fashion.

Watching him attend his mother, Livia raised her eyebrows. She found his attentions touching. "How very curious! I believe my father said that she doesn't speak, either?"

"No, not really."

The Roman girl's eyes danced. "Well, I wager I can make her say something. Just watch me." She spoke with the assurance of a pampered and petted child who had never been refused anything.

Throwing herself down at Vesi's feet, Livia caught the woman's hands between her own and gazed earnestly up into the impassive face. "How lovely you are," she said. "At least you would be if you were tidied up a bit and had your hair curled. I have pots and pots of cosmetics, some from as far away as Crete and Aegypt. My father is a trader, you know; he imports all sorts of things. Would you like me to paint your face for you?"

Vesi's vacant eyes stared through her.

Nonplused, Livia tried again. "Why were you wearing rags last night? I thought Etruscan women were always exquisitely dressed. I see Mother has loaned you one of her gowns, but mine are much nicer. You will have your choice of my best. Which would you prefer, my pleated yellow linen or my Aegyptian cotton with red embroidery around the hem?"

Something flickered at the back of Vesi's eyes.

"Aha—I told you," said Livia triumphantly.

Horatrim knelt in the dust beside Livia and took his mother's free hand. Maybe this was what she needed; female company.

Vesi's jaw sagged open and her features began softening like wax in the sun. An altered bone structure appeared beneath the flesh, subtly changing the shape of the face.

Livia dropped Vesi's hand as if it were hot.

Vesi's skin darkened and coarsened. Her throat muscles began to work, but the voice when it came was not Vesi's. Nor was it any of the voices Horatrim had heard before. Slurred, sibilant, it rose and fell in an eerie cadence that raised the hackles on his neck.

In her tomb among the Campanians, your mother's mother sleeps in a peplos *of fine wool, with amber at her breast.*

Livia gave a gasp. "What was that? Who spoke?"

Horatrim said honestly, "I don't know. But it was not my mother."

He would have been relieved that someone else heard the voices speaking to him through Vesi—had it not been for the fact that this was such a frightening voice.

He had walked away from fear once, but now it closed around his heart like an icy hand. Fear not for himself but for Vesi. Yet he could not have said just what he feared.

He said, "I've never heard my mother speak like that before."

"But I made her talk," Livia insisted shakily. "Didn't I?"

"Yes. Yes, I suppose you did."

Delighted with herself, Livia left Horatrim with his mother and rushed into the house to boast of her achievement.

But when she related the incident—and Vesi's puzzling words—to Delphia, the Roman matron gave a shriek. Followed by her baffled daughter, she ran outside.

Delphia bent over Vesi. "How did you know?" she demanded, grabbing the other woman by the shoulders. "How did you learn my grandmother was entombed at Campania? I never told anyone she was not Roman. And what gave you the idea that her funeral dress was a woolen *peplos?* Or that she wore an amber brooch? Nobody knew that, not even my husband."

Vesi stared up at Delphia.

"You're frightening my mother," warned Horatrim. He stepped between them, gently but firmly pushing Delphia aside. But Vesi did not look frightened. Nor were her features misshapen; the distortion had faded, as had the peculiar dark hue. She looked like herself again, except . . .

Except that once or twice, he thought he saw something move in her eyes. Something peered out of them. Something terrible.

Until that moment Pepan had been unaware of any change in Vesi. When Horatrim ran to answer the Romans's cry for help, Pepan had gone with him, fearing he was in danger. Then once Horatrim joined the Romans, their Otherworld signal, a strident blare of horns, had blotted out any other music. So Pepan had not detected the loss of the solitary pure note that identified

Repana's daughter. Now he realized it was gone. Instead she emitted a faint but ceaseless sibilance.

Pepan was horrified. He had failed in his self-appointed duty; he had not protected his beloved Repana's daughter against invasion by a malign force.

When he sought to discover what had possessed her empty shell, his efforts were rebuffed by a solid core of blackness within Vesi. The voices of the ancestors, who had found it easier to speak through her unresisting mouth, were silenced, driven out.

Though Pepan had thought himself beyond human emotion, he was stricken with guilt and the terrible feeling of helplessness.

He had failed Repana and Vesi once, and now he had failed Vesi again. This time the cost would be much higher.

When Delphia told her husband about the incident, Propertius said, "The woman must be what the Etruscans call a seer. Such people are holy, beloved of the gods."

"I thought you had no religion. 'Sacrificing livestock to stone statues is a waste of saleable meat,' you said. 'I'm too practical to be taken in by hysterical priests and clouds of incense,' you said."

"I am practical. Practical enough to recognize an opportunity when it is beneath my very roof. This Etruscan pair is exceptional. It only remains to decide how best to exploit their assets to our advantage."

"What assets? I suspect they are fugitives; we've seen such people before. Perhaps Vesi made an unpopular pronouncement and fell out of favor with her tribe. I'm sure Horatrim will tell us the story when he feels he can trust us enough. In the meantime they have come away from Etruria with nothing more than the clothes on their backs."

Propertius gave his wife a pitying look. "Those rags are the least of their fortune," he told her. "I think we are going to hold a banquet, Delphia. A feast in honor of our rescue and our rescuers—and to introduce our pet Etruscans to a few select members of Roman society."

"Banquets are costly. Not that I'm objecting," she added quickly. "We don't entertain as much as any of the other Senate families. Do you plan to invite the king?"

"Of course."

Delphia stared at her husband. "Then the banquet will be twice as costly. There must be something in it for you aside from the expense?"

"Oh, yes," Propertius assured his wife. "Yes, indeed there is." He was positively glowing with anticipation.

The household was thrown into a frenzy of preparation. Horatrim found himself very much in the way; everyone seemed to have something to do but him. Within the walls there was no place where a boy used to the silences of the forest could find peace and quiet.

The front door of the Roman house opened directly into one large, rectangular room where most daytime activities took place, including meetings with Propertius's business clients. Off this were several cramped cubicles that served as bedchambers for family and guests. Slaves had to be satisfied with sleeping on the floor in the kitchen or in one of the overcrowded storerooms at the rear.

The house was stuffy and poorly ventilated, with only small windows high up under the eaves to keep passersby from peering in. In spite of the lamps that were kept burning throughout the day and polluting the atmosphere with malodorous smoke, the interior remained dark and gloomy.

As he walked around the rooms, Horatrim could not

help but imagine the alterations he would make if the house were his.

Like all meals, the banquet was to be served in the main room. Couches were arranged around a large table so guests could recline as they ate. Horatrim was not sure he approved of eating while lying propped on one elbow. His mother and grandmother had done so, but Wulv had always insisted on squatting on his haunches while he ate, claiming it made the food easier to digest.

"I miss Wulv," he was saying to Vesi when the slaves Delphia had assigned arrived. It was their duty to bathe her and dress her and make her presentable for the king of Rome.

Horatrim wondered what a king would look like.

A dozen other guests arrived before the man known as Tarquinius Superbius was expected to appear. Several of them were members of the Senate, identifiable by the broad purple stripe on their elaborately folded and draped togas.

"Only kings and senators wear purple," Propertius had explained to Horatrim beforehand. "The color is very rare and precious because ten thousand murex shells must be crushed to produce a usable quantity of dye. Whenever you meet a Roman wearing purple you must show the utmost respect."

"What is so special about senators?"

Propertius was surprised that anyone could be so naive, but replied patiently, "Every senator is the head, the *paterfamilias,* of a leading Roman family. Upon the death or discredit of the king, it is the function of the Senate to nominate a new king from among our own class, the *patricians.* The nominee is then voted upon by an assembly of the people, but in my time Rome has never failed to accept the choice of the Senate. Although the king has supreme power, the senators serve as his advisors. Our influence therefore is considerable."

Horatrim, who understood only a little of this, had contrived to look impressed. "So you are really the power behind the king?" he asked.

"But of course," Propertius lied.

As his guests arrived, Propertius introduced the Etruscans as if they were at least as important as senators. "These are our valued friends," he would say, while Delphia chirped, "They are of the Rasne, you know, the Silver People. The oldest and most noble line in Etruria."

Horatrim smiled politely and tried to remember names, but Vesi responded as usual, with no response. She merely stood, powdered and perfumed and silent.

When Propertius's brother Severus arrived, he proved to be as tall and lean as the trader was short and stout. He was accompanied by a fine-boned man with a dark complexion and a closed, enigmatic face. "This is Khebet, an Aegyptian, a trusted and honored associate, who is visiting me for a time on a matter of business," Severus announced to the other guests, "so I brought him along."

Propertius already seemed to know Khebet; the two exchanged brief nods. The Romans took the Aegyptian's appearance for granted, but Horatrim could not help staring at him like any small boy confronted with marvels. Khebet wore a narrow gown of striped, lustrous fabric fitted very close to his lean body and cinched at the waist with a broad swath of supple leather. Folds of white cloth formed an elaborate headdress, completely covering his bald head. But his clothing was not the most remarkable thing about him, Horatrim decided. Never before had he seen a man whose eyes were outlined with kohl, nor whose lips were touched with some red cosmetic. The young man briefly wondered if Khebet could be a woman.

Introductions concluded, Severus caught Propertius

by the elbow and led him off to one side. "Are you mad, brother? Whatever made you bring such a pair into your home?" he asked, nodding toward Horatrim and Vesi. "People you know nothing about—did it never occur to you they could be spies?"

"Would you know a spy if you saw one?"

"I am sure I would."

"And would the Etruscans send a mute woman and a mere youth to do their spying?"

"Perhaps not," Severus reluctantly conceded. "But they look hungry to me, particularly the woman. They look like the sort of beggars who will rob you blind."

"You always were a good judge of character," Propertius replied sarcastically.

"And here you are displaying your foolishness to the rest of the Senate and in front of the king."

"As it happens, Severus, that young man over there saved my life. That's all the recommendation he needs. In addition, however, he has some very interesting talents. You'll be sitting next to him at table tonight; I suggest you ask him what he thinks of Rome's streets." The trader gave his brother a cryptic smile.

When at last a yellow-haired slave announced "Tarquinius Superbius, King of Rome!" Horatrim turned eagerly toward the door. The person who entered was a profound disappointment. Although he wore a robe of royal purple and was flanked by a towering pair of Numidian slaves, Tarquin the Superb was a skinny little man with a nose like a vulture and the eyes of a ferret.

"So that is what kings look like," Horatrim whispered to Propertius.

The Roman chuckled. "That's what *this* king looks like, but he's hardly typical. Anyone with the right bloodlines can become king if he's determined enough or crafty enough or wealthy enough."

"Which is Tarquinius Superbius?" Horatrim wondered. "Determined, crafty, or wealthy?"

"All three," Propertius replied. "In addition, his father

was once king of Rome himself. He was the late lamented Tarquinius Priscus of the tribe of the Tarquins."

As soon as the king had been greeted effusively, all females with the exception of the hostess were ushered from the room. This, Horatrim understood, was the Roman custom, although Livia threw a wistful parting glance over her shoulder as she left and made sure Horatrim saw her flutter her eyelashes at him.

One other female did remain however. When a slave tried to lead Vesi away, her eyes came alive.

I stay, said that peculiar, sibilant voice.

The slave threw a questioning look toward Propertius.

That one has no power over me, the voice announced.

A silence fell over the room.

When the moon hangs by its horns, a trader will pass through the gate and a king will dance with the black goat.

Now all heads were turned toward Vesi. The voice did not seem to come from her mouth in the normal way, for her lips did not move. Rather, it issued from some cavern deep within her, echoing eerily as if it had traveled a great distance through subterranean passageways.

Khebet the Aegyptian sat bolt upright on his couch.

"What did she say?" Tarquinius demanded to know, blinking shortsightedly at the woman. "Is there something wrong with her?"

Delphia immediately shoved the slave aside and put her own arm around the Etruscan woman. "Vesi," she told the king, "is a seer of visions. She described my grandmother in her tomb with details she could not possibly have known."

Propertius added, "This is a very holy woman, Lord Tarquinius. One of the reasons for tonight's banquet was so you could meet her. I had planned to have her join us again after the meal, you see, and. . ."

Tarquinius was not listening. With his bodyguards hovering close on either side, he approached Vesi.

For a moment her eyes glittered like black stones seen through a thin layer of ice.

"Do you know who I am?" the king demanded.

Although her gaze turned in his direction, he had the disquieting feeling that she was not seeing him.

"I am Lucius Tarquinius Superbius, King of Rome."

The gleam began to fade from Vesi's eyes, and her head drooped.

"Explain to me what you meant by what you just said about a king dancing with a goat?" Catching hold of Vesi's chin, he raised her head. But the eyes into which Tarquinius glared were dull and lifeless, all intelligence extinguished.

Tarquinius turned toward Propertius. "What's the matter with this woman? Is she a fool? How dare she refuse to respond to me!"

"She was badly injured some time ago, lord," Propertius hastened to explain. "But she is a holy woman, I assure you. A prophetess, as you have seen. It's just that her gift . . . ah . . . comes and goes. I fear it is not under anyone's command, even a king's. While we await its return, perhaps you would care to sample the feast we have prepared for you?"

Giving Propertius a threatening look that indicated Vesi's "gift" had better reappear before the evening was over, Tarquinius allowed himself to be shown to the table. But he insisted the Etruscan woman remain in the room. "Stand her over there where I can see her," he ordered.

Pepan was dismayed. The arrival of the king of Rome had thrown the Otherworld entities into a frenzy. *Hia* who had never been incarnated in the flesh were able to see past and future as one and therefore were aware of

Tarquinius's destiny. Something about his future excited them unbearably.

Will he die soon? Pepan wondered. *Are they hoping to capture his* hia*?*

The atmosphere darkened, portent of a struggle.

Pepan hovered close to Vesi and Horatrim in order to protect them from whatever was to come. But he knew he could really offer little protection. Horatrim's gifts were formidable and he was learning more about them all the time. Soon he would need no help from anyone. As for Vesi . . .

She stood where the slaves had stationed her, half a dozen paces away from the table. Her blank gaze stared off into space. But she was no longer empty. Pepan was all too aware of the darkness within her, the seething blackness that roiled and hissed.

The banquet Propertius had prepared was the finest the house could offer. As the guests reclined on couches around the table, slaves served the first course, which consisted of bowls of black and green olives and platters of dormice seasoned with poppy seeds and honey. This was followed by hens in pastry, horsemeat boiled with juniper berries, and an enormous roast pig.

When the pork was presented, Propertius scowled in monumental displeasure and shouted at the slaves carrying the platter, "This pig has not been properly gutted! Send for the cook."

The cook was a handsome yellow-haired slave from Thessaly who appeared at a trot. Propertius repeated the charge. Bowing low, the man replied, "Oh, but it has been gutted, my lord. I would never embarrass my master with improperly prepared food."

"If you lie I will have you flogged. Slash open the belly and prove your words if you can."

Producing a large knife with a dramatic flourish, the cook slashed open the belly. Out tumbled a vast quantity of spicy blood puddings and steaming sausages, overflowing the platter and spilling onto the table. Propertius and the cook burst into laughter at the guests' amazement.

Even Tarquinius smiled. "Well done, Propertius. I trust you will breed more pigs like that and have them delivered to my kitchens?"

"As soon as they can fly," the trader assured him. Laughter rippled around the table. Horatrim's childish whoop was the loudest of all.

Flagons of wine and beer were kept refilled as course after course subsequently appeared, offering everything from globe artichokes to bulls' testicles. By watching the other guests, Horatrim discovered how to eat both delicacies. He was quite enjoying himself, though he was uncomfortably aware of his mother standing like a statue in the background.

He had been placed between Severus and Delphia. Between courses, Propertius's brother turned to Horatrim. "For some reason known only to himself, my brother suggests I ask you about Roman streets?"

New concepts leaped into Horatrim's mind. He began describing drainage and paving techniques, sketching ideas on the edge of his toga with a finger wetted in red wine, while a rapt Severus listened and watched. "You could use the same method on the approaches to the city," the young man elaborated. "Paved roads leading to Rome would surely improve trade."

Overhearing, Tarquinius leaned forward. "Does he know what he's talking about, Severus?"

"I think so, my lord. I've never seen that type of paving myself, but I believe it is common in Etruria, where the streets have stood the test of centuries."

"Maybe I should order them built, eh?"

At that moment an eerie, sibilant voice rang through the room.

He who builds that which endures, becomes immortal.

Tarquinius sat bolt upright as everyone turned to look at Vesi. "That prophecy was meant for me! Did you hear what she said; she said I could become immortal. I must have that woman!"

TWENTY-EIGHT

A demon follows its child.

Though the *siu* could not feel love, it was bound to Horatrim by invisible bonds that could not be severed while the child lived. And while the child lived, it remained a danger to its sire.

Of all the creatures that were stalking Horatrim, the *siu* was the most deadly. It was in no hurry to close with its quarry however. Once the *siu* picked up the trail, it was confident Horatrim could not escape. Vesi was a handicap the youth could not overcome. The capture could be made in its own time; the kill in its own way. The *siu* followed the young man patiently, savoring the luxury of anticipation. Enjoying, too, the opportunity to observe the changes that had taken place in the world since it last walked upon the earth with human feet.

Its human life had always been characterized by intellectual curiosity.

* * *

The walls of Rome did not impress the *siu.*

He recalled a much grander city, a citadel of unrivaled splendor where once his name had been almost as respected as that of the Great King, the Lawgiver. He had walked its streets in those long-lost days when he wore flesh, holding his proud head high while people excitedly pointed him out to one another.

"There he is! Bur-Sin, with the light of genius in his face. See the wealth of the jewels on his breast, the gold and glass and lapis lazuli. They are gifts from the Great King, small payment in return for the fabulous creation he is erecting."

A small return indeed, Bur-Sin had thought. As the days passed and work progressed, he had been increasingly aware of how unique, how spectacular his achievement would be when it was finished. Nothing remotely like it existed in the Kingdom of the Two Rivers or even beyond.

As chief designer and architect, Bur-Sin had labored for years over the plans before building began. On countless mud tablets he had drawn elaborate construction details. When his plans were finally approved by the Great King, he had become responsible for training and overseeing the laborers who did the actual building. At the same time he had personally searched the land for the rarest, most beautiful plants, jewels to be placed in the setting of the Hanging Gardens of Babylon.

Tier upon tier the gardens rose. They did not actually hang in the air, but were roof gardens built within the walls of the royal palace. Laid out in a series of ziggurats, or pyramidal towers, they were irrigated by pumps of the architect's own design, drawing water from the Euphrates River.

Almost every day the Great King came to see them. At intervals he would bestow another gift upon the architect, more jewels or a supple dancing girl with honeyed hips. The Great King knew his architect had an insatiable passion for women.

Then Bur-Sin began to notice that in conversation, the Great King invariably referred to the gardens as "my gardens." The name of the man who was creating them was never mentioned.

A thousand slaves labored, a thousand times the sun rose and sank, and still the Hanging Gardens were not completed. The Great King grew impatient. "How soon can I dedicate my gardens?" he demanded to know.

Bur-Sin lost his temper. "On the day when they bear my name, the gardens will be finished!"

The Great King had responded with a burst of temper of his own. "Arrogant servant, how dare you usurp the royal prerogative!"

"I am entitled to recognition for my work. It is not too much to ask. The people of Babylon already know who is responsible for the gardens. They will remember and revere me long after I am dead. I merely request that when foreign dignitaries come to view the gardens, as they will, they too should honor the builder's name."

"I am the builder!" thundered the Great King.

Bur-Sin had felt his rage turn to ice. "Then complete the Hanging Gardens yourself. As for me, I will offer my services elsewhere. Perhaps the Aegyptians will appreciate me. I can erect an equally splendid construction for them."

The Great King's rage knew no bounds. "I will never allow you to build a rival for my gardens! Seize him!"

Guards had tried to grab Bur-Sin, but he ran. He fled through the halls of the royal palace until at last he came to the Inner Temple, the private precincts where the Great King offered sacrifices to the god Marduk. In an alcove curtained with crimson silk the image of Marduk stood, an upright crocodile sheathed in gold.

Bur-Sin had prostrated himself before the statue. "Great Marduk, deliver me!" he pleaded.

They had found him there, cowering at the feet of the gilded saurian. Breaking the laws of sanctuary, the guards had dragged him away and taken him before the

Great King. Then did Hammurabi the Lawgiver, the Just and Wise, pass the most unjust decision of his life.

"Put out his eyes," he said.

That was long ago. Now the *siu* who was once Bur-Sin walked again, not the ancient avenues of Babylon, but the muddy streets of Rome, stalking its prey.

TWENTY-NINE

The woman was red-eyed and weary. Since sundown she had been in and out of *tavernae* soliciting business, but the loins of the Romans were not responsive to her decayed charms. She hated the prospect of going home. Home was a tumbledown hut at the foot of the Palatine Hill. Built into the hillside above were a number of tombs, bleak reminders of mortality. On the summit stood some of the finest houses in Rome. Their sewage combined with noxious liquors seeping from the tombs to rot the footings of her walls. She had grown so used to the smell that she no longer noticed it.

Her shack was dark and lonely, and without a client for the night, Justine could not even buy oil for her lamp. There was nothing to eat either, but that scarcely mattered anymore. Her teeth were so rotten she could hardly chew and had to stifle her hunger pangs with soggy bread and overripe fruit when she could get them.

There was little pleasure in such a diet. At last she admitted defeat and set out for the Palatine.

The night seemed darker than any she could remember. "I am too old for this," she said, talking to herself for company. "When I was young and beautiful they all wanted me; oh yes, I could command any price then. Now they laugh at me."

Almost every statement she made was prefaced by, "When I was young and beautiful," until the phrase had become a joke. "When you were young and beautiful that old she-wolf was still suckling Romulus and Remus!" her listeners would jeer.

People could be so cruel. Justine's eyes brimmed with self-pity. Once she had laughed at older harlots who were glad to settle for marriage to some rough farmer from the country and the security of food on the table every night. In her youth she had believed such women were foolishly sacrificing freedom for the drudgery of slavery. Now she would have accepted an offer of marriage from even the most impoverished goatherd or lime digger and been grateful, but the offers had dried up with the last of her beauty.

"This winter I'll be forced to get a bowl and beg," she muttered to herself. Then a remnant of almost-forgotten pride surfaced. "No, I won't beg. I'll kill myself first. I will. I'd rather be dead."

In the enveloping darkness, something snickered.

The woman froze. "Who's there?"

Silence. But the silence was not total; she could swear she heard breathing close by. She reached into the neck of her gown and fumbled between her scrawny, sagging breasts and produced a sliver of metal. "Who's there, I say. I warn you, I have a dagger here and I know how to use it."

This time there was no mistaking the low chuckle. The sound came from off to her right, in the direction of the marshy waste ground that comprised much of the valley between the Capitoline and Palatine Hills. The path she usually took home lay across that space, but she felt a curious disinclination to follow it. "Perhaps if I go back to that last tavern my luck will turn," she murmured to herself.

Facing around, she began to retrace her steps. The breathing followed her.

Other sounds accompanied it now, whispers and murmurs and obscene smacking noises. She felt a sudden relief. She was being followed by young boys then, males still embarrassed by their burgeoning sexuality and resorting to childish games. But she knew how to deal with them.

Halting abruptly, she threw wide her arms. "That's all right. You needn't be afraid. Step up and show me what you're made of. I'll be good to you; I'll break you in right. Come now," she wheedled, "come to me."

Out of the darkness, something came.

Justine had thought nothing could shock her anymore, but she was wrong.

From the shadows swarmed amorphous apparitions that hissed and growled and sniggered, writhing obscenely as they advanced. Some appeared as gaping mouths with slimy tongues or slobbering lips that mimicked sucking. Others were oversized genital organs, a phalanx of throbbing phalluses advancing on the horrified woman. Still others were mere sparks of sulfurous light that gave off the stench of carrion.

Central among them was a figure who appeared human yet moved in rhythm with the disgusting phantasmagoria. He chuckled again.

"You called me?" asked the *siu.*

Justine tried to run. He caught her before she had gone more than a few steps and threw her to the ground. Gibbering, the other horrid forms closed around them in anticipation.

"You must forgive my admirers," the demon growled. "From time to time they follow me like shadows, and they are just about as useful. Let us dispense with them, shall we?" He whirled on his companions with such a ghastly roar that they faded into the night, leaving him alone with his prey.

Justine fought with all her strength and the experience of too many years spent on the streets. She knew how to hurt a man. She kicked and clawed until he pinned her wrists with one hand, squeezing them tightly enough to block circulation. He stopped her from kicking him by the simple expedient of throwing his full weight on top of her.

To her surprise, he was not nearly as heavy as he looked. But he stank abominably.

She tried to scream then. He covered her mouth with his own and swallowed the scream, then drew back enough to say, "I suppose it is too much to hope you might be a virgin?"

Before she could reply he chuckled again. The sound was mirthless and cruel. "No, I suppose not. A pity."

"Do whatever you want; just don't kill me!"

"Kill you? I assure you, the mere thought of a corpse disgusts me." Justine felt a shudder run through the body pressed against her own.

"I'll do anything. . . "

"Good, very good. I appreciate compliance in a woman. Tell me, what do you want most in all the world?"

"To get away from you!" she snapped.

"Oh, we can't allow that. Try again. Consider your situation. You are a harlot, I suspect, and thus in the business of selling yourself. If in exchange you could ask for anything you liked, no matter how impossible, what would you ask for?"

Her frantic mind skittered sideways and she said the first thing that popped into her head. "I'd ask for my youth back."

"Better, much better. I think that could be arranged."

"Don't be ridiculous. I'm old; I'm thirty," Justine

confessed in a whisper. She turned her head to one side, trying to avoid his fetid breath.

As if he read her mind, he said, "Do you dislike my odor? Someday you will smell even worse, unless you find a way to stop time. That is what I can offer you. In exchange for something I require, I can make you half your age and keep you young forever."

"You're mad."

"The gift I describe is in my power to give, I assure you."

"Only a demon could do such a thing!"

He stroked her sunken cheek. "And what do you think I am? I can make this flesh bloom again and do more besides, much, much more. In return, however, I have special needs that must be satisfied."

Justine could not imagine what "special needs" this repulsive being might have. She was convinced he was mad and dangerous as well. In her years walking the streets of Rome she had met any number of madmen and learned it was best to placate them whenever possible.

"Just let me get up," she urged, "and we can talk. I'm not used to doing business like this."

He chuckled again. "On the contrary, I should say this is the very position in which you are most accustomed to doing business. But you may get up. If we are going to be partners, you deserve that courtesy."

Partners. The idea repelled her. But if she could stall for time, perhaps she could find a way to escape. A few minutes ago she had been ready to consider dying; now she wanted most desperately to live.

"Do you indeed?" he asked abruptly, reading her thoughts, which were a clarion call in the Otherworld. In one lithe movement he was on his feet and reaching down to offer her a hand up.

Although she tried not to, Justine shrank from his touch. His hand was icy cold and very dry, the skin rough and flaking. His sharp nails bit into her palm like tiny fangs. "Take me home with you," he said. "We can talk there."

The last thing she wanted was to lead this lunatic to her home, but she had no choice. With fast-beating heart she made her way across the fetid waste ground at the foot of the hills. He followed close behind her. She did not have to look back to know he was there. She could smell him. Just knowing he was there made the flesh burn on the back of her neck. In fact, her skin felt peculiar all over, as if she had been in the sun too long. A hot flush radiated from the top of her head to the soles of her feet. She toyed with the idea of claiming disease—a trick a Scythian whore had taught her in her youth—then remembered that he could read her mind.

In the end she simply kept walking. For so many years she had done as men asked; the habit was deeply ingrained.

At last she came to the pitiful shack that was her home and tugged open the splintery door. There was no lock; she had nothing to protect, so she could not slam the door in his face and lock him out. But he was too close behind her anyway. She felt him brush past her into the darkness. Then she heard the scratch of fingernails on pottery.

"I have no oil for that lamp," she started to say just as her one small lamp flared into light. He stood holding it in front of him while its flame threw eerie shadows on his face.

The sight made her nauseous.

"Do you not find me handsome?" he asked sardonically.

She could not bear to look at him. In the wavering light, his face was the color of putrid meat. "You must be diseased. Your skin is flaking off."

"Unfortunately that is correct, but not because of disease."

She could not resist asking, "Does it hurt?"

"You dear child. So tenderhearted."

"I'm not a child and I'm not tenderhearted either."

"But you would help me if you could?" he persisted.

"Of course, but I don't see how I. . . "

"In return for your youth, you will do anything?"

"Anything."

" 'Tis done, then. Now it is your turn." Reaching for her with one hand, he caught her by the wrist and drew her closer to the light. "Look down," he commanded. "Dear child."

Justine looked down.

The arm he was holding had been sunburnt and scrawny, scored with old scars; but even as she watched it began to change. The contours grew as plump and prettily rounded as in her youth. Her gnarled fingers became white and supple once more; then the broken fingernails were whole again, forming perfect arcs.

He slowly moved the lamplight along her arm, then across the front of her body. "Observe yourself, Justine."

She did not ask how he knew her name. Her attention was focused on the full, firm breasts plainly visible in the low neck of her gown.

He released his hold on her. Her discolored metal mirror appeared in his hand and he held it before her face. "What do you see, Justine?"

"Is that me?" she asked tremulously, lifting a wondering hand to her cheek.

The girl in the mirror copied her gesture exactly. The girl was barely fifteen, with eyes like sloes and a ripe, red mouth. Not a line marred her perfect complexion; she was vibrant with life.

Staring into the mirror, Justine said, "I used to look like that."

"You look like that now. And you will forever, unless I withdraw my gift. Or . . . if we should fail to conclude our business arrangement.. . . " He twisted the mirror away, then held it back. This time Justine found herself gazing upon the old familiar face that greeted her each morning, haggard and wrinkled, with pouches under the eyes and an apathetic expression.

She caught his hand. "Ah no, bring her back!"

"Are you certain?"

"Yes. Yes! I will do anything. Anything."

His lips quirked into a smile. "Somehow I thought you would," the demon said.

THIRTY

Horatrim was dismayed to hear Tarquinius demand possession of Vesi. But before he could leap to his feet in protest, Delphia caught hold of his arm, squeezing firmly. "Don't be rash. The king's bestowing a great honor on her. Your mother will live in the royal palace and be treated like a queen."

"I won't let my mother be any man's harlot!" Horatrim had never heard the word before, yet it suddenly burned through his mind.

Tarquinius overheard the outburst and blandly replied, "You misunderstand my intention, Horatrim. I don't need her for my bed; I have plenty of willing women. I want to install her as my personal soothsayer."

Slowly Vesi turned her head and met her son's eyes. For a single instant he thought he saw his mother's true expression: terrified, lost. Then it faded and was gone.

* * *

It was close to noon the following morning when a sedan chair arrived at the house of Propertius Cocles and obsequious slaves offered their bowed backs for Vesi to step upon so she could climb in. She seemed quite content to go.

Severus had been too drunk to go home after the banquet, so he and Khebet had been given beds for the night. They now joined the party gathered at the door to wish Vesi farewell. Severus had a cloth soaked with vinegar wrapped around his head, but the Aegyptian showed no sign of a hangover. He was bathed, shaved, and neatly dressed, every hair in place. Even his fingernails were buffed and shining, and he exuded a throat-catching aroma of pungent herbs and exotic spices.

"I charge you to take good care of my friend," Delphia told the king's servants.

"And remind him that it was I who found her for him," added Propertius. Turning to Horatrim as the sedan chair disappeared down the street, he said, "You could not possibly have made better arrangements for your mother's welfare. Relax and be happy for her."

"But she speaks so rarely," Horatrim protested, "and when she does much of it is so obscure."

Severus interjected, "No matter how obscure her pronouncements, they will be taken as messages from the gods. Propertius doesn't set great store by the gods, but I assure you Tarquinius does. As does my friend Khebet," he added, indicating the Aegyptian.

Severus continued, "Unfortunately the rest of us have to work a bit harder at pleasing the king. I want to hear more about these paving ideas of yours, Horatrim. Propertius, do you mind if we take your guest on a little tour of the city? Perhaps the air will help clear my head."

"Go right ahead," said the trader with an indulgent wave of his hand. "I thought you would find Horatrim interesting. Just remember who introduced you to him."

"He will probably try and charge me an introduction fee," Severus grumbled as they strolled out into the street.

Rome by daylight was sprawling and squalid but still seethed with energy. The earliest settlers had been farmers who built their huts on the hills overlooking the Tiber in order to leave the fertile river valley free for grazing and cultivating. With the passage of time the pastoral settlement had gone through several transformations, becoming a market town for local produce, then a regional market involved in both export and import, then finally the headquarters of a fledgling bureaucracy devoted to managing the wealth of Rome. Now ambassadors and trade delegations from friend and foe alike made frequent visits to the city on the seven hills.

Horatrim noticed other kohl-eyed Aegyptians. Khebet even bowed politely to one, acknowledging recognition though nothing was said between them.

Khebet, it appeared, was a man of few words. He and Severus exchanged an occasional remark, but for the most part he was content to pace sedately beside the others. The only obvious interest he showed was in the new Temple of Jupiter, Juno, and Minerva that crowned the stony Capitoline Hill.

"I built that," Severus said proudly. "Completed it within the time allowed and under budget. Observe the Etruscan-style portico. That was to please Tarquinius, of course."

Rome was a city of wonders to Horatrim. He had never seen so many people in his life, and he was becoming increasingly aware that each person emitted a distinctive musical sound, a barely audible chime or lilt or even percussive beat. Some were pleasant, others discordant. Because he knew no different, Horatrim assumed that everyone else could hear this music, too.

"Listen!" he exclaimed.

Severus and Khebet stopped and looked at him quizzically.

"Do you hear that?"

"Hear what?" asked Severus. The Aegyptian said nothing, merely raised one eyebrow.

"That!" Horatrim insisted, turning his head from side to side. He was trying to identify the direction of the martial music he was hearing, a sound as of trumpets in the air. His gaze fell on a side street just as an unusually tall, strikingly handsome man came striding out into the sunlight. The man, who appeared not much older than himself, walked as if the earth was hardly good enough for him. He was followed by a company of ceremonial bodyguards wearing plumed helmets and carrying highly polished spears at a uniform angle. They too moved with arrogance and grace.

The tall man's eyes met Horatrim's. They were a clear green with no gentleness in them. Theirs was the look of an eagle. They examined the young man, then flickered across Severus and the Aegyptian . . . and dismissed them.

He strode past and was gone.

"Who was that, Severus?" Horatrim wanted to know. The force of the tall man's personality had jolted him across the space between them. "And wasn't he . . . splendid!"

"Him? He's Lars Porsena, a prince of Clusium."

"Clusium?"

"Hill country in Etruria, which makes him one of your own in a manner of speaking. He's visiting the king as head of a trade delegation. My brother knows him; Propertius knows everybody."

"A prince," murmured Horatrim, "from Etruria." He turned to watch the bodyguard march away up the street. They were tautly muscled, clean-shaven, well-drilled. He thought them more impressive than the Romax . . . Romans. "Were you ever a warrior?" he asked Severus.

"Me? I'm not such a fool as to be willing to lay down my life for someone else."

"But surely to be a warrior is a noble calling."

"I'm a senator. We do battle in a different way. When it comes to physical combat I prefer to be a spectator. I go to the arena whenever there's a performance scheduled and wager on my favorite fighter—or the bear—but I have no interest in risking my personal hide."

Eyes fixed on the fast-disappearing Lars Porsena and his men, Horatrim said, "I think I would like to be a warrior."

"You're a bit late. The Etruscans have lost their enthusiasm for warfare."

The young man smiled almost dreamily. "We might find it again."

"Better not let the king hear you say that. Our Tarquinius boasts of his noble Etruscan forebears, but he's really a Roman at heart. He truly believes the accident of having been born here makes him superior to anyone else, be they Hellenes or Carthaginians or even Etruscans. The welcome he gives trade delegations is all on the surface, good business for the city. If Lars Porsena or his warriors so much as waved a spear out of turn they would never see Etruria again.

"And speaking of Tarquinius . . . since we've come to a particularly steep street, why don't you show us what you mean about laying paving, so I can discuss it with the king?"

They spent the early afternoon wandering around Rome. The Aegyptian, Horatrim eventually learned, held an exalted position in his own country. "I am a priest of Anubis, the Jackal God," Khebet elaborated, briefly breaking his silence.

Severus took up the conversation. "Aegyptian priests are experts in mathematics, the science of numbers. They build quite remarkable temples by relying upon complex calculations no one here understands. Propertius knows Khebet through his trade connections in Aegypt, so he arranged for him to come and work with me for a time, instructing my men."

Khebet gave a faint smile, the merest tightening of his lips over his teeth. "In return you pledged sacrifices to Anubis, remember."

"Yes, yes, of course!" Severus hastily assured him. "Bounteous sacrifices, just as we agreed."

As they continued their stroll Severus called Horatrim's attention to the situation of various streets and asked for comment. In responding, the young man displayed a knowledge of construction that led the Roman to remark, "You certainly learned a lot in the cities of Etruria."

"I've never seen the cities of Etruria."

Severus's jaw dropped. Then he grinned. "Surely you jest with me."

"It's no jest. I was born and raised in the Great Forest. Rome is the only city I've ever seen."

"But that's simply not possible! How could you concoct such ideas out of nothing?"

"They don't come out of nothing. I . . . it's difficult to explain this, Severus. But I simply know these things. And sometimes I hear voices."

Khebet turned and gave him a penetrating look.

"Doesn't everyone hear voices?" Horatrim asked, surprised by the expression on the Aegyptian's face. "They tell me what to do. Sometimes," he added ruefully, thinking of the girl Livia.

Severus hardly knew how to react. On rare occasions, perhaps once in a generation, someone produced a totally new idea. He had heard of such god-gifted geniuses, though he had never met one himself. Yet if Horatrim spoke the truth he was one of that number. "If your knowledge originates in your own head," he told Horatrim, only half-joking, "we must be careful to see that no one chops it off."

Late afternoon found them approaching an expanse of damp, rat-infested waste ground in the valley between the Palatine and Capitoline Hills. Here was dumped every sort of rubbish from oyster shells and dead dogs to aborted infants. Around the perimeter stood an assortment of makeshift shacks, some little more than rotten planks leaning against each for support like drunkards leaving a tavern.

Horatrim remarked, "If this were drained you could build decent houses here. Or a market square or even some fine public building."

"How would you suggest draining it?"

The young man squatted on his haunches, picked up a stick from the ground, and began drawing diagrams in the mud. Severus and Khebet leaned over his shoulder, watching. From time to time the Aegyptian gave a murmur of approval.

His first diagram concluded, Horatius went on, "As for the river, I am surprised you have no substantial bridge across it. Surely it would be to the city's advantage to unite both banks by something wider and more stable than that flimsy wooden structure you have now. Look here. You could span the Tiber like this, starting at this point, using arches for support. . . "

Lost in his work, he drew furiously as the two men watched him in silent amazement.

At last Severus found the voice to say, "I want you to work for me, Horatrim. In fact, I insist upon it."

"Work for you? Why?"

"I'm the king's personal builder, his architect. When Tarquinius wants something constructed he commissions me to draw up the plans and contract materials and labor. There's always a nice profit to be made; he never questions the costs I quote him. No business head at all," Severus added with a wink. "While you, my young friend, have a quite remarkable head. If you're willing to come up with ideas exclusively for my firm, I will reward you handsomely. Very handsomely." He winked again.

"You want to buy my ideas?" Horatrim asked incredulously.

"Something like that, yes. An arrangement rather than a purchase however; one that would benefit us both. You would be apprenticed to me to learn the building trade, and in time you might even have a share of the business. A very small share, of course. What do you think?"

A short time ago Horatrim had been a primitive child living in the Great Forest. Now he was being accepted as a man and offered work of importance in the city of Rome.

For one wild moment he almost laughed, but he was afraid they would misunderstand. With an effort he kept his face serious. "My mother foresaw this, Severus. She said my future was here, though neither of us had ever been here and we did not even know any Romans. But she insisted we come. You know the rest."

The older man gave a low whistle. "She is obviously a great seer. But for great seers to survive, they must temper their pronouncements with discretion. I wonder what she'll foresee for our Tarquinius."

As the day wore on the three men were too preoccupied to think of food. Only when a bank of dark clouds swept in over the river did Severus realize how late it was. "We had better go back to my brother's now, Horatrim. If I don't deliver you in time for dinner he'll suspect I've kidnapped his guest or begin charging me for your time."

When they reached the house, the first person Horatrim saw was Livia. The Roman girl was sitting casually by the door as if she had just paused there for a moment. In truth, she had spent an impatient day awaiting the young man's return. At sight of her, all of Horatrim's plans and designs went out of his head. Once more his inner voices failed to guide him, but he was beginning to feel more confident.

I can do this myself, he thought.

But when he attempted to strike up a conversation with the girl over dinner, the presence of so many other people in the room was a serious distraction. Severus was talking to Propertius; Khebet was wandering around the room, thoughtfully stroking his chin and ignoring everyone else; Delphia was instructing the steward; other slaves were preparing the table and couches for the evening meal; Livia's younger brothers and sisters were scampering back and forth or hovering close, giggling whenever Horatrim paused to talk to the girl, laughing aloud when she tried to open the conversation. There was no such thing as privacy.

"Is there somewhere else where we can talk, Livia?" he finally asked with an air of desperation.

"We could always go outside, but it's getting dark and the air smells of rain. Rain will ruin my hair." She patted her carefully arranged curls and smiled disingenuously. "You wouldn't want to see these disarranged, would you?"

"Ah, no. Of course not. They are . . . beautiful. But . . . is there no place else? Inside?"

"Only the sleeping chambers, and I share mine with my two sisters. If we go there they will come after us immediately out of curiosity."

"This is no way to construct a house."

Livia's laughter was gently mocking. "I suppose you know a better one?"

Now they came to him unbidden, singing through his blood.

"A house should be built around an unroofed courtyard so it forms a hollow square," said Horatrim, echoing his inner voices, hands moving to shape the design. "The exterior wall is blank, but every room opens onto the courtyard which lets light and air into the interior."

He could see it so clearly; as clear as a personal memory. "The house is two houses, really. The front portion is the public one, with a large reception area rather like your main room now, only much more elegant and comfortable. To provide additional light to this space there is an opening in the center of the ceiling. The tiled roof above slopes down on all four sides, throwing rainwater through spouts into a marble pool set in the center of the floor. This gives a sense of coolness and peace, while the reflection of the sky in the water provides an ever-changing work of art."

The girl was looking at him wide-eyed. The young man's voice had deepened, become stronger, more commanding, with the faintest hint of an accent.

"Off the principal reception area are chambers for dining or playing games and dice, whatever entertainments the host wants to provide for his guests. Or in fine weather he may take them into the courtyard, which has a columned portico down either side. Behind this portico are the servants' quarters, readily accessible to either part of the building. The rear half of the house comprises the private residence, with ample apartments and bathing facilities. Here the women of the family can enjoy themselves while the men conduct business and entertain clients at the front. The entire structure is light, airy, spacious, and affords total privacy within, no matter how busy the streets beyond its walls," Horatrim concluded.

He was so rapt in his vision he was unaware of Delphia, who had abandoned her task and come to stand slightly behind Livia. She listened to him with fascination. When he stopped speaking she turned and called, "Propertius, come over here at once! This young man has just described the perfect house. Every matron in Rome is going to want one like this. I know I do. You must build it for us, Severus."

After that Horatrim had no opportunity for a private conversation with Livia. The evening was spent with Severus and Khebet extracting every bit of construction information they could from him, while Propertius insisted on talking about how best to market the design and how much money could be made building the houses.

When everyone was exhausted and a yawning

Severus finally announced he was going home, Propertius said abruptly, "We will expect a sixty percent share of the profits of this venture, of course."

Severus was suddenly wide awake. "What do you mean, we? Horatrim's going to be working for me. I'm the builder."

A bland smile spread across Propertius's face. "So you are. But while you were wandering around the city today, I paid a little visit to the royal palace. The king is delighted with Vesi. He believes having his own personal oracle will enhance his stature enormously; and when I pointed out that I had found her for him, he was in a humor to grant me any reasonable request."

"And you made a reasonable request?"

"I asked to be allowed to adopt Vesi's son."

Horatrim turned to look at Propertius.

"Horatrim is henceforth to be known as Horatius Cocles, and this family is entitled to share in whatever he earns. As *paterfamilias,* I demand you pay him sixty percent."

"Fifty."

"Fifty-five."

"Done!" cried Propertius. With a grin, he turned to Horatius. "Welcome to my family!"

THIRTY-ONE

The hour was late; the rain had long since blown over.

Horatrim was sharing a stifling cubicle off the main room with Propertius's sons. Three were much younger boys. The fourth, Quintus, was a sullen fellow of his own age who resented having so suddenly acquired a new brother.

They slept on pallets on the floor in order to be cooled by any stray draught of air, but no air was stirring. Only Horatrim's thoughts were churningly active. Horatius Cocles, he kept saying to himself. I have become a Roman!

For a while that evening he had feared Propertius and Severus would come to blows, but eventually they had struck upon a mutually acceptable arrangement. Horatrim was certain each man privately thought he had the better deal. No one asked the new Horatius what he wanted.

So much had happened to him so fast, the old patterns

were breaking down. Childhood was sloughing away like dead skin. He could not sleep, there was no point in trying. He wanted . . . he needed . . . when he ran his hand down the length of his body there was an immediate stirring in his groin.

He arose from the pallet, wearing only the tunic in which he had slept, and went out into the main room of the house. The front door stood invitingly ajar. He stepped outside. And found Livia. As he knew he would.

She was there, leaning her back against the wall beside the door as she gazed up into a star-spangled sky. She was aware of him but did not look around, allowing him the pleasure of looking at her.

She wore a shift of sheer Aegyptian cotton, exposing her arms to the shoulder and her legs almost to her groin. He could smell quince-seed pomade on her hair. He was achingly aware of her, an unsettling experience for one who had so recently been a child.

"You came to us a stranger, yet now you are my brother," Livia remarked. "You will live here with us. Your fortune is assured, and with that fortune your place in the Senate. Using your ideas, father and uncle plan to bring new glory to Rome. Furthermore, work will soon begin on a new house for us with a private apartment of my own where I can entertain you." She spiced this last remark with a mischievous grin.

"How? I mean, entertain me how?"

She gave her trilling laugh. "Not with games or dice. Surely we can find something much more pleasurable." Turning toward him, she ran one speculative fingertip along his arm. A thread of invisible flame sprang up in the wake of her touch. With languid grace she tilted forward to lean on Horatrim instead of the wall. For a moment he staggered, more from surprise than the weight of her body. He could feel the heat of her flesh through the fabric of her shift. Then his arms closed around her and he held her close. When she lifted her face to his, her breath smelled of wine and honey.

Horatrim had never exchanged a kiss with a woman. He only knew how to plant a childish pucker on his mother's cheek. But Livia allowed him no time to be awkward. She pulled her arms free of his embrace, cupped the back of his head with her hands, and pressed her open mouth to his.

"I know what you are; you're a demon," Justine accused. Pointing to the immense phallus, erect and throbbing, between them, she said, "*That* gives you away. I've seen enough of the other kind to know it isn't human."

The *siu* glanced down. "Oh, I assure you it is—or was. During my human lifetime my member was a great source of pride. An abundant sex does not make one a demon, dear child. In my time this was not considered unusual, though nowadays I believe that males are less generously endowed. Even the gods have gender, although it may have been attributed to them originally by humankind, an example of man making gods in his own image. But now deities take as much pleasure in their sexuality as any human—more. Appreciating that sex is the quintessence of creation, the ultimate magic, they celebrate passion with a splendor you cannot even imagine. Even such a one as Marduk, the Crocodile God, is famous for. . ."

He paused.

They were lying together on a heap of rags and straw that passed for a bed in her miserable hovel. Justine had just taken part in a sexual act outside of anything in her prior repertoire, a comingling of pleasure and pain that exploded her senses with ecstasy while filling her mind with revulsion. She did not ever want to repeat the experience.

And yet she knew she would again . . . and again . . . and again. . . .It was the price she must pay.

Meanwhile she hung on his words with professional interest. How many harlots had ever heard a demon describing the sexual lives of the gods?

"Yes?" she urged. "What about Marduk?"

His voice was dark with anger. "There was a time when I prayed to Marduk to save my life. Seeking protection from the Crocodile . . . I was a fool to ask! I lived, but he let them put out my eyes with a hot poker. The pain was indescribable, yet that was not the worst. I who had been an architect, the designer of great palaces and magnificent gardens, was nothing without my eyes. Less than nothing—a beggar with a bowl. I who had been so proud!

"In fear and fury I turned against Marduk then. If one god fails you, I reasoned, try another. There are a multitude of gods; the trick is to find one who suits. I redirected my prayers to the goddess Pythia, a deity from the land of the Nile, because I had always been fond of females. Restore my sight, I promised her, and I will be your slave forever.

"Pythia did indeed restore my sight. When I awoke the next morning and gingerly touched my cauterized eye sockets, they were swelling with new orbs. A miracle! Within a few days the first dim glimmers of light appeared to me. I was so grateful I never thought to ask the cost. No gift, even one freely given, is without its price. This would be a salutary lesson for you, dear child, were it not too late.

"The price Pythia demanded proved to be more than I wanted to pay. The dark goddess restored my sight—and allowed me one night and a day to enjoy it. I went to bed one night strong and healthy and with a beautiful woman beside me.

"But the morning never came. While I slept the dark goddess extracted my spirit from my body as neatly as you would pull a tooth. I found myself stranded in the Otherworld, a disembodied being still tormented by an insatiable appetite for life. It was even worse than being blind.

"It should have been the end of me. But it was not.

"In the Earthworld, people who had admired me while I lived continued to revere me. They passed on my legend to the generations who followed them, telling the story of the builder of the famous Hanging Gardens and adding their own flourishes as the years went by. Eventually the Babylonians began to make statues of me and offer sacrifices.

"But because a human spirit cannot be so idolized without incurring the wrath and jealousy of the gods, deities I had once worshipped transformed me into a demon. Unfairly," he added bitterly. "I deserved to be worshipped myself; I had been an extraordinary man!"

Justine bit her lip and said nothing, desperately concentrating on the sagging ceiling, unwilling to allow the *siu* to read her mind.

"Pythia should have protected me," he went on in an aggrieved tone, "or at the very least argued with the other gods on my behalf. But she allowed them to abuse me. Finally, when it was too late and I had become the demon you see, she took pity on me and adopted me as her personal servant. But perhaps pity is not the right word. I think she took pleasure in my abasement. When I realized this I vowed to be revenged upon the dark goddess. I bided my time, always pretending to be devoted to her, while centuries passed in the Earthworld."

Justine smiled in the darkness. Men—either from modern Rome or ancient Babylon—never changed. They always wanted to talk about their favorite topic: themselves. "Did she never suspect you?" she asked.

He replied with his bitter chuckle. "Gods are not as omnipotent as they want us to believe. I was able to deceive Pythia because in her arrogance she thought herself above deception. And at last I found a way to even the score with her.

"From the dark goddess I stole enough power to clothe my spirit in flesh, enabling me to live once more in the Earthworld. Such transformation is within the gift of the gods, although they hoard it jealously. But I wanted my life back. I had a right to it!

"The power I took from Pythia was sufficient to form a tangible body through sheer force of will, so I undertook to re-create my own self. Alas, however, I am not a god. I did not perform a perfect act of creation. The body I attempted to restore proved to be a rather blurred copy of my original form. I became what you see now.

"I experimented with other forms, sending my spirit into the body of a beast—a beast that was soon slain, unfortunately. I tried to use the body anyway, and the result was disastrous. For a time my spirit went mad. When I recovered, I returned to this body resolving not to make the same mistake again. My next mistake was almost deadly; I consumed dead flesh . . . and the madness that overtook me once more almost engulfed me.

"Maintaining my hold on the Earthworld is difficult. In spite of all I can do, I feel my body fading. Every day it becomes less substantial; and as you have remarked yourself, the skin is flaking off. I look leprous. I do not blame you for being repelled by me, Justine.

"Nourishment is vital to me, nourishment of a very particular sort. But very soon I am going to require another body to inhabit. Something young and strong and original, not a copy of one long in the tomb."

He smiled. She found his smile more sinister than his chuckle.

"I have been seeking a perfect body for a long time, and now, at last, I have found one. Tell me, dear child—are you familiar with the royal palace?"

THIRTY-TWO

The royal palace of Rome stood some distance from the Tiber in order to avoid the smell of the river. As the city expanded, its river was becoming an open sewer. The intense heat of summer caused the water level to fall alarmingly, exposing mud flats that added their own stench to the effluvium. But the city could not grow without Father Tiber, which provided access to the sea and thus to foreign markets.

Like every Roman household, the palace served a number of functions. In addition to being the residence of the king, it provided guest apartments for visiting dignitaries such as the prince, Lars Porsena.

This evening's entertainment included an appearance by Tarquinius's latest discovery. "From now on, the king of Rome will have his own personal holy woman to interpret messages from the gods," he had informed his chief steward. "I want to present her after the banquet and under the best possible circumstances. Arrange a high seat for her in a private chamber. Surround her with all the trappings appropriate to one of her calling."

Guests in the palace on this particular occasion included not only the young prince from Clusium but also a wealthy Sardinian shipowner, the leaders of a trade delegation from Smyrna, and a major Aegyptian dealer in slaves and exotic beasts. After dinner they were shown into the windowless chamber where Vesi waited. While Tarquinius watched with a proprietary air, they gathered around a tripod supporting a huge bronze bowl. Within this peculiar perch sat a woman.

She was dressed in a gown of bleached linen, cross-banded beneath her breasts. Her arms were bare, her head crowned with a laurel wreath to signify honors. On either side of the tripod were bronzed laurel branches, and at the feet of the stool was a brazier filling the room with clouds of white smoke and the fragrance of bitter herbs. The effect was every bit as impressive as Tarquinius desired.

"Speak to us, O Prophetess!" he intoned.

Silence.

Vesi sat immobile in her bronze bowl and stared over his head.

"Speak, I command you!"

Something came alive behind her eyes. Something terrible.

No mortal commands Pythia, said a voice that seemed to come from very far away.

Vesi's lips did not move.

When he heard the name of the dark goddess, the Aegyptian slave dealer blanched beneath his olive skin. Pythia was not a major deity in the pantheon of his people, but she was an horrific one, her name invoked rarely and always with trepidation.

Tarquinius bowed low before the woman on the tripod. "Forgive us our presumption. We merely seek wisdom."

Wisdom is a tree with ten million roots that feed on blood while the branches die.

Tarquinius cleared his throat. "Ah . . . indeed." He had never heard the number ten million before.

The Aegyptian, however, was impressed. Turning to the king, he said, "What you have here is something remarkable. I commend you. Where did you find such a valuable commodity?"

The king of Rome knew enough to refrain from divulging gratuitous information to trading partners. Airily waving one hand, he said, "She is from Etruria, of course. Who else has such an affinity with magic and mystery? Who else converses regularly with the gods? And she's not for sale, if that's what you're hinting. She's like one of my own family."

The Sardinian shipowner was skeptical. "I never heard the name Pythia mentioned in connection with any Etruscan tribe." He glanced accusingly at the Aegyptian. "Pythia's one of yours, isn't she?"

"We have a goddess by that name, I believe," the man replied warily. No one could see his fingers clutching the amulet sewn into his robes in an attempt to ward off evil.

"Well, I've never heard of her," Tarquinius said with a shrug. "But I dare say the name will become famous in time. This woman merely needs a larger audience, which I will provide. Have any of you questions you wish put to her?"

Uncertainly at first, then with growing fascination, the party addressed the woman seated on the tripod. Sometimes she did not answer. Then for no apparent reason she would fall into incoherent raving. Seizing the bronze laurel branches, she shook them wildly as she chanted. Out of the chaos an occasional phrase would make stunning sense to one or another of the men in the room.

Her most cryptic comment was reserved for the handsome prince of Clusium, Lars Porsena. When he stepped close to the tripod to get a better look at the woman through the smoke, she fixed her eyes on his face and solemnly declaimed, *Beware the empty nest. That which hatches from the eagle's egg will rain fire on the wolf's cubs.*

When the evening was over Tarquinius was euphoric. The Etruscan woman had far exceeded his expectations. "Having her entertain my guests was a brilliant idea, positively brilliant," he confided to his favorite body slave as he took his evening bath. Beaming with self-congratulation, the king absentmindedly fondled his genitals in the warm water. Recognizing the signals, his slave ran through a mental list of the concubines, trying to guess which one Tarquinius would want tonight.

But his master's mind was still on the Etruscan woman. Though her pronouncements had been few, they had been relevant. It would be but a short step from the genuine prophecies of the seer to those he would have her make for political reasons. In a month, perhaps less, he would announce that she had proclaimed him the son of a god and that his line would rule for a thousand years. Then she would really earn her keep.

"Do you wish a woman sent to you tonight?" his slave inquired as Tarquinius emerged from his bath. "Perhaps the yellow-haired one you bought last spring?"

But Tarquinius was too overstimulated for anything so ordinary. "No, I'm not in the mood. Bring me the seer instead, so I can talk with her privately. Perhaps she will have some prophecy for my ears alone."

The slave bowed low so the king would not see the smile on his face. He could imagine the type of conversation Tarquinius had in mind.

They brought her to him in the anteroom that led to his bedchamber. The ruler of Rome was casually attired in a robe of orange silk dyed in Syria. Vesi wore a sheer, pleated gown of the sort favored by the palace courtesans, and scented pomade had been used to dress her hair. In the soft light of the oil lamps, which rendered the gown virtually transparent, she appeared surprisingly youthful . . . and innocent. Tarquinius liked his women young. Suddenly he was interested in something more tangible than her oracular abilities.

Rising from his bench, he led her through the doorway into the next room. She followed without resistance. A massive bed waited half-hidden behind swathes of sheer fabric that could be drawn to keep out biting insects. Tarquinius drew the curtains back and, still holding Vesi by one wrist, stretched himself upon the bed. She continued to stand at the edge of the bed until he tugged imperiously at her arm, then she lay down beside him and closed her eyes. When he released her wrist she folded her hands across her breasts.

Seen thus, she looked like a corpse.

The image was troubling. "Open your eyes," he requested.

She did not move.

"Open your eyes, I said!"

She raised her lids to reveal huge dark eyes that held not the slightest hint of intelligence. Tarquinius was excited by her docility. She was his; he owned her.

"I appreciate your cooperation tonight," he said. "You will be amply rewarded, as are all my favorites. But you must reserve the true prophecies for me. You understand that, don't you? Anything of real importance that the gods tell you, you are to divulge only to me. And in a little while I will need you to make certain prophecies for me."

She lay unresponsive. Seen from this close she was even younger than he had thought. How could that great hulking Horatrim be her son? The king's eyes strayed to her hips. They were full and rounded, with swelling pubes clearly visible beneath the soft fabric.

"Do the gods really speak through you?"

Tarquinius had never possessed a holy woman before. What divine visions might present themselves to her when the king of Rome entered her body? He was thrilled at the idea of being so close to the gods, entering a vessel they had so recently vacated. Perhaps a vestige of their godhood would have remained, a scrap he might claim for himself. Gently, with respect, he attempted to arouse her.

But she was as indifferent as a statue. He began to feel insulted. He was Tarquin the Superb; what right had she to ignore him? His anger and his lust grew together. When he could control them no longer, he caught the neck of her gown and ripped it open.

In one of the guest apartments, Lars Porsena was still wide awake. He was young and virile, but he had deliberately refused the king's offer of a woman for the night, just as he had been careful not to drink too much wine. In the morning there would be complicated negotiations with the king present. It was best to keep one's senses sharp when dealing with Romans.

In the meantime he was mentally preparing himself by going over the moves and countermoves to come. One must be prepared to be firm, yet flexible. He lay on his couch with his fingers laced behind his head, gazing at the ceiling and calculating just how much grain he was prepared to give in exchange for the goods his people wanted. The flickering light cast by the lamp beside his bed cast weird shadows on the walls around him.

Then he heard the scream.

Since even a *hia* could not be in two places at the same time, Pepan had chosen to stay with Vesi rather than with Horatrim. She was all but lost; whatever had possessed her was too old, too powerful for him to combat. All he could do was stay close to her and hope for an opportunity to help her.

The Rasne lord found the palace of the king of Rome as disappointing as the houses of his subjects. Pepan thought the royal residence resembled a glorified rabbit warren, with countless chambers and passageways tacked onto one another as need dictated. There was no coherence to the plan, merely a cancerous growth sprawling unchecked. *Perhaps Horatrim will improve the place,* he thought. There was a delicious irony in having a Rasne design the capital of the Romans.

While Vesi entertained the king's guests, Pepan watched. He was perfectly aware her mysterious mouthings did not originate with the girl he had known. She was being well-treated, however, which was his immediate concern. He could only hope that sooner or later he would find some way to free her from the black miasma enveloping her spirit. If the spirit of the girl Vesi still existed at all.

When Tarquinius Superbius took her body into his bed, Pepan was distressingly aware of his inability to prevent rape. And it would be rape; Vesi was incompetent to give her consent. Yet something in her recognized the impending violation—and screamed.

A scream carries on the night wind, and the senses of an embodied *siu* are far more sensitive than those of an ordinary human. Any cry of pain can draw a demon. To their kind, pain is food and drink.

"Hurry!" he ordered Justine. "We may be just in time!"

Lars Porsena was on his feet before the woman's scream stopped echoing through the halls of the palace. He raced in the direction of the scream. As he came around a corner he surprised a pair of guards who tried to intercept him, but he seized the spear from one and slammed its shaft against the temple of the other, knocking him unconscious. The first man hesitated, reluctant to fight the tall Etruscan nobleman alone. That moment's pause cost him dearly, for Lars Porsena hit him a blow on the jaw that laid him on the floor beside his companion. The Etruscan leaped over them and entered the king's private chamber.

Tarquinius looked up, enraged by the intrusion. "How dare you burst in here! Where are my guards?" Lurching to his feet, he started toward the door to summon them.

Lars Porsena moved to block his way, towering over the much smaller Tarquinius. "I heard a scream."

"Nothing to do with you," Tarquinius snarled.

Lars Porsena looked over the smaller man's head. The Etruscan seer lay stretched on the bed unmoving, her gown shredded around her.

"What are you doing to that woman?" he demanded to know.

"I already told you it has nothing to do with you. Now get out of here or Clusium can forget about ever doing any business with Rome."

Hot blood flamed the Etruscan's cheeks. "You can't threaten me!"

"I just did. Now get out."

On the bed, Vesi moaned.

Forgetting the king, Lars Porsena whirled around and went to her. "Are you all right?" he asked solicitously. "Has he hurt you? I'll make him pay for insulting one of. . ."

Tarquinius hit him over the back of the head with a bronze lamp.

Lars Porsena collapsed without a murmur.

Panting, Tarquinius stooped over the woman on the bed. The incident had shaken him. He was not accustomed to being thwarted, certainly not in his private chamber. Now he was determined that nothing should stop him. Taking hold of Vesi once more he roughly thrust her legs apart. He was not looking at her face. But then something in the way her body felt to his hands alerted him and he raised his head.

The expression in her eyes was the last thing Tarquinius saw before she tore him apart.

In the early years of her harlotry, Justine had been beautiful enough to command high prices and count some of Rome's most powerful names among her clients. On a number of occasions she had visited the royal palace, and even after so many years, its rooms and passageways remained clear in her mind.

At the gates she presented herself as a whore answering a royal summons. "And this," she said, indicating a figure swathed in robes, face hidden, "is my protector and bodyguard."

"With that body, you'll need one," leered the guard.

Her restored beauty was sufficient. Justine and Bur-Sin were swiftly passed through.

Once inside, she led the way to the king's apartments. Each time a guard challenged them she flashed a dazzling smile. "Tarquinius Superbius sent for me," she would say. The king's tastes in young women were well known, so no one questioned her.

When they reached the royal chamber she was astonished to find two guards lying unconscious outside the door. "Be careful," she started to warn Bur-Sin. Then she laughed. How foolish to warn a demon! With him close behind her, she entered the chamber.

The room was like an abattoir.

A tall man lay unconscious in the middle of the floor. On the bed a woman in a torn gown crouched in a pool of blood. Her hands were hooked into talons clutching gobbets of flesh. The light of madness burned in her eyes.

There was blood everywhere, spurted in long streaks up the walls, dappled across the ceiling, pooled on the tiles. Half on the bed and half on the floor sprawled a mutilated body, so badly disfigured that it took Justine several moments to recognize the king of Rome. She gave a moan of horror.

The *siu* hardly glanced at the corpse—or the woman. All his attention was fixed on the unconscious Etruscan. He bent over him and stroked his face with a lover's touch. "See how strong he is, how healthy! Dear child, this is a gift," Bur-Sin chuckled, "from the gods."

Pepan could feel the whirlpool of energies swiftly gathering around the embodied *siu*. He knew him now, knew his name and his history. This was Bur-Sin, architect in life, lover of the goddess Pythia in death. He was now somehow trapped in rotting human flesh, his very presence in the Earthworld an abomination. His current state of existence disturbed the delicate web of energies that linked the worlds, creating pools and vortices of discord.

All of Pepan's strength was necessary to keep from being sucked into one of the vortices. A low humming sound filled the room. The air grew cold, colder, freezing.

Justine hugged herself. Her lips were turning blue. "Let me out of here," she pleaded.

The woman on the bed whimpered. Then with an effort she got to her feet and began to stagger toward the door.

The demon rolled his eyes in her direction. His features were livid; with every movement of muscle, more skin pulled loose. Completing the transfer would require his total concentration, but even so he was briefly distracted by something he saw on the woman's face. Something familiar.

He had no time to think about it now. "Yes, go, Justine," he managed to say in a voice distorted by the collapse of his vocal cords. "Go to that shack of yours and take the woman with you. I will come for both of you soon. Soon."

"Where will you be?" asked Justine.

"I'll come to you presently. I have some work to do here first. Go!"

Justine caught Vesi by the wrist and fled.

THIRTY-THREE

The slaves who came to prepare their master for bed were alarmed to find the guards unconscious on the floor outside. They hurried into Tarquinius's chamber. What they saw sent them gibbering in terror.

Flavius, captain of the royal guard, arrived at the run, sword in hand and a company of men at his back. One look inside the chamber was enough to tell him the king had no further use for his services. His body had been torn apart. Flavius shrugged. He had always known that one day he would find Tarquinius slain.

His constant prayer had been not for the king's safety but that he himself would not be in the way when the assassination attempt was made. Obviously, the gods had answered that prayer. He must go to the temple when he had the opportunity and offer a sacrifice of thanksgiving.

At the foot of the bed was a small heap of decomposed meat, as if someone had thrown a meal on the floor and left it there to rot. Flavius stepped over it, idly wondering what it was doing in the king's bedchamber.

Then he crouched down beside the nobleman from Clusium. From the general condition of the chamber, he expected to find Lars Porsena dead. But the Etruscan was still alive, although he appeared dazed and groggy. Flavius helped him to his feet. "What happened here?" he demanded.

Lars Porsena slowly opened his eyes. "We were talking. Someone burst in. . . " His pupils rolled back in his head, showing only the whites before his eyelids drifted down again and he fell silent.

Flavius's men had by this time restored the guards in the hall outside to consciousness and marched them into the room. They looked at the dead king and then at Lars Porsena with expressions of shock and horror; but before either could speak, the Etruscan said, "The king was attacked by a band of assassins who must have sneaked into the palace. The two guards stationed at the doorway fought valiantly but were unable to overcome them. They should be commended; I have never seen anything so brave. If they were mine, I would make them both officers."

His eyes were still closed.

The guards kept their mouths similarly closed. The word of an Etruscan nobleman would be believed before the testimony of two lowly plebeian guards. Better to be lauded as heroes than condemned for failing to save the king.

"What of you, Lord Porsena?" asked Flavius. "How did you manage to survive?"

"I defended your king to the best of my ability," the other replied. Then he opened his eyes and looked down at his right arm. He extended it for Flavius's inspection. The arm was badly lacerated and a purple bruise was appearing from his temple to his jaw. "I am afraid my best was not good enough, although I would gladly have given my life for Tarquinius. He was one of us, you know, a man of Etrurian blood," Lars Porsena added with convincing sincerity.

Flavius was examining his wounds. The longer the captain looked at them, the more horrific they became. "Your defense of Tarquinius does you credit," he said. "Do you know what became of the assassins?"

Lars Porsena shook his head. "Sadly, I do not. I was struck a blow on the side of the head and everything went black. The next thing I knew you were helping me to my feet. Will you allow me to assist in searching for them? If I get my hands on them, I will do to them what they did to . . . to. . . " He indicated the mangled body of Tarquinius with a nod, obviously too emotional to speak further.

Pepan was aghast at the turn of events. Watching helplessly from the Otherworld, he had observed the serpentine shadow wrapped around Vesi's spirit. He had seen the ancient evil peering through the empty eyes of Repana's daughter and knew it for what it was.

He wanted to warn Horatrim, but his first duty under the circumstances was to Vesi. Abandoning the gore-spattered chamber, he followed the fleeing women. He was aware that the strength to do the deed had not come from Vesi herself. The girl he had known would never have been capable of such horror.

She was different now. Possessed. But not totally lost. Not yet. Faintly, very faintly, wind-blown and weakened yet persistent in its grip on life, came the thread of sound that identified Vesi's *hia*.

In the Otherworld Pepan also could hear the tonal discord surrounding the beautiful young woman called Justine. She was not possessed but she had been warped in some way; her song was distorted and off-key. Having Vesi in her custody was worrying. Pepan didn't sense any malice in the woman, however . . . only greed and a deep sadness.

Pepan hovered close to them as they made their way through the warren of corridors. Justine knew the palace well; she managed to avoid each point at which guards were stationed and in time led her charge safely through a side entrance and out into the night.

No one in the palace was paying much attention to women anyway. The guards were concentrating on finding a band of assassins. Foremost among the searchers was the wounded Lars Porsena, who valiantly ignored his injuries as he ran up one corridor and down another, indifferent to danger, inspiring the men who followed him.

Streaks of angry red light appeared in the eastern sky before Flavius reluctantly conceded the murderers had escaped them. "We should summon the Senate immediately," he said.

"What will happen now?" asked Lars Porsena. The prince from Clusium looked very tired, with dark circles under his eyes. Yet those same eyes were fever bright.

The captain shrugged. "It will be up to them to decide what to do next. It's not the first time we've had an assassination, nor I fear will it be the last. Being king of Rome is a lifetime occupation, but sometimes that means having a rather short life." He stopped, and looked intently at the wounded prince. "Of course, certain kings—those who inspire the respect of the military—tend to live a little longer."

By the time Justine and Vesi reached the harlot's shack, the Etruscan woman's energy was exhausted. In spite of the fact that the slain man's blood was drying to a stiff paste on her hands and clothing, Vesi tumbled onto the rags piled in the corner and was asleep at once.

Justine stood looking down at her for a time, wondering what Bur-Sin wanted with her. She was not attractive by Roman standards; just mute and god-touched. Justine's own brother, in their distant childhood, had been god-touched. He howled at the moon every month with white froth bubbling on his lips. One morning she had awakened to learn that their father—or the man they assumed to be their father—had given him to the Tiber.

Justine blew out the lamp and stretched herself beside Vesi. Strange, she mused, she had not thought of her brother in a long time. Just then a sudden, sickening chill washed over her. The ancients believed the sensation presaged death. In the gloom, her teeth flashed in a grim smile. She was not going to die. Not now. Not for a long time. She had a demon on her side.

Pepan waited nearby until Justine feel into a troubled sleep; then he turned and fled back toward the palace.

Horatrim awoke with a start. At first he did not know where he was. Then he was not sure who he was. Slowly, memory came dribbling back. He was in Rome. And he was no longer Horatrim. He was Horatius Cocles. Propertius's adopted son.

And he was a man. Last night Livia had kissed him. The memory was sudden and vivid. The man in him knew there had been the promise of more . . . the boy in him was unsure what the promise entailed.

The pale lemon light of an early Roman morning was beaming through the one small window. The other "sons" with whom he shared the room were already up and gone. Yawning, Horatius rose from his pallet. He stood tall, stretched, yawned again. Where was everyone?

He jangled the string of silver bells that hung by the door, but no slave came running to dress him. After waiting for a time, Horatius began to laugh at himself. The sound was strangely hollow in the quiet room. "I've dressed myself all my life," he remarked aloud. "I can do it now."

He fumbled awkwardly with the folds of the toga, trying to achieve a fashionable effect, then gave up and simply twisted the cloth around his tunic as best he could. He gave the sandals a long look, then decided to leave them for later. After a life spent barefoot it would take a while to get used to having his feet encased in leather.

Next he splashed his face with water from a pottery bowl on a nearby stand. Lifting the bronze razor Propertius had given him as a gift, the young man looked at his reflection in the mirror beside the bowl and decided that he really should practice scraping the hair from his face. Roman men did not have facial hair, unlike the Teumetians, who prized it as a sign of virility.

"Horatius," he said, practicing the name as he scraped the blade across his cheekbone.

Horatrim.

His old name echoed in his head.

"Horatius."

Horatrim.

The sound was louder, clearer.

He squinted into the mirror. His image was curiously blurred. Bending his arm, he scrubbed the polished silver with the sleeve of his toga. "That's better." He raised the razor again and looked into the mirror.

A face gazed back at him—but not his face.

Horatrim, your mother needs you.

The razor slipped and cut a deep gash in his cheek. He brushed at the wound, then ran his bloody fingertips over the silver, leaving a crimson streak.

The face in the mirror solidified.

Your mother needs you.

"But my mother is safe in the royal palace!"

She is no longer there, and she is far from safe.

"Where is she then? And who are you?"

Vesi was taken from the palace during the night. She is in grave danger.

"Who are you?" Horatius repeated, his voice rising. "Are you one of the gods?"

Alas, I am no god. Nor do I have a physical body with which to save hers. That is why I need you to . . .

"But I can see your face!"

You see my memory of my face. I am—I was Pepan—and now I am what you would call a ghost, I suppose. A spirit without flesh. Throughout your life I have watched over you out of love for your grandmother.

Suddenly Horatius became aware of noise outside; people were shouting to one another in the street beyond the window, and there were distant horns blowing.

"My grandmother? Repana? You knew her?"

I knew them both. Listen to me, Horatrim. You must go to your mother and make her safe.

The razor dropped forgotten from Horatius's fingers. As soon as he turned his back on the mirror Pepan could no longer appear to him. He hovered at the young man's right shoulder; invisible, calling but unheard.

Horatius ran from the room as the noise outside grew louder.

In the Otherworld Pepan was almost overwhelmed by the brazen blare of Rome's voice.

Propertius's house, Horatius quickly discovered, was empty. Even the servants were gone. He opened the front door to find the street crowded with people milling about and calling questions to one another.

"Something terrible has happened; I just know it," a woman was saying anxiously. "I heard an alarm just now."

Horatius caught hold of her shoulder and turned her to face him. "What alarm?"

"Horns blowing at the palace."

Horatius began to run. The face in the mirror had told him that Vesi was in danger . . . and now an alarm was sounding from the palace. The two events could not be unconnected.

Where was Propertius? He must find the Roman. Propertius would know what to do. Elbowing people aside, Horatius pounded off down the hill, intent on reaching the palace, unsure what he would do when he got there.

Then he turned a corner and ran headlong into someone he knew.

Khebet the Aegyptian staggered under the impact.

Horatius caught the man before he could fall. "Have you seen Propertius?"

"I have not," Khebet replied, rubbing his bruised chest. "I was looking for Severus myself. He was summoned from his house abruptly; I thought he might have come up here to his brother."

"There's no one in Propertius's house, but people are saying there's some sort of trouble at the palace. I'm going there now. My mother is . . . but she may not be . . . I must find her!" Horatius cried, increasingly frantic.

Khebet was practiced at remaining calm when others were emotional. Observing that a slash across Horatius's cheek was oozing blood, he touched the wound with his long, slender fingers.

When Khebet, priest of Anubis, made contact with Horatius's blood, his third eye opened.

The Jackal God always responded to blood.

Never before, however, had mystical vision come as vividly. Khebet found himself staring at a veritable horde of beings, male and female, old and young, clustered so tightly around the young man that their forms overlapped into an ever-changing, fluid shadow. They had no bodies, merely the memory of flesh.

Khebet knew he was looking at the naked *ka,* the soul. Scores of souls, hundreds of souls, generations of souls, every one of them interlocked with the spirit of Horatius. Beside the young man, standing by his right hand, was a powerful *hia* who wore the flickering form of a Rasne lord.

For once even the imperturbable Aegyptian was astonished.

But his long years of training in the temples along the

Nile stood him in good stead. He appreciated the w[illegible]der of what he was seeing and understood that he was in the presence of a very special human being.

Recovering his poise, he put a hand on Horatius's shoulder. "Thou art blessed," he said in the secret and formal language of the temple, an archaic tongue long-forgotten by ordinary Aegyptians. "Doubly blessed," he added, looking at the lordly shadow beside Horatrim.

His astonishment returned, Horatius replied in the same language, "I do not feel blessed, Khebet. I am so worried about my mother and. . . " he broke off abruptly. Moving past the Aegyptian, his eyes had fixed on a large metal ewer standing on the counter of a streetside shop. Reflected in the polished metal of the ewer, Horatius saw the face that had stared at him out of the mirror. When the Aegyptian turned to follow his gaze, three faces were momentarily reflected in the metal.

"Do you see that?" Horatius whispered.

"I do."

"Then it is real?"

"Very real."

Horatrim pointed toward the third face. "Just a little while ago he told me my mother was in danger, and that I should go to her."

Khebet nodded. "Believe him."

"Will you help me, Khebet?"

With grave courtesy, the Aegyptian bowed. "I would consider it a great honor," he replied.

THIRTY-FOUR

As members of the Senate, Propertius and Severus were among the first to be informed of the king's murder. They were wakened in the dawn by messengers who spoke in hushed whispers. Hastily throwing on their clothes, the two men came at the run from their separate houses and arrived almost simultaneously at the palace.

"Stop blowing those cursed horns!" Propertius shouted to the guards on the palace wall.

Unless the horns were silenced, all Rome would soon converge on the palace, he knew. Once news of Tarquinius's assassination was public knowledge, vast crowds would besiege the gates, either to declare their undying loyalty to the dead king or to learn who was going to replace him, more often the latter. Every foreigner in Rome would be trying to arrange for passage home at a time of social upheaval. Army officers would come pouring into the city, hopeful of improving their individual power bases. In the midst of all this, enterprising vendors would be hawking sausages and dates anc ened bread baked in the shapes of dogs, and taking w gers as to the name of the next king.

Pandemonium. There might well be riots—and riots were bad for business.

Any sensible, reasoned plan of action would be rendered impossible.

"Stop those horns, I said!" Propertius screamed at the guards.

The strident horns fell silent, but the air was still torn. Tarquinius's wife and concubines were in full mourning; their shrieks and wails echoed from the palace. Meanwhile companies of grim-faced warriors continued to search the grounds, although no one really believed the assassins were still inside.

"A dark day," Propertius panted to his brother by way of greeting.

"It is for a fact." Severus wiped sweat from his brow. "Have you ever noticed that just when you think you have everything going right, it all goes wrong?"

The trader nodded. "Hubris."

"Eh?"

"The Hellenes have a word for everything, you know. *Hubris* means never count your accomplishments or you tempt the gods."

"I thought you didn't believe in the gods."

"Things change," retorted Propertius. "Do you recall what the seer said at my banquet the other night?"

"Aaah . . . not precisely, no."

"She said, 'When the moon hangs by its horns, a trader will pass through the gate and a king will dance with the black goat.' Last night there was a crescent moon. I'm a trader, and I'm about to pass through the palace gate. And in Etruria a black goat is a symbol of death. I believe the gods spoke through that woman, Severus. Her prophecy is already . . . Ho, Antoninus!" he broke off to call to a passing warrior. "You certainly got here fast!"

n strode briskly toward Propertius.
city anyway to make a report to the
ite bizarre happened at the northern
ago, and we thought he should know
n't be telling him anything now."

"Not u... ou care to follow him across the Styx. Have you been inside yet? Do you know what's happening?"

"The captain of the guard is questioning Lars Porsena right now."

Propertius raised his eyebrows. "The prince from Clusium? Why, is he a suspect?"

"Far from it. He tried to fight off the assassins and was badly injured in the attempt, so he's quite the hero now. Flavius is hoping he can identify the murderers."

Severus spoke up. "They must be taken alive. It will be up to the new king to execute them once they are captured."

Propertius was thinking fast. "The new king indeed. The Senate will want to choose a nominee before news of the murder is made public, so we must ensure that not a word of what has actually happened gets out, at least for the present. A panic is the last thing we need. We will have to warn the servants and swear the guards to secrecy. Quiet those caterwauling women inside. Keep out everyone who does not have legitimate business in the palace. We can't afford to deny all entry though; that would look suspicious. Antoninus, will you pass us through the gates?"

"I'll take you in myself; but I warn you, the place is in chaos."

"I'm a trader; I'm used to chaos. Come, Severus. There is much to do."

Antoninus conducted the brothers into the palace. However he seemed less interested in talking about the assassination than in describing some peculiar incident on the frontier. ". . . and hacked off what he thought was a leg," he was saying, "but it proved to be a snake. Or part of a snake. It actually crushed the wrist of one of my men and. . . "

They passed a small antechamber just as Flavius, captain of the palace guard, came out. Over his shoulder they could see Lars Porsena inside. At the door Flavius turned and bowed low to the prince of Clusium. Very low indeed, Propertius noted.

Taking Antoninus by the elbow, he said in an undertone, "Would you mind arranging it so that we have a few moments alone with Lars Porsena? Just to discuss a bit of trading business. I will, ah, make it worth your while the next time I cross the northern frontier."

Antoninus promptly engaged Flavius in animated conversation and steered him off down the corridor. As soon as they were gone, Propertius beckoned to Severus to follow him then entered the chamber. "I understand you're the hero of the day," he greeted the Etruscan.

Lars Porsena looked at him blankly.

"I'm your old friend, Propertius! We've done business together. I bought a quantity of fine silver jewelry from your craftsmen just last summer. Paid above the going rate for it, in fact. Under the table, of course."

Something shifted behind Lars Porsena's eyes. "You must forgive me; I took a blow to the head last night. Now I remember you, Propertius. A man of my own stripe."

The Roman took this as a compliment. The prince was, he thought, looking unwell, with sunken eyes and a faintly greenish cast to his skin. "If Flavius has finished questioning you, Lars Porsena, have you time for a word or two with us?"

"I already told Flavius what I know."

Propertius gave an impatient wave of his hand. "I'm sure you did, and they will or will not catch the assassins and we'll have a grand trial and a splendid execution and that's the end of that. It really doesn't matter. What is important is the future."

"Forgive me again, but I do not understand what you mean."

"It is the responsibility of the Senate to nominate a new king as soon as we can agree on one. But that may take time. In the manner of all politicians, we're more inclined to disagree. Furthermore, there are very few at the moment whom we would consider suitable candidates. But you, as a hero, a man who like Tarquinius can claim the most ancient noble blood . . . you are well-qualified to be king, Lars Porsena."

Severus looked at his brother with awe as he realized what was coming next. The plan was extraordinarily audacious, a plan worthy of Propertius in his youth, when his boldness and cunning had made his fortune.

"I don't think we could nominate you right now because you're not well enough known."

"You are suggesting making me king! But I was not born in Rome," Lars Porsena protested.

Propertius shrugged. "A minor handicap. Such inconveniences can always be overcome if one is determined. If we can stall the deliberations for long enough, Severus and I may be able to bring the other senators around to our way of thinking in time. I trust you would not be averse to rewarding us for acting on your behalf?"

In the eyes of Lars Porsena laughter sparkled, as if at some dark and secret joke. "Perhaps I have a better idea," he said. "We can discuss the repayment of obligations later."

By the time Horatius and Khebet reached the palace, there was a crowd at the gates being held back by noncommittal guards. No one knew what disaster had occasioned the sound of the brazen horns, but every imaginable rumor was being floated. Some said the king was ill; others claimed there had been a military revolt. As the people grew increasingly frustrated in their efforts to gain information, they were turning sullen.

The Aegyptian sensed danger in the air. Though his

face remained impassive he tensed inwardly, wanting to turn back. "If your mother may no longer be in the palace," he remarked to Horatius, "why did you want to come here?"

"Because this is the last place she was." His eye fell on a familiar face in the crowd. "There's Quintus!" Horatius pushed his way through the throng to his new brother. "Is Propertius here?"

Quintus turned a sullen face in his direction. "You mean *my* father? He's inside with Uncle Severus. Why?"

"I need his help."

Quintus said smugly, "They'll never let you go in to him. No one's being allowed inside but senators and a few foreign officials. Important people," he added. "And in spite of my father's recent action, you are simply not important."

Horatius drew himself up to his full height. "Is that a fact?"

Within a matter of minutes he and Khebet were inside the palace.

The Aegyptian remarked, "I have never been introduced to palace guards as an ambassador before. And as for calling yourself the son of a member of the Senate . . . !"

"I am. Now."

"That may be, but it only worked because the courtiers are so distracted. Something is seriously wrong here. What do you want to do first, look for Propertius?"

"First, I want to find out where my mother was kept. Perhaps I can pick up her trail."

"This is no forest; there are no tracks to follow."

Horatius replied incomprehensibly, "Wulv taught me how to read all sorts of spoor."

"Wulv?"

The young man did not answer but set off down the nearest corridor, sniffing the air. Khebet hurried along in his wake. When they were challenged by a guard, Horatius cried, "Make way for the Aegyptian ambassador!"

The guard bowed as the imposing Aegyptian swept past in a cloud of almond perfume.

"Do you know where we're going?" Khebet asked in a low voice.

"No, but I have noticed that all of these Roman houses and palaces are built to a similar design. I'm hoping that the king's chambers will be down. . . " Suddenly he skidded to a halt. "In there; she was in there!" Darting through a doorway, he entered a spacious chamber. This opened into one still larger, where a bed stood on a dais enshrouded with badly torn draperies. Khebet followed, slipping one hand up the sleeve of his other arm. In a moment more there was a knife in his hand.

The bedchamber reeked of blood. The cloying stench hung heavy on the air, a sweetish-rotten odor that made Horatius gag. But after one shocked inhalation, he relaxed. "That isn't my mother's blood," he said. "Her scent is still here though. And something else, an awful stink. . . "

The Aegyptian's nostrils dilated. "The smell of a demon," Khebet said hoarsely. One step at a time, fearful of what he might see, he approached the ruined bed and drew the curtains aside. The linen sheets were soaked with clotted gore. On the floor beside the bed was a veritable lake of blood.

For a long moment Khebet stared down without speaking. Then he crouched beside the pool and used the tip of his knife to crack the hardening surface of the blood. His lips began to shape an incantation. "Accept this gift, great Anubis. Not spilled in your name, but freely given to you. In return, I ask for the revelation of the blood."

The surface of the blood, already darkened by coagulation, turned black as jet.

Khebet leaned closer as a vision began to form. Shaping itself from the essence of lost life, an image appeared of a woman on the bed with a man bending over her. Then another man rushed into the room and a scuffle ensued. Fascinated, the Aegyptian watched the recurrence of deeds whose sinister vibrations still resonated within the chamber. Once he gave a gasp of alarm.

"What is it?" asked Horatius, peering over his shoulder. "What are you looking at?"

But the blood revealed its secrets only to the priest of Anubis. Horatius saw nothing more than a tar-colored puddle. Khebet, however, made a choking sound and waved his hands as if warding off some invisible horror. The smell that he had identified as the stink of a demon grew stronger in the room. The surface of the blood began to bubble. "Oh, wretched being," Khebet moaned, "thou art evil, evil!"

Suddenly Horatius had a sense of immense vistas just beyond his gaze. A singing thundered through his bones. Unconsciously using the Aegyptian tongue, he said, "What are you seeing, Khebet? You have to tell me; I command you!" No longer was he a child asking questions. Power resonated through him, the imperious force of a hundred chieftains.

Even a priest of Anubis could not resist. Bowing his head, Khebet murmured a different incantation and swept his hands in circles over the boiling pool. Its black surface quieted slowly. Then, just as slowly, gleamed silver.

"Look," said the Aegyptian as he moved aside to make room for Horatius. "This is the blood lore, the tale of life carried in the red liquid of life. See the past through the generosity of Anubis."

THIRTY-FIVE

The king's death would have far-reaching ramifications for Rome's trading partners and her military alliances. The most immediate effect, however, would be upon the Romans themselves. Although politically conservative, they were emotionally volatile. Without someone strong in charge, they could stampede like cattle in a thunderstorm. The assassination of Tarquinius was tantamount to a major thunderstorm.

The members of the Senate who gathered on the morning following the king's death were aware of the precariousness of the situation. There was always the possibility that the assassination had been carried out by some ambitious *patrician* outside their own circle, who would then attempt to capture the allegiance of the Roman military. It had happened before. If successful, he could be declared king by popular acclamation. And if he was not one of their own, he might abolish the Senate altogether. That too had been threatened before. The ultimate power rested with the king.

As soon as all the senators had arrived at the palace, an urgent meeting was convened. Propertius and Severus were last to enter the large chamber—walking on either side of Lars Porsena. His presence excited a buzz of conversation. They went to the head of the room and stood facing their colleagues. While they waited for conversation to die down, Lars Porsena said to the brothers in a low voice, "Remember our deal. You help me, then I help you."

"Agreed," Propertius murmured.

"Absolutely," echoed Severus. "We have your word on this?"

"You have my word. And you know how much I value it." Lars Porsena smiled.

The room fell silent.

Lifting his arms, Propertius announced, "Today we stand at a crossroads. We can undertake to nominate a new king immediately, knowing that suitable men of sufficiently noble blood are in short supply at present. The best are too old, too young, or simply unwilling to take on the responsibilities and hazards of the office.

"Or we can consider something else."

His fellow senators stared at him dumbfounded. "But Rome must have a king," someone said.

Severus pointed out, "The Hellenes have no king."

"Oh, well, the Hellenes," came the dismissive reply. Roman contempt for the Greeks was well known.

"I am not suggesting we adopt a democracy," Propertius went on, his mouth shaping the word with disgust. "However kingship offers many opportunities for abuses. I, as much as any of you, prospered under the reign of Tarquinius Superbius, but ultimately he behaved in a way that could only bring discredit to Rome."

Turning to Lars Porsena, he said, "Please tell us what happened last night. What really happened."

The prince from Clusium cleared his throat. "I did not wish to make this public out of respect for the kingship itself," he said, "but my friend Propertius has persuaded me to do so. The statement I originally made concerning the king's death was not accurate."

A low murmur ran around the chamber, like surf beating on a distant shore.

"I am Etruscan, as was Tarquinius. As indeed was the prophetess he recently brought into the palace. Last night, while relaxing in my chamber, I heard a woman scream. I ran to the king's chambers only to find him raping the seer. Brutally raping a holy woman!

"I lost my head and attacked him. I have no excuse other than my revulsion at what he was doing. I attacked my fellow Etruscan to prevent him completing an act that would have brought undying shame upon his name, his race, and the kingship of Rome. But even as I was dragging him off her helpless body, the gods of Etruria intervened.

"You have been shown the body, and many of you remarked that nothing human could have wrought such terrible damage upon it. You were right, wise Senators.

"It was the *Ais* who tore Tarquinius to pieces. I was helpless to stop them, though I tried and was wounded in the attempt. Who can prevent the gods doing anything? Thereafter I could only watch in horror as they delivered their terrible punishment.

"When it was over, I did what I could to make it look like an outside assassination. Not out of fear for myself, but to keep from having to reveal the king's wickedness. I did not want the proud line of the Tarquins to suffer humiliation."

Lars Porsena's speech was met with a stunned silence. After a suitable time, Propertius said humbly, "We are very much in your debt, Lars Porsena. If the king's depraved attack upon a holy woman became public knowledge, it would severely undermine governmental authority."

"Governmental authority is already undermined," Lars Porsena replied. "The king of Rome has insulted the gods. The gods know even if the people don't. And now that the gods have turned their eyes to Rome . . . we must be very careful.. . . "

Severus was nodding agreement. "Following such an event, whoever replaces Tarquinius must be absolutely above reproach," he told the other senators. "It could take months, even years to find such a man. To allow us adequate time, the prince of Clusium has offered an alternate suggestion that we feel has great merit."

"For the immediate future, Rome might be better off with a division of power," explained Lars Porsena. "While waiting for the right king to manifest himself, appoint two men from your own ranks as joint interim governors. Surely no one is better equipped to rule Rome than its senators."

The *patricians* in the chamber responded with flattered smiles. But one toward the rear called out, "What about Tarquinius? He's dead, no matter how it happened. We have to deal with that issue first."

Propertius said, "Under the circumstances, the less that becomes known about this shameful affair the better. Publicizing the king's death would serve no constructive purpose. I suggest we announce that, as a result of unspecified abuses of power, Tarquinius has been expelled from Rome by a unanimous vote of the Senate. The people will see that we have acted in their best interests and their trust in us will be enhanced."

The prince of Clusium nodded and bowed his head. An almost palpable tension radiated from him, but those who noticed put it down to simple nervousness, the discomfort of a warrior mired in a puddle of politicians.

Severus clapped a hand on the prince's shoulder to lend him support. A spark leaped from Lars Porsena's skin, nipping the builder's fingers sharply enough to draw blood. At the same time the prince shot a sidelong glance at Severus, who blinked in surprise.

The light in the chamber briefly reflected in his eyes, turning them a vivid green. Lars Porsena smiled; the color faded.

The prince bowed his head and folded his arms across his chest, holding his body tightly. An invisible wave emanated from him, a tide that rippled across the room in concentric waves. Its greatest influence was felt by those closest to him at the front of the room, the oldest and most respected members of the Senate.

"What we have heard makes sense," a venerable, silver-haired *patrician* said thoughtfully. "You know that I have always advocated such a path." The other senators looked at him in astonishment. They had never heard him say any such thing. "Perhaps it is time the Senate took control of Rome. I move we appoint two consuls to serve as joint governors."

Another suggested, "Why not elect consuls annually until we find a new king? That way they won't have a lifetime lock on power."

"And if we give them the right to veto each other's actions," said the man to his left, "their decisions will have to be taken in concert."

But one lone senator at the farthest edge of the room remained dubious. "We would have to be certain the two we chose could work together. We must not rush into anything, my friends. Calm deliberation is required here. Reasoned debate. Perhaps we should name a committee to look into the matter further and draw up a list of possible candidates."

A suddenly impatient expression flickered across the face of Lars Porsena. Lifting his head, he fixed his coldly burning eyes on the silver-haired senator who had spoken first. After a moment the man exclaimed, "There is no time for committees and lists. But you are right, we need two men who can work well together; I nominate Propertius Cocles and his brother, Severus, to be consuls of Rome. And we'll vote on them here and now!"

THIRTY-SIX

Horatius was badly shaken. The scene Khebet showed him in the pool of blood was horrific beyond his imaginings. As the two men stared at the shocking vision, Khebet said in a surprised voice, "I recognize that man, Horatius. You saw him in the street, remember? Severus identified him as an Etruscan prince called Lars Porsena."

"I think I remember him," Horatius said vaguely, "but he is nothing to me. We just saw my mother dragged away, perhaps to some awful fate. That's all that matters. Come on, we have to find her!" He bolted for the door.

With the greatest reluctance, Khebet followed him. The priest's horoscope for this moon had promised revelations and excitement and the prospect had tempted him. Now he was beginning to wish he had stayed in Aegypt, where he knew how to avoid danger to his person.

Throughout his career Khebet had stood apart from every murderous court intrigue and repeatedly shifted allegiances within the jealous ranks of the priesthood to be certain he was on the safe side. Let others suffer the assassin's dagger or the poisoned cup.

Fear of death was not something an Aegyptian priest could admit. His people considered death the brilliant climax of life, the blazing sun following life's pallid moon, and spent fortunes to prepare for the Afterlife. Yet the idea of dying terrified Khebet. His real reason for joining the priesthood of Anubis had been hope that the god of death might relent for one of his own priests.

He had promised to help Horatius and so he would. For the moment, pride was as strong in him as fear.

Horatius ran straight for the palace gates. Khebet pounded along at his heels. When a guard challenged them with a leveled spear, Khebet summoned enough priestly authority into his voice to shout, "Urgent business! Aegyptian ambassador!"

The disconcerted guard stepped back and the two men ran out into the chaotic streets of Rome.

They did not go alone. Pepan, the invisible companion, hovered close to Horatius as he had done since early that morning. The Lord of the Rasne was even more desperate than Vesi's son. He had a better idea of what was at stake. *Hurry!* he kept urging, although Horatius could not hear him. *Hurry!*

Whenever they passed some reflective surface there would be a brief glimpse of an aristocratic face with an aquiline nose and a beard composed of two long, corkscrew curls, a face whose anxious gaze was fixed on Horatius. The young man was too distracted to notice. But the observant Aegyptian saw the image clearly, just as he had seen the shades that were joined with Horatius's spirit.

* * *

The skills Wulv had taught the boy Horatrim proved invaluable. Horatius was not far from the palace before he caught a whiff of her scent, that particular combination of skin and hair that would always mean Vesi to him. For a time he was able to follow the trail through the narrow, crowded streets, but then he lost it again. The smells of Rome coming awake on what promised to be a hot morning overwhelmed the scent of one woman. Horatius cast back and forth like a hunting dog, desperate to pick it up once more.

Fate seemed to be conspiring against him. A cartful of fish blocked an exceptionally narrow street; a crowd of children playing a ball game ran into Horatius and Khebet full tilt, then swirled around them, shouting and laughing, hindering their progress.

As he accompanied them, Pepan could hear the sibilant hiss that had replaced Vesi's identifying music. Sometimes it seemed to be getting closer, then again it faded when Horatius took a wrong turn. Pepan knew exactly where Vesi was, but the knowledge did him no good. Try as he might he could not transmit it to Horatius.

Then he became aware of another being hurrying toward Vesi. Mortals on the streets of Rome that morning noticed only a tall Etruscan prince emerging from the palace and setting out across the city. They gave way before him out of respect for his size . . . and the air of purpose and menace he exuded.

But seen from the Otherworld, there was no mistaking the *siu* that now occupied the prince's body. Bur-Sin reveled in the strong, virile flesh. This body, he promised himself, he would keep and enjoy for a long time.

Just as Horatius found Vesi's trail again, his nostrils were assailed by an appalling stench. He recoiled in disgust. Khebet cried, "I smell a demon!" But in the crowded, narrow streets they caught no glimpse of Lars Porsena.

The smell evaporated or was drowned in a hundred other odors.

Horatius resumed the search, instinct and the unseen urging of his invisible companion drawing him on until they eventually came to the edge of the fetid waste ground below the Capitoline Hill. Suddenly Horatius stiffened and threw up his head. With a broad grin he broke into a run. "Thank the *Ais,* I've found her, Khebet!" he called over his shoulder. He was sprinting toward a shack at the foot of the Palatine Hill on the far side of the waste ground.

Before he had covered half the distance he was attacked.

They came out of the heaps of refuse, and they came in their hundreds. An army of huge black rats swarmed toward Horatius as if guided by a single mind. The first few to reach him hurled themselves at his bare feet and ankles and began to gnaw furiously.

Horatius gave a violent kick but only succeeded in casting off two or three while still more ran up his other leg. Razor-sharp teeth bit deep into his upper thigh. A questing head rummaged beneath his toga, seeking his genitals.

Horatius screamed in defiance. Springing high into the air and simultaneously pummeling them with his fists, he at last dislodged his attackers and leaped clear of them—but only temporarily. Within a heartbeat they were on him again.

Meanwhile Khebet, badly frightened, ran back to the edge of the waste ground. The rats paid no attention to him. Their fury was concentrated on Horatius.

The young man fought with extraordinary agility,

moving, moving, always in constant motion, knowing that if he stood still he would die. He used two broken lengths of wood to strike at the rats that came too close. Horatius leaped across a fetid pool. The rats in his wake poured into it, those behind landing atop those already in the water, pushing them down, until the pool was thick with bodies. Still the vermin came.

Horatius was tiring.

Khebet found it hard to believe that any human could battle so many rats at one time and stay on his feet. Summoning all the courage he could muster—and furious with himself for being in this situation in the first place—the Aegyptian looked around for a weapon. There was nothing but broken planks and bits of stone. He seized the nearest piece of timber and tried to make himself go to Horatius's aid . . .

. . . as a second army appeared on the scene.

This one was composed of thousands of warriors in armor, black, jointed armor. Individually each was the length of a man's forearm; together they formed a dark sea of chitinous terror. They waved audibly clashing pincers while their curving tails dripped poison.

"Scorpions!" Khebet froze where he stood. Although normally scorpions were solitary individuals, these were acting in concert. What malign force controlled them the Aegyptian could not say, but it was obvious they had a single, deadly purpose.

When the rats saw the scorpions they ceased their attack on Horatius. They gathered around him in a semicircle—and waited. The scorpions hurried toward them. Rat and scorpion bracketed the young man between them. Inexorably, they began to close on him.

Khebet shouted an unnecessary warning; Horatius was fully aware of the danger. He dodged to one side toward a perceived opening, but the rats were even faster than he. They filled the hole with their bodies and kept coming.

Horatius turned in the other direction, but the scorpions wheeled and blocked the opening. Then, when they were almost close enough to touch him, they inexplicably halted.

He took a tentative step. They reared up and menaced him with clashing pincers and he stopped.

The rats swiftly moved in behind him.

He was completely encircled with vermin now. Their ranks had grown so deep that even the most spectacular leap on his part could not clear them. He turned all the way around, slowly, looking for the tiniest avenue of escape.

There was none.

The rats watched, eyes fixed and unblinking. He noticed that their eyes were green—but did rats not usually have red eyes? When he turned to look at the black carpet of scorpions, he saw that they too were sheened with a greenish hue.

Now that they had him trapped, Horatius expected them to attack from every direction. But they did not move.

He cast a frantic look toward Khebet. "Help me! I have to get to my mother, don't you understand?"

"Yes, yes, of course. I understand *now,*" the Aegyptian added. He did not know the reason, but he recognized the magic. There was only one way to fight magic.

Throwing back his head and lifting his arms toward the sky, the priest of Anubis began to chant.

"Great Anubis, Jackal Lord, god of the dead, hunter of souls, devourer of *kas*! Hear me!"

Moments ago the sun was high in a cloudless sky, but suddenly black clouds came boiling out of the south. Across the waste ground a warm wind began to blow sharp particles of sand that stung Horatius's skin like a million tiny insects. But there was no desert close to the city.

The wind blew harder, hotter. Howled out of a black sky.

The earth rumbled beneath Horatius's feet. A quiver ran through the hills of Rome, a shaking of the earth that grew steadily stronger. Carried but faintly on the howling wind came the terrifying ululation of a hunting dog.

A jackal.

Within the tombs on the Palatine hillside, something stirred.

Something awoke.

One by one, the heavy stone doors of the tombs were pushed open from the inside. Out into the day shambled a parade of decaying forms, bodies phosphorescent with decomposition. Bodies long since vacated by their spirits, but obedient to the command of the god of the dead. Many were so rotted they had no discernible gender. Some were child-size; others still bore remnants of white hair clinging to their emerging skulls.

Step by awful step they came down the slope.

THIRTY-SEVEN

The rats were the first to notice. They lifted their heads and sniffed the air curiously, then began an excited chattering among themselves. A moment later the scorpions responded, turning in unnatural unison to see what was happening.

Following their movement, Horatius looked in the same direction. At first his mind could not comprehend what his eyes were reporting. Scores of dead and rotting bodies were making their way down the hillside toward him. They could not be described as walking, for many no longer had feet to walk upon. Yet they were capable of a form of locomotion. Staggering, sliding, dragging themselves as best they could, they set out across the waste ground toward Khebet. The smell of death went with them, wafted on a hot wind.

The Aegyptian never stopped chanting. "Great is Anubis, god of the dead! Eater of souls. Heart-render. Bone-cleaner. Skull-crusher. Flesh-shredder. Great is Anubis."

As the rotting bodies drew closer, the army of rats found the charnel odor too tempting to resist. Abandoning Horatius, they scurried in pursuit of the corpses. After a moment's hesitation the giant scorpions scuttled after them. The young man promptly seized the opportunity to run in the opposite direction, toward the shack.

As soon as Horatius was free, Khebet ceased his chant. The dead bodies promptly collapsed where they stood; the vermin swarmed over them.

The Aegyptian hurried to join Horatius, hands pressed to his ears to drown out the disgusting sounds of feeding.

Above it all, the jackal howled with delight.

The tall man filled the doorway, blocking the light.

When his shadow fell across Justine, she instinctively recoiled.

Lars Porsena laughed. "You are not glad to see me, dear child? Do you not recognize me? I have transformed myself for your pleasure. Think what delights we can experience together with your renewed youth and this fine strong body."

The lovely girl sitting on the pile of rags said nothing. The woman lying beside her moaned, however, deep in her throat.

Crossing the room in two long strides, Lars Porsena bent over Vesi. He took up Justine's lamp and studied her face. "Yes, she is who I thought she was," he said with satisfaction. "Excellent! This is excellent. He is searching frantically for her—and I have her. If he wants her, he must come to me. How very convenient."

"What are you talking about? Who is she? And who's searching for her?"

"I never knew her name, but I knew her body—briefly. Some time ago. Now her son is searching for her. She is the bait he cannot resist, but I must not let him find her. Not yet and not here. First I need to separate him from any possible ally so I can destroy him without interference."

"Why do you want to destroy him?"

He ignored the question. "We must go now, and quickly, before he catches up with us. I have put barriers in his way but they may not hold him for very long. On your feet, Justine, and the woman with you. I must admit there is a certain inconvenience to having a body; it has to be physically moved from place to place and that takes time and effort. But in my opinion the pleasure of solid flesh far outweighs its disadvantages. Come on!" He gave her arm a cruel tug.

Horatius found the door ajar. Stepping inside, he discovered one small room furnished with bits of rubbish scavenged from the waste ground. A cracked *amphora* contained the dregs of sour wine, but there was no sign of food. The place was much poorer than Wulv's old hut. The thought of his mother in such squalid surroundings sickened him. Vesi, who had already been through so much. His throat burned with grief for her sake.

He was almost relieved to find her gone.

A faint trace of her scent remained, however, lingering in spite of the pervasive odor of burnt cloth. A pile of rags in the corner was smoldering where a lamp had been hastily overturned.

"Is she here?" asked a voice from the doorway.

"I'm afraid not, Khebet. See for yourself."

The fastidious Aegyptian had no intention of entering the shack. Pressing his perfumed sleeve to his nose and mouth, he swept his eyes around the interior but remained resolutely outside. "Was she ever here?"

"Yes, and quite recently too."

"You were deliberately prevented from getting to her in time," said Khebet. "But I wonder why they did not overwhelm you when they had a chance."

"You mean the rats and scorpions? Who could make vermin obey them?"

The Aegyptian allowed himself a modest smile. "With the aid of Anubis I was able to make the bodies of the dead obey my will. Magic is all around you, Horatius. You yourself have more than one shadow."

"What are you talking about?"

But before Khebet could reply, another being finally succeeded in making himself heard.

From the smoke of the smoldering rags that had once been Justine's bed, Pepan formed a body. It was not much of a body, hardly substantial enough to exist for more than a few moments, but by using all his strength he was able to give it a voice. *Vesi,* he said, forcing a simulation of sound through a simulated throat.

Horatius whirled around to confront a shadowy figure vaguely resembling a man, a man with a face he remembered. Had it been only that morning? In the mirror?

Vesi, said Pepan again.

"I tried to find my mother and make her safe, as you said. I fought to get here only to find her gone. She should have known I would come," Horatius complained to the creature of smoke. "She should have waited!"

Khebet thought Horatius sounded surprisingly like a small boy who has just discovered that the world is not fair and one's best effort is not always rewarded. He liked the young man better for it. But the image in the smoke said, *Do not be unreasonable; she could not wait for you. They have taken her to the caves.*

"What caves?"

The Caverns of Spasio, east of Rome. If you follow her, there is grave danger to yourself. You must be on your guard every moment. Use the protections I have given you. It is not Vesi he wants, but you.

"Who? Who is doing this?"

Before Pepan could reply, the tiny fire that fueled the smoke finally died.

Horatius turned to Khebet. "Was that what you meant about my having other shadows?"

"He is but one of many, not all of them benign."

"Why are they following me?"

"I can only speculate. Some may have something to share with you; others may want something of you. As a priest, I find your situation most intriguing."

Horatius felt his temper fraying like old rope. "My situation isn't important; it's my mother I'm worried about! Those caves he mentioned—have you ever heard of them by any chance?"

"As a priest," Khebet repeated with emphasis, "I know a lot about the Caverns of Spasio. They are believed to be one of the entrances to the Netherworld. I had not been long in Rome before I made a point of seeing them—from the outside only, of course."

"Take me there, Khebet. Please!"

The Aegyptian shook his head. "I knew you were going to say that. Revelation and excitement," he added cryptically.

Later, four inhuman hunters crowded together at the doorway of the shack, peering in. The atmosphere inside still trembled with vibrations but he had gone. Yet at last they were closing in on him. The long hunt would soon be over.

Pythia would be pleased.

THIRTY-EIGHT

The country was rocky and rough, the trackway all but invisible. They were walking single file along the path, with herself in the lead and Vesi in the middle. From the rear his voice guided, "Left here. Now up through that defile, then off to your right. Move faster. I want to reach our destination while there is still enough light for him to follow."

"Where are we going?"

He responded with the familiar, demonic chuckle that had nothing of Lars Porsena in it. "My plan is simplicity itself, dear child. We are taking the mother to a place where the son can only follow by dying."

Suddenly Justine knew. Her stomach contracted with terror. "The Caverns of Spasio!"

"And through them to the Netherworld," he replied.

"You can't take me with you; I wouldn't. . . "

"Survive? Not under normal circumstances, no. But with sufficient power I can keep both you and this woman alive in the Netherworld for a time, just as I can maintain this body. I merely need a little nourishment. We spoke before about my nourishment, remember? That is why I need to keep you with me—even there."

Half-fainting with fear, Justine felt her knees give way beneath her. Then to her astonishment the mindless woman behind her reached out and caught her. *"Courage,"* she whispered in a voice only Justine could hear.

"What can he possibly intend to do with my mother, Khebet?" Horatius asked over his shoulder as he trotted along the road the Aegyptian had indicated.

Khebet was struggling to keep up. He was a lean, fit man, as Aegyptian priests were inclined to be, but Horatius's speed and stamina excelled his. "I cannot say, but he is evil, Horatius, evil. Whatever he means to do can only harm her."

"Yet the face in the smoke said it was me he wants."

"What better way to lure you into a trap than this?"

"I don't care if it's a trap," Horatius said stubbornly. "I have to go to her; I don't have any choice. No one else can help her."

His fiercely possessive attitude toward his mother once again reminded the Aegyptian of a small boy. When boys became men and found women of their own that emotion was tempered. But although Horatius had a man's body, the spirit within was still immature.

"Look sharp," Khebet said aloud. "Somewhere up ahead there is a turnoff. Watch for a narrow path partially obscured by hemlock and cedar."

No mortal was needed to guide the four. That fragment of Pythia which possessed Vesi provided a sufficient beacon. They were hampered by a lack of physical speed, but they were relentless. They would eventually catch up with their quarry.

Four cloaked and hooded figures glided along a Roman road, speaking to no one. When they encountered a man on a horse the animal shied so violently it threw its rider, who sat cursing in the dirt and shaking his fist at them. They never stopped, never even looked around.

The dark goddess was waiting.

In the late afternoon sunlight Justine looked deep into Vesi's eyes, just for a moment. Then Lars Porsena gave them an impatient shove from behind. "Go on, go on! We are almost there."

"I thought I was going to faint."

"Gather your courage, dear child. I expect better of you than fainting. What is about to befall you is a simple transaction, nothing more. You need only think of something else and it will soon be over. Surely in your former line of work you were accustomed to thinking of something else during business transactions?"

Justine shuddered. His insinuating voice tore the scabs off old wounds.

The Caverns of Spasio were a series of interlinked caves extending into the bowels of the earth. Initially very large, they became smaller as they went deeper. Unlike other caves, a constant flow of air moved through them, claimed by the Romans to be the breath of the Netherworld. Through the caverns wound a river of black water. In its lightless depths no fish swam. The Romans believed that it was a tributary of the Styx.

Everyone knew the caverns had been fashioned by the gods at the dawn of the world. No human had ever explored the caves fully; no sane human wanted to. The few who did—brave or foolhardy, drunk or mad—had never returned. One cave led to another, then to another, all the way to the Kingdom of the Dead. If one went too far, one could never get back.

The entrance to the foremost cave was screened by scrub cedar and a tangle of white-flowered hemlock. Lars Porsena caught the hemlock and drew its blossoms to his face, inhaling the fragrance. "Wonderful," he breathed. Then he pushed the shrubbery aside to reveal a great dark cavern like a gaping mouth waiting to devour Justine.

"I can't." She screwed her eyes shut and clutched Vesi's arm. "I can't. I'm too afraid!"

"You can," insisted the demon's implacable voice. "Step inside, Justine. I grow impatient for my meal."

Pepan stayed close to Horatius and Khebet. He found no further way to communicate; so many restrictions applied to a disembodied *hia* in the Earthworld. Yet he remained within an arm's length of Vesi's son at all times, hoping Horatius would somehow sense him there and draw strength from his presence.

As they drew nearer the caves, his anxiety increased. First he heard a ripping noise and then a shrill screech, the unmistakable sound of pain transmitted through the Otherworld. Shortly thereafter, Vesi's identifying sound began to grow faint; fainter . . .

Hurry, Pepan urged Horatius, *hurry, before it is too late!*

But he feared it might already be too late. Death was only the least of what might happen to Vesi.

By the time Horatius and Khebet reached the caverns the daylight was beginning to fade. Peering through the opening into the first cave, they saw only darkness until their eyes adjusted. Even then the interior of the cave was grimly shadowed.

Horatius drew a deep breath. "I smell my mother's scent; she was here recently. Now her trail leads deeper into the caverns. She's going away from me all the time,

Khebet; what shall I do?" he asked in the voice of a desperate child who expects adults to have all the answers.

"She has led you to a very dangerous place, Horatius. I most urgently suggest we turn back."

But no sooner did the Aegyptian speak than Horatius felt the familiar singing in his blood, filling him with knowledge and certainty.

We never turn back, he replied.

It was not his voice.

Khebet closed his eyes in a moment's silent prayer. *Great Anubis*, he thought, *do not desert me. I am in the presence of wonders*. "Horatius, please listen to me. We cannot pursue her through these caves. They lead to the Netherworld. Do you understand what I'm saying?"

"I do understand. But if that's where they've taken my mother, that's where I must go. Now you can come with me or stay here. It's all the same to me. You have a choice. I do not." The young man shoved his way through the shrubbery and disappeared into the cavern.

"Nor do I," Khebet murmured. Perhaps this was a punishment, though he could not recall any deed of his so heinous. Some unpropitiated crime in a previous life perhaps? "The only way I know to enter the Netherworld is through death," he argued as he reluctantly followed. "The *ka* must leave its body in order to cross the Styx. If your mother has been taken that far she is already dead, so there is no point in your. . . "

Horatius turned to face him. In the dimly lighted cave he stood with his hands on his hips and his feet wide apart. "I won't let her be dead," he said stubbornly.

"You have no choice!" the Aegyptian cried in exasperation.

"I do. I'm going to go get her and bring her back."

Khebet rolled his eyes skyward. "Anubis help me!"

"*You* help me, Khebet. You can work great magic. You brought the dead back to life."

"No, I did not. You saw dead bodies move, which is

not the same thing. They were briefly animated through the power of Anubis, whose priest I am."

"Then when I bring my mother back from the Netherworld, you can do the same for her."

"You do not want an empty shell!"

"There is little more than that of her now," Horatius remarked ruefully. "I'm going after her, Khebet. Help me or not as you will."

The Aegyptian drew a deep breath. "Very well, I will do what I can. But if you have faith in my magic, you must obey me completely. Agreed?"

Horatius hesitated. Wulv was the only man he had obeyed. At last he said in a low voice, "Agreed."

The Aegyptian began to pace back and forth, talking as much to himself as to Horatius. "We cannot let you attempt the journey in your physical body; it will have to remain here, so you have something to come back to. I will release your *ka* to travel to the Netherworld. First I will need hemlock from those bushes outside to make a potion and some of the niter from the walls of this cave. Then. . . "

"Will you go with me?"

Khebet shook his head. "I cannot. I must remain behind to stand guard over your untenanted body. There are many malign spirits who would possess it otherwise."

"When my spirit leaves my body, will I be dead?"

"Not if the ritual works." The Aegyptian hesitated. "But I must be honest with you, Horatius. I have never performed this ritual before. It was old when the world was young, and only the greatest of priests would ever dare attempt it. Alas, I am not the greatest of priests," he added ruefully. "If I cannot reunite your *ka* with your body once you return from the Netherworld, you will be dead. Worse than dead, because while your *ka* wanders lost in the Otherworld, your body may be possessed by some foul spirit. There are many such who are always eager to seize uninhabited flesh. The gods alone know what crimes may be committed by something wearing your face and form."

Horatius shrugged. "I have no fear of death." That much was true. The other horrors Khebet described however . . .

He swallowed. Hard. "I trust you to bring me back," he told the Aegyptian. "But if you cannot, then you must destroy my body so nothing can use it. Promise me this."

"I promise."

THIRTY-NINE

At first the way through the caverns was all but lightless, yet Lars Porsena never faltered. With one hand locked on Vesi's wrist and the other on Justine's he plunged ahead, down and down and down, dragging the women with him.

Beside them ran the river. Merely an inconsequential trickle along the floor of the first cave, it broadened with each cavern. Try as she might, Justine could not discover any tributaries feeding the river, yet it continued to gather strength as it descended until the caverns echoed with a mighty roar. The sound beat against her skull. The water gave off a foul, disgusting odor like rotten eggs.

Once when Justine whimpered with pain, Lars Porsena pulled her to its very brink. "You can have a drink if you like," he said.

She turned her face away.

He laughed. "Come then, we have a distance yet to go."

They went on; her pain did not lessen. He had hurt her very badly and she marveled that she was still able to walk. As if he read her mind, he remarked, "You can stand an extraordinary amount of pain, you know. You are young. And I chose you because you are strong. You had to be, to survive the life you led." He chuckled. "If you think you suffer now, just wait until we cross to the other side of the river."

"I can't cross that river; it's the Styx."

"Have you so little faith in me? I told you—you will survive. You both will survive for as long as I need you to. Come now, dear child, do not scowl at me. I have restored your beauty. Why ruin it?"

"What are you going to do to me after we . . . after we cross the river?"

"I have not yet decided. The Netherworld offers many opportunities for pleasure; what I call pleasure, that is. You may not agree. But you will be able to explore at first hand aspects of your sensual nature whose existence you have hidden even from yourself. Does the prospect not intrigue you?" he asked archly.

"Of course not!" she shot back. Yet she was lying and he knew it.

The dishonesty of her reply pleased him. As a reward he lessened the severity of his grip on her wrist. "All mortals lie," he said. "Only the hopelessly mad, like our friend here," he jerked his head in Vesi's direction, "are innocent. Hers is the purity of mindlessness."

But Justine had looked deep into Vesi's eyes. There was a mind behind them, a cold, calculating mind that watched everything—and understood.

As they went deeper the caverns did not become darker. Instead a pale gray light, barely discernible at first, grew stronger as they progressed. By this light Justine was able to recognize a change in the life-forms within the caverns. At first there had been numerous common spiders scrabbling over the damp stone. Past a certain depth the spiders disappeared to be replaced by creatures that never saw the light of day. Translucent land crabs scuttled sideways at their approach, and albino bats hanging in packs from the ceilings mewled at them like cats or chewed the finger-thick white slugs that lurked in stony crevices.

Deeper still, the shadows partially concealed beings of such frightful, distorted shape that Justine could not bear to look at them, but averted her eyes and hurried past. Bulbous forms leaped from the dark river and fell back with a squelch rather than a splash. Once or twice long, sinuous tentacles broke the surface and waved hungrily, questing in the air for a moment before retiring to the depths again. Once one brushed against Lars Porsena and recoiled with a hiss.

"What sort of creatures live down here?" Justine asked him in a ragged whisper.

"Live? You can hardly say anything *lives* this close to the Netherworld, dear child. Beings do occupy this region, but their existence is very different from yours."

Something huge and hairy came bounding forward to press itself against Justine like an affectionate dog, but within the hair it had no bones, merely a jellylike form that molded itself disgustingly to her leg. She gave a gasp of horror and pulled away, almost breaking free of Lars Porsena's grasp.

His fingers swiftly tightened again on her wrist. "You do not want to do that," he cautioned her. "If you break contact with me I cannot keep your body alive, not down here. Look ahead and you will see light. We have almost reached our destination, dear child. Blessed art thou among women, for you are about to experience wonders."

FORTY

Khebet sat beside the body of Horatius, trying not to look down at the emptied face.

I should have gone with him, thought the Aegyptian. Or I should go back to Rome. In fact, I should never have come to Rome.

Regrets were futile. He could not leave the comatose body. He could only sit and wait.

Daylight beyond the mouth of the cave, already partially blocked by shrubbery, gradually disappeared. The creatures of the night began to make their presence known. Owls hooted, predators emerged from their burrows and began to take prey. A tiny voice shrieked in pain.

Khebet sat cross-legged on the floor of the cave in the dark and waited. Thirst began to torment him. He found himself dreaming of golden barley beer with beads of moisture running down the side of the cup or crystal flagons of melon and pomegranate juice or a great pitcher of cool water from the well in the temple courtyard. And rain. Slanting silver rain replenishing the Nile, making all things green.

When he ran an exploratory tongue over his lips they were cracked and dry.

When this was over, he was going to return to his own land and immerse himself in the Great Mother of Rivers until her water soaked into every pore of his skin.

He had used water from the tiny stream that ran through the cave to make the potion he had given to Horatius, preparing the mixture in a naturally hollowed-out stone the size of an infant's head. The water had seemed pure enough, though foul-smelling, but he was strangely unwilling to drink any of it himself. A priest of Anubis could surely overlook such a small inconvenience as a dry mouth.

The body he guarded was indifferent to discomfort. It merely waited.

Periodically Khebet put his fingertips against the broad, strong throat. The faintest sluggish pulse beat there, like a candle guttering just before it goes out. So far the ritual had worked, but Khebet knew full well the hardest part lay ahead, if Horatius returned at all.

He heard someone approaching. Rustling bushes betrayed the presence of several large bodies.

"Who is out there?" called Khebet. "I warn you, I am armed!" His hand dropped to the hilt of the small ceremonial knife he always carried tucked in his sash.

The rustling of the shrubbery ceased. Something was breathing out there, a stertorous breathing that did not sound quite human to the alarmed Aegyptian.

Khebet bent and fumbled on the floor of the cave, searching for the hollowed-out stone that had contained Horatius's potion. Then he slipped his knife from his sash and held the blade between his teeth. Untying the sash, he knotted one end of it around the stone.

Now he had two weapons. Yet he had never been so afraid.

The four outside the cave conferred silently with one another. Those whom they sought had gone within; there was no doubt of it. They must follow. But there was an obstacle.

Their leader thrust his body through the shrubbery until he stood in the entrance to the caverns. At that moment there was a silken, whirring sound; then a missile struck him a painful blow on the side of the head.

He staggered backward out of the cave.

"Got one!" Khebet gasped around the knife he still held in his teeth. He could hear them milling around and was not comforted by the fact that they did not speak aloud. The sounds they did make were sufficiently alarming. To Khebet's anxious ears it seemed as if something very heavy was being dragged through the undergrowth. And there was a curious dry sibilation like that of scaled bodies rubbing against one another.

Khebet was reminded of a nest of newly hatched snakes he had disturbed on the banks of the Nile in his boyhood, long before he learned serpents were sacred . . .

. . . and the glee he had taken in throwing brush down upon them and setting fire to the nest, watching the little snakes twist and writhe in agony.

No sooner had the image flashed through his mind than there was a concerted rush at the mouth of the cave. Flinging up his arms, Khebet spat out his knife so he could cry with all his might, "Great Anubis, empower me!"

A jackal howled.

* * *

Fire.

And the Little Ones burning.

The four had responded in fury to the picture in Khebet's mind. Sacrilege! The dark goddess would never forgive them if they did not punish the perpetrator of such an obscene act. Gathering around their leader, they attacked the cave with every intention of slaughtering the person inside. Pythia was always pleased by sacrifice.

As they filled the entrance a wall of fire blossomed just in front of them.

So intense was the heat that Khebet staggered back, but he did not lower his arms. He had called the flame from the living rock through the power of Anubis. This was the most potent of magics. He had secretly believed himself incapable of such great work. Thankfully, he was wrong.

When he felt Horatius's body against the back of his ankles, he shuffled his feet to push his friend farther from the flames. But Horatius was powerfully built, not easily pushed. Khebet would have to take hold of him with his hands and drag him, and that he dare not do. If he lowered his arms, the flames would die.

And so would he and Horatius.

The obedient flame roared upward to the ceiling of the cave and licked along it greedily, seeking out and feeding upon the tiny lichens that clung there. The fire-voice roared.

"Great Anubis, Jackal Lord, all praise to you from this your servant!" shouted Khebet to be heard above the fire.

Maintaining the wall of flame required a vast expenditure of physical energy. The Aegyptian could actually feel the heat being drawn from his body, even while it radiated back to scorch his face. He did not know how long he could continue to provide the barrier. His fingers were growing numb, pins and needles radiating down his arms, locking his wrists and elbows into knots of pain.

Then through a momentary break in the flames he caught a glimpse of the four hooded strangers. They lurked just inside the cave mouth, waiting, waiting. Only the fire could drive them away.

Khebet tried to summon courage. When he acted it was not bravery, however, but terror that impelled him. He would die unless he made himself move. He stepped forward toward the four, driving the wall of flame ahead of him into their faces.

There came a hiss of pain and the stink of scorched cloth.

When the fire bellied out to meet them they tried to hold their ground, but nothing living could resist flame. Tiny blue lights danced on their oiled skins and they retreated beyond the mouth of the cave and stood huddled together there, trying to decide what to do next.

Within the cave the Aegyptian desperately held up his tiring arms and wondered what to do. It was getting hard to breathe. The fire was using up the oxygen in the cave and drawing in replacement air from the lower caverns. Air that smelled of sulfur; noxious air that lay heavy in the lungs.

Khebet was wracked by such a fit of coughing he momentarily lowered his arms.

The flames dipped; the four beyond the cave mouth glided forward.

"Back!" screamed Khebet, recovering. His arms stretched high once more; the flames leaped higher.

The four stopped.

The man within the cave shivered violently in spite of the fire. "I do not want to die here, Lord Anubis," Khebet said in a hoarse whisper. "Not here, so far from the valley of the Nile. This is not my place, and the cause in which I fight is not my cause. Have mercy on this your servant!"

FORTY-ONE

He was dead.

Yet not dead.

The boy within him knew he should be terrified. But since that dreadful day when he'd left personal fear behind, only insatiable curiosity remained, untempered by caution or experience.

He could still feel fear for others however.

Vesi had been the hub of his life. Although his body was entering manhood, the child inside was still far too young to imagine life without her. To restore her to himself he would undertake anything, even the ritual that made him dead and notdead. For a fearless child the prospect was a great adventure.

There had been a brief, unsettling moment after he emerged from his fleshly shell when he found himself staring down at his own body. Khebet was crouching over him with long fingers pressed to his throat. In his other hand the priest still held the drinking vessel he had fashioned of huge leaves, containing the dregs of narcotic poison.

The Aegyptian twisted around to look up with his third eye at Horatius's *ka.* Khebet's lips did not move, but the young man clearly heard the ancient language of the Black Land. "May the gods speed you on your mission."

Horatius had then begun the journey from which no one ever returned.

The way to the Netherworld was far from straightforward. The caverns comprised a passageway disorientingly located between different planes of existence. To complicate matters, being a disembodied spirit did not allow Horatius the ease of movement he had expected. In order to make any progress he had to force his *hia* forward through sheer concentration. Although he had no physical body this required a tremendous amount of effort.

Water was both a conduit and a barrier between the worlds of the living and the dead. He followed the course of the river because Khebet had told him it was the surest guide to his destination, but whenever he drew too close he sensed he could not cross.

Down he went, and down, ever farther from light and sun.

Horatius was still aware of physical surroundings: the walls of the caverns, the increasing volume of the river, the sulfurous stench that wafted upward from the depths. But behind stone and earth and water he saw, as if in a clouded mirror, another world.

Otherworld.

And the deeper he went, the farther away from light and life, the clearer it became.

This was a place of spirits and shades, of the ephemeral and the immortal. The Otherworld was a realm of dreams and nightmares, yet in its own way more real than the world he had just left behind.

Here myriad intangible figures swirled and danced in

complex patterns much older than man. With a sense of mounting amazement, Horatius realized that earthly life as he knew it was nothing more than the skin on the surface of a sea of incalculable depth. Within that sea were glowing multicolored constellations inhabited by multitudes of spirits. Some were gorgeous; some were shocking. All were occupied with pursuits far removed from the interests of humankind. Their existence underlaid and even collided with his, yet until that moment he had known nothing about them.

Horatius was swept by an almost irresistible desire to join their seductive dance. Without the burden of a human body he could spend an eternity exploring the wonders of the Otherworld. The adventurous small boy inside him was sorely tempted. It would be so easy to leave the river and wander off. But instinctively he knew that if he did so, he would never return to the body that awaited him or rescue his mother.

Abandon her now and she will be forever lost, said a familiar voice.

A face swam toward him out of the darkness. A narrow, aristocratic face with long-lidded eyes and a distinctive beard on its chin.

Horatius's mouth worked, but no sound came out.

You have no need of a physical voice in this place. Think your words, imagine your phrases. This is the place of words made flesh.

"Who are you?" Horatius asked in his head.

"In human life I was Pepan, Lord of the Rasne. As I told you before, I was a friend of your grandmother and of your mother."

"And you are with me now?" This business of talking in one's head was intriguing.

"I have always been with you. No one walks alone. You have been reinforced more than most, however, and you will need still more help if you are to succeed in your mission. Come, we have not far to go."

"Are we near the Netherworld, Pepan? I hope to catch

up with my mother before they—whoever they are—take her across the Styx."

"You cannot. You are at too much of a disadvantage here, neither totally alive nor truly dead. Be patient. Once you enter the Netherworld we will be able to give you appropriate armor and weapons. Then you can fight for your mother with some hope of winning."

Horatius said stubbornly, "I don't want to wait; I want to save her now!"

Pepan sighed. "You do not realize what you challenge. Right now Vesi is little more than an empty shell used by one of the *Ais,* a goddess who sometimes speaks through her defenseless mouth. She is also the captive of a *siu,* a demon of formidable powers. Few mortals have ever been more at the mercy of the Otherworld."

"A goddess? A demon?" Horatius struggled to understand. "Why have they chosen my mother?"

"Who can explain the motives of such beings? They play elaborate games according to their own rules. No human can understand them. But we are not without powers of our own, that is what I am trying to tell you. Once you are across the Styx . . . see ahead, where the river narrows and then rushes downward through an opening like a gullet? At that point we make our crossing."

"Will I be truly dead then?" It was a small boy's question.

"Truly dead."

"And dead forever?"

"Nothing is dead forever."

Horatius could sense the increased momentum of forces rushing toward the narrow opening. The mouth of the tunnel was formed like a skull with jaws agape. Stalactites and stalagmites resembled jagged teeth. Turbulent rapids were created as black water boiled with the effort of trying to force too great a volume through the open jaws. Back through the tunnel came the deafening roar of a mighty waterfall beyond, a wailing as of a million souls in torment.

In spite of himself Horatius hesitated. "Do you mean we have to go through there?"

"That is the only way. Are you afraid?"

"I haven't been afraid since Wulv and my grandmother were killed," Horatius boasted. "I was told to walk away from my fear and I did. But . . . this is different."

"Yes, this is different. Until you make your decision, the only help I can offer is to assure you that you are not alone."

"My decision . . . are you suggesting . . . I could turn around and go back?"

"There is still time," Pepan replied, "if that is what you want."

"More than anything else—except to save my mother."

"Your decision is already made then."

Suddenly Horatius felt as if a great burden was lifted from him. How liberating it was to fix on one star and let all else follow! "Yes, my decision is made. I choose not to be afraid. And I never go back."

"Good," Pepan approved. "Now we have to get you across the Styx. Look closely. Just before the river plunges downward you will see a tiny pier and a boat. The boatman is called Charun. Once you pay your fare his boat will carry you through the rapids, into that tunnel, down the waterfall that lies beyond, and deposit you safely on the opposite shore."

"Where will I be then?"

"In the Netherworld. And I will be there to help you."

"How am I to pay Charun? I have nothing."

Pepan laughed. "Usually a coin is placed in the mouth of a person at the time of their Dying in order to pay the boatman. Since you had no proper Dying, I will provide you with a coin. I am Lord of the Silver People after all. Otherwise you would have to tell Charun a secret; sometimes he will accept that as a fare."

As they drew near the pier and the boat, Horatius saw Charun waiting for them, tapping his foot impatiently. The boatman had the appearance of a very old man with a morose visage, cavernous eye sockets, and overly developed arms and shoulders. In his right hand he held a heavy hammer. As they approached he raised his left arm, hand outstretched.

A shadowy arm reached past Horatius and dropped something shiny into the boatman's open palm. Charun hefted the coin, judging its weight, then closed one eye and squinted at the silver through the other. At last he spat through a gap in his teeth and nodded. "This will do," he said grudgingly. "Passage for one. Who stays?"

Neither. A second coin fell into his hand.

"Passage for two to the Netherworld." Charun's nostrils flared and he inclined his head toward Horatius. "Are you sure this one is dead? There is the stink of life about him."

"He is ready for the Netherworld," Pepan replied, not answering the question.

"Are you being met? If you set off on your own through the Netherworld, you'll regret it. Satres rules there as god, but the only sure safety is with Veno, Protectress of the Dead. And you'll need someone to guide you to her, you know."

Pepan hesitated. "Our situation is different from most."

Charun shrugged. "Not being met. The more fool you then. But come ahead; it's nothing to me."

For such a turbulent voyage the boat seemed very small and flimsy. Horatius and Pepan had no physical bodies to entrust to its care, but their spirits could not make the crossing unaided.

"Water is too powerful for a *hia,*" Pepan explained.

"Water has life of its own and is holy. Our spirits must be carried across."

They did not step into Charun's boat; rather, it folded around them. Its sides were curiously spongy, giving Horatius the impression of a huge stomach. "We can't see!" he protested.

"Believe me," Charun assured him, "you don't want to look down into the waters of the Styx." He stood at the rear of the boat, hidden from Pepan and Horatius by its upcurving sides, and began to pole them through the water.

The small boat bucked like a fractious horse. Horatius had not thought the river wide, but they seemed to travel for an age, tossed violently about in the rapids. After the first few moments Horatius became accustomed to the motion and even began to enjoy it. He listened with fascination to the sounds coming from the water: horns blowing, pipes playing, wild laughter, somber weeping, voices of seductive beauty calling. More than once he wanted to peer over the sides, but Pepan warned him, "Charun is right; do not look into the Styx. What waits there could capture your spirit forever."

As the boat leaped and spun on the current they could hear Charun mutter to himself like any disagreeable old man. When he let loose with a particularly colorful expletive, Horatius could not help laughing. At once Charun snarled, "Are you not afraid of me?"

"Should I be?"

"I am Death!"

Horatius laughed again. "Why should I fear Death"?

The tunnel was a shock. The boat suddenly upended and dropped prow first with frightening speed. Nothing could be heard above the roar of the cascading water but the sound of endless screaming, as if multitudes were forever falling. Horatius wondered what it would be like to spend an eternity falling . . . falling . . . falling.

As they plunged downward he was thankful he had no solid body. Even so the sensation was sickening.

I am not afraid, he told himself firmly. I am not afraid!

Abruptly they hit bottom. The boat struck the surface of the river below the falls with a juddering impact, seemed about to overturn, then righted itself. A few moments later they felt it grate on the shore. The sides unfurled, falling away like drooping petals. From being a devouring belly, Charun's boat had been transformed by the journey into something resembling a giant lily.

Horatius scrambled from the boat. From the riverbank he turned and called to Charun, "When I return, will you take me back across the Styx?"

The boatman gave a derisive snort. "Return, you say? No one ever returns."

"I shall return," Horatius promised.

The young man found himself on a pebbled bank that gave way to rolling hills. A well-worn path meandered away from the river. Before setting out upon it, Horatius paused to look back.

To his surprise there was no sign of Charun or the boat, only the black waterfall roaring down into the black river.

He resolutely faced forward and set out along the path. "Are you still with me, Pepan?" he called over his shoulder.

"Of course. I told you, I am here to help you find your mother. You will not be able to track her in the Netherworld as you did on earth, but I can. I promise to stay with you as long as you need me."

"And then . . . ?"

Pepan did not answer.

Horatius followed the path to a promontory overlooking a small, tranquil lake of opalescent water. Around the lake grew a variety of trees resembling giant ferns, with graceful, drooping branches. From the trees unseen birds called in piercing voices. When Horatius looked up he saw no sky. Instead there was an arching ceiling far overhead, like the top of an immense cavern, lit with a reddish glow. Across this background occasional streaks of gold blazed and died abruptly, briefly illuminating what looked like cursive lines of script. The boy in him wanted to know who had written those gigantic words on the distant ceiling.

"Here we are at last," said a voice close behind him.

Turning, Horatius saw an elegant, middle-aged man in a close-fitting white robe with a dark red mantle over one shoulder. His face and curling beard looked familiar.

"Pepan?"

"I am." The man smiled and held out his arm. Horatius hesitated before reaching for it.

"But you're flesh and blood!"

"In the Netherworld all spirits are materialized. Those who have lived Earthworld lives take on the memory of the last form they possessed."

Horatius reached out to touch Pepan's bicep. "This is only a memory? It feels so solid!"

"I am as substantial," replied Pepan, "as everything around us. Only the Otherworld is insubstantial. Yet it has the greatest power of all," he added mysteriously. "Welcome." He wrapped his hand around the younger man's right forearm, and Horatius repeated the gesture.

"I have waited so long to meet you," Pepan said with genuine warmth. "So long to do just this."

Realizing he was feeling what seemed to be living flesh, Horatius looked down to discover his own familiar form. He was dressed in the badly folded toga he had put on this morning—so very long ago! Or was it?

He had lost all sense of time.

Extending his arms, he turned his hands palm up and studied the lines. "This is me all right, Pepan. But I don't understand. What about my other body, the one back in the cavern with Khebet?"

"Your Earthworld flesh remains intact where you left it. As long as it is not destroyed, there is the possibility of your *hia* returning to it. But make no mistake, the Netherworld form your *hia* now inhabits is vulnerable and must be protected. Here there are countless varieties of vicious beings with no desire but destruction. You will require weapons from your armorers."

"What armorers? I see no one but ourselves."

"No one?" Pepan echoed. Reaching out, he pressed the palm of his hand against Horatius's breast. "Although you now bear a Roman name, you are destined to become the greatest of all the Etruscans. Everything we are or were is carried forward in you. As I told you before, you have never been alone."

FORTY-TWO

At first the pearly waters of the little lake were warm against Horatius's skin. Concentric ripples spread across its translucent surface as the young man waded out from the shore.

"How far do I need to go, Pepan?" he called over his shoulder.

"To the heart of the lake. There, that's it. Now. . . "

"Now?"

"Crouch down."

"Is that all? Just crouch down?"

"Stop asking questions, Horatius, and do as you are told. Crouch down until the waters close over your head. Then you may stand again."

Closing his eyes tightly, he took a deep breath although he was not sure if he would need it. Was breath necessary in the Netherworld? So many unanswered questions. . . .

"Do as I say!" called Pepan.

Horatius bent his knees until he was submerged. The

lake at its center was much warmer than elsewhere, and swirled in sluggish tides about his body, thick and cloying, more like honey than water. It insinuated itself into every orifice; almost at once his belly knotted with cramp. He hugged himself against the pain and stood up again . . . to discover that he was not alone in the water.

Another man emerged with him, a man who bore a discernible resemblance to Pepan. He wore military dress, including a breastplate of highly polished bronze that reproduced every muscle of his torso.

He responded to Horatius's look of astonishment with an amused smile.

"Fear me not, lad. I—and those who follow—are your ancestors; we are your past. I am called Zemerak and was your grandfather's grandfather. Under my leadership Etrurians stood shoulder to shoulder with Athenians and Corinthians, and beat the warriors of Carthage to their knees. As a trophy of victory I returned home with the splendid breastplate I wear, which I personally removed from the commander of the Carthaginians." He began unfastening the armor. "No weapon was ever able to penetrate its surface. I now bequeath it to you."

As he handed over the breastplate, Zemerak gazed deeply into the young man's eyes. Across his noble features a momentary regret flickered, for the life that had once been his. Then he smiled. "Hail and farewell, Horatius." Between one breath and the next he was gone.

"Give yourself to the water again," instructed Pepan from the shore.

Once more Horatius bent down, felt the lake close over his head, felt the cramping under his heart. This time when he stood up he was facing a stocky man with long-lidded, drowsy eyes. After a moment, however, Horatius realized their expression was deceptive. They watched him with a keenness he could feel in his bones.

"I am called Emnis, and I too was a warrior," said the stocky man. "In my time the tribes of Etruria were establishing themselves in many lands. From each of these we took the best and adapted it to our own use. The shield I carry is my favorite example." He held up a long, slightly curved rectangle of highly polished blue metal with a grooved bronze rim. "When the edges of several of these are fitted together they form a covering like the shell of a turtle, and several men can shelter beneath.

"Take this to protect you from your enemies, Horatius. Equally important, be generous in sharing it with your allies." The man smiled. "Enjoy your life, Horatius. Live every moment fully. Hail and farewell."

After his next submersion in the lake Horatius was joined by a lantern-jawed man with laugh wrinkles and a merry mouth. He clapped the young man on both shoulders. "So this is what my line has become! I am not displeased. My name is Tarxies. Long before Emnis was born I was a famous horse-warrior. I led raids as far away as the land of the Lydians, and took many captives . . . mostly women," he added with a wink. "A man astride a horse needs to protect his exposed legs from the knives and spears of his enemies, so I developed these greaves."

Tarxies reached down and fumbled beneath the surface of the lake, then came up with a pair of dripping shin guards. "These are molded of boiled leather so they cover the entire front of the leg from kneecap to foot, yet do not hamper mobility. You will find they fit you perfectly. While your wear them your legs at least will be invincible," he broke into a grin, "whether you have a horse between them or not. Hail and farewell, Horatius."

Horatius had barely raised his head when his next ancestor appeared in a fountain of bubbling water. "Mastarna," the man said simply, and the young man did not know whether it was a greeting or a name. Water dripped in pearly globules from the highly polished edges of the great two-headed ax he carried.

Horatius took a step backward in spite of himself. The man with the ax smiled grimly.

"They called me Mastarna of the Minoans," he said, "because I conducted a profitable trade with the sea kings of Crete. When I saw this double-bladed ax in the palace of Knossos I coveted it for myself. One head faces to the right as you can see, the other to the left. Both blades are looking for blood." He tapped the blade with a fingernail. It sang high and pure. "The metal is bronze sheathed in gold; the haft is ebony. A ceremonial weapon consecrated to the gods, it ultimately cost half my fortune and almost my life as well. But it was worth it. Now it belongs to you, Horatius of Rome." With a curiously mocking bow, he held out the ax.

When Horatius closed his hands around the haft he gasped at its weight. Turning away from Mastarna, he tried an exploratory swing. The gleaming weapon was perfectly balanced, and sang effortlessly through the air like the very voice of death.

"Well done," commented Mastarna. "I am relieved to see my prize is in strong hands. Use it well and often. Hale and farewell, Horatius."

The next donor was not a man, but a woman. Horatius could only gape at the sinewy female who rose from the lake beside him. A wealth of brown hair was twisted atop her head and held in place with a skewer of ivory that might have been animal bone. Her broad cheekbones momentarily reminded Horatius of Repana, but this woman's eyes were as wild as those of any animal in the forest. When she bared her teeth, they were very white against her deeply tanned skin.

"Bendis," she introduced herself succinctly. "The Huntress. I understand weapons. I give you my favorite." She handed Horatius a long strip of woven cloth, wide in the middle but narrowing at the ends and reinforced throughout its length with strings of supple rawhide. "You know how to use the sling," she said. "I watched you." Next she gave him a small doeskin bag and instructed, "Fill the bag with stones from the shore of this lake. Use them only when you must, but be assured you will never miss. Hale and farewell."

"Again," Pepan called from the shore, "bend down again."

The figure that emerged from the water this time bore little resemblance to the others. He was a stooped, emaciated man with only one tuft of white hair remaining at the back of his skull, sticking upright like the crest of some exotic bird. His skin was yellow with age, his nose thin and beaky, his lips so narrow he seemed to have no mouth. Across his arm he carried a folded hide.

Nodding gravely to Horatius, he said, "Among the Etrurians I was known as Waylag the Traveler, but over a long lifetime I answered to many names in many lands. Some of these names are now legend, not only to my people, but to others you may never encounter. In the reign of Atys, Son of Ghosts, I ventured to explore the First Kingdom of the Kush. There I learned forbidden secrets.

"In those days the animal kingdom was composed of our brothers, and shared its wisdom with us. One of my greatest teachers was Pardus the Cunning. When he died he left me his skin, the book in which his wisdom may be read. Clothe yourself with it; learn both patience and guile from your long-dead brother."

Reaching out, Waylag draped a magnificent leopardskin around Horatius's shoulders. "You travel in a new direction," he said. "Your feet will create paths no one has walked before. I envy you, Horatius. Never stop traveling. Never stop looking, and learning, and seeking. The answers do not matter, remember that. But the questions are all-important. And now—hale and farewell."

The young man stroked the silken pelt. It was as supple and glossy as if it had just been removed from the leopard and instantly warmed his chilled flesh. But once more Pepan gestured to him to immerse himself.

This time he had to wait until he felt as though his lungs would burst before the familiar cramp wracked him. Gratefully he surged to the surface and drew a deep breath.

The figure who emerged from the water beside him was barely half his height. Wild, coarse hair grew over most of its visible body. In appearance it reminded him, with a jolt, of the thing that had attacked Propertius on the road to Rome.

Automatically he lifted the ax. But Pepan cried out, "No, Horatius! He is the first of us!"

Without taking his eyes off the shaggy man, Horatius called, "What do you mean?"

"From that primitive creature's loins sprang the seed that one day became the Etruscans. The gift he brings you is perhaps the most potent of all."

The shaggy man did not speak; perhaps he had no words Horatius could recognize as language. But there was intelligence in his deep-set eyes beneath their shelflike brow. With great dignity, he drew something from the leather strip tied around his waist and held it on both outstretched palms.

Wedged into an antler-prong handle was a blade made of flint. When Horatius reached for the primitive dagger his fingers grazed the edge of the blade. He drew back with an exclamation. The weapon was incredibly sharp.

"Nothing cuts like flint," Pepan observed from the shore. "With tools like those our distant ancestors carved out a civilization."

Horatius cautiously reached for the dagger a second time. When he held it up to examine in detail, he was struck by the craftsmanship of the weapon. The flint blade had been painstakingly chipped into a perfect cutting edge. The antler handle was incised with a complex pattern carved into the bone. Using only the raw materials of nature, its maker had created both beauty and utility.

He looked at the shaggy man with new respect. The other gazed back across untold centuries. As their eyes locked Horatius felt a change taking place within himself. *The Silver People began with this man,* he thought, *and all the men and women who followed him. I have just met some of them. Each has given me the gift they value the most.*

For the first time in his life Horatius felt the humility that marks the beginning of true maturity. He bowed his head.

The shaggy man grunted in response.

Slowly, with a sense of ceremony, Horatius raised the flint dagger and pressed it first to his forehead, then to his lips.

Its maker understood. Light leaped in his deep-set eyes. Reaching toward Horatius, for the briefest of moments he rested his palm on the exact center of the young man's chest.

Then he too was gone.

Horatius stood alone in the water.

"Come out now," Pepan called to him. "You have everything you need to be a man of the Silver People."

FORTY-THREE

"I knew he would follow her!" Lars Porsena crowed in triumph. "I knew the fool would never desert his mother. Let this be a lesson to you, Justine. Love is the greatest weakness of the human race."

"I should have thought," she replied, "love was one of our greatest strengths." She was beginning to know his mind. He liked to give lectures and expound upon his philosophies. Justine had known men like him before; men who paid for her time simply to talk. Lonely men. She found herself wondering if the demon was lonely.

The trio were crossing an arid plain beneath a crimson sky. The ground beneath their feet seemed firm enough, yet toward the horizon it wavered as if unstable, like the shimmering of a mirage.

Vesi walked between Justine and Lars Porsena with one of them holding each of her arms. When they first entered the Netherworld she had whimpered a time or two but now she was silent, docile.

They were accompanied by an ever-changing assortment of muttering, snarling entities, beings that lurked at the corner of the eye but were too frightening for Justine to turn and face. Some, she recognized. They were similar to the creatures who had inhabited her worst nightmares. Lars Porsena seemed unconcerned about them however. From time to time he even asked them questions and apparently received answers, though in a language Justine could not understand.

"There is no strength in loving," the demon was now saying to her with conviction. "Caring for anyone is always a mistake. That fool boy just proved it by walking into my trap. Love makes humankind vulnerable."

"Did you never love?"

"Only myself. I was the only person I ever found worthy."

The faintest tremor passed through the arm Justine held, as if some violent internal struggle were taking place far below Vesi's placid surface. Justine cast a swift glance at Lars Porsena but apparently he had not noticed, being preoccupied with his own discourse.

He went on describing the ways in which love invariably failed humans, but Justine was no longer paying attention, though from time to time she murmured a syllable of approval. Her mind wandered back over people she had loved—or thought she'd loved—times when the world seemed joyful. There had been many dark days in her existence and only a few bright moments. Those were the ones she wanted to remember. *What a shame,* she thought, *there were not more of them.*

"Love is the ultimate trap," Lars Porsena announced conclusively. "For the sake of love men march willingly to horrible fates, as that boy behind us will discover."

Justine awoke from her reverie. "Are you going to attack him soon?"

"Not yet. First I have some business to conduct in order to facilitate my actions here. Then I want to lead him far away from any possible help before I confront him. The Netherworld is a vast realm, most of it violent and unstable. You are already aware of some of its natives. There are others far worse.

"Satres, god of the Netherworld, makes no effort to control its inhabitants. He enjoys and even encourages their worst behavior to amuse himself. But Veno, Protectress of the Dead, provides a sanctuary of delight for those who manage to reach her. I have no intention of allowing that boy's spirit to find safe haven.

"If he gets close enough to Veno's realm, he will be able to call upon whatever kin he has there for aid. But if I catch him out in the open, I can call on allies of my own. All the advantage will be mine. I will tear his immortal essence to shreds."

"You never told me why you want to destroy his spirit," said Justine. "I can understand killing a living human for revenge, but to destroy the *spirit*. . . "

"Not easily done," the demon interrupted. "But possible. And in this case, necessary. Suffice it to say that while his spirit survives it poses a threat to me. I had long been looking for him. When I discovered his mother in the palace, I realized the weapon for his destruction had fallen into my hands."

"How did you know she was his mother?"

"I did not . . . at first. But I have an infallible memory, Justine, and soon recalled her face. I forget nothing. You would be wise to remember that yourself."

There was a chilling undertone in his voice. Justine was suddenly anxious to change the subject. "Have we far to go?"

"A distance yet. The Netherworld is much larger than the Earthworld."

Justine glanced over her shoulder. "What if he catches up with us before you conduct this business of yours?"

Lars Porsena turned to look at her over Vesi's head. In the lurid crimson light, his handsome features were strangely distorted, his wild, uncombed hair suggesting horns. "You are a clever girl. A woman with a mind—

what a peculiar idea. We need something to slow him down of course. An impediment . . . ah, I know!" Releasing Vesi's arm, he raised his face to the blood-lit sky and clapped his hands together twice.

"Children of Rak-Sar-Shu! Attend me!" he called in a ringing voice.

Singly, then in small clusters, then in a blazing cloud, they formed out of the scarlet sky, the crimson light. Brilliant yellow-white sparks swirled and darted toward Lars Porsena like so many fireflies. But these insects made a sinister hissing sound as they approached. The cloud of malign spirits that had accompanied Lars Porsena fled in terror.

"What are those things?" whispered Justine.

"Fire fiends," Lars Porsena replied casually. "Infernal servitors of a Babylonian fire god now long forgotten. Only his minions remain."

When the burning sparks reached him and the others, they began circling the trio with ever-increasing speed. As they flew they grew larger until each was the size of a man's fist. The sound they made became a muted roar, the roar of a fire on the verge of exploding. The air smelled of molten metal.

Justine shrank back against Lars Porsena. "Will they hurt us?"

"Not as long as they are under my command," he assured her.

"Are they like you?"

He chuckled. "No one is like me, dear child. These fiends are very minor imps that have never been human. They possess almost no mind. Like fire they are obedient to anyone who can control them. Such beings have their uses however. Because they have little intelligence and are incapable of emotion, they are perfect tools for my purpose."

Addressing the moving balls of fire, he commanded, "Return along the way I just came until you find a young man trailing me. Surround him, harry him, do whatever is necessary to slow his progress without causing him to stop altogether."

He paused as if listening to the fiends, then chuckled his cruel chuckle. "I doubt if you have enough power to kill him," he said, "and I forbid you to try. Hurt him all you like but do him no fatal injury. He is mine. I will not rest until I have torn his spirit apart personally."

FORTY-FOUR

Waiting in the cavern with Horatius's body, Khebet listened anxiously to the sounds of the four regrouping outside. He was keeping Anubis's fire alight, but just enough to be a warning. In time his energies would fail and the fire would go out. What might happen then he could not imagine.

From time to time he looked at Horatius. The young man lay supine on the floor of the cave with his hands folded on his breast and his calm face upward. In the light from the magical fire he looked asleep. Beneath his closed lids the eyeballs moved constantly however, as if scanning the landscape of dreams.

Then, as Khebet watched in the flickering firelight, a change took place.

The landscape of the Netherworld was not a constant. As Horatius and Pepan advanced, the scenery changed dramatically. No sooner did they leave the lake than they entered into a parched, arid country. Stunted trees clawed the reddish atmosphere as if desperate for air, and the ground was baked to a hard crust. As Pepan had said, Earthworld tracking techniques were not possible here. Yet with the Lord of the Rasne at his side Horatius always knew which direction to take. From time to time Pepan would cock his head as if listening, then point. "We go this way," he would say with certainty.

"What do you hear?" Horatius asked.

"The music of her soul," was Pepan's cryptic explanation.

Horatius wanted to question him as to what he meant, but there were so many other new things to see, experience, learn. . . .There would be time later, he thought. Once Vesi was safe. Then he would sit down with Pepan and have a wonderful conversation. He would learn all about his mother and his grandmother and the land from which they came.

As he strode forward Horatius made a striking figure: a lean, muscular young man wearing a warrior's breastplate and the pelt of a leopard over his damp toga. The shield was strapped to his arm, the greaves covered his legs to the knee, and he had used the cloth sling to fashion a pouch holding the bag of stones from the Styx and his flint knife. The pouch hung round his neck within easy reach. Most impressive of all was the glittering two-headed ax he carried nonchalantly on his shoulder.

Horatius's clean-shaven face was calm, his eyes were clear and confident. Purpose was implicit in every line of his body. The bursts of childishness that had, understandably, still been part of his character seemed to have been left behind in the warm waters of the lake. Horatius Cocles was indeed a man.

I wish he were my son, Pepan told himself.

No sooner had the thought crossed his mind than he saw Horatius tense and flex his knees, dropping into a defensive crouch.

"What is it?"

"Look there, coming toward us over that hill." Shifting his grip on the haft of the ax, Horatius pointed with his free hand. A cluster of bright specks like blazing embers had appeared in the distance. They rapidly drew nearer. As they approached, the two men could hear a low, sinister hum coming from the fiery swarm.

That sound told Pepan all he needed to know. "Beware, they are dangerous. By their very nature most natives of the Netherworld are inimical to life."

"I am armed."

"You are," agreed Pepan, "but your arsenal is not proof against fire."

The specks had become spinning, blazing balls that hurtled through the air at tremendous speed, trailing streamers of black smoke in their wake. Horatius stood his ground. "They may pass us by, Pepan. There is no point in worrying until. . ."

Suddenly one of the balls swerved toward Horatius. A second and third followed, then halted in midair to hover in front of him, blocking his path. When he took a step sideways the globes of fire moved with him. The others gathered until there were twenty or thirty forming a burning barrier. They would not let Horatius pass, yet neither did they force him backward.

"See if you can get around them, Pepan."

But when the Rasne lord attempted to move to one side the fiery spheres took up an orbit around himself and Horatius, effectively penning them in. As they circled the pair they continued to spin at great speed individually, throwing off more sparks. A few caught and flared briefly in the dry grass. There was an immediate smell of carbon, acrid on the tongue.

Horatius narrowed his eyes in thought. "He did this before, Pepan."

"What are you talking about? Who did this before?"

"The man who stole my mother. He sent rats and scorpions that threatened me but apparently did not intend to kill me. Well, I'm not waiting to see what these things will do!" Clenching his jaw, Horatius took a step forward.

Pepan started to say, "Be very caref" then stopped. The burning globes in front of Horatius had given a tiny amount of ground. They allowed him to move forward one small step at a time, no faster.

Horatius looked over his shoulder. "It's all right, Pepan. Apparently we are allowed to advance as long as we go slowly. But why should we go slowly?"

As if in reply something sang through his blood, the wisdom of a wise old warrior recognizing an enemy strategy. "We are being delayed because those we pursue need more time!" exclaimed Horatius. "Time to give themselves an advantage . . . right! Let's go, Pepan. Run!" He raced forward.

Instantly the low hum became a furious roar. The globes of fire launched a concerted attack on Horatius, coming at him from every direction. He plunged ahead, through the fire, through the smoke, grimly holding on to the haft of the useless ax, possessing no adequate weapon against the flames but his own courage.

The spinning balls narrowed their orbit until they were close enough to singe hair, but Horatius never hesitated. He ran as fast as he could, with Pepan hurrying after him. In an effort to slow him, the balls of fire began mindlessly hurling themselves at Horatius's body. The first struck his breastplate a glancing blow and went spinning away. The next one hit harder, only to explode in a gout of flame and a shower of sparks. A tiny, insanely raging entity fled unnoticed from the holocaust. Undeterred, the other fiends pressed the attack. Another ball hit the breastplate and burst, the flames spinning off at an angle to graze the exposed underside of Horatius's arm. The flesh turned an angry red as a long blister erupted from wrist to elbow.

Ignoring the pain, Horatius ran on.

* * *

As Khebet watched over his body in the cave, one of Horatius's arms turned crimson. The Aegyptian lowered his own arms long enough to lift the limb and examine it, finding a huge, watery blister rising on its underside. Almost at once a second blister appeared on the upper arm. The hair on the arm crisped and smelled scorched.

There was only one conclusion: Horatius was being injured in the Netherworld.

And if he was injured, he could be slain. Khebet lifted his arms and cried to Anubis, "Great Jackal Lord, protect this man who now roams the dark realms! Let him survive this ordeal, allow him to return safely and I will offer you sacrifices of a splendor to rival that of the pharaohs!"

He made the promise wildly, rashly, with no idea how he would keep it but knowing he must find a way somehow. The gods always demanded that promised sacrifices be delivered.

But he had a more immediate worry. During his brief lapse of concentration the fire across the entrance had died down enough to allow the four to get into the cave.

FORTY-FIVE

The moon pool in the long, oval hall began to bubble. There were no mortal eyes present to see the figure that partially emerged. The multibreasted Pythia rose briefly through the white water, looked around, found herself unattended, and submerged again. But she did not leave the pool, need not leave it in order to travel from her Earthworld temple to her Netherworld palace. Water was a conduit.

Among the many palaces belonging to gods in the Netherworld, Pythia's was neither the largest nor the most spectacular. Each palace was a reflection of the nature of its builder. Some employed Cyclopean architecture on a scale beyond Earthworld comprehension, with massive walls and immense towers that bespoke granitic power. Others were as tiny and exquisite as jewels, refracting rainbow prisms from crystalline pinnacles where silken banners fluttered gaily.

Pythia's stronghold in a shadowy valley between two brooding mountains possessed a sinister quality all its own. Even among the gods, who could scarcely afford to condemn any of their own for misbehavior, Pythia's name was enough to provoke a shudder of distaste. At the dawn of Humankind she had interfered with Man and Woman in the Birth Garden, tempting them to an intellectual independence that altered the entire relationship between *Ais* and human. For this she was ostracized.

In response she had made defiance her coda. Her palace reflected her truculent attitude. A vast circular structure surfaced with overlapping scales of metallic black, the mansion rose level upon level, coil upon coil, to dominate the valley. Any who wished to traverse the region between the two peaks found their way blocked. Should they be so foolhardy as to venture into Pythia's realm, they could expect to find agony.

As a result the coiled black palace had very few visitors. Sumptuously furnished in onyx and obsidian, the building echoed hollowly whenever the goddess was not in residence. At its heart was another pool whose waters were as thick as curdled cream and as black as tar.

Here Pythia resurfaced.

A flat forehead, a long narrow jaw, a slash of a mouth. In the Netherworld, however, Pythia was not blind. Her keen eyes were like buttons of polished jet. Turning her head slowly on its long, slender neck, she surveyed the hall surrounding the pool. Her tongue briefly flickered through half-parted lips. "Attend me!" she cried.

Servants hurried forward. Like her Earthworld acolytes, these had serpentine forms. In their case, however, the shape was natural rather than an imposition of the goddess. Pythia was fond of capturing humans and warping them to suit her fancy, but those who served her in the Netherworld were snakes at heart and had never been anything else.

"You command, we obey, Great Goddess," they replied with superficial deference as they approached the tarry pool. They did not share the fear of the Earthworld acolytes that prevented them from looking at their deity. They looked at her openly, almost insolently, as if measuring her usefulness and wondering if they might find a god more worthy.

"Have you any news of the traitor Bur-Sin?" the goddess demanded.

They writhed in indecision, urging one another to go forward. Finally one was shoved to the front. "Even now," the reluctant messenger related, "he is approaching your palace, Great Pythia."

"What! He is coming here? Deliberately?"

"So it seems. With him he brings two females from the Earthworld. Two living females. He maintains their fleshly bodies by using the power he stole from you, an act of appalling audacity. Possibly he thinks to use them to do you harm."

"Harm me? What wretched demon could possibly harm me?" With a great upward surge, Pythia began to emerge from the pool. Beads of moisture clung to her polished skin. She rarely left the water completely because her form was repellent even to herself. Once she had been as beautiful as the loveliest human woman. But in punishment for her misdeed the other gods had put a mark upon her forehead and cursed her to crawl forever in the dust.

She found it easier to hide her shame within the shelter of opaque water. For some acts, however, she must commit to dry land.

Up she came, and up. The slender column of her neck gave way to sloping shoulders, then a grotesque cluster of swollen breasts with their ruby nipples—and one withered breast, empty and useless. The elongated torso that followed was muscular and sinewy, without waist or hips. As more of Pythia emerged from the water her resemblance to anything human disappeared. Her undulating body was broad and thin, like that of a monstrous eel, and of astonishing length.

With a final convulsive heave she cleared the water

and lay stretched upon the floor of the hall, half-filling the room, her many bosoms heaving. Gathering herself, she swiftly coiled into a huge and deadly spiral.

Her servants recognized their danger then and tried to slither backward. Before they could escape she reared up until the forepart of her body towered high above them. A broad hood of mottled black flesh unfolded from either side of her neck just below the jaws. Then she dipped her head and played her flickering tongue over the one who had spoken.

Pythia's jaws opened; fangs shot out, dripping a paralytic poison onto the hapless servant. Her victim could only watch with eyes bulging in horror as her jaws unhinged enough to clamp around his entire head . . . and rip it from his body.

The others fled. Alone in the central hall of her palace, the giant figure of Pythia swayed back and forth. Softly she hissed to herself, "Why? Why has he burdened himself with women?"

FORTY-SIX

The fire fiends continued to hover close, but Horatius would not be deterred. The burning globes did not attack him again however. "They seem more inclined to hinder you than to harm you," Pepan remarked.

"Perhaps I can't be harmed in the Netherworld."

"Make no mistake; you can. Only in the Kingdom of the Dead is there total safety, and you're not dead."

"What about you?"

Pepan replied, "As long as I remain outside the kingdom I too am vulnerable."

"Yet you choose to remain with me?"

"I do."

Horatius paused for a moment and turned to look the other man squarely in the eyes. "I owe you a debt," he said.

"You do not. I am atoning for failing your mother and grandmother a long time ago. I made them a promise I could not keep. Now, through you, I have a second chance. If anything, it is I who am in your debt."

They struggled on. In time they found themselves skirting a broad plain that stretched almost to the horizon. The ground was littered with immense slabs of limestone like a giant's paving stones. Leafless, spiny plants thrived in the gaps between them.

When Horatius tried to go over for a better look, the fire fiends closed around him, attempting to prevent him. Stubbornly he forced his way forward. When he reached the first of the stones the burning globes drew back. "It looks as if they can't follow us here. We can escape them now, Pepan! Come on!" He ran onto the limestone plain and began leaping from one stone square to another. Pepan hurried after him.

The fire fiends hung in the air at the edge of the rocky expanse like a swarm of frustrated hornets. The tiny plants growing between the stones crisped and flamed, only to immediately reappear, then burn again.

The rough-surfaced stones were split and fissured, frequently unstable, shifting underfoot. Running proved impossible and Horatius and Pepan were forced to slow to a walk. The young man felt an uneasy prickling at the back of his neck. Beneath the lurid red sky that was not a sky, the plain had an eerie, haunted quality. "What is this place, Pepan, do you know?"

"I cannot say I do, much of the Netherworld is unexplored, but . . . look over there, Horatius."

Pepan was pointing toward a massive framework emerging from between two slabs of stone. Like the ruin of an ancient building, a set of curved vertical timbers clawed at the sky. Horatius went to take a look. Moments later he called over his shoulder, "These are bones, Pepan!"

The Lord of the Rasne hastened to join him. Together the two gazed down at the ribcage of a giant skeleton, crushed and broken, slowly being freed by natural forces as the stones shifted and the soil wore away. Once a creature of monstrous size had been buried there. Now all that remained was its decaying frame.

"What was it, Pepan?"

The older man studied the bizarre shape, running his hand over the hard surface. "No creature you or I have ever seen. Nor are these actually bones, not as we know them. They are made from some other substance entirely. Not stone, but not bone either."

"Can you say what the creature looked like when it was alive?"

"I cannot even say if it ever was alive. This is the Netherworld, remember. Earthworld life is alien here. I . . . where are you going?"

"There's another one over there!" Careless of his footing, Horatius trotted off at a tangent across the stony expanse.

Pepan caught up with him as he bent over another recumbent form. This one was much smaller and of a different shape. It included a skull of vaguely human proportions but with curving tusks and a bony crest across the top. From the shoulder blades spread a fan of bones that might once have supported wings. The entire skeleton reminded Pepan of something only glimpsed in dreams.

They found another, a human skeleton, with the skull of a bull and curving horns. Beside it lay a creature that had the body of a horse, but the foreparts of a man. A few paces farther on was a huge skull that possessed three sets of eye sockets, three gaping mouths.

Pepan crouched to rub his hand over the three-faced skull. "May the *Ais* forgive us," he whispered. "I believe we have stumbled into a graveyard of the gods."

"But the gods are immortal, surely." Horatius was staring down at the perfectly preserved skeleton of a man—but a man four times taller than a normal human. He tried to imagine a limit to immortality and failed.

The two continued on their quest. Horatius was troubled by what they had seen. From time to time they found other relics, each hinting at some mystery, some legend. He paused by each one, struggling anew to understand the mystery.

Gods die.

And if gods can die, what hope for man?

He was turning to put the question to Pepan when he heard a low groan. The sound was soft and musical, so sweet that at first Horatius thought he was hearing a song or a melody played by the wind moaning through the bones of dead gods.

When it came again, he followed the sound to its source.

At the foot of a towering vertical stone that pointed to the crimson sky was a pit littered with bones. A huddled figure lay in the bottom of the pit. "Pepan! Look here!"

The Lord of the Rasne hurried over to put a cautionary hand on his arm. "It might be a trap."

"Or it could be someone in pain," argued Horatius. As if to confirm his words, another moan sounded from the pit. He shook off Pepan's hand and jumped down. His companion could only follow, shaking his head.

When Horatius and Pepan tossed aside the piled debris of ancient bones and knelt beside him, the being opened his eyes. Orange eyes. Star-shaped eyes set in a pale but perfect oval face, surrounded by a mane of curling, golden hair like the petals of a flower. He was very beautiful but he was not human.

When he saw them he groaned again and closed his eyes.

"Who are you?" Horatius asked gently. "Can we help you?"

The voice that answered was very weak. "You cannot help me. I am dying."

"Are you wounded?"

"No, merely starved."

"We have no food."

"I need no food."

"Who are you?"

"Why do you care? But if you do—I am what you call a god. A once-god."

Pepan tensed. "Be careful, Horatius."

"You need not fear me." The orange-eyed being attempted to sit up. "I am the one who should be afraid of you. My enemies have sent you to mock me in my weakness. I take satisfaction from knowing that their time will come. One day they too will lie here and wait for oblivion."

Horatius crouched beside the god. With tender care he gathered the being into his arms and stroked the pallid brow, brushing strands of golden hair away from the extraordinary eyes. "We have no intention of mocking you; we are not cruel. But if you are a god, why are you not immortal?"

"I am immortal; I have always existed and always will. But not with this face and form. Their substance was created by the imaginations of humans who long ago conferred godhood upon my spirit. They encased me in this image. Now humans no longer worship at my shrines. My temples have fallen; no power of faith sustains me. My beauty is dying and I grieve for its loss."

"Of course!" exclaimed Pepan. "Horatius, long before there were Etruscans other people walked the earth, people who worshipped very different gods from ours. When those folk died out, their vision of the gods must have died with them. Here we see an example of someone's god dying because the belief has died. Don't you see? The *Ais* need us as much as we need them!"

Horatius was deeply moved by the beautiful, fading creature. "Is there no way I can help you?"

The orange eyes gazed up into his. "Believe in the reality of me. As long as I am real to you, the form you see will survive. In return I will give you my help in your hour of greatest need."

"You have my pledge," promised Horatius. "May I know your name?"

"Some have called me . . . Eosphorus."

"Eosphorus," Horatius repeated, his mouth full of the word. "Eosphorus." Even as he said the name, the creature in his arms began to change. A glow appeared beneath the clear skin, then grew in power until Eosphorus was radiant. His beauty became so great Horatius had to turn his face away. "I cannot look at you; you dazzle me."

"I was once known as the Shining One," the god in his arms said.

FORTY-SEVEN

When he saw the two mountain peaks rising ahead of him Lars Porsena smiled. "We are nearing Pythia's palace," he told Justine.

"Is that where we're going? But you told me she hates you and wants to harm you."

"She does. I am tired of fleeing however. I want to put an end to the quarrel between us and rid myself of fear. Cowardice ill becomes me, dear child."

"So you are going into her den to confront her?" In spite of herself, Justine could not keep a throb of admiration from her voice. Hiding from trouble, or running from it, or not admitting its existence—these were her ways of coping. They had failed her miserably, as her life proved. Yet the one time she had taken her courage in both hands and faced a tormentor, it had proved to be this demon at her side.

Lars Porsena uttered his demonic chuckle. " 'Den' is hardly the word I would use for Pythia's palace. She is lazy and likes her comfort, as you will soon see. Her taste is a bit bizarre, perhaps, but reflects her true self. There, just ahead. Those gates in that high wall are hers. Beyond them is a long road that leads to her, ah, den."

The gates were made of metal bars cunningly contorted to resemble a tangle of briars. Large, needle-sharp thorns protruded in every direction. Anyone who attempted to force the gates open, or climb over them, would be badly lacerated. But there was a handle; a single smooth handle shaped into a serpentine curve.

"Try it," Lars Porsena suggested.

Brushing past Justine, Vesi reached forward and took hold of the handle.

From somewhere among the thorns came a dry, menacing rattle.

Vesi, unintimidated, twisted the handle until both gates swung open. Lars Porsena's eyebrows shot upward in surprise, but he recovered to reward her with a sweeping bow. "After you," he said.

Once the three had passed through the gates they heard them slam shut. Justine glanced back. No visible agency had closed the gates, and there was no handle on the inside.

Ahead lay a road that wound down a dark valley between two somber peaks. No light reached that road; it lay in eternal shadow.

"This place frightens me," Justine whispered.

"So it should," Lars Porsena laughed. "This is the Valley of the Shadow."

They had gone some distance before Lars Porsena stumbled. Then, visibly faltering, he stumbled again and came to a halt. "I am growing weaker," he complained to Justine.

"Surely not here, not so soon."

"Yes, dear child, right here. Right now! I dare not approach Pythia unless I am at my full strength. And for that I need you. It is your reason for being. Come to me now," he said in a seductive voice. "Come to me."

The demon opened his arms.

* * *

Afterward Justine walked in a daze for a time. When at last she took notice of her surroundings she discovered they were approaching a round, oily-looking black building that rose layer upon horrid layer, each successive coil smaller than the one below. There was no peak at the top of the structure, no tower, no turret. Merely an awful emptiness.

"Pythia's palace," announced Lars Porsena, striding forward.

Scale-cloaked and hooded figures guarded the double doors that led into the palace. Although their faces were concealed by the enveloping hoods, Justine sensed they were apprehensive at the arrival of the visitors.

Lars Porsena said brazenly, "Tell the dark goddess her favorite acolyte has returned. Announce the arrival of Bur-Sin of Babylon."

The guards drew back; the doors swung wide.

A second set of figures wrapped in iridescent, scaled cloaks appeared from within the palace to usher Lars Porsena and the two women into a large audience chamber. The room was devoid of furniture aside from benches of obsidian and onyx lining the black walls. Sullen yellow flames flickered in bronze braziers. Pythia's servants indicated silently that the new arrivals were to seat themselves. Then they all but ran from the hall.

The central feature of the audience chamber was a circular pool brimming with black liquid. From time to time a lazy bubble surfaced, glistened, broke. Justine found herself gazing at the pool as if hypnotized. Her mouth was dry, her tongue thick with an ancient and irrational fear of the unknown.

A disturbance destroyed the apparent tranquillity of the pool, a slow roiling that gradually intensified, a sense of some mighty body moving below the surface.

When Pythia's head emerged from the pool Justine gasped and opened her mouth to scream, but Lars Porsena's fingers tightened in a savage grip over her jaw. She choked on her fear in silence.

Vesi sat unmoving, looking straight ahead.

The goddess rose from the water just far enough to reveal the upper curve of her breasts and fixed unblinking eyes on Lars Porsena. "You."

"Yes."

"You never fail to surprise me, Bur-Sin; I suppose that is why I tolerated your insolence and your insubordination for so long," said Pythia in a terrifyingly soft and sibilant voice. "But this time you go too far. Or have you returned to submit to the punishment you so richly deserve?"

"No, Pythia, I have a different resolution of our conflict in mind."

"What could you possibly suggest that would give me more pleasure than reducing you to blubbering madness?"

"A sacrifice."

Justine's stomach contracted with fear. But instead, Lars Porsena gestured toward Vesi. "I have brought you this woman as an offering. Visit upon her whatever punishment you had in mind for me."

Justine observed that Pythia had yet to look at Vesi. "Why should I accede to your request, Bur-Sin?" the goddess inquired. "What makes you think she would be a sufficient substitute for you?"

"Because she is not just any woman, Great Goddess. She is quite remarkable: an oracle, a seer. I personally witnessed her prophesying for the king of Rome. We both know that oracles are favored by the gods. Therefore she is a very valuable sacrifice and one that should more than repay my, ah, misdeed."

At last Pythia transferred her gaze to Vesi. "An oracle, you say," she continued in the same conversational tone.

"Unless my eyes deceive me, she is also an Etruscan. She certainly has Etrurian features; the race beloved of the gods, or so they claim."

"Therefore she is twice valuable, Pythia. And in addition—just so you will know how much I am willing to pay for your forgiveness—she is the mother of my child," Lars Porsena finished triumphantly.

"Indeed! You would do that, surrender the mother of your child to me? An impressive sacrifice, Bur-Sin. But"—the tongue of the goddess flickered fretfully between parted lips—"is one woman enough to atone for your crime against me? Even if she is all you claim."

"Oh, she is, Great Pythia! I can prove it." Lars Porsena caught Vesi by both shoulders and clamped his fingers painfully deep into her flesh.

"Say something," he growled at her. "Look into the future and tell us what you see."

Vesi did not move, did not blink.

"You are trying to deceive me, Bur-Sin," drawled Pythia. "I expected as much."

"This is no deception! She is a seer, I tell you! If you once hear her speak, you'll be convinced."

"Oh, I have heard her speak," replied Pythia in that unmistakable voice. But the words did not come from the goddess in the pool.

They came from the lips of Vesi.

Lars Porsena snatched his hands away from her shoulders as if burned by her flesh. "I have not only heard her speak," the voice went on, "but I have spoken through her. I even used her as a tool to tear apart a human for my amusement. Bur-Sin, you fool, you have brought me my own plaything as a sacrifice. The mother of your child, indeed! How ironic, since my minions have exhausted themselves searching for your son. Once they found him, he was to be used as a lure to draw you: and I then thought I might kill him in front of you as part of your punishment. But now that I have you in my coils, I do not really need him. I can punish you

the Netherworld you could have materialized here in any form you chose. But unfortunately, your insatiable appetites prompted you to steal a second Earthworld existence for yourself. A great mistake, Bur-Sin; the gods disapprove of demons incarnating on earth. They invariably try to claim our prerogatives there.

"You say you came here to offer me the woman as a sacrifice, so I accept her—but my acceptance does not imply forgiveness. Far from it. There is no atonement for what you did to me, Bur-Sin. I merely take her for my own amusement, and I will keep the young one as well. To survive what you have done to her she must have an exceptionally strong spirit. I am sure I can find an interesting use for such a spirit. Entering my service will mean the irrevocable destruction of their Earthworld bodies, of course, but no matter.

"As for you, Bur-Sin. . . " Pythia hesitated in order to prolong his agony. "As for you, obviously you will have no use for either of them any longer. You have sacrificed much for that body you prance around in, but your days of enjoying human flesh in all its forms are over. I mean to give you *exactly* what you deserve."

Surging upward, she began to leave the pool.

With a great shout Lars Porsena shoved the two women toward the goddess and ran.

FORTY-EIGHT

Again the landscape of the Netherworld changed. Guided by Pepan, Horatius entered a billowing desert striated by different colors of sand, ranging from ochre to yellow to a strange, burning white. A hot wind blew continually, stirring up clouds of sand.

At first a few pinnacles of eroded stone were the only landmarks, but these eventually merged into a wall of low, rugged cliffs pierced by occasional dark defiles. Pepan found the sullen atmosphere of the region disturbing, the scenery of nightmare.

Horatius felt differently. "I must admit, I miss green," he remarked to Pepan. "My eyes are hungry for green and blue and clear, cool colors. But this is a remarkable place all the same. The Netherworld contains more wonders than I ever imagined on earth."

"I doubt if you're aware of a fraction of the wonders that exist on earth," Pepan replied. "Only when you enter the Otherworld and leave human limitations behind do you fully appreciate the beauty of the Earthworld. To hear the music of a living spirit. . . ”

“Of course, you spoke of this before. The music of her soul, you said. But I don’t understand what you mean.”

“How do you think I am following Vesi? Every *hia* sings a song unique to itself that cannot be heard in the Earthworld, but is clearly audible once you leave.”

“You can actually hear my mother? Can I?”

“Perhaps. Listen for the particular song of her human spirit, a single pure note, tempered by experience and age, altered by pain, heightened by love. Open your heart and listen.”

The young man shrugged the ax off his shoulder in order to concentrate more fully. “I think I hear . . .” Sudden alarm leaped in his eyes.

Accompanied by a curious, gobbling noise, a dozen or more grotesque beings came into view making their way among the sand dunes. Standing smaller than an average man, each possessed one head, two arms, and two legs but there any resemblance to humankind ended. Their skin was the color of rust and composed of innumerable small bubbles. They traveled with an awkward, loping gait, and as they moved the bubbles lost cohesion and burst so that bits of their surface continually sloughed away, leaving a sluglike trail in their wake.

“What are those things?” asked Horatius with disgust.

Pepan shook his head. “I have no idea and no desire for a closer look. Let’s head for the cliffs, there at least we have a chance of getting away from them. Out here on the desert we’re too exposed.”

Trying not to call attention to themselves, the two set out for the cliffs at a brisk walk. The creatures immediately changed direction and followed them. At this ominous sign Horatius and Pepan broke into a run, but by the time they reached the cliffs the pack was closing fast. Their smell preceded them on the hot wind. They stank like the bowels of someone in the last stages of disease. A momentary wave of nausea doubled Horatius over, retching.

The pack swiftly caught up with him then. The leaders flung themselves upon him, clinging to his torso and arms like lichen on a tree. The rest encircled him to keep him from running away. They had no faces other than thick-lipped mouths in the center of their heads from which poured a foul-smelling, yellowish drool. Their slobbering mouths held curving fangs, their two-fingered hands ended in long talons that they could use either as claws or as crablike pincers. The bubbling skin was too slimy to grasp; Horatius could get no hold on them to tear them off. Against so many the shield was merely an impediment on his arm. Neither were his weapons of any use, for with the creatures crawling over him he could not swing the ax nor even get to the knife in his neck pouch.

When they discovered they could not tear through Horatius's breastplate they turned their attention to his head. They attempted to gnaw his ears from his skull, their talons slashing for his eyes. He tried as best he could to fend them off but there were too many of them.

Pepan was dismayed. To come so far and risk so much, and then fall victim to this loathsome horde . . . "No!" cried the Lord of the Rasne. Unarmed, he threw himself on Horatius's attackers and dragged the young man free. Pulling him by the straps of his breastplate, he hauled him into the mouth of a narrow defile. Then tossing Horatius behind him into the shadow, he stood squarely in the mouth of the defile and faced the creatures.

His fists sank from sight in slimy bubbles, he could find nothing solid to hit. But he screamed and kicked and flailed his arms, driving them back with the sheer fury of his attack. The creatures hesitated momentarily to regroup. "This is your chance, Horatius! Run for it, go through the defile to whatever is on the other side. I'll hold them here until you can get away. And listen for your mother's music!"

"I can't leave you alone!"

"I told you they are dangerous to life, but you forget—I'm not alive," Pepan argued. "Run, I tell you. Run!"

The young man staggered to his feet. "I cannot desert you."

"And I will never desert you," Pepan lied. "Now go!"

Horatius ran.

Sooner or later, Pepan thought as the young man disappeared into the cleft in the rock, *he will remember my telling him that I am vulnerable here too. But by that time he will be safely away.*

I do this for you, Repana. So that he can save your daughter.

The creatures attacked. Their curving talons cut through the air with an unnerving, scythelike motion, or closed into pincers attempting to rip his flesh from his bones. As if they knew how unmanning their breath was, they deliberately belched great waves of gaseous stench in his face.

There were too many to attack him all at once. Half their number were clinging to his body while the rest capered around him, gobbling hungrily, mouths opening and closing, the jaws and chests wet with noxious saliva. Pepan had no illusion about their plans for his flesh.

If only he had a weapon.

He ruefully recalled lending his favorite ebony-handled knife to Repana, so long ago. There must be some weapon he could use now; anything! But as he looked frantically around he saw nothing but sand.

Stooping, Pepan snatched up a handful of sharp grains and hurled them deep into the nearest open mouth.

The creature choked, clawed at its throat, fell writhing to the ground. To Pepan's disgust the others promptly turned upon their companion and devoured it alive, shoving chunks of bubbling flesh into their mouths even as they resumed the attack on the Rasne lord.

Since his death Pepan had learned much about the laws that controlled the three disparate planes of existence. But he did not know how much damage a Netherworld body could suffer and still host a living spirit. If his body was destroyed his *hia* would be set adrift alone and unprotected in this dreadful place. He would surely fall victim to the predators of the Netherworld long before he could find his way to sanctuary with Veno. Only the gods themselves knew what he would become.

Pepan fought to control his fear, but he was tiring. One of the creatures behind him took a terrific swipe at his back. A pain like a bolt of lightning drove him to his knees.

Repana, he thought again as he struggled to his feet.

He did not know if he spoke aloud.

His attackers were tumbling over one another in their eagerness to destroy. The pain rose to a dazzling crescendo.

So this is how it will end. What sort of destiny is this for a prince of Etruria?

Claws slashed his chest, pincers ripped flesh from his shoulders and thighs. The creatures were grunting with excitement at the prospect of a kill. In another moment they would overwhelm him with sheer numbers, but he was determined to go down fighting.

Then at an invisible signal the entire pack flung itself upon him at once. Pepan fought back with fists and elbows but the outcome was inevitable. Under their massed weight he staggered and fell sideways. He managed to get to one knee only to be knocked down again, sent sprawling by a crashing blow to the back of the head.

He could not get up again. Curling into a ball, he attempted to shield his head with his arms for as long as possible.

As he lay huddled on the ground memories flickered through his mind like a brilliantly colored ribbon. Images of his childhood, his gentle and affectionate mother, his aloof and lordly father. He recalled his youth, his first love, the taste of her lips. His initiation ceremony into manhood, his leadership of the Rasne. Wife, children.

Repana.

Above all others, Repana.

So many people, so many faces. Many of them now safe in the Kingdom of the Dead, whereas he . . .

So many images, so many lives and loves, so few regrets . . .

Repana.

When the other faces had vanished into the pain, Repana's remained. He struggled to hold onto that memory to carry with him into the darkness. Perhaps if he could take her image with him into the night, it might sustain him.

Then through the gobbling and grunting of the creatures tearing at him he heard a single sound: a rich and melodious note that went straight to his heart. Twisting around, he managed to peer through the legs of the creatures in time to see two figures appear out of the shimmering heat.

One was a woman dressed in an Etruscan gown.

Behind her, hulking huge, loomed the shadowy form of a massive bear.

The woman . . .

Pepan tried to focus on her face but he was swiftly losing consciousness. Gray mist swirled through his head. He squinted, struggling to see for just one heartbeat longer . . .

. . . as the great bear launched itself upon the creatures, roaring in righteous fury as it savaged them.

* * *

"My lord, can you hear me?" She bent closer until her face was almost touching his. "Open your eyes and speak to me."

Pepan made himself ignore the excruciating pain in his back long enough to lift his eyelids.

A face appeared. A beloved face. Younger than he remembered it, bright with youth and alive with love.

"Repana?" His voice was very faint.

"Yes, yes, my dear one."

"But I thought . . . you were safe with . . ."

"With Wulv? I was. Together he and I made our way to Veno. We faced many hazards on the way but he overcame them all for my sake. At last the Protectress opened her arms to us and we were safe in a realm of delight. But then we heard your call. And here we are."

"You left the security of Veno's realm for my sake?" Pepan asked incredulously.

"Just as you eschewed it for my sake, and Vesi's. I know what you did for us. Even in death, you remained with us, watching over us. But don't waste strength talking now. We must get you away from here before any more harm can come to you." Raising her voice, she called, "Wulv! Is it over?"

"Almost," came the reply.

The immense bear shambled into view, holding a torn body in his paws. From the body streams of tiny bubbles ran onto the ground, forming a puddle that emitted a nauseating odor.

"Get rid of that," commanded Repana, "and help me carry Pepan."

"Carry me!" the wounded man retorted indignantly. "Where?"

She smiled down at him. "To Veno, of course, where you will be forever safe with us."

Pepan tried to sit up. "But your grandson needs me."

With a firm hand, Repana pushed his shoulders back

onto her lap. "You have done all one could possibly do to help him."

"How do you know?"

"Veno allowed us to watch from our sanctuary."

"You took a great risk by coming to save me."

Repana laughed, the warm, low laugh he remembered from long ago. "Ah, when one is with the redoubtable Wulv, one is in little danger."

At the sound of his name Wulv, in human form, came trotting up. There was yellowish ichor on his hands and soaking into the tunic of skins he wore, but his eyes were very bright. Pepan noted that his face was no longer ridged with scars. He was almost handsome.

"Best battle I've had in ages," the Teumetian commented happily. He bent down and helped Pepan to his feet.

"You do not have to carry me," said the Rasne lord with a hint of his old authority. "I can walk."

"Of course you can," Repana replied. "You always were a strong man. We will each take one of your arms, though, just to steady you." She smiled into his eyes. "Come, my love. It is time to go home."

FORTY-NINE

The fire of Anubis had subsided to a row of flickering tongues of flame just inside the entrance to the caverns. Twice the hooded figures had gained access; twice Khebet had fought them back. One now lay unmoving within the mouth of the cave, its body partially consumed in the flames. There was no fight left in the Aegyptian, nor magic either. The next time they attacked they would leap the low flames and kill him.

Khebet felt hollow inside, numb as with some appalling cold.

According to the tenets of his religion, a luxurious Afterlife awaited him. Gold and silver and attentive slaves, sweet wine and silken couches and beautiful women.

His teeth began to chatter uncontrollably.

He could hear the remaining hooded horrors moving around outside. Why did they not talk to one another? Their silence was as sinister as their intent. The agony of anticipation was unbearable.

Khebet thought of the sacrifices he had to offered to Anubis over the years, the trussed-up calves and lambs and kids with garlands of flowers around their necks that he had placed upon the god's altar. The animals had gazed at him with such innocent, despairing eyes as they awaited their fate, but their emotions had been of no consequence to him—then.

Now he wondered if they had been as terrified as he was tonight.

"If I survive this," he murmured to give himself the comfort of a human voice, "I vow I will never again offer a blood sacrifice to the Jackal."

Not only his teeth were chattering. His whole body had begun to tremble.

He had not succeeded in placating the gods after all. His life had been misspent, his priesthood a fraud. With death imminent, Khebet was shocked to discover he did not even believe in the Afterlife.

The realization should have increased his fear, but instead a sort of desperate peace came over him.

His trembling abated.

"Die bravely, Aegyptian," Khebet whispered to himself in the echoing cave. "If all else is lost, give yourself that much. Die as a hero, like Horatius."

FIFTY

The defile in the cliffs widened into a canyon, then eventually opened onto a broad plain. The surface of this tableland resembled black marble polished to a high gloss. Pausing at the mouth of the canyon, Horatius gazed out across the desolate landscape and tried to decide which way to go. There was nothing here that could serve as a trail, no way he could track Vesi. He needed Pepan and the musical sound the other man had followed.

Pepan . . .

Pepan should be behind him . . . and then he inhaled sharply. "But he told me he was vulnerable in the Netherworld too!"

Suddenly he understood. Pepan had offered himself as a sacrifice. Horatius turned and ran back through the defile, ax in hand. This time he would be ready for them. He would hold his breath and not breathe their poison.

But the sandy plain was deserted. There was no sign of the creatures, though the ground was encrusted with slime. There was no sign of Pepan either, only a puddle of blood.

Crouching, Horatius studied the scene. The congealing blood told him nothing. But then the pervasive, lurid light changed slightly and he made out an unusual indentation on the ground a few paces away. He got swiftly to his feet and went to look.

Moving in a straight line across the sand toward the horizon were blurred marks more nearly resembling the tracks of a bear than those of a man. They were accompanied by the footprints of naked human feet, high-arched like a woman's. Between them were the unmistakable prints of Pepan's Etruscan sandals.

Horatius raised his ax in silent salute to the man he had known so briefly—the man who had been with him all his life.

Then he retraced his own footsteps back through the defile, in the direction Pepan had sent him. His journey was not yet over.

No sooner had he set foot on the gleaming black plain than he became aware of something moving beneath him. When he glanced down he discovered his own reflection, as if he walked on a mirrored surface. At first the effect was unsettling. He kept looking down to see his face looking back at him.

Raising his eyes, he tried to estimate the distance to the horizon. But perspective was unreliable here. At one moment it seemed quite close, then when he looked again he was gazing across an endless blackness beneath a lurid red dome. The infrequent streaks of gold that blazed across the faraway roof of the Netherworld were also reflected in the black marble. Like fireflies, they provided nervous flashes of light that were gone before he could focus on them.

Nothing else moved on the dark plain.

Perhaps because he was alone now, Horatius felt increasingly apprehensive. And yet the ax was on his shoulder, the knife and slingshot close to hand. None of these had been of any use against the creatures with the bubbling skin but they were a comforting reminder of Pepan's words: *You have never been alone*.

He walked on for a time.

An interminable time.

The landscape, and himself as the solitary figure in it, was unutterably depressing. What he had seen of the Netherworld was no place for a human spirit, he thought. What would the Kingdom of the Dead be like? Surely it was better than this. But he had no idea in which direction it lay, any more than he knew where to find his mother. He could only keep going forward, ever hopeful of discovering something—anything.

Perhaps that is what faith means, Horatius told himself.

Then in the distance he glimpsed a single figure that flickered in and out of his vision, now discernible, now seeming no more than a trick of the light. As he watched, he realized the figure was coming in his direction. Soon he could tell that it was bobbing back and forth as if running in an erratic pattern, then crouching and half-turning to look back.

These were the actions of prey fleeing a predator.

Hefting the ax, he scanned the horizon but saw nothing else moving.

As it came closer, the figure gradually resolved itself into that of a man. Every movement he made indicated terror. Horatius set off toward him, impelled by the instinct to help a fellow being in distress. Then he paused. There was something disturbing about that figure. Although manlike in every proportion, he was running too fast for any human.

Horatius took the ax from his shoulder and balanced it warily in his two hands.

Now the other noticed him, turned toward him. The unnatural speed slowed to a normal pace.

Horatius called out, "Are you in trouble?"

The man threw up one arm and waved. "Stay where

you are," he called, "I will come to you." He trotted toward Horatius.

As he approached Horatius was astonished to see a face he knew: the clear green eyes, the piercing gaze of an eagle.

Lars Porsena.

The Prince of Clusium—here!

Then at once he realized that although the creature wore the handsome visage of the prince, this was no human.

At the same time Lars Porsena reacted to him. He stopped, shocked. His handsome face hardened into a look of implacable hatred. "I know you," he said through clenched teeth as he approached. "Oh, but this is good . . . good. Surely the *Ais* are playing with me. This is some jest. I know you," he repeated almost with disbelief. "You have your mother's sound."

Horatius was caught off guard. "How do you know about my mother's sound?"

Lars Porsena bared his teeth in what might have been a smile. "I know all about your mother; at least, all I need to know."

"Have you seen her?"

"Seen her? I just left her—back there." With a jerk of his head he indicated the direction from which he had come. Then unaccountably he chuckled.

"I have to go to her," Horatius began, but before he could take a step Lars Porsena blocked his way.

"You are going nowhere," said the demon in a voice vibrating with menace. "You pitiful puling pup, the gods have delivered you into my hands after all. I can snatch victory from the very fangs of defeat. When I finish with you there will be one less thing for me to worry about. When I have done with you, I may even go back and confront Pythia."

Faster than thought, the Etruscan body melted into a different form altogether. Instead of a human being Horatius was confronted with a man-size ball of metallic-looking spikes. The ball rolled toward him, pulsing rhythmically, while from its midsection two green fires burned like eyes. A spiky tentacle shot out to take a savage swing at Horatius.

He dodged sideways, barely avoiding the tentacle, feeling it brush against his hair. "What do you want?" he cried with a sense of outrage. "I've done nothing to you!"

From within the ball the voice of Lars Porsena replied, "You exist. That is your crime against me and the punishment is death."

"That makes no sense!"

The demon chuckled. "You expect logic? The rules of existence are different once you leave the Earthworld. You are totally in my power here."

Not totally, thought Horatius. *Hit me; strike my breastplate.*

With an act of purest faith, the young man stood firm. When the demon reached for him he met the blow with his chin up and his head high. The spiky tentacle snapped out, catching him full in the chest. It rebounded harmlessly off his armor.

But it suffered dreadful damage in return. A ripple of blue fire ran up the appendage from the surface of Horatius's breastplate. There was a blinding flash of light and a great crash like the voice of Tinia the lightning god. With a howl of pain, the spiky ball disappeared.

In its place stood a beautiful woman, nursing a bruised arm.

The transformation was so abrupt, the contrast so total, Horatius could only stare. She was the most compelling creature he had ever seen. A mane of honey-colored hair cascaded down her shoulders, framing naked breasts. The curve of her unclothed hips was an invitation; the golden nest at the base of her rounded belly was a lure. Meltingly green eyes smiled languorously at Horatius. "I want you," she whispered.

The young man's body responded with a surge of mindless desire.

Opening her arms, the woman urged, "Come to me. Be my lover and you will know the heights of passion."

Unconsciously, Horatius stepped forward and the woman moved to meet him.

"I will teach you wonders," she promised in a voice throbbing with invitation. But as she spoke the hair on her head began to move, to writhe and twist with a horrid life of its own. The light in her green eyes became an insane glare that held nothing of human warmth.

Fighting the lust still scorching through him, Horatius held his shield at an angle so he could catch the woman's reflection in the metal surface. What he saw was no woman at all. Instead his enemy was revealed as a figure of putrescent horror, holding out arms that dripped with the rot of the grave.

Shuddering, Horatius swung the shield in front of him to cut off the vision.

A silence fell then. He might have been alone in all creation. The loudest sounds were the roaring of his blood in his ears; the thudding of his heart. He waited, trying to prepare for the unguessable, but nothing further happened.

When he could stand it no longer he peered over the top of the shield and saw only the black plain, the red sky. Then he heard something moving and looked down.

On the ground before him crouched a monstrous lizard longer than a man. The body was the color of flame, the head saffron yellow surmounted by a serrated crest of orange cartilage. From the shoulders sprouted leathery black tendrils that waved like weed beneath the sea.

The saurian's eyes were clearest green.

Fixing a cold gaze on Horatius, the lizard vented a roar that reverberated across the plain. Its open mouth revealed a double row of pointed teeth, each one as long as a man's thumb, set in muscular jaws. The creature continued to roar as it lashed its tail from side to side, building momentum for the attack.

Horatius held his shield to one side, arms spread as if inviting destruction.

The lizard lunged forward.

Fearsome teeth clamped on the young man's shin. The beast bit down; the teeth shattered like glass against the greaves.

The lizard's roar became a squeal of pain as splintered shards tore its mouth and tongue. Black blood spurted. The monster writhed at Horatius's feet and . . .

. . . was transformed into an immense bull.

The roar of the lizard was as nothing compared to the bellow of the bull, a creature half again as large as any Earthworld beast. The hide was dead white with large patches of red, like splotches of blood, on the back and belly. A pair of sharp black horns curved out from the forehead—but it was not a bull's forehead. The beast's massive shoulders were surmounted with an outsize human head. The face was a distortion of Lars Porsena's.

Pawing the ground and snorting in rage, this grotesque brute fixed baleful green eyes on Horatius. It was powerful enough to charge through his shield. Even his breastplate could not turn so huge an adversary.

Had not one of his ancestors mentioned bulls?

Horatius spread his feet to give himself a more secure stance and hefted the gold-plated ax just as the bull charged.

Horatius neatly sidestepped the charge and put his full weight behind the swing. The ax sang with a voice of its own, a somber whirr of death. The glittering blade sliced into the muscular neck of the bull just below the human jawbone. There was a momentary resistance of tough flesh, but nothing could deflect the sacrificial ax.

At the moment it sliced through the brute's jugular, Lars Porsena changed again.

In place of a bull with a man's head an even more improbable hybrid appeared. Crouching on four clawed legs was a creature with the body of a great, tawny lion—and with wings. This time the head was that of an eagle, a green-eyed eagle. The pitiless, predatory eyes burned into those of Horatius.

He swiftly took half a step backward and lifted the ax for another blow. Before he could strike, the creature unfolded its broad wings and sprang into the sky.

The ax sang harmlessly through empty air.

Tilting back his head, Horatius saw the thing hovering above him out of range of the ax. When it screamed its voice was like nothing he had ever heard before. Then it extended its clawed feet and dived toward him.

The mighty wings beat the air so hard they almost knocked Horatius down. One of the feet caught the ax, tore it from his grasp, and carried it high into the crimson heavens. Screaming triumphantly, the monster climbed into the sky again and prepared for another dive. With gaping beak and downbeating wings, the brute could plummet to the ground with enough force to break Horatius in half.

Horatius whipped the pouch from around his neck. Tucking the flint knife into his belt, he twisted the cloth into a sling that he armed with a stone from the Styx.

The monster dived.

Horatius fired.

The stone struck between the savage green eyes. The brute, stunned, lost control and fell spinning out of the red sky.

When it hit the ground it vanished. In its place a human figure lay crumpled at Horatius's feet. The figure moaned and struggled to rise, then turned a bloody face toward the young man. "Help me," implored Pepan, reaching out. "Help me get up."

Horatius automatically extended a hand. Pepan got to his feet with an effort, wincing in pain. "What have you done to me?"

"I don't . . . but . . . I don't understand . . ." stammered Horatius. "You . . . I mean he . . . I thought you were a monster."

"I am and always have been your friend," Pepan replied reprovingly.

Embarrassed, Horatius dropped his eyes . . . and noticed two reflections on the gleaming black surface where they stood. His own was familiar, but the image beneath Pepan did not resemble the Rasne lord. It belonged to a very different man in a very menacing posture.

Horatius swiftly dropped to one knee and snatched the flint knife from his belt. Raising his arm, he struck a mighty downward blow. The weapon fashioned by the earliest Etruscan sank to the hilt in what appeared to be solid stone—and pinned the demon's reflection to the ground.

Pepan's form dissolved into that of a furious Lars Porsena. He tried to lift first one foot and then the other from the ground, but they were held securely in place. Even demonic strength could not free them from their reflection.

He was trapped.

His green eyes gave Horatius a look of such concentrated hatred that the young man took a step sideways, out of Lars Porsena's reach.

The demon bent to draw the knife from the stone himself, but when his fingers touched the handle a shudder ran through him. He convulsed with pain. White smoke coiled from seared flesh.

"My mother!" Horatius cried. "Where is she?"

Through clenched teeth the demon snarled, "I'll tear you to bits!"

"I think not. We just proved I am more than a match for you. But I might be prepared to release you in exchange for information about my mother."

With a visible effort Lars Porsena arranged his features in a slightly more amiable expression. "What do you want to know?"

"How can I be sure you're telling me the truth?"

"I have no reason to lie to you."

"You have no reason to kill me either."

"Ah, but I do. Did. If you release me I will consider matters settled between us however."

"First you'll have to tell me about my mother and where to find her. Did you have anything to do with her kidnapping?"

"I?" Lars Porsena sounded genuinely offended. He splayed the fingers of his right hand across his chest in a gesture of sincerity. "I dearly love women, I would cause no harm to any of them. Trust me."

"Trust you? I had as soon trust a viper. I don't know just what you are, but . . ."

As Horatius said the word *viper*, Lars Porsena went pale. His green eyes were no longer fixed on the young man's face; they were staring over his shoulder with a look of total terror.

At first Horatius suspected a trick, but it was obvious that Lars Porsena's fear was genuine as he redoubled his efforts to free himself. He was almost sobbing with terror.

Horatius turned to follow the direction of his gaze. Coming over the horizon was a huge, dark figure that appeared to glide forward, halt long enough to gather itself like a coiled spring, then glide forward again.

"No," Lars Porsena gasped. "No no no no no!"

"What is that?" asked Horatius.

"Pythia."

The name meant nothing to Horatius, but the way the creature was moving was unnerving. It advanced with astonishing rapidity. By the time it had halved the distance between them, he could make out details.

He stared in disbelief at the largest serpent he had ever seen.

The upper part of her body was female, though not human. In her coils she carried two human women. She was so huge that their bodies did not impede her progress in the slightest.

"Don't let her get me!" begged Lars Porsena.

Horatius started to ask, "What does she want with you?" but the words dried on his tongue as he recognized one of the women caught fast in the serpent's coils.

"Mother!"

At the sound of his voice Vesi opened her eyes.

"Horatrim," she called softly.

She was looking down at her son from a height, for the huge serpent was holding the two women far above a man's reach. Both women were alive and conscious. The muscular coils of the creature possessed unimaginable power, but also great delicacy. Pythia could have crushed Vesi and Justine if she chose. Instead she held them almost tenderly.

"Bur-Sin," she hissed.

The being Horatius knew as Lars Porsena crouched on the earth in abject terror.

"Did you think to escape me?" Pythia inquired of him. "You demons are so arrogant." Her glance flickered toward Horatius. Her eyes were as cold as the spaces between the stars. "I am the goddess Pythia. Release this cringing thing to me at once."

The young man calculated swiftly. Although the being before him was awesome, obviously she had some limitations or she would not have asked him to release Lars Porsena. She would have done so herself.

"I will release him to you on one condition," he replied. "Give those women to me. Then he is yours."

"No!" screamed Lars Porsena. Neither Pythia nor Horatius paid any attention to him. He had become a mere object for barter.

Lowering her head on her sinuous neck, Pythia brought it close to Horatius. Her forked tongue flickered over his face in a curious, questing gesture. He shrank inwardly from her touch but stood his ground.

"Ah," she said at last. "So that is who you are. What extraordinary gifts you possess! Bur-Sin underestimated you, I suspect. He always underestimates others: his opinion of himself is so great he assumes everyone else must be inferior. In truth there is nothing superior about him. He is a thief, a bully, and a coward and deserves whatever punishment I choose to give him. Let me think . . ."

Her voice sank to a hiss more awful than her anger. "Bur-Sin is so proud of the form he now wears. I will make it human again, mortal again, with his *hia* still inside—and kept totally under my control this time. Then I will send him back to Rome to serve as my minion there. He will have no free will, of course, but . . ."

Lars Porsena clasped his hands together in an attitude of prayer. "Great is your mercy, Goddess!"

"Your gratitude is ill-founded, Bur-Sin. Your body will be vulnerable to the pains and tortures you have inflicted upon others, and when it dies I will simply put your *hia* into a new one to suffer again. And again. You will have a most interesting future. I will make you the scourge of Rome . . . and Rome in turn will scourge you."

Lars Porsena's eyes widened with horror.

Pythia addressed herself to Horatius. "By what name are you known?"

"Horatius Cocles."

"Very well, Horatius Cocles. Give me this pitiful wretch and you can have one of the women in exchange."

For the first time Horatius took a good look at the second woman in Pythia's clutches. She was beautiful; even Livia would have seemed plain by comparison. And she was gazing at him with enough pleading in her eyes to melt iron.

But so was Vesi.

"Choose," demanded Pythia.

"I will take them both."

"Oh no, I am not inclined to be that generous. You must choose one and relinquish the other to me, together with your captive."

Horatius folded his arms across his chest. "Both, I say. If you do not agree, free him yourself." He stepped back, gambling that the serpent had no more power over the flint knife than did the demon.

If he was wrong. . . .

For a long moment she stared at him, her tongue flickering lazily between her lips. Then, with agonizing slowness, Pythia began to lower the two women to the ground. As their feet neared the gleaming black surface the serpent loosened her coils.

Horatius darted forward to catch Vesi before she could fall. "Mother!"

The face she turned up to his was haggard and exhausted. "My son," she whispered. She raised one trembling hand to touch his cheek. "Make her release me *completely*."

Though he did not understand, he called to Pythia, "You must release her completely!"

"Very well," was the grudging reply. "You drive a hard bargain."

Horatius felt his mother shudder in his arms. Then she drew a deep breath of relief and nestled her head gratefully against his shoulder.

The beautiful girl stumbled toward them, moaning with every step she took. Horatius reached out in pity and drew her into his embrace as well. "We must get away from here before she changes her mind," he told the two women.

Pythia drawled, "Oh, I will not change my mind. Unlike demons, the gods usually keep their word. I do not need you anyway. My little games with Bur-Sin will keep me as entertained as a cat with a mouse. Just remove that knife, Horatius Cocles, and you are free to go wherever you like."

Over the heads of the women, he told the goddess, "We don't belong here, we must return to the Earthworld. But the way is long and difficult and these two are very weak. We need help."

Pythia replied with vast indifference, "What is that to me?"

"You are so powerful that even a demon fears you. Surely you could do this small thing."

"Flattery only works on fools. Remember that in the future, Horatius Cocles. But yes, I could transport you if I chose." She hesitated as if weighing various considerations. Then the great coils shifted with a liquid sound of scales sliding against one another. "I will help you on one condition: that you ask me for nothing else. Ever. Make even the smallest request of me in the future and I will strip you of everything you possess, do you understand?"

"I do."

"Very well then." Opening her mouth wide, Pythia vomited a large pool of alabaster liquid onto the black plain. "Here is your roadway. Release Bur-Sin to me. Then dive into the pool with your women and let the current carry you to the Earthworld. Do it immediately; I offer you only the one chance."

"Be careful," urged the girl. "It might be a trick!"

But Horatius could not be frightened. Releasing the two women, he crouched down, grasped the handle of the flint knife, and tugged.

The knife slid out of the shadow on the stone.

Lars Porsena staggered backward.

Pythia responded with a triumphant hiss. The huge coils shifted again; the black form lifted toward the red sky.

Horatius gathered the women into his arms again and strode to the brink of the pool. Before he entered the water he took one last look back.

With dreadful clarity he saw the great serpent towering high above the demon, her body bent into an S-curve. Her eyes blazed with a murderous lust beyond human comprehension. Extending her flaring hood Pythia spread its dark shadow over the figure cowering below her.

Lars Porsena's frantic green eyes met those of Horatius. "Do not abandon me to her!" he screamed just as Horatius leaped into the pool.

"I am your father!"

FIFTY-ONE

The opaque water was as warm as milk. No sooner had it closed over their heads than a current seized Horatius and the two women and dragged them deeper, then swept them inexorably forward. When Horatius could not hold his breath any longer he was astonished to discover that he did not choke. Breathing the water was like breathing air.

The two women he tightly grasped were making the same discovery. Vesi relaxed, but the girl writhed and kicked in a futile attempt to swim under her own power.

As Horatius was carried along, faces swirled at random through his memory.

Wulv. Propertius. Pepan.

Lars Porsena.

I am your father!

Horatius shuddered.

The demon had lied to him countless times. No doubt it would have told him anything in a desperate bid to escape the vengeance of the dark goddess.

I am your father.

Nonsense.

But the seed of doubt was planted.

As the warm white flow sped them back toward the Earthworld Horatius fell into a sort of dream. He was imagining the future. He would work for Severus, become prosperous, build a house for his mother, marry someone . . . Livia . . .

Livia seemed very far away however. Held close to his side was a different and even more beautiful young woman. As she struggled he felt her full breast against his arm; her legs entwined deliciously with his own. The gods had thrown them together. What did this mean?

Before he could speculate, the current roiled wildly around them and tore Justine and Vesi from his arms.

A moment later a geyser of alabaster liquid spewed Horatius into a clump of hemlock at the entrance to the Caverns of Spasio.

His spirit was sucked from his Netherworld body like a seed being sucked from a grape. There was a sickening swoop, a jolt . . .

Horatius opened his eyes to find himself lying on his back on the floor of the first cavern. After a momentary confusion his mind cleared.

Khebet, battered and bloody, was straddling him and trying to fight off three hooded assailants. A fourth lay unmoving by the entrance. The sound of the Aegyptian's harsh breathing filled the cave. Although he did not yet feel settled in his Earthworld body, Horatius drew up his knees and swung them to one side then swiftly rolled up onto his feet. "Enough!" he cried.

The hooded figures froze.

Khebet was at the end of his strength. He managed to mutter, "Thank the gods," then let himself slump to the ground, gasping for breath.

Horatius hurled himself on the nearest figure. He

smashed his fist into a shadowy face beneath a hood. His knuckles struck a snout; cartilage crumpled. There was a grunt of pain. The other two recovered from their astonishment and joined the fight.

The three creatures were formidable, yet Horatius would not have cared if there were six—or sixty. He had the advantage of surprise. He also had a young and healthy body that had benefited by a good rest. Dancing on the balls of his feet, he pummeled each opponent in turn, taking savage joy in the release of tension. With every blow he struck his confidence grew. He did not need magical weapons, he did not need the aid of the gods.

"I'm Horatius Cocles!" he shouted, whirling, leaping. "I've been to the Netherworld and come back alive!" Kicking, battering. "I cannot be beaten by cowards who hide their faces!" He landed five blows for every one he took. He seemed to be everywhere at once and growing stronger every moment. The cave was full of him, larger than life, angry and joyous and brilliant.

Pythia's minions panicked. Abandoning their fallen comrade, they fled from the cave.

Horatius tossed a lock of hair out of his eyes. He was not even breathing hard. "By the gods, it's good to be alive!" He bent to help the Aegyptian to his feet. "We did it, my friend! We did it!"

"Did you get what you went for?" Khebet asked weakly. His legs were trembling; he had to sit back down.

Just then a shadow fell across the scorched opening of the cave. Khebet tensed—until two women entered. Vesi was leaning on the shoulder of the lovely girl Horatius had rescued from Pythia.

Horatius gave a sigh of relief. "Yes, Khebet. I brought back all that I sought—and more."

Khebet was injured and the women were exhausted. There was no point in leaving the caverns until they were able to travel, so Horatius gathered enough firewood to keep the cave warm and went looking for something to eat. Nuts, berries, a bird shot out of the sky with an improvised slingshot, a rabbit taken in a snare made of vines—with these he provided for his charges. Once more Wulv's training came to his aid. Soon he had created a comfortable little camp where they could spend a number of days if need be.

"I've made a discovery," Horatius confided to Khebet when the Aegyptian began to take a little interest in something other than his aches and pains. "Our ancestors and our friends are our true riches."

"My people store up riches for the Afterlife," Khebet said, "but what if there is none? You are right, Horatius; at least we can be certain of the past and present."

Thinking of Lars Porsena, Horatius chuckled. "I can assure you there's an Afterlife as well, at least for some of us. The only thing is it may be horrible."

"I am in no hurry to find out," the other told him.

"Will you be returning to Aegypt?"

"I am in no hurry to do that either, Horatius. I used to think I knew everything and was in control of my destiny, but I was mistaken. I would like to stay with you for a while longer, if I may. I suspect you have much to teach me."

Horatius laughed. Laughter came easily to him now, bubbling up like a fountain. "I can't teach you anything. You're a priest, an educated man."

"I am not even sure about being a priest," Khebet said with a shake of his head. "But I do believe I am more of a man than I was."

The girl called Justine was also regaining her strength. She took over the chore of caring for Vesi, bathing her face with fresh water, urging her to eat, trying without success to get her to talk. As Horatius watched them he was touched by her devotion to the older woman. It was inevitable, he decided, after what they had been through together.

One evening as they finished their meal beside the

fire Horatius noticed that Justine was beginning to look haggard. Perhaps she was doing too much too soon. "Are you ill?" he wanted to know.

"Why do you ask?"

"Your face, it's . . ." Horatius paused, not sure what to say next. He did not want to insult her. Perhaps it was a mere trick of the light.

Justine raised a hand to her cheek. Was there the slightest loss of firmness? "But he promised!" she cried, aggrieved.

"Who promised?"

She bowed her head but did not explain. She did not want this extraordinary young man to know what a fool she had been, believing the word of a demon.

In Rome there were plenty of wealthy old men who would buy the finest creams and lotions for her in return for her favors, and perhaps enable her to retain her recaptured beauty. But she knew she would not seek them out. Having seen Horatius, Justine could not bear to think of returning to her past life.

She willed slackening flesh to cling tight to bone and flashed him her warmest smile.

Horatius smiled back. As the firelight leaped his smile caught someone's else's attention.

"Horatrim?" Vesi said hoarsely. It was the first word she had spoken since the Netherworld.

Horatius caught her in his arms and rocked back and forth, holding her head against his shoulder as if she were the child and he the parent. "Yes it's me, Mother. It's me."

"But you are . . . so big."

"And you are so little. I never realized how small you are, Mother."

"A long time must have passed . . ."

"Do you not remember?"

She shook her head. "Only flashes. Bright bits in a darkness. They make no more sense than a shattered mosaic."

As gently as he could, Horatius recounted their recent history to his mother. Khebet and Justine filled in their parts of the puzzle, though Justine was careful to edit hers. Occasionally Vesi asked questions; hesitantly at first, then with growing comprehension. Her bright spirit, so long submerged, began to peep through her eyes like sunshine when dark clouds roll away.

"You have restored me to myself," she said at last. The recital had tired her but it was a happy weariness. "I don't know how to thank you. All of you."

The Aegyptian said, "Thank the gods, who must truly love your son."

At the mention of the gods Horatius gave a start. "Eosphorus!"

"Who?"

"Someone I met in the Netherworld, Mother. I made him a promise. Wherever we go, we are going to set up a little shrine to Eosphorus. Once each day we will remember him and call his name."

Vesi managed a faint smile. "If it pleases you. I would like to sleep now, I think." Her eyes drifted shut. Tenderly, Horatius carried her to the bed he had made for her of fallen boughs and soft mosses.

Then he returned to Khebet and Justine, who were still by the fire. Justine was playing idly with a stick that had fallen away from the flames. "What are your plans, Horatius?" she asked as he sat down beside her.

"I'm going back to Rome with my mother and Khebet. My future is there." Taking the stick from her, with its burnt end he began drawing on the floor of the cave. Squares, rectangles, cubes. Houses and buildings. He gazed thoughtfully at the images, then turned toward the girl. "Have you a family somewhere worrying about you?"

Justine bit her lip. "I have no one. No one anywhere."

"Then you'll come with us. Having gone to all the trouble to bring you back from the Netherworld I'm not about to abandon you now."

"You know nothing about me!"

"I've seen how kind you are to my mother. And you're very beautiful. That's all I need to know."

"But . . . I will grow old, I will . . ."

Horatius laughed. "I may be old before you are. I seem to be aging more rapidly than other men."

"That will not matter to me."

"Then why do you think it will matter to me?"

Fearful that someone in the city would recognize her, she started to protest further. Then she remembered how much she had changed. *If happiness is enough to keep a woman beautiful*, Justine thought to herself, *perhaps I have a chance.*

"In Rome I can make a good living," Horatius was saying, "and you can be a companion to my mother. Perhaps one day . . ." he stopped and shook his head. There would be time for that later. When he understood women better. "At any rate our worries are over," he concluded. "We can enjoy some peace from now on."

Khebet raised an eyebrow. "Peace? In Rome? I doubt that. Rome is many things—raw, new, greedy, exciting—but I cannot imagine it being peaceful."

Rome, mumbled Vesi. They had thought she was asleep. When she spoke her voice was so low, so strange, that at first they could not make out what she was saying.

"Your mother has not yet thrown off the effects of her terrible experience, Horatius," Khebet suggested. "She is still haunted by it and having nightmares."

Vesi stirred uneasily on her bed and spoke again. This time Horatius heard her clearly. She was repeating the words Pythia had said to Lars Porsena.

I will make you the scourge of Rome . . . and Rome in turn will scourge you.

EPILOGUS

We Ais do not always have things our own way. The fate of humankind is written not on stone, but on the wind. Man himself—blind, ignorant, irrational Man—has more power over his future than we do.

We do not want him to know this. As long as he leaves his destiny in the hands of the gods we can control him.

Control is a two-edged weapon however.

Some of us are genuinely fond of humans and seek to protect them from their own worst natures. Others perversely encourage the destructive tendency in humankind.

But if Man dies, so die the gods.

We would all do well to remember this.